The author of over 50 novels, Anna Jacobs grew up in Lancashire and emigrated to Australia, but still visits the UK regularly to see her family and do research, something she loves. She is addicted to writing and she figures she'll have to live to be 120 at least to tell all the stories that keep popping up in her imagination and nagging her to write them down. She's also addicted to her own hero, to whom she's been happily married for many years. In 2006 one of her novels, *Pride of Lancashire*, won an award for the Australian Romantic Novel of the Year.

THE TRADER'S GIFT

Bram Deagan has a gift for matchmaking and wishes to see his friends Dougal and Mitchell happily married like himself, so he doesn't hesitate to suggest they find wives. When her ailing husband dies, Eleanor Prescott wonders if she dare return to Western Australia. Will Dougal still want her after nearly a year? And Mitchell has asked his cousin in England whether he knows any suitable lady. For one widow, desperate to keep her young son from a cruel relative's clutches, Mitchell's invitation is a lifeline she will grasp with both hands. Both Eleanor and Jacinta bravely take a huge risk on the chance of happiness and set off for Australia. But for Jacinta at least, the troubles of her old life can't easily be left behind . . .

ANNA JACOBS

THE TRADER'S GIFT

Complete and Unabridged

CHARNWOOD
Leicester

First published in Great Britain in 2013 by
Hodder & Stoughton
London

First Charnwood Edition
published 2015
by arrangement with
Hodder & Stoughton
An Hachette UK company
London

ISBN 978–1–4448–2421–6

Published by
F. A. Thorpe (Publishing)
Anstey, Leicestershire

Set by Words & Graphics Ltd.
Anstey, Leicestershire
Printed and bound in Great Britain by
T. J. International Ltd., Padstow, Cornwall

This book is printed on acid-free paper

This book is dedicated to the memory of Mrs G.C. Jacobs ('Blondie') who lived an exemplary life of love and hard work in equal measure. She is sorely missed by all of those who knew and loved her.

Thanks once again to Eric Hare,
my nautical mentor, whose input
is invaluable.

Prologue

Western Australia: March 1870

Bram finished his evening meal and looked round with a sigh. 'I do miss having the other children around.'

His wife smiled. 'They were only living with us for a short time. And though they've moved out, they and their new family live a mere two streets away, so you'll still be seeing them most days. You're never satisfied, Bram Deagan.'

He shrugged. 'You know it's my dream to have my family join us in Australia, Isabella darlin'. Why else do we have this fine big home but to fill it with people we love?'

He leaned across to give her a quick kiss on the cheek, then looked thoughtful. 'And I like to have friends round me, as well as family. I do wish Mitchell and Dougal would find themselves wives.'

'You know Dougal met someone on his last voyage. His voice still goes softer when he speaks of this Eleanor.'

'She's no use to him, though. She's married already, and she's gone off to live in England.' He began to drum his fingers on the table. 'We should start looking round for someone who'd suit him. Sometimes people need a bit of a nudge.'

'Leave him to find his own wife, Bram.'

1

'He's nearly forty and he hasn't got one. And there's Mitchell to think of, too. He needs another wife to help him bring up his son and give him other children.'

'Well, there's a shortage of suitable ladies here in the Swan River Colony, so how's he going to do that?'

'They're calling it Western Australia now. It's not as pretty a name, is it? Now, about Mitchell — '

'Bram, don't!'

He ignored her, still counting off his unmarried friends on his fingers. 'And what about Livia? If ever a woman needed a husband, it's her. That makes three of them.'

Isabella grabbed his arm and gave him a shake to get his attention. 'Darling, you can't interfere. Both Mitchell and Livia have been married once and are over thirty, and Dougal is old enough to manage his own life. If any of them want to marry, they're quite capable of finding someone without your help. Besides, you have enough on your plate with our trading business.'

'I can keep my eyes open, can't I?'

'You're a hopeless romantic.'

He gave her a quick hug, laughing as he had to lean over the stomach full of his baby. 'That's because I have the best wife in the world, and will soon have three children. I do hope the new one will be a girl. Ah, you've made me very happy, Isabella darlin'.'

'And you me. You've such a gift for loving people.'

They sat for a moment or two longer, clasping

hands and smiling tenderly at one another.

But Bram's frown returned when his wife went up to check on their young son and the little girl they'd adopted. He'd managed to distract her and avoid talking about his troublesome ice works investment, though he'd meant what he said about their unmarried friends.

Isabella kept the accounts for his Bazaar, but he hadn't told her yet that some new ice-making machinery needed more money putting into it if it wasn't to fail, because she'd been against getting involved in the ice works from the start.

He hated to leave the venture unfinished, was sure there would be a profit in it one day. Besides, the ice had saved his son's life when the child had a fever, and never mind the money, he wanted the ice available for other children in need. He sighed. His partner would have to wait a while longer for the money, though. He just didn't have any to spare at the moment.

Ah, something would turn up. It always did.

★ ★ ★

The very next day Bram ran into Mitchell in town and seized the moment. 'Just the man I want to see.'

'Do you need some more timber? Surely you're not going to extend the Bazaar again.'

'No. You and your carpenter have finished my new house beautifully. It's you I'm worried about, Mitchell. You've been talking for a while about finding another wife, but you haven't done anything about it.'

3

'Actually, I have.'

Bram looked at him in surprise. 'Oh? You've met someone?'

'No. After we talked last time, I did as you suggested and wrote to my family in England, asking if they knew any lady who might be willing to come out to Australia to marry me.'

Bram clapped him on the shoulder. 'Good man! Good man! Did you send them a photograph of yourself as well?'

'Yes. Of me *and* my son. I wanted there to be no mistake about what someone would be taking on.'

'You're a fine-looking man and he's a sturdy lad. I'm sure your family will find someone suitable.'

'What does 'suitable' mean? I don't care about the woman's looks. I told them that. She can be as ugly as you please. What I care about is finding someone who's kind and practical, someone who'll help me make a home for my son and give me other children. I doubt I'll ever fall in love again. I chose so unwisely last time that I no longer trust myself. The trouble is . . . ' He sighed.

'What?'

'After I'd sent the letter to my cousin, I had second thoughts. How can anyone else choose a wife for me, Bram? How can I be sure she'll be kind and pleasant-tempered without meeting her? Only it was too late by then to get the letter back.'

Bram hoped he hadn't allowed his satisfaction to show. 'Well, you'll have to leave it to fate now, won't you?'

4

'Yes, but what if my cousin sends someone who's unsuitable?'

'You'll give her a chance, surely? Not judge her on a first meeting, when she'll be nervous. She can stay with us at first, just to keep things respectable.'

'I can do nothing else but give a woman a chance if she comes all the way to Australia to meet me. *If* anyone comes, that is.'

As Bram walked away, he decided he wasn't going to tell Isabella about Mitchell's doubts. He'd just give her the good news that his friend had asked his family to find him a wife.

1

England, March 1870: Eleanor

The journey from Australia to England had taken nearly double the usual two months, because of Malcolm's mistakes. By the time the ship docked at Southampton on a cold day in March, Eleanor Prescott had no doubt that her husband was in far poorer health than he'd admit. He looked shocking, like a walking skeleton, his skin yellowish white, his eyes sunken.

'Stop fussing, Eleanor,' he snapped when she suggested seeing a doctor. 'I'll be all right once we're on dry land again. Just like last time.'

'But you've hardly left the cabin during this voyage.'

'Because I've been conserving my strength to help my brother. I pray Roger will still be alive when we get there. As he wrote in his letter, he needs us to act as guardians to his children now that he's mortally ill of a growth. So sad that his wife died in childbirth, the baby too. Those other two children will be left orphans.'

She watched him sit down and rest. It was true that after the interminable voyage to Australia, Malcolm had slowly improved in health once they disembarked. But he'd still been frail the whole time they were in Melbourne. And he'd been much worse on the journey back to England.

What did he see when he looked in the mirror? Did he really believe that he'd get better? Who knew? She'd never understood how his mind worked, had made such a bad mistake marrying him.

She could only hope Malcolm would live long enough to sort things out with his brother. He wouldn't make old bones, that was sure. She'd be happy to take on the task of rearing their niece and nephew . . . afterwards.

Her more immediate worry was that she and Malcolm had so little money left now. She didn't know what they'd do if Roger didn't make suitable arrangements to help them before he died. Emigrating to Australia had been even more of a disaster than the other business ventures in which her husband had got involved.

She could have done better with their money, she knew she could, but Malcolm didn't believe in women having anything to do with business. He'd refused even to discuss his financial plans with her, let alone listen to her advice.

★   ★   ★

Eleanor and Malcolm arrived at Courtlands late in the afternoon. It was a pleasant country house in Hampshire, about a hundred years old and showing its age in its sagging roof and paintwork which needed attention.

As they got out of the cab they'd taken from the station, he smiled up at the house. 'You know, I still think of Courtlands as home. We

7

had such a happy childhood here, Roger and I. We were like twins, since he's only a year older than me.' He moved forward, tossing over his shoulder, 'Make sure all the luggage is brought in, Eleanor.'

But the cab driver was already attending to that, so she joined her husband at the top of the three shallow steps.

He tugged the bell-pull beside the door and somewhere in the house a bell clanged, the sound faint and muffled. Just as he was about to pull it again, they heard footsteps and the door was opened by an elderly maid, who must have been new there because he didn't recognise her from his last visit, when a butler had opened the door.

'I'm Malcolm Prescott. I've come from Australia to see my brother.'

'I'll deal with this, Bertha.' A lady in her middle years appeared behind the maid, who nodded and went to stand waiting at the rear of the hall.

The newcomer was clad in black silk and didn't so much as smile at them. 'Roger said he'd written to you asking you to come back, but I hoped you hadn't been able to do that.'

Malcolm gaped at her. 'I beg your pardon? I don't understand what you mean. And who are you to say such things?'

'I suppose you'd better come in so that I can explain. Leave the luggage. Bertha will see that it's brought in. I suppose you'll have to stay for a night or two.'

She didn't wait for an answer, but led the way

8

to what had once been Malcolm's mother's sitting room.

'Please sit down.'

'I'd rather speak to my brother. We've come a long way to see him.'

'I'm afraid Roger died two months ago.'

Malcolm didn't even make it to a chair. He turned such a sickly white, Eleanor moved to stand nearby, in case. He'd had a couple of fainting fits in the last two weeks and he looked as if he was about to have another one. Sure enough, his eyes rolled up and he would have fallen had she not been ready to catch him and ease him down on a nearby armchair.

'He looks ill,' her hostess said bluntly. 'Very ill.'

Eleanor couldn't deny that. 'Sea travel doesn't agree with my husband. He'll be better now we're on land.'

The woman's expression as she studied Malcolm said she wasn't fooled by this. 'Where are you going to be living once we've settled matters here?'

'We were promised a home *here* on condition we looked after Roger's children. We have nowhere else to go now.' Malcolm had insisted on selling everything before they left England, so that he had money to invest when they reached Australia. He'd been so sure he'd make a fortune.

'Well, I'm afraid there's no permanent place for you here. I'm Roger's widow, Daphne, by the way. He married me so that *I* would be able to look after his children once he died. I used to be their governess. I'm very happy to raise them,

9

but I didn't promise to look after you two and what's more, I won't do it.'

Eleanor looked meaningfully at her husband and moved across to the bay window. Daphne took the hint and followed.

There was nothing for it but to speak frankly. Eleanor kept her voice low. 'We don't have any money left, except for a few pounds. We spent the last of what we had on the journey back to England.' She flushed and under the steely gaze of the widow, felt compelled to explain, 'Malcolm wasn't good with money and he took us to Australia on a wild-goose chase, thinking to get rich quickly.'

But since *she* was better with money, she still had a little hidden in her luggage that Malcolm didn't know about. If she'd told him about it, he'd have taken it from her and spent it, and then where would she be?

She'd expected Daphne to get angry, but her hostess merely sighed and replied in an equally low voice, 'A family trait, then. Roger didn't handle his money well, either, so I've not been left well provided for. But with economy and sensible management, I mean to put the children's inheritance in order so that they can have a decent start in life. *And* teach them to handle money properly.'

'Very . . . um, admirable.'

'I'm *not* going to make myself responsible for you two as well, however.'

As Malcolm began to come to his senses, Eleanor could only repeat, 'But we don't have enough money to go anywhere else. I'm not

10

asking for much, we can live frugally, but we do need your help. There's nowhere else to turn.'

The only answer was an angry huff of air, so she went back to her husband's side.

He was looking from one to the other in bewilderment and she quickly explained to him that he'd fainted on hearing of his brother's death.

'Roger!' He hid his face beneath one hand, fighting tears, his shoulders shaking.

Daphne watched him with a scowl. 'You can stay here for a little while, as long as you don't demand much attention from the servants. You'll have to see if you can nurse your husband back to health, then if — when he recovers, he can find himself a job.'

Malcolm didn't seem to be taking this in, so Daphne addressed Eleanor, 'He should be able to manage something clerical, surely, enough for you to live on modestly?'

'But — '

'You are *not* going to move in here permanently . . . whatever happens.' She got up and rang the bell. The grey-haired maid appeared.

'Ah, Bertha. Mr Prescott's brother and his wife will be staying for a few days. Put them on the second floor. They can have their meals in the schoolroom, unless I invite them to join me.'

Malcolm was now sitting with his head in his hands, weeping openly, muttering his brother's name again and again.

Daphne turned back to Eleanor. 'You may think me hard, but it's a cruel world and I have

11

two children to think of. You look like you've got more backbone than your husband, I'll say that for you. Now, take him upstairs and don't come down again today. There are books in the schoolroom, if you need something to occupy yourself with, and meals will be brought up to you. Can you sew?'

'Yes, of course.'

'Good. I'll find you some mending tomorrow and you can make yourself useful while you're here. Heaven knows, there's plenty of it needing doing. The house has been very poorly managed. I had to sack the housekeeper.' She went to hold the door open.

Eleanor helped Malcolm up the stairs and he at once lay down on his bed, closing his eyes, leaving everything to her — as usual.

She turned to the dour maid. 'I'm sorry to be a trouble, but is there another bedroom I can use? My husband is ill, you see, and doesn't sleep well.'

The maid studied him, then nodded. 'He's very like his brother, isn't he?'

'Yes. Very.' She couldn't keep the bitterness out of her voice. It was Roger who had encouraged Malcolm to invest in the ridiculous enterprise in Australia and travel out to reap the benefits.

'I'll have to ask madam if that's all right.'

Which showed, Eleanor thought, how much in control of her own life Daphne was. She envied her sister-in-law that.

Bertha came back a few minutes later. 'The mistress says you can have the bedroom next to

12

this one. But you'll have to make up the bed and keep the room tidy yourself.'

'I'm happy to do that.'

Malcolm refused a proper meal, contenting himself with sops of bread in warm milk.

Bertha nodded silent approval when Eleanor carried their trays back to the kitchen herself, one by one, refusing help and using the servants' stairs.

Not until it was dark and she was safely in her own bed did Eleanor allow herself to weep.

Her tears flowed even faster as she remembered Dougal McBride. The ship's captain had been a true friend to her and she still missed him. Now there was a man worthy of love. *He* wouldn't have taken to his bed and left her to do the impossible. *He* wouldn't have left her so poorly situated she had to beg for shelter from a stranger.

Well, it was no use thinking of what might have been. Dougal would have sailed back to Australia in the *Bonny Mary* by now and Eleanor was still tied to a dreary life with Malcolm.

Surely Daphne would agree to help them in *some* way or other? Perhaps there was a cottage in the village? Perhaps Eleanor could act as sewing woman here. There was always plenty of mending to do in a big house, especially with children around.

Tears flowed again. To be always a dependant! To have to be grateful for help that was begrudged!

Damn you, Malcolm Prescott!

13

Eleanor met Roger's children again the following morning when she went to the schoolroom to beg the loan of a book to distract her from her troubles. Malcolm had stayed in bed, taking only a cup of tea and a piece of dry toast for breakfast, and ordering her to leave him to mourn in peace.

The children had grown beyond recognition since she'd last seen them over three years ago. They were a lively pair, Jonathon now eight and Jane six. They seemed as fond of Daphne as the widow was of them.

This pleased Eleanor in one sense, because she wished them well, but it emphasised that she and Malcolm were not needed here.

When she went to check that he was all right, he lay there staring into space, not even responding to her questions or attempts at conversation.

A pile of mending was brought to her bedroom just before midday and she was left to herself for the rest of the day. She didn't mind helping in this way. At least it gave her something to do with her hands.

About three o'clock, Bertha brought her a tea tray and an invitation for her to dine with her hostess.

'I'd be happy to. Could you please explain how things are done here? I wouldn't like to offend.'

The maid nodded. 'Mrs Prescott likes to dress for dinner. Nothing too fancy, but something better than in the daytime.'

14

'May I come down and iron one of my better outfits, then? I have a grey silk, but no blacks, and I'm afraid my clothes are rather old-fashioned now.'

'I'll iron it for you, Mrs Prescott.'

'No, no. I can manage. I just want to mend it first. I tore it last time I wore it. I don't want to be a trouble.' She was terrified of being thrown out of the house, didn't know what she would do.

'You're very little trouble, ma'am. And from the mending you've done already, your sewing is better than mine or anyone else's here, so leave the ironing to me. Just bring the dress to the kitchen when it's ready. If you stay for a few days, we'll catch up nicely on all the mending. Apart from the household linen, which is wearing out, those children are always tearing their clothes. I'll tell Mrs Prescott how good your work is. She'll be pleased about that.'

Eleanor was glad of the maid's support. 'I prefer to have something to keep me occupied. My husband seems to be doing nothing but sleep.'

'He's failing,' the maid said bluntly. 'He has the look of death on him. You can't mistake it. You do realise that?'

'Oh, yes. I've known for a while.'

When she took out the grey silk, Eleanor decided an hour or so of work would bring it into a more modern style and hide the tear. She'd noticed as soon as they arrived in England that fashionable ladies were no longer wearing crinolines, and now had the material of the skirt

15

pulled to the back, some of the skirts being draped in very intricate arrangements. She could manage a simpler version of this style quite easily, because without the crinoline, her skirt was too long.

She worked quickly, draping the old-fashioned skirt, so that the material was pulled towards the back. She'd have to make it more secure tomorrow, but her stitching would hold for this evening.

When Bertha came back, she examined the skirt and nodded approval. 'That's clever.'

'The bodice will have to do as it is. But I can alter my other skirts. I like sewing.' It was one thing to enjoy sewing but quite another to make a living from it, however. Seamstresses who worked for other people were paid a pittance, she knew.

When Eleanor went down to dinner, Daphne was waiting for her in the small sitting room. She too had changed her clothes. She studied Eleanor's outfit quite openly. 'Bertha told me you'd been altering your skirt. You made a good job of it. No one would know it wasn't designed that way.'

'Thank you.'

'And you've worked hard on the mending too.'

'I'm happy to help in any way I can.'

'Malcolm still hasn't left his bed, I gather.'

'No. I can't get him to eat or drink much and he won't talk, let alone decide what to do.'

'Bertha says he's failing. She can always tell.'

'Yes.' It was a relief not to have to pretend any longer.

16

Thankfully, her hostess didn't pursue that subject but led the way into the dining room. Dinner was a simple meal but perfectly cooked, and it was served on good china.

Daphne led the conversation, questioning her about everyday life in Australia.

Without meaning to, Eleanor revealed the fiasco en route back to England that had cost them most of their remaining money.

'Your husband is even more of a fool than I'd thought. And the captain took advantage of you.'

To hear Dougal maligned was more than Eleanor could bear. 'On the contrary, Captain McBride went out of his way to help us and if it hadn't been for him, we'd not yet have reached England.'

Daphne stared at her thoughtfully. 'You jump to the man's defence and your whole face softens when you talk of him.'

Eleanor could feel herself flushing and was unable to control it. 'I don't like to hear friends spoken ill of. Malcolm and I had a lot of reasons to be grateful to Captain McBride.'

Daphne's smile showed she hadn't been fooled about Eleanor's feelings. She seemed interested in anything and everything, and continued to ask about their travels. By the end of the evening Eleanor felt wrung out.

As the dessert was cleared away, Daphne said abruptly, 'I enjoy a glass of port after a meal. Will you join me?'

'I'd love to.' Though in truth, Eleanor had had two glasses of wine with the meal and oughtn't to drink any more, not with such a sharp-eyed companion. But she didn't want to go back to the small bedroom. It was cold and she felt closed in and uncomfortable there.

They moved to sit on two armchairs in front of the fire.

'Has your husband made plans for after he dies?' Daphne asked abruptly.

Eleanor's hand jerked, but she managed not to spill the port. She stared down at the ruby liquid. 'I'm not sure Malcolm understands how ill he is.'

'Oh, I think he does. I saw the same thing with Roger. Towards the end, he simply gave up trying to get well. He and his brother are very much alike, don't you think?' She stared at Eleanor and laughed suddenly. 'You don't think I fell in love with Roger, do you?'

'I . . . believe that's your own business.'

'I saw a need, made myself useful and secured my future. Roger got a good bargain in me, and I *will* look after the children, bring them up properly.'

'I can see that you're fond of them.'

'I am. And I think they have some affection for me. But what are we going to do about you once your husband dies?'

Eleanor shook her head. 'I don't know. I lie awake and try to think of something. I suppose I'll have to seek a position as governess or . . . lady's companion. I can't think of anything else.'

'What about the captain? What was his name?'

'Dougal McBride. What about him?'

'Is he married?'

Eleanor shook her head.

18

'Was he as fond of you as you clearly are of him? Would he have married you if you'd been free, do you think?'

Blood rushed into Eleanor's cheeks again, but her embarrassment only seemed to amuse her companion.

'Well, would he? Or are you just imagining things?'

She raised her head, annoyed by this. 'He said so, yes. But I'm not free, am I? And even if I become free, Dougal is in Australia and I'm here in England.'

'Well, you're clearly fond of him, so after Malcolm dies, you must go back to Australia and see if your captain meant what he said. That would be your best hope for the future.'

Said so brutally, it upset Eleanor. 'Dougal will probably have met someone else by then. It takes months to get to and from Australia. And Malcolm may linger for some time.'

'I doubt it. Never mind him. You told me they're short of women in the Swan River Colony. Even if Captain McBride has got married, you'll soon find yourself another husband there, I'm sure. If I can do it here, with my plain face and dumpy body, you'll manage it easily in Australia with your lovely face and slender figure.'

'I don't like the idea of going back to offer myself to Dougal. It would seem so . . . brazen.' Though he had asked her to go to him if she ever could.

'She who dares wins.' Daphne smiled and got up to refill their glasses with port.

19

Eleanor tried to refuse another drink, because she was afraid of giving too much away.

'I'm not your enemy, you know. Here. It's very relaxing to take a glass or two at night. No wonder the men enjoy their port.'

'Well, all right. Thank you.' Eleanor watched the ruby liquid swirl into her glass.

Daphne took another sip. 'This is what we'll do: I shall pay your fare to Australia and then your future will be in your own hands. It'll suit me to have you leave the country, because you won't be able to turn to me again. I won't support you for the rest of your life once Malcolm dies, however much mending you do.'

'He's not even dead yet! How can you talk like that?'

Daphne threw back her head and laughed. 'Because I was a governess and I escaped. It's not a pleasant life, teaching other people's children. One is neither family nor servant. And it's very lonely, too. Don't do it except as a last resort.'

She took another sip, rolling the sweet liquid round her mouth with relish. 'Weak women give in to what life brings them, strong women find a way to better themselves. Which are you?'

Eleanor put down her wine glass, surprised to find it empty and stood up feeling the room sway around her. 'I don't think I'm weak.'

She didn't wait for a response but walked out of the room. As she closed the door and rested her hand on the wall for a moment to steady herself, she heard Daphne laughing softly.

When she reached the second floor, she went

20

to check on Malcolm and found him sleeping soundly.

Suddenly she hated him, admitted to herself that she wanted him dead quickly. He was weak and selfish and stupid, and he'd not only ruined her life, but was leaving her a pauper. Why had she ever thought him kind and gentle? Why had she married him?

Because she'd met no one else willing to take a penniless woman without any close family, that's why.

But did she dare travel all the way to Australia . . . just in case Dougal hadn't forgotten her . . . hadn't met someone else? She wasn't sure she was strong enough to face the humiliation of offering herself to him and being refused.

She didn't weep that night. Was beyond tears. Just wanted this whole business to be over.

★   ★   ★

It took Malcolm Prescott longer to die than anyone had expected, two months to be precise. Daphne grew tight-lipped but didn't try to turn them out.

Eleanor undertook most of the care of her husband, to make sure they caused as little trouble as possible for the household. It was over a year since he'd acted as a proper husband, so at first she was shocked to see how skeletal his body had become.

She took time each day to go for a walk if the weather was at all fine, or simply to sit quietly in her room if it was raining. Without those brief periods of privacy, she didn't think she could have endured the strain.

When she went into Malcolm's bedroom one sunny morning in early June to begin her distasteful duties, she found him dead. She could only stand there in shock for a moment or two, unable to think what to do next, unable to believe that her ordeal was over at last.

She went to close his eyes and said a dutiful prayer for his soul. As she turned away, she acknowledged that it was relief she felt most, not sadness. But the relief was tempered by anxiety. What would happen to her now? Would her sister-in-law really send her to Australia?

Did she dare go to Dougal? She'd swung first one way, then the other as she thought about that during the past couple of months, and though she thought she'd go, she still wondered if it was the right thing to do, if it had all been a foolish dream.

It was still early, so Eleanor went down to the kitchen to find Bertha and ask her to tell her mistress when she woke that Malcolm had died during the night.

'We'll go and check that, if you don't mind.'

The bedroom was as still and sour-smelling as ever, and the maid nodded as she pulled the sheet back from Malcolm's face. 'Yes, he's dead. Has been for a while.' She turned to the widow. 'Are you all right, ma'am?'

Eleanor looked at her in surprise. 'Yes, of course. Why should I not be?'

'You've been under a lot of strain ever since you got here. You've lost weight and excuse me for saying so, but you look exhausted.'

'I'm not going to collapse, if that's what you're worried about.'

'What *are* you going to do?'

She knew Bertha wasn't prying, but was genuinely concerned, so she answered frankly, 'I'm not sure. Your mistress made one suggestion, but I haven't been able to come to a final decision about it. I was too busy looking after my husband.'

She turned to the bed and couldn't hold back a shiver. 'I'd better start laying him out, I suppose.'

'I'll do that, if you like.'

She looked at Bertha in surprise. 'Why should you?'

'I've done it many a time before. I laid out his brother, too. It means nothing to me, because *he* means nothing to me. I think it would upset you more than you realise.'

It was already upsetting her. Eleanor felt sick at the mere thought of cleaning his dead body. 'But what would your mistress say to that?'

'She won't mind, as long as the neighbours know everything's been done properly. Why don't you go and sit in the morning room? I'll get Patsy to bring you some tea. Madam won't want hers for another twenty minutes. I'll start on him after I've taken it to her.'

'Thank you. I'm very grateful for your kindness.'

Eleanor felt guilty to be sitting with nothing to do. But she couldn't raise the energy to pick up a book or even to glance at yesterday's newspaper, lying neatly folded on a small table.

Within five minutes Patsy brought her a tray with some shortbread and a pot of tea. 'Bertha says you're to eat something, ma'am. She says you need to build up your strength.'

But Eleanor couldn't force down more than half a biscuit. Anxiety was roiling around inside her about her future. She couldn't settle, so went to stand by the window and stare out at the flowers, then sat down and leaned her head back, closing her eyes for a few seconds.

She jumped in shock when someone spoke nearby.

'Bertha was right. You're utterly exhausted.'

'Daphne!' Eleanor stared at the clock in surprise. 'Is it really nine o'clock? I must have fallen asleep.'

'No wonder. Come and join me for breakfast.'

Daphne tucked into the food with her usual hearty appetite, pausing to say sharply, 'You need to eat more than that. Never mind whether you're hungry or not. Force something down. I don't want *you* falling ill on me next.'

'I shan't do that. I'm never ill.'

'Nonetheless, humour me.'

They didn't chat, because Daphne was opening her mail, sorting it into two piles. Once the meal was over, she picked up the papers. 'We'll go into my sitting room to talk. Patsy needs to clear up.'

Feeling like a prisoner about to be sentenced, Eleanor followed her.

'We'll have to think how best to get you to this captain of yours.'

She'd expected them to discuss Malcolm's funeral, so this remark startled her and she didn't know what to say.

'He's your best chance of happiness and you'd be a fool not to go to him.' Daphne drummed her fingers on her chair arm, frowning. 'Does he have money? Or is he still making his way in the world?'

'He owns two ships and a fine house in Fremantle, in the Swan River Colony.'

Another silence, then, 'It's worth a try, then.'

Eleanor couldn't hold back a protest. 'But if he's changed his mind, I'll be penniless and alone in a strange country.' That was one of the main things holding her back.

'The country can't be that strange. You lived there for two years.'

'We lived in Melbourne. The Swan River Colony is nearly two thousand miles from there, and very different.'

She saw that Daphne was waiting for more information and searched her brain. 'There isn't even a road between the two places. You have to go round the coast of Australia by ship. People in Melbourne are very scornful about the Swan River Colony, say it's a backward place and no one ever stays there willingly. Some call it the Cinderella colony. Malcolm and I were only in the west for a couple of nights and he was ill, so we didn't see enough to — '

Daphne held up one hand. 'You're prevaricating. All you need to tell me is: do you have the courage to do this or are you going to sentence yourself for the rest of your life to the misery of being a governess, of never having children or family of your own?'

Eleanor bent her head, avoiding that piercing gaze. She was finding it so hard to think clearly.

'I can see you need time to think about it, now your burden has gone.' Her sister-in-law gestured towards the door. 'I'll arrange the funeral. I know how things are done round here. Why don't you go for a walk round the gardens? You can tell me what you've decided at dinner tonight.'

As Eleanor opened the door, the sharp voice followed her.

'It's a harsh world for women. We have to seize every opportunity there is to better ourselves. Wait!'

She turned to look at Daphne.

'One more thing. I'm only paying for you to travel steerage. I'm not made of money.'

'Very well.' In the hall, Eleanor hesitated, then went outside without fetching a bonnet or shawl. It was a beautiful day and many flowers had opened, filling the whole garden with colour. The sight of them made her feel better immediately.

She strolled round to the summer house, her favourite place. Such a pretty structure, painted white, with seats inside. Sitting there, she looked out at the rose bed, but the flowers became a blur, because tears filled her eyes. Malcolm had only been thirty-six. She was thirty-one. How long would she live?

Dougal was older, she thought, but such a vigorous man he'd looked far younger than Malcolm. She could remember that last night

26

with Dougal so clearly, every word he'd said, the loving way he looked at her.

Eleanor, if you are ever free, or even just in need of a friend, it will always be my privilege to help you . . . You're the only woman I've ever wanted to marry in my whole life, so it's not likely now that I'll meet anyone else.

Could she trust herself to those words?

He'd given her instructions on how to find him again, had said he'd send money to England to pay for her passage to Australia. If he'd done that, it'd be in the care of a lawyer whose name he'd written down. If he'd done that . . . he'd meant what he said. Surely?

She could imagine nothing more wonderful than to marry him, so why was she hesitating now?

She raised her head and squared her shoulders. 'I'll do it,' she said aloud, 'I really will.'

But before a minute had passed, she was reminding herself not to hope for too much, even if the money was waiting for her at the lawyer's.

Life had a way of playing tricks on you, as she'd found out after marrying Malcolm.

★   ★   ★

Eleanor returned to the house to find an empty coffin being carried inside by two burly fellows, supervised by a gentleman in black with long crepe weepers hanging from the back of his top hat.

She hesitated near the front door, watching as

27

they carried the coffin upstairs.

'Come in here,' Daphne hissed from across the hall. 'And don't come out again till they've gone. We'll need to find you some mourning clothes or it'll look bad.'

So Eleanor waited out of sight until the men had taken away the coffin, heavier now, causing them to puff and pant as they eased it round the turn in the stairs and through the front door.

Daphne led the way out into the hall, watching the men load the coffin on to a hearse drawn by four black horses. As it pulled away, she turned to Eleanor. 'I hope you didn't want to keep the body here to gaze at.'

The words escaped before she could control them. 'I hope I never have to see Malcolm's face again.'

'I don't blame you. I have never understood the fascination some people have with their dear departeds' bodies.' Daphne waved one hand in a dismissive gesture and changed the subject. 'Now, let us be practical. I've remembered that there are some old clothes in the front attic, including quite a few black garments. You're welcome to take any of them you can use, but you'll have to work quickly to alter something for the funeral, which will take place the day after tomorrow.'

'Thank you. I'm grateful.'

Daphne shrugged. 'They're no good to me. They're too small for me anyway. Besides, I'm never going to wear cast-offs again.' She stroked her silk skirt and smiled down at it, then looked

28

up at her guest. 'Take any of the old clothes you wish. I'm only going to throw them away. Some of them should fit you. You get to that part of the attics by the stairs near the schoolroom.'

Eleanor nodded and went up, surprised to be left to her own devices to do this. She found some beautiful silk gowns, so old-fashioned they'd be laughable, which was no doubt why Daphne had dismissed them as useless. But the material was still perfect, even under the arms, so they couldn't have been worn much. She could easily alter them.

She went through them methodically, sorting out clothes which looked suitable, then went through again, sorting out anything which might be useful later.

Afterwards she looked at the piles with satisfaction. She could take enough clothing from here to wear on the voyage to Australia and for many years to come. And altering them would occupy the long hours of the voyage.

It was only then that she realised she'd finally made up her mind. She was going to go to Dougal. She was willing to risk everything to see if Dougal had meant what he said. Because nothing could make her happier than to become his wife.

She went down to check with her hostess, just to be sure. 'Did you mean it, that I can take as many clothes as I want from the attic?'

'I never say anything I don't mean. I have no need of them and would only throw them away.'

Eleanor knew her sister-in-law well enough by now to realise that Daphne didn't want to seem too soft-hearted, so she didn't comment on the kindness of this act.

She returned to the attics, bringing an armful of clothing down to her bedroom and going back to the attic for more, because there were undergarments there too, as well as shoes and shawls.

She would alter only one black garment, however, because if she boarded the ship in deepest mourning, she would be expected to keep herself to herself for the whole journey, as a recent widow.

She'd had enough isolation because of Malcolm and his stubborn pride, wanted to live a full life now, meet people . . . marry, have children if it was still possible.

If it was wrong of her not to stay in mourning, she didn't care. She hadn't loved Malcolm for a long time, wondered if she ever had. But she'd *liked* him when they first married, she was sure of that.

After they were married, he'd never talked of his feelings for her. She'd just accepted that he must care for her, or else why would he have asked her to become his wife?

Eleanor intended to ask Bertha if her most worn garments could be given to the poor. They were welcome to the horrid things. She'd had enough of looking shabby.

Was she mistaking this act of Daphne's for kindness? Perhaps it was merely a way of ensuring that she'd leave here properly equipped to find another husband and thus never come back?

Well, her sister-in-law need have no fear of that. There had been a freedom in Australia for women, ladies or not, that there wasn't in England. Perhaps because even the ladies worked harder in the Antipodes, many doing menial chores because they had trouble finding domestic help. That brought people closer together, somehow.

She suddenly remembered the lawyer. She must contact him immediately. Dougal had said he'd pay for her passage. If he really had sent her some money, surely that was a sign? She'd write to the lawyer this minute and ask for it to be put in the post quickly.

Whatever happened, she didn't intend to travel to Australia in steerage class, however. She knew only too well how little privacy or comfort that offered. She intended to travel cabin class, although a second-class cabin would be adequate.

If both Daphne and Dougal's lawyer helped her, surely she'd have enough money left to manage on after her arrival? If she needed to.

★   ★   ★

She heard back from the lawyer two days later. Dougal had indeed sent money and Mr Saxby was at her service. He had now moved to London, but was going to Western Australia himself shortly. They could travel together if she wished.

Feeling immensely relieved, she wrote back giving him the name of the hotel Daphne had recommended in London. She could have managed on her own, of course she could, but people always preferred to deal with a gentleman and it would make things easier to travel with Mr Saxby.

For the first time she felt hopeful. And excited.

2

England, June 1870: Jacinta

Jacinta was conscious mainly of relief when her elderly husband died, but of course she hid that. She was an expert at hiding her feelings by now.

As she accompanied the doctor to the door, he said gently, 'I shall not, of course, be charging you for my attendance, Mrs Blacklea. I know how you're situated. May I ask — what shall you do now?'

'Bury Claude, then seek the help of his family, since I have no family left.'

He nodded. 'Very wise. I'll call at the parson's on my way home and tell him about Claude. You'll need to arrange the funeral.'

She took a deep breath and said something that was unthinkable for a gentleman's widow. 'I can't afford to pay for one, so it'll have to be a pauper's funeral.'

His mouth fell open in shock and it was a minute before he spoke. 'Are things so bad, then?'

She nodded. 'They've been bad for a while. Ben and I are almost penniless now. We need the little that's left to pay for our journey to his relatives.'

The doctor stared at the ground, brow wrinkled in thought. 'Well, I'm sure the Squire will join me in paying for the coffin, and for a simple funeral. Claude was a friend of ours, after all.'

His tone was disapproving, as if she were somehow to blame, but she ignored that and tried to sound grateful. 'Thank you. You're very . . . kind.'

She'd rather have had the money for her son, though, and left Claude to the pauper's burial, because that was all he deserved.

'What about his books?'

'I haven't thought.'

'I should be happy to buy them from you. As you know, Claude and I shared similar tastes in reading material. How much would you be asking?'

'I'll accept whatever you think fit. I have no idea of their value.' She lowered her eyes and added, 'I know a gentleman like you won't cheat me.'

'Hmm. I'll give it my consideration.'

When she was alone again, she went back to the still figure on the bed and with a sigh, set about preparing his body for burial. It wasn't as bad touching him in death as it had been submitting to his attentions in bed when he was alive. She still had nightmares about it, had been thankful when he stopped wanting her in that way.

As she worked, she glanced occasionally towards the other downstairs room in their tiny cottage, where her son was playing quietly in front of the fire with a toy dog she'd made him from some rags. He was a bit old for such a toy, but as he wasn't allowed to play with the village lads, it was very dear to him.

Just before dusk she felt a desperate need for

34

fresh air, so took Ben out for a walk, speaking cheerfully, not attempting to curb his high spirits and need to run to and fro. He'd had to be quiet so often during the long month his father had taken to die. Now he deserved to run about and play like any other nine-year-old.

She supposed she should find a way of setting up a gravestone marker of some sort, but she wasn't going to spend a penny on Claude, if she could help it.

As she was passing the rear of the church she noticed the pile of planks that had been lying there for over a year and stopped to study them. Grass had grown between them and died in the winter, leaving the new grass to push through a tangle of dry stalks. She walked across to them, leaving Ben to investigate a spider's web and poke a stick at its occupant.

Did she dare take a couple of planks? Would anyone mind? Whose were they anyway?

She looked round but there was no one else about, so she began to poke among the pieces of wood, finding two of the right size to make a cross. She was glad the gathering dusk hid her theft.

It was a struggle to drag the bigger plank home on her own. Ben managed to drag the shorter one, thinking it a fine game.

Luck was on her side, for once, and they didn't meet a soul. Whether any of the neighbours could see what she was doing from behind their curtains, she couldn't tell. If they were watching, they didn't come out to interfere. Or to help.

Claude had always made it clear that even though he lived in a humble cottage, in what he called 'reduced circumstances' and she called 'poverty', he considered himself far above his neighbours in status and wanted nothing to do with them. That had kept her and her son so lonely, though she hadn't always obeyed his edict to have nothing to do with the villagers.

Before she prepared their meal, Jacinta went to knock at the carpenter's house just along the lane, intending to beg the loan of a saw, hammer and a few nails. Surely it couldn't be all that difficult to cobble together a rough cross?

'What do you want them for, if you don't mind me asking, Mrs Blacklea? I don't like lending my tools to people who aren't used to them.'

She hesitated, then explained.

Mr Ketch looked at her gravely. 'I'll come round and do it for you, shall I?'

'I can't pay you, I'm afraid.'

'I'm not asking for payment, any more than you did when you helped me nurse my wife last winter.'

Her voice wobbled as she thanked him, because kindness was a rarity in her life and doubly precious to her now. By the time they got back to her cottage, she was in control of herself again, had to be, for her son's sake.

When Mr Ketch had finished making the simple cross, he looked sideways at her. 'Do you have some paint for the name? I'm no good at carving.'

'No. I'd thought to burn it with the poker. I used to do pokerwork when I was a girl, so I know how.'

He smiled. 'If you don't mind my saying so, Mrs Blacklea, you don't seem much more than a girl to me now.'

'I don't feel young any more, Mr Ketch.' Hadn't since that dreadful day she'd been married off to elderly Claude Blacklea.

When Jacinta's parents had died suddenly of a fever, her aunt had waited till after the simple funeral, then said bluntly, 'You'll have to marry, Jacinta. And I've found a man for you.'

'Who?'

'Claude Blacklea is looking for a wife.'

'Not him. Please, not him!'

'He's the only one offering. I mean what I say. Your parents left you no money, only debts, and I have daughters of my own to provide for. You're too pretty to live with us. You'll damage their chances.'

'But — '

'If you refuse, I'll throw you out of my house and leave you to beg on the streets. If you marry Mr Blacklea, he'll pay the debts and look after you. Well, marriage or begging? Which is it to be?'

So Jacinta had married Claude.

And it had been as bad as she'd expected . . . except that he'd given her a son to love. And that made up for the rest.

Was she only twenty-nine now? She felt much older. Maybe once she'd made a new life for herself and her son, she'd feel younger again. If his family would just make her a small allowance, she could manage. She was good at managing on very little money.

She realised Mr Ketch was speaking again. 'I

beg your pardon. What did you say?'

'You've had a hard few months, Mrs Blacklea. I hope things will brighten for you in the future.'

She could only nod and wish he'd stop being kind. She wasn't used to kindness and couldn't afford to break down and weep when she had so much to do.

★   ★   ★

The following morning, it took Jacinta an hour to burn the words on the wooden cross with the tip of the poker. Ben watched in fascination, dying to have a try, but she didn't want him burning himself. And anyway, she wanted to get this over and done with as quickly as possible.

She wrote the words to appease others. The sign ought to have included the word Fool, but you couldn't put that on your husband's grave, however much he deserved it. But no true gentleman would have ignored his family's needs as Claude had. He'd not wanted a wife, only a servant who didn't need paying any wages.

> Claude Blacklea
> Scholar and Gentleman
> 1807–1870

The next afternoon she attended the brief burial ceremony, paid for by their wealthier neighbours. When it was over, the doctor slipped an envelope into her pocket, an envelope that clinked.

'It's a fair amount,' he said quietly. 'I'll send my man to collect the books tomorrow morning before you leave.'

'Thank you.'

She nodded farewell to him and the trio of gentlemen who had attended, then laid one hand on her son's shoulder. 'Come along, Ben.'

No one offered to help her with anything else.

Unfortunately, Ben was in a contrary mood that day, unsettled by the strangeness of everything. 'I want to go and walk in the woods.'

'Not today, dear. I have some people coming to see me.'

He opened his mouth to protest, caught her eyes and shut his mouth. But he looked sulky.

Her visitors were waiting for her already, the woman standing by the door, the young man peering through the window. He turned as she approached, not looking in the least ashamed of his rudeness. Well, he was a Prynne, from the meanest family in the village. Jacinta knew she'd have a fight on her hands to get a fair price out of them.

'Sorry about your loss, Mrs Blacklea,' the young woman said, but her eyes had already taken on a possessive gleam as she followed Jacinta into the cottage.

'How much do you want for your furniture?' the man asked.

'Fifty pounds.'

'We can't afford that. I'll give you twenty.' His smile was smug, as if he was certain he was about to get a bargain.

The fact that they were intending to take advantage of her desperate need only stiffened Jacinta's resolve. She let them knock the price down to forty pounds, which she'd expected, then drew herself up and stared him in the eye. 'Any lower would be grossly unfair and well you know it, Mr Prynne.'

'I'm not a rich man. I'm surprised you need to haggle with poor people like us. You're gentry, after all.'

So she told him what she'd kept secret for years. 'My husband lost all our money, so I have almost nothing left. And I'm so angry about your low offer that I'll *burn* the furniture rather than let you profit from my distress.'

He gave her a disbelieving look, so she picked up the Bible, knowing how much the Prynnes prided themselves on being good Christians, and brought it to her lips. 'I swear that on this holy book.'

They both gaped at her, then he said, 'You can't mean it!'

She brandished the book at him. 'Oh, but I do. Have I not sworn an oath on this Bible? How can you in all conscience cheat a widow with a small son to support and no other money coming in?'

As they exchanged glances, she folded her arms and stared stonily back at them. 'I really will burn everything if I don't get my price. Forty pounds is a bargain and well you know it.'

He took a deep breath. 'Throw in the rest of the bits and pieces, including his books, then

40

we'll give you thirty pounds.'

Jacinta shook her head. 'Those pieces are promised to other people who have agreed to pay my price, and I've sold the books to the doctor. Forty pounds and not a penny less.'

'Thirty-five, then.'

'I am a desperate woman, Mr Prynne. If you won't, in all Christian charity, deal fairly with me, then at least I'll make sure you don't profit from my distress.' She picked up the Bible again and clutched it to her bosom.

'Thirty-five is all we can afford.'

She let the silence pool around them, then walked across to run her fingers across the gleaming wood of the dining table. 'This will burn quickly, with all the wax I've polished into it.' She waited then repeated, 'Forty. You know they're worth double that.'

The young man sighed, exchanged glances with his wife, who looked at him pleadingly. 'Oh, very well. Forty. I'll pay you ten on account and the rest after we have the furniture.'

Jacinta wasn't that stupid. 'We have no bargain unless you pay all the money now.'

'But you'll still be in possession of the furniture.'

She cast him a withering look. 'What do you think I'm going to do, spirit the things away during the night? It'll be here waiting for you tomorrow morning. Ben and I are leaving on the carrier's cart at eight o'clock, so that we can catch the train to London.'

'We'll be here before you leave, then, to check.'

'If you must.'

When they'd gone, she unclenched her fingers from the money he'd counted out and sat down for a moment or two. She was feeling unaccountably tired, she who usually had boundless energy. It was the worry of it all, she supposed. And the lack of food.

She now had just over a hundred pounds. Some would call it a fortune, but she knew how hard it would be for a woman with a small child to earn any more, so she wasn't spending a farthing of it, if she could help it. Not till she knew where she stood.

She hadn't written to her husband's family when he fell ill because they'd disowned him years before. She reckoned she'd stand more chance of getting their help now if she went in person and threw herself on their mercy.

She would beg, plead, do anything for her son. Anything at all, except marry another cruel old man who took pleasure in beating his wife.

★ ★ ★

The following morning, as Jacinta buttoned Ben's overcoat and set his cap on his soft blond curls, Mr Ketch's son arrived with a handcart to collect the books for the doctor.

It was Ben who was upset by this. 'You've given away all Papa's books. He said they'd be mine one day.'

She kept her voice low. 'Ben, I've let you choose one and that's all we can take. I've explained about the money and how we have to leave. I can't carry the books, only our clothes.'

42

Her heart ached for him, but pity would do no good if she was to build into him the strength of character that had been lacking in his father. At just turned nine, he should be concerned only with his playmates and his lessons. Instead, he'd been living a lonely life in a small cottage, taught by his mother, forbidden to speak to the village lads, let alone make friends with them.

'I am a gentleman,' Claude had said loftily when she protested. 'The children of common labourers are not suitable companions for *my* son.'

'And I'm a gentleman's daughter, but that doesn't stop me being obliged to mop my own floor, or cook and wash for you. You don't complain about that, do you? Claude, please reconsider. Children need companions of their own age. What harm can it do to let him join in their games?'

'I forbid it and I won't hear another word on the subject.'

After which she could have talked herself blue in the face without receiving a response from him, though he'd have used force if she'd tried to go against him, had done in the past.

How unhappy her marriage had been. And yet — Jacinta's eyes lingered on her son — she wouldn't wipe it out, for it had given her Ben. A son like him was worth any sacrifice.

As she was picking up her shabby portmanteau, she saw Mr Prynne come striding up the path, followed by his wife, who was having trouble keeping up with him.

He walked in through the open door without

43

knocking, his eyes darting here, there and everywhere, then held out one arm to bar her way when Jacinta would have left. 'I intend to check everything before you go.'

At that, fury boiled over within her and she shoved him away good and hard. 'Don't you dare touch me! I haven't cheated you, or anyone else.'

As Prynne hesitated, she swept past him with Ben, carrying the portmanteau and walking briskly towards the village inn. Their two shabby trunks had already been taken there by Joe Ketch.

The carter arrived soon after they got to the inn. He and Joe heaved the trunks on to the cart, then he told Ben to climb up on to the bench seat beside him, and indicated the second bench behind him. Jacinta took her place next to a woman with a basket on her knee containing eggs well cushioned by straw.

Ben was excited now by the thought of going on a train journey for the first time in his life and pelted the carter with questions about the places they were passing through. The man was clearly used to children and answered him with good humour.

'Sorry about your husband, Mrs Blacklea,' the woman said.

Jacinta forced out a suitable reply. It was a lie. *She* wasn't sorry, not at all. She was glad.

Surely she could make a better life for her son and herself now?

★ ★ ★

44

Hours later, with dusk falling rapidly and her stomach growling with hunger, they arrived in Berstead, the small village in Hertfordshire, where her husband's family lived.

Claude might have refused to ask his family for assistance when they fell on hard times. But she wasn't too proud to beg their help now, if only for Ben's sake.

In Berstead, Jacinta had to spend some of her precious coins to hire a cab to take her and her luggage from the station in Watford to the Hall. She could only hope pride in the family name would at least impel them to house her tonight.

She didn't know what she would do if they refused to help her. There was no one else to whom she could turn, because her aunt was dead now and she'd lost touch with her cousins.

Apart from the money she'd made by selling their household goods, her only other possessions of any value were the narrow gold band on her finger and her mother's locket. The latter meant far more to her than the ring.

Claude had tried to steal the locket once, so that he could sell it and buy some books he'd particularly wanted for his never-ending study of an obscure Latin poet, but she'd stolen it back, then kept it well hidden. Even though he'd beaten her black and blue, she'd refused to tell him where it was.

Whatever happened, she vowed now, she'd find a way to survive, but she wanted more than survival for her son, which was why she'd come here first. She wanted Ben to be brought up decently and properly educated, so that he could earn his living as a lawyer, or in some other gentlemanly profession.

The cab drew up at a large, comfortable house, set in well cared for grounds. Her spirits rose. If Claude's family were rich enough to own a place like this, then they could surely afford to offer her some modest help.

She woke Ben and paid the cab driver, ignoring his scowl at the lack of a tip. Two minutes later she was standing in front of the door next to her luggage, listening to the cab horse trot away. A maid opened the door and gaped at the sight of her and her son. Well, it must have looked strange to turn up unannounced with their luggage.

Head spinning, Jacinta leaned against the doorpost for a moment to regain her breath. She should have eaten something, but there had only been enough bread left to give Ben his breakfast and take the rest for him to eat during the journey. She hadn't had time to buy more.

'I'm Mrs Claude Blacklea, a distant relative of the family. I'd like to speak to your master, if you please.' When the maid still looked puzzled, she asked in sudden, sharp panic, 'Mr Gerald Blacklea does live here?'

'Yes. Um . . . is he expecting you?'

'No. But I'm sure he'll see me.' As the maid still looked reluctant to let her inside, she said it baldly. 'His cousin has just died, and I'm left with my son and nowhere else to turn.'

She thought she saw a flicker of pity in the young woman's eyes.

'Please come inside, ma'am. If you'll take a

46

seat in the hall, I'll find out if the master is free.'

'My luggage?'

'I'll get the gardener to bring it in.'

If it hadn't been for Ben, Jacinta might have broken down and wept with sheer relief at having got past the door. But it had terrified him to see her crying during Claude's final illness, when she found out how little money he had left, so this time she didn't allow herself to give way.

Ben, who had been standing behind his mother, suddenly spied a dog pattering across the far end of the hallway and ran after it. He adored animals and had tried to bring home several, but for the past few years they hadn't been able to afford even the trifling extra expense of feeding a puppy.

Jacinta tried to grab him, but caught only air and would have fallen had she not clutched a nearby door-post. Everything wavered round her.

The dog vanished through a doorway and Ben ran after it.

Then he let out a sudden cry. Terrified someone had hurt him, Jacinta found the strength to rush down the hallway.

Inside the room she found Ben crouched on a hearthrug next to the dog, looking up at a tall gentleman. The latter bore some resemblance to her late husband, but was several years younger and looked more powerful. He was staring down at the boy as if he couldn't believe his own eyes.

The maid cleared her throat to get her master's attention. 'Sir, this lady says she's the widow of Mr Claude Blacklea, and this is his son.'

There was a moment's silence, then, 'Very well. Take the boy to the kitchen and see that he's fed. He looks hungry. Then take him up to the schoolroom.' He turned to study Jacinta. 'And bring some tea and cake to us here.'

'I'm so sorry to burst in on you like this,' she began. 'I'm afraid Ben ran after the dog before I could stop him.'

'I don't understand why you're here. You must surely know that the family disowned Claude — paid him to stay away, in fact. He was such a fool.'

She felt herself flush under his scornful gaze. 'Yes, sir. And he remained a fool, for he lost all his money. When he died, I was desperate and didn't know where to turn. I'm not greedy. I don't need much, but I beg you'll help me, for my son's sake. Ben doesn't deserve to go hungry. He's such a good little fellow.'

Mr Blacklea looked at her thoughtfully, not saying anything.

She felt utterly humiliated by the scrutiny. It was worse than she'd expected to come here and beg, and she was feeling quite stupid with tiredness after her long day of travelling with a fractious child.

The tea tray arrived.

He gestured to a chair. 'Will you pour?'

She forced herself to pick up the teapot and check that the tea was adequately brewed, then poured him a cup, afterwards offering him the plate of little cakes first.

48

Her stomach betrayed her by growling with hunger.

Another of his searching looks, then he asked, 'How long is it since you've eaten?'

She flushed, unable to meet his eyes.

'How long?'

'Yesterday. There wasn't much bread left and I couldn't let Ben go hungry.'

'Hmm. Eat some cake.'

When she'd finished, he said abruptly, 'I'll need time to consider what to do. If you'll kindly pull the bell?'

She did that and when the maid returned, he told her to find a bedroom for Mrs Blacklea.

Jacinta was shown up to a comfortable bedroom, but there was no sign of Ben or his things there.

'Where's my son?'

'In the schoolroom, ma'am, like the master ordered. The governess will look after him. Children don't come down to the main floors.'

'I'd like to see him, check that he's all right.'

'He's had something to eat.' The maid led her up to the next floor and she found Ben sitting at the schoolroom table with a little girl. A lady stood up as they came in, a governess by her appearance.

'Mrs Blacklea wishes to assure herself that her son is all right,' the maid said.

She turned to Jacinta. 'This is Miss Foresby, and this is Miss Elizabeth, Mr Blacklea's daughter. My goodness, is that the time? We'd better get ready. We don't want to upset the master.'

Jacinta sighed and blew a kiss at her son, then followed the maid back down the stairs.

'Dinner is served at seven o'clock sharp, ma'am, and the master doesn't like people being even a minute late. You'll wish to wash and change, I'm sure.'

Jacinta could feel herself blushing with embarrassment. 'I . . . don't have anything suitable to change into. My husband . . . didn't provide well for us. My clothes are all . . . sturdy, like this.' And worn, but she'd no need to say that. It must be obvious.

'I'll consult her ladyship's maid.'

She returned a few minutes later with an elderly maid, neatly dressed in black.

The lady's maid bobbed the slightest of curtseys, studying Jacinta with a scornful expression. 'I can find one of her ladyship's old gowns for you, ma'am. It would be better for you to be properly dressed. The master believes in keeping up standards.'

No time to be standing on her pride. 'Thank you. It's very kind of you. I'm — er — my husband died recently. So it can't be a colour.'

The maid was back in a few minutes with a black gown. It was silk and it fitted beautifully when the other woman helped her into it. But when Jacinta reached up to stroke the material, her rough hands caught on the fabric. She hated to see them so red and raw; she used to be told she had lovely hands.

Dinner was in a small dining room and to Jacinta's relief, there were no other guests, just Gerald Blacklea and his wife.

50

'Maria, my dear, this is Claude Blacklea's widow.'

The woman by his side, frail-looking and immaculately dressed, inclined her head slightly, without even a hint of a welcoming smile, let alone a word of welcome.

During dinner, Mr Blacklea led the conversation, questioning Jacinta about her life and background. She had nothing to be ashamed of, so answered freely. Her father had been a curate, a respectable man, if not wealthy, but his annuity had died with him, so he'd not been able to leave her anything.

When the meal was over, Mr Blacklea said, 'I can see you're very tired and I need to think carefully about your future. I'll talk to you tomorrow morning and let you know my decision then. You may breakfast in the nursery with your son.'

He made her feel diminished, as if she was only a puppet and he could pull the strings in any direction he wished. She didn't like him at all. And his wife seemed utterly cowed, poor thing.

In fact, Jacinta was beginning to wonder if she'd done the right thing in coming here. But where else could she have sought help?

Damn you, Claude Blacklea!

★　★　★

When the widow had gone, Gerald turned to his wife. 'What do you think of my idea now, Maria?'

51

'I'm . . . not sure. She looks . . . Did you see her hands?'

'The hands of a woman who has worked hard. Nothing *she* needs to be ashamed of in that. It just proves that my uncle was right to disown Claude, if that's how he looked after his family.'

Another thoughtful pause, then he added, 'She and the boy were immaculately clean when they came to us. That isn't easy for people in reduced circumstances.'

'The boy was polite enough when I went to say goodnight to Elizabeth. And he speaks well. I think he's been better fed than his mother. Did you see how gaunt she was?'

'Yes. That also speaks well for her care of him. I doubt there's any bad blood on her side.'

'But to take the boy into our home. Gerald, are you quite sure?'

'It would be a good solution to our little problem, Maria.' He scowled at her. 'Especially since *you* can't provide me with a son. There is plenty of time to mould his character.'

'But it's clear how much she loves him. I'm sure she won't want to — '

His voice grew sharper. 'Leave it to me to arrange that, my dear. I know best what is needed — and how to achieve it.'

She sighed and bowed her head. 'Yes, Gerald.'

3

Quentin Saxby stared out of the window at the rain, then looked back at the letter from Dougal McBride, a close friend of Adam Tregear, who was like a son to him. Adam had suggested Captain McBride contact him. If he vouched for this McBride, then Quentin would do his best to help the fellow.

As the family lawyer, he'd supervised the care of Adam for years after the lad's mother died and had seen the youth grow into a fine man. He'd been sad when Adam moved to Australia in order to claim an inheritance, happy when Adam had found happiness in marrying Ismay Deagan.

He missed Adam greatly, but he missed the young man's adopted Aunt Harriet even more. Why hadn't he gathered his courage together and asked her to marry him? They'd been close friends for many years. Why had he let her leave England and move to Australia with Adam?

Because he was a coward, that's why. But no longer.

He'd been so restless after they'd left Liverpool that he'd sold his practice and moved to London, unable to bear the familiar surroundings without her.

The letter from Dougal had been forwarded from his old address, had probably crossed his own letter to Australia detailing his move. He was now working with a lawyer friend and renting a house near some cousins and their families.

But his cousins hadn't become as close as he'd hoped, because they were very high church and very starchy about the proprieties. They pulled prune faces when he talked of his work and life with the sailing fraternity and their tales in foreign lands.

Saddest of all, he suspected what the cousins mainly cared about was that he'd one day leave his money to them.

This Dougal McBride was asking him to help a young woman, who might or might not contact him around the time he received this letter. Dougal was another man who'd lost the woman he loved, it seemed, and Quentin felt a great deal of sympathy for him, he did indeed.

If this Eleanor Prescott got in touch, Quentin was authorised to draw upon a bank draft that was enclosed in the letter to help her get to Australia. He'd be very happy to help her.

More people were going to the Antipodes these days, because the journey wasn't nearly as hazardous in steamships as it had been by sail. And since the Suez Canal had opened last year, it didn't take much more than two months to get there.

Some went to visit family out there, but many went to stay, so that they could be with people they cared about. Why should he not join Adam and Harriet for the same reason? Whether she wanted to marry him or not, she would still be his friend, he was sure.

From his letters Adam sounded to be

54

extremely happy, his only sadness being that he had to leave his wife with his aunt while he travelled to and from Singapore. Some wives sailed with their husbands, it seemed.

Well, if Quentin was living there, if he married Harriet, maybe Ismay could join her husband, if that was her wish.

He stared at the letter and suddenly let out a gasp as the world wavered around him for a moment or two. He was having one of his feelings that it was right to go to Australia. And when he felt something this strongly, it always happened as he'd 'seen' it in his mind's eye.

That came from his Scottish grandmother who claimed to have 'the sight'. He'd never told anyone except her that he had it too. Let alone few people would have believed him, who'd want to employ a lawyer who claimed such a gift?

But his instinct, or whatever you called it, had helped him a time or two in his legal dealings, and had kept him from being cheated in investments too.

Now, it was telling him to go to Australia, telling him it was the right thing to do. Dare he leave everything and go there? If Eleanor did get in touch with him in time, he could escort this young woman to the other end of the world at the same time.

He stared blankly out of the window, seeing nothing but a blur, concentrating only on the tangled thoughts that filled his mind, the actions he needed to take. He was suddenly quite sure she would contact him, so he'd get ready to act, by finding out all the necessary information and purchasing the clothes and other things he'd need for the journey.

Excitement filled him. Well, why should he not go to Australia? He had more than enough money, could do what he chose in his later years.

He hoped Harriet would agree to marry him. Just because he'd never married before didn't mean he was impervious to love and she was the reason he hadn't married. He'd loved her for so many years, ever since they were both young, but she'd loved and married another man, his best friend, so he'd had to keep his feelings to himself.

As the visions vanished, happiness filled him. No more evenings spent sighing over a book in his lonely armchair. No more tedious hours.

He was going to be very busy indeed. You were never too old to have an adventure.

★ ★ ★

The morning after her arrival at Berstead Hall, Jacinta was summoned to see her host in the library. Gerald was sitting behind a desk, looking very much master of all he surveyed. He gestured to a hard, upright chair in front of it with a flick of one hand.

He hadn't stood up as she came in, so wasn't according her the respect due to a lady and guest. Why not? What was he going to say to her, do with her?

She sat down and waited, hands clasped in her lap.

He let a few moments pass before starting to

speak. 'I cannot allow a Blacklea like your son to live from hand to mouth, without education or family support.'

He steepled his hands, moving slowly, and rested his chin on them, staring at her assessingly, holding back the words, letting the silence continue till she thought she would scream.

'You, however, are not a Blacklea and I do not feel the same responsibility for your future.'

Her mind started racing as she tried to work out what he meant by this.

He waited, watching her as a cat would watch a mouse before pouncing.

In the end, she realised he wasn't going to speak until she did, so said quietly, 'I don't understand what you mean, sir. I'm the boy's mother and I'm a Blacklea by marriage.'

'Yes. But you married the son cast off by his family. Poor judgement on your part, as you no doubt found out. Claude was a fool. I worry about the similarly poor decisions you may make concerning your son's upbringing.'

Her hands felt clammy and her throat was dry. It sounded as if . . . as if he intended to take her son away from her. Surely he couldn't be so cruel?

'I'm willing to accept Benjamin in my home, to raise him as my son and heir, since my wife is unable to bear me any more children. He will have every advantage and will be well educated, as befits the future master of this house.'

Jacinta tried to work out why he'd do this. 'But you have a child.'

He waved one hand dismissively. 'A daughter. I don't believe in women inheriting property. They cannot handle money. But if my daughter were to marry your son, they would both benefit, and I'd have made sure by then that he knew how to manage the estate, how to live as a Blacklea should.'

His gaze was scornful as he studied her. 'However, I don't want you interfering in your son's future life. I have therefore decided to help you find employment as a governess, or some such thing . . . in one of the colonies would be best. You have my word that I'll bring up Benjamin in the manner befitting a gentleman's son, and that he will want for nothing.'

Oh, how she hated those words 'gentleman's son', which Claude had thrown at her so often! And how she was beginning to hate this man.

'But I shall do this only on condition that you give me your solemn word never to return to England or try to contact Benjamin.'

Jacinta felt like a frozen creature, unable to move or speak, only able to stare at him in disbelief at such cruelty.

He leaned back and waited, looking bored and impatient, not seeming to care at all that he was trying to destroy her life.

It took her a while to gather together the courage to say, 'I'm afraid I can't give up my son.'

'You're being selfish, not thinking about how greatly this arrangement will benefit him. Women don't think clearly and logically. I shall therefore allow you time to consider this offer more carefully. Let us say three days. That will give you time to say your farewells to Benjamin properly.' He held up one hand as she would have spoken. 'Do not say another word. Not — one. It would be unwise till you've had time to think.'

Something in his chill voice silenced her protest. He had been nothing but polite, and yet, she didn't dare protest any further. Just . . . didn't dare.

He stood up, looked at her with his icy grey eyes narrowed, and added, 'I will leave you with one more thought: having decided to take the boy into my household and family, I shall do so, because I always achieve what I set my mind to. *Always*. There are ways of getting rid of you that are far less kind than sending you to the colonies, believe me.'

He was like a different person from the urbane host who had led the conversation at the dinner table. He was a monster, someone to be feared. And she was indeed afraid of him. Terrified.

'Go away now and think about how sensible it will be to accept my offer, how wonderful this opportunity will be for the son you claim to love so dearly. I suggest you take a long walk. It's a beautiful day and the village is only a mile away. You can pray for guidance in the church there.'

She bowed her head. Now was not the time to argue. She'd made a big mistake in coming here without checking what Gerald Blacklea was like. He had all the power now, because she'd delivered her son into his hands: the power of money *and* the power of evil.

No wonder his wife was so quiet and meek.

Well, a man like that wasn't going to bring up Ben, whatever Jacinta had to do to prevent it.

Desperately wanting some time to think, time away from his presence, she went to fetch her bonnet and left the house, setting off in what the maid said was the direction of the village.

She already knew she wasn't going to accept the offer without first trying to escape. Only, how was she to do it? How could she get Benjamin away from here?

And if she did succeed in that, how was she to keep her son safe from this monster in gentleman's clothing?

He'd come after them. She was quite sure of that. He'd use his power and money to find them. She had to plan how to avoid being captured by him, or it would do her more harm than good to flee, and then where would Ben be?

★   ★   ★

When she got to the village, Jacinta stopped, not certain where to go next. In the end, she took Gerald's advice and made for the church.

Her spirits were at a very low ebb, because she hadn't had a single idea about how to save her son, though she'd racked her brains as she walked.

The church was small but pretty, with a square Norman tower and narrow stained glass windows. She went inside and paced slowly down the aisle, finding a tiny side chapel that seemed more private.

When she sat down, the tears she'd been

60

holding back overwhelmed her and she wept, rocking to and fro, struggling desperately to keep quiet, so as not to draw attention to herself.

'My dear young lady, take this.'

A handkerchief was thrust into her hand and she used it instead of the soggy square of threadbare cotton lawn she'd been wiping her face with.

She blew her nose hard in an attempt to control her emotions and for the first time looked at the man next to her. He was about ten years older than her, with a tranquil face, thinning silver hair and a kindly expression.

'I'm Peter Stanwell, vicar of this parish. Are you new to the area?'

She hesitated, worried that if she confided in him, he'd go straight to Gerald Blacklea with the tale.

'Anything you say to me will be held in the strictest confidence, I promise you, but perhaps it'd be better if we went into my inner sanctum first, where we can be truly private. I believe some of the ladies from the village will be arriving shortly to arrange the new flowers.'

He stepped back and offered his arm, so she took it, not knowing what else to do. She could feel her hand trembling on the superfine worsted of his elegant morning coat, and couldn't seem to stop her fear showing, however hard she tried to control her emotions.

He didn't say a word as he led her through a narrow panelled door at the side of the church. The short corridor led to an elaborately carved wooden door, which opened into a room filled

61

with coloured light from two stained glass windows perfectly placed to catch the morning sunshine.

He gestured to them. 'Beautiful, aren't they? These are modern copies of the old windows in the church. I was so fortunate to be given this parish, which has always housed its parsons in comfort. Please take a seat.'

She sat down, feeling limp and drained, and since she couldn't clutch him now, she clasped her hands together.

'I'd get my housekeeper to bring us a cup of tea, but if you wish to keep your visit here secret, it'd be better not to do that. No sooner does a thought pop into poor Jean's head, than she lets it out of her mouth.'

'I do wish to keep my visit to you secret. And . . . will you promise not to say a word to anyone if I tell you why I'm so upset?'

He laid one hand on his Bible. 'I swear to repeat nothing that you tell me without your consent.'

She'd have trusted him even without the oath, because his expression was gentle and kindly, so she began to explain her problem, stopping from time to time to mop away more tears.

He was silent for so long after she'd finished that she thought he was trying to find a way to tell her he couldn't help. Then he looked up, his expression grim.

'I'm putting myself in *your* hands now, my dear young lady. A parson should not despise anyone, but Gerald Blacklea becomes more arrogant with every year that passes and I do

62

despise him. He is the canker in the bud as far as this parish goes, he and that henchman of his. Blacklea opposes any efforts of mine to lighten the burdens of the poor, though he's happy enough to keep the church in excellent repair. As if stones and glass are worth more than the souls and bodies of those who come here, as if it doesn't matter that his tenants and the villagers go hungry!'

She looked at him, grateful for his sympathy.

'So you see, feeling as I do, I'm not likely to betray you to such a man, Mrs Blacklea.'

Jacinta nodded. 'But I don't see how you can help me. I don't see how anyone can. Gerald Blacklea is . . . frightening. Only, I don't know how I'll bear it if I lose my son. Ben has been my one consolation during the past few years, and my joy.'

After a moment's silence, she added, 'What's more, I don't want a man like that raising him, training him to be ruthless and uncaring.' She waited for Mr Stanwell to speak, praying he would find a way to help her.

'Then we must do something about the situation. It's not going to be easy, I know, because Gerald Blacklea is both ruthless and clever. Still, there must be a way.'

She watched him stare into the distance, as if trying to marshal his thoughts, and his lips moved, as if he was praying for guidance. Then his face slowly brightened.

'I'm not sure, and it may not work, but there could be a way to provide for you.'

'And for my son? To keep Ben with me?'

'Yes. And for your son as well.'

She took a deep breath. 'Whatever it is, I'll do it.'

'Wait until you hear what I'm offering.' He stood up. 'I need to fetch something from the house. Please wait here. And don't leave this room. In fact, I'll lock both the doors, if you don't mind, so that no one will disturb you.'

Jacinta searched his face, trying to read his character and he stared gravely back at her. Surely he wasn't trying to keep her here while he fetched Gerald? No, she couldn't believe that of a man with so kind a face.

After a moment, she nodded.

Mr Stanwell paused by the outer door to say, 'No one can see inside because of the stained glass. You'll be quite safe.'

When he'd gone, she sagged against the back of the chair, praying as she'd never prayed before that she'd read the parson's character correctly.

When the key turned in the outer lock, she jumped in shock. She'd been so deep in thought she'd lost track of how much time had passed on the neat little clock ticking away on the mantelpiece.

Mr Stanwell came back in, locking the door behind him. He was carrying a small package and took from it what looked to be a letter. 'Please read that.'

She took the piece of paper and unfolded it.

My dear cousin,
    As I said in my last letter, I'm now settled in the Swan River Colony and

64

making a good life for myself here. My son Christopher seems to have recovered fairly well from his ordeal, though he does occasionally have nightmares about it.

I hardly know how to say this, but a dear friend has been urging me to find myself a wife and I've been giving the idea some consideration.

Easier said than done in a place where men outnumber women ten to one. I think my friend is right, though. A man isn't made to live alone, and I do need a woman's help in raising and caring for Christopher.

I'm not sure whether you can help me find someone, but you're the only one I'd trust with this task. Do you know any lady who'd be prepared to come to Australia and marry me?

She need not be beautiful, nor even pretty, but she must be kind, that above all, and of a motherly nature, willing to look after Christopher.

You can explain to her how cruelly my son suffered at the hands of his own mother and her paramour. I hate even to think about it, let alone set it down on paper.

The lady must be prepared to be a wife to me, in all senses of the word. I would dearly love to have other children. If she is a widow and has a child already, then I'd be happy to take in the child as well.

In return, I would promise to keep her in modest comfort and do all I could to make her life here happy.

Am I asking too much? Is it possible to find such a lady, do you think?

I've enclosed a photograph of myself and Christopher, taken recently. You'll be surprised at how much he's grown. Perhaps this will reassure her that I'm not a monster — though I look somewhat grim, don't I? But it's hard to stay perfectly still for a whole minute while a photograph is being taken.

The timber yard is thriving, and I've extended my business into renovations and building work, which I enjoy. I'm constructing a new house for myself next to the timber yard, and it'll be completed by the time you receive this letter.

Fremantle is a pleasant little town, rather small considering it's the main port for the capital of Western Australia. Perth lies inland, about twelve miles up the river Swan. Both towns (they're not really cities by English standards) have approximately three thousand inhabitants.

I've made good friends here, who'd welcome a wife into their circle. Indeed, it's my dearest friend, Bram Deagan, who has urged me to write this letter. He's a trader, with a gift for friendship and kindness, and his wife is charming. She works in their business, selling silks imported from Singapore.

It's not unusual for someone in the colonies to send home for a wife, so if you find a suitable lady, she need not fear being a cause for gossip.

I'll trust in your good judgement, my dear cousin. My son is like a plant growing wild, which needs tending to make it flourish. And I'm lonely. I need a companion as much as a wife.

I've written this letter three times and this is the best I can manage to explain everything. Please ask any lady reading it to forgive me if I've expressed myself badly.

If you find someone, please take the enclosed letter to my bank and ask them to give you the money to pay for her passage. Make sure she has a comfortable cabin.

My thanks for any efforts you can undertake on my behalf,

Your cousin,

Mitchell

PS I nearly forgot to say: should the lady not wish to marry me after we've met, I promise to see that she's looked after till she can find another husband. There is no shortage of men here.

Jacinta read the letter again, more slowly this time. It was the admission that this Mitchell Nash was lonely that won her over, and the PS. Not many men would be that generous. The confession that Mitchell had found it difficult to

67

write the letter pleased her, too.

She looked up. 'May I see the photograph?'

Peter took it from the package and handed it to her.

Mr Nash had dark hair and a serious expression, grim even, as he'd said. But his hand lay possessively on his son's shoulder and the lad was leaning confidently against him. She couldn't imagine a lad leaning against Gerald Blacklea, son or not.

'You know your cousin, Mr Stanwell. If you think I'd be suitable, I'd be willing to travel to Australia to marry him. My only worry is how to get Ben away from that man. And I'm quite sure Blacklea will pursue us.'

'Could you get out of the house during the night, do you think?'

'He locks the doors carefully.'

Mr Stanwell smiled. 'I have a friend, a recluse who has been badly treated by Blacklea. His manservant, who also bears no love for Blacklea, used to be a poacher. If anyone can get into the house, Tam can.'

'I won't be able to bring our clothes and our other possessions.'

'I can give Tam enough money to buy you new ones. My cousin used to live nearby, so I can go to his English bank this very day. There is still time to withdraw the money.'

'You must hate Gerald Blacklea.'

He sighed. 'I try not to hate any human being. But I do believe that man is completely without conscience, acting only in his own interests. I don't believe it's right to separate a mother from a son, especially not when she loves him as much as you clearly love Ben.'

He patted her hand. 'I came to the conclusion a while ago that I won't stand by and allow Blacklea to ruin any more lives if I can do anything to help. Now, we have to plan carefully.'

He continued to frown and she waited patiently.

'I shall have to stay here, or he'll suspect I've been involved, but my friend's manservant will get you away. Tam will enjoy doing that, I believe, and he's an enterprising fellow. It'd be best for you to go at once, before that man thinks to lock you in your room at night.'

'Very well.'

'As soon as the household has settled tonight, go down to the kitchen with your son and wait for Tam Bennett to come for you. Take nothing with you that you can't carry easily.'

She nodded.

'Now, you'd better give me back my handkerchief. It bears my initials. There must be no sign that you and I have met. I'll go outside first and check that there's no one around. If you follow the path through the copse at the rear of the church, you'll come to the Hall.' When he beckoned, she followed his instructions.

As she walked back to the house, she made no attempt to hide the fact that she'd been weeping. It was only to be expected, after all. She saw the curtains move in the library window and guessed *he* was watching her.

She spent the day in her room, but was allowed to take Ben out for a walk round the garden that evening, supervised by one of the grooms. She didn't tell her son what she was planning to do.

Blacklea was waiting for them as they re-entered the house. 'Run along to the nursery, Benjamin.'

The boy shot him a quick look that told Jacinta he didn't like his relative, either.

She let herself sob and mopped away a tear.

'You may take him for a farewell walk tomorrow evening. As long as you do what I wish, I shall be as kind to you as circumstances permit. I don't want him to have bad memories of you or to think ill of me.'

She forced herself to thank him, but it came out as a whisper.

That seemed to satisfy him because he continued, 'The day after that, you'll be escorted to a place of safety and will stay there until I have your passage booked to Australia or Canada.'

She felt as if his eyes were boring into her back all the time she was climbing the stairs to her room. She was glad to shut the door on that feeling of being studied like an insect about to be crushed.

When the dinner gong rang, a maid came to fetch her.

'I'm not hungry.'

'It'd be better to go down, Mrs Blacklea. The master has asked you to dine with him.'

★ ★ ★

70

Jacinta spent an excruciating two hours, forcing herself to eat, if only to keep up her strength, and listening to Gerald talking about his plans for the future of her son. What an unhappy life Ben would lead if he stayed here! He was a lad who loved the freedom of the countryside, not hours of careful study.

When she could at last go to bed, she got undressed only as far as her underclothing. She put on two of everything she could, in case she had to abandon her luggage, then slipped her nightgown over the top, lying in bed with her back to the door.

She could hear noises here and there in the house. Then she heard a chorus of 'Goodnight, sir, madam.' Doors closed on the floor below, which had to be the doors of the bedrooms occupied by Gerald and his wife, because they were the only occupants of that floor.

Footsteps went up to the attics. The last of the servants, she hoped. Doors closed there too.

She lay for what she judged to be another hour, then built up a mound of covers in the bed, which she hoped would seem like a person sleeping.

After bundling some of her clothing in a pillowcase, she took a moment to pray for success in getting her son away. She began her escape by opening the door a little and listening intently for several minutes before she even peered out.

When she'd heard and seen nothing, she crept across the landing to the elegant sweep of stairs. She moved to stand by the banisters, looking down, then moved to look up at the narrower servants' stairs in a corner of the second floor. No lights seemed to be showing anywhere in the house, but nonetheless, she stood there for several minutes, listening carefully. There were no sounds of movement from the main bedrooms just below her or from the attics above.

Only then did she creep along the corridor to her son's bedroom.

He woke with a start as she knelt by the bed, but she placed one hand across his mouth and whispered, 'Shh. It's me. Darling, we have to escape.'

'Good. I don't like it here.'

'I know. I don't, either. Be very quiet.'

He nodded. There had been times when he'd had to be quiet or his father would have grown angry. The poor boy knew only too well how to be quiet.

'It's an adventure, my darling. We mustn't make any noise until we're far away, or that man will catch us and try to take you away from me. Let me help you get dressed.'

She made him put on two layers of clothing, then bundled some of the rest in another pillowcase.

When they were ready, she turned towards the door, letting out an involuntary gasp as someone started to open it.

Had she been discovered already?

She stared at the person standing in the doorway. The governess.

They stared at one another for a moment,

then the woman turned away without a word.

A minute later a nearby bedroom door closed with the faintest of clicks.

Jacinta shuddered in relief and it was a moment or two before she could move again. In the darkness she reached again for her son's hand, murmuring, 'Shh.'

Ben squeezed her hand and she decided to continue. She let go and leaned down to whisper, 'Follow me and don't make any sound at all. Move slowly and carefully.' Then she led the way towards the back stairs.

The stairwell was dark. This one had no grand windows to let the moonlight in. She began to feel her way down it, checking occasionally that her son was still behind her.

When they got to the next floor down, she stopped, bending to whisper, 'Wait a minute.' Her heart was pounding and she felt as if every nerve in her body was jangling as she listened for the sounds of someone else moving round the house, following them.

But all was silent.

The stairs ended just outside the kitchen. The door opened quietly, well oiled to prevent the servants from disturbing their master. As they went through it, Jacinta looked round. She had no way of knowing what was expected from now on.

'We'll go and wait outside,' she whispered.

But the outer kitchen door had big bolts on it and she hesitated to open them, sure they'd make a noise.

'Psst.'

She spun round to see another dark figure across the room. A man this time.

It took her an eternity — or was it only a few seconds? — to realise it wasn't Gerald Blacklea. The man beckoned and she seized Ben's hand and walked across to him, carrying her bundles in one hand. If this was someone keeping guard for Gerald, she'd rather get the confrontation over with before her heart burst with the anxiety.

The stranger leaned forward, his voice low in her ear. 'I'm Tam Bennett, ma'am. Parson sent me. Let's get out of here as quickly as we can. We'll go through the laundry. No bolts on that door.'

His teeth were a paler line in the dim light as he smiled. 'This way. We'll be very quiet, won't we, lad?'

Jacinta could feel Ben nodding, see the eagerness in his whole body as he started after the man who was to guide them. To the boy, this was an adventure. To her, it felt more like a matter of life and death to get away from that man.

Gerald's threats hadn't been specific, but she wouldn't put it past him to have her murdered, if it was the only way to get what he wanted. He was so chill and arrogant, she couldn't imagine him respecting other people's lives.

She followed the others through the laundry door.

Tam held up one hand to tell them to stop and moved past her to shut the door into the kitchen.

As they moved outside through the laundry, he jiggled with the outer door's lock and something clicked. Turning, he smiled again, before leading the way across the garden into the woods.

She had nothing but the clothes she stood up in, two bundles and the money she'd gained from selling the furniture and her husband's books, which was inside her stays.

But she had her son, and that mattered more than anything.

★ ★ ★

The half-moon shed enough light for Tam to lead Jacinta and Ben across the fields of the home farm without needing a lantern. A horse and cart were waiting in a little used lane on the other side of the final field. The driver didn't speak and had his hat pulled down, plus a muffler round his neck, as if to hide who he was.

'We'll ride in the back,' Tam said in a low voice. 'Then I'll tell you what I've planned, Mrs Blacklea.'

There was a lad a few years older than Ben sitting in the back already. He grinned at them and made room for the smaller boy to sit next to him.

Tam waved one hand. 'This is my eldest, Johnny. He looks younger, but he's fourteen and got a bit of sense in his head — most of the time anyway.'

As the driver told the horse to walk on, Tam went on, 'Make no mistake about it, Mrs Blacklea. *That man* is to be feared. He'll stop at nothing to have his own way — nothing! — and he's cunning enough to get away with murder, if necessary.'

Jacinta shivered at having her fears confirmed. 'I know. He threatened me when he told me he intended to take Ben away from me, said he would get what he wanted, with or without my agreement. I took that to mean he'd have me killed if necessary, because he looked at me as though I was less than nothing, just an obstacle that could be crushed and removed without much difficulty.'

'I'm glad you believe me about him. Now, listen carefully. This is what the parson and I have planned. My Johnny's a smart lad. He'll go to London on the same train as you, but he'll take Ben with him. Two brothers travelling together, don't you see? If *that man* starts asking questions, no one will have seen a lady and her son.'

'Yes. That might work.'

'We'll dress Ben in rougher clothes — the parson sent some from the poor box — and the two lads will sit in a different carriage from you. They won't come near you at all, so the people who work on the railway will never see you and Ben together, if they're asked. Even when you get to London, you must walk right outside of the station before you rejoin your son.'

She nodded reluctantly, seeing the sense of this, but not wanting to let Ben out of her sight for even a minute.

'My wife's sent some ragged clothing for you as well. We'll stop soon and you can change behind some bushes, then put your other things in this old portmanteau. You're to look as old as you can. She's put in a little packet of flour, says to rub it into your hair to make it look grey.

Keep a shawl over your head and bend your back, moving slowly.'

Jacinta nodded again. She could do that.

'I wish I could come with you, Mrs Blacklea, but I need to be around here as usual, so that *he* doesn't suspect me of being involved in your escape. But he won't think of Johnny helping out, I'm sure. I doubt he even knows who any of the children in the village are.'

'I'm grateful.'

'I like to help people, especially when it's to stop *him* hurting someone else. I'll put you on the early milk train and you should be well away from here before they even realise you've left the house. The main trouble will be getting a ship to Australia. We don't know when the next ship sails. Mr Stanwell's given me some money to pay for your two passages, cabin class, but you'll have to book them yourself.'

'He's so kind.' Jacinta was relieved that she'd not have to travel steerage, and just as relieved not to have to pay for the passages herself. She needed to be very careful with what little money she had left, just in case she disliked Mr Nash.

'He does a lot of good, though not always openly. You know that ships leave from Southampton, so you'll have to get a train there from London? Good. My Johnny will have to leave you in London, though.'

'Yes. Of course.'

'Mr Stanwell has written a letter for his cousin in Australia. He says you're to go to him, even if you change your mind about marriage.' Tam pulled out a package and a small leather pouch with a drawstring. 'This is the money and the various letters and photo. Now, let's stop and you can change your clothes behind those bushes. I think everything will fit in that portmanteau.'

When they were rumbling along again, she said without thinking, 'It's ironic that I should be going to Australia. Gerald Blacklea talked about sending me there.'

Tam looked at her in dismay. 'He didn't!'

'Yes, he did.'

'Then I have to warn you . . . He'll probably send someone to look for you in Southampton when he can't find you in the district. He'll leave no stone unturned, that one, and his henchman will do anything for money. Bernard Pearson, he's called, tall with grey hair, about my age, has a scar on his chin about here.' He touched his own chin to show her. 'You watch out for that one. He's as ruthless as his master.'

She felt shivery with fear and her words came out as a whisper. 'What am I going to do if I have to wait weeks for a ship?'

'Take new names and work out a disguise. Not a widow's veils. That'd look suspicious straight away. Perhaps you should hire a man to guard you both and see you on to the ship. There is enough money if you're careful.'

'Tam, I'm truly grateful for what you've done.'

'I'm happy to help you.'

She had a lot to think about after that and hardly noticed where they were going. She'd do anything, short of murder, to get her son away from Gerald Blacklea.

Or die trying.

4

When Eleanor Prescott's letter arrived, Quentin was delighted that his presentiment had been correct, though not surprised. If Dougal McBride had bothered to get Adam's help and send the money to his friend's lawyer, he must have been sure that the woman he loved would want to travel out to join him once her ailing husband died.

He was so eager to get on with his move that he considered going to the expense of three shillings to send her a telegram, saying he was ready to help her and she should let him know immediately where he could find her in a week's time. But he found there wasn't a telegram delivery service to the village where she was staying, so contented himself with a letter, which would be delivered one day later, after all.

He received another letter from her by return of post, giving the name of a hotel in London, to which she would move in three days' time. She thanked him for replying so quickly and would very much appreciate whatever help he could give her.

She'd be surprised when she found out he was going to Australia as well, he thought. He caught sight of himself in the mirror over the mantelpiece, grinning and looking almost boyish — as far as a man of sixty-two could look boyish.

It seemed a long time since he'd felt so good about life.

★ ★ ★

Eleanor showed the letters to Daphne, because she knew by now that her sister-in-law was much more helpful when she knew every tiny detail of what was going on.

Daphne even paid Eleanor's fare to London and gave her the money for a steerage passage, plus ten pounds 'for expenses'.

When the morning came to leave, Eleanor felt so anxious she couldn't eat any breakfast. For once her hostess didn't try to persuade her.

Daphne walked to the door with her as she left.

'I should be interested to find out how you get on, if you have time to write to me, but I shall not be giving you any more money.'

'No. I understand that. I'm grateful for all you've done for me.'

'It was the correct thing to do.' She hesitated, then added, 'And I was happy to help another woman who doesn't sit and wail about her fate.'

As the train rattled away towards London, Eleanor leaned her head against the upholstered back of the seat. She felt numb. The last year had been turbulent.

She was committed to going to Australia now, but couldn't help wondering whether Dougal would be glad to see her or whether he just felt obliged to look after her, given the offer he'd made.

Had they truly fallen in love? It had happened so quickly.

Even if Dougal still wanted to marry her, it might be better to wait until they knew one another better. The few weeks on board his ship, with her husband lying sick in the cabin, now seemed very unreal to her. A marriage needed more than a romance carried out only by words and quiet conversations. Why, Dougal had only ever kissed her once, as a farewell!

She could only hope things would work out between them. Most of the time she felt they would, felt the two of them had a good chance of finding happiness. But every now and then she couldn't help worrying, wondering if she was deluding herself.

Well, if things didn't work out, she'd manage. She always did.

★　★　★

Eleanor booked a room at the Stourby Hotel, one of the cheaper rooms on the third floor, and sent a message round to the hotel where the lawyer had said he would be staying, saying she'd arrived. It seemed that fate was on her side, because Mr Saxby too had now arrived in London.

After that, she changed out of her black mourning clothes and donned a dark blue outfit, one of only two others she'd finished altering. She didn't intend to remain in mourning for Malcolm because she felt she'd lost him years ago.

To her surprise, a short time later the hotel's bell boy brought her a message that a gentleman was waiting for her in the lobby, a Mr Saxby. The lawyer must have come as soon as he'd received her message.

After a quick glance in the mirror, to make sure she looked respectable, she followed the boy down.

An older man stood up as the bell boy led her across the lobby.

'This is Mr Saxby, ma'am.'

'Thank you.' She reached into her pocket for a tip, but the lawyer held up one hand to stop her and dropped a penny into the lad's outstretched hand. 'Could we have some tea and cakes?' he asked.

'Yes, sir. Straight away, sir.'

He turned to offer his hand to Eleanor. 'I'm Quentin Saxby.'

She took it, finding his grasp firm and his smile warm. He was studying her openly in his turn and gave a little nod, as if pleased with what he saw. Offering his arm, he said, 'I gather we can go and sit in the residents' lounge now that you're with me, Mrs Prescott.'

'Yes, of course.' To her relief no one else was using the lounge. She took a seat and gestured to him to do the same. 'I don't know how much Captain McBride told you.'

'We'll be frank, shall we?' At her nod he continued. 'He said that your husband was gravely ill, and Dougal hoped to marry you once you were free. He hoped you'd trust him enough to do that, and wouldn't be afraid to travel back

82

to Australia on your own, since he'd find it extremely difficult to leave his ships and come to England to fetch you. Though he'd do that, if necessary.'

'Oh.' She could feel herself blushing. 'I . . . wasn't sure whether he might have changed his mind or not.'

'He sounds very determined about this. I've not met the man, but if he's a friend and partner of Adam Tregear, who is like a son to me, then I know the captain must be a good man.'

She was finding it hard to concentrate on what the lawyer was saying, because she felt so happy that Dougal hadn't forgotten her, still wanted her.

The tea and cakes arrived just then, but though she sipped some tea, Eleanor was too happy to eat anything.

'How long ago did your husband die?'

She hated to turn her thoughts away from Dougal. 'Three weeks ago. But he'd been ill for years, so it was a merciful release. And . . . I don't intend to wear mourning. I did my duty, cared for my husband in his final illness, but I hadn't been happy in my marriage for a long time.' She looked at him, hoping desperately that he wouldn't scorn her for this.

His voice was gentle, his gaze sympathetic. 'That must have been a great strain.'

She decided on frankness. 'Yes. During the last few months Malcolm was very . . . difficult.'

'And you're quite certain you wish to travel to Australia, to join Captain McBride?'

'Yes, I am. I need to see if the — the attraction

83

between us still exists. I can't promise to marry him until I've spent time with him, got to know him better. I won't rush into marriage this time. I have to be certain it's the right thing to do.'

'Very sensible.'

As he smiled at her, Eleanor could feel herself relaxing. 'I'm rather worried about taking Dougal's money for the journey.'

Mr Saxby smiled. 'You needn't worry. Captain McBride clearly isn't short of a pound or two. This is a good opportunity for you both, one not to be missed, even if you don't rush headlong into marriage once you get there. Believe me, life can be very lonely as you get older if you have no one to care for you, no children.' His expression saddened for a moment or two.

She let out her tension in a long, low sigh. Children. How she hoped it wasn't too late for that!

'Now, let's deal with the practicalities. There's a ship leaving Southampton in a few days' time. Can you be ready by then?'

'I'm almost ready now. I just have to buy a few more bits and pieces for the journey.' Sewing materials, above all, to alter the underwear and outer garments that filled two whole trunks.

'Good.'

As he leaned back, he gave her a twinkling smile that made her catch a glimpse of the boy he had once been. She liked the man already.

'I have to confess that I'll be travelling on the ship as well.'

Eleanor looked at him in surprise.

'Adam's Aunt Harriet went to Australia with

him. She was my dearest friend and I miss her so much I've decided to go and visit her. I may even stay there if . . . if things work out as I wish. I have no close family left in England, after all.'

'It'll be good to know someone on the ship.' There was something very kindly and comforting about Mr Saxby. If only she'd had a father like him, she wouldn't be in this difficult situation, she was sure.

He finished his cake, took a final mouthful of tea and stood up. 'I'll go straight to the shipping agent, then, and confirm that we shall definitely want the two cabins I asked them to keep for us.'

She stood up with him. 'Um . . . about the money you've given me.'

'That's yours to buy what you need. I'll deal with our passages and let you know the details once they're booked. Perhaps we can travel down to Southampton together?'

'I'd like that.'

She sank down on the chair once he'd left, feeling strangely boneless. She'd done it now, committed herself to going to Dougal in Australia.

★ ★ ★

As Jacinta hobbled away from the train in London's Paddington Station, still pretending to be an old lady, people walked past her on the platform as if she didn't exist, their eyes sliding away to more interesting sights. That made her decide to keep her old woman's disguise for the journey to Southampton.

A surreptitious glance in the window of a shop on the station itself showed her how tired she looked — well, she *was* tired, no need to feign that. It was only mid-morning still, but she felt as if she'd been travelling for ever, after having no sleep the previous night.

The two lads ignored her and walked off the platform and out of the station, chatting to one another. She followed them, not liking to let Ben out of her sight, relieved when they stopped to wait for her round the second corner, out of sight of the station.

'Can we go and buy something to eat, Mother?' Ben asked at once.

She had to start thinking carefully before she acted. 'In a minute.' She turned to Johnny. 'What are you going to do now?'

'Get something to eat, then catch a train home.'

'Let's all eat together. That way no one will remember a woman and boy.'

'Good idea, Mrs B — '

'Mrs Jackson,' she corrected quickly, taking the first name that came into her head. 'Let's find a workmen's café.'

They found a place which served hot meals for sixpence each and had food ready to serve.

'Eat quickly,' she said in a low voice. 'We need to leave as soon as possible.'

Afterwards, she made enquiries and discovered she had to go to Victoria Station to catch a train to Southampton. She found a cab, and in keeping with her appearance, asked how much it would cost before getting into it.

'A shilling for you, ma,' the cab driver said.

It was a small open cab and he was close enough to chat as he drove them through streets so crowded with vehicles, she didn't know how he managed.

'The new railway line's only recently been completed, you know. Where are you going?'

She'd said Southampton before she thought and was instantly angry with herself. If only she wasn't so tired.

'You'll find it a very smooth journey on the new line, none of the delays there used to be. Going to visit family, are you?'

'Yes. My cousins live just outside the town.'

'Why did you choose the name Jackson?' Ben whispered to her.

'I don't know. Can you remember to be Billy Jackson from now on?'

'Yes. It's exciting, isn't it? I'm so glad we got away from that horrible man. Everyone in the house was frightened of him . . . and I was too.'

'We won't have got away until our ship has left Southampton.'

He looked at her. 'You're frightened of him catching us, aren't you?'

'Yes. So we have to be very careful. Don't talk to people unless you have to, and don't tell anyone where we're from.'

'Here we are, ma,' the driver called.

She paid the fare, gave him a tiny one penny tip, as if paying it hurt her, and hurried her son into the station.

★ ★ ★

87

As the cab driver had said, the train journey passed very smoothly, even in third class, and they were in Southampton by teatime.

She abandoned her attempt to appear old, but didn't resume a lady's clothing. They found respectable lodgings near the harbour, then she took Ben out for something to eat.

He was already yawning as they got back to the room they were sharing, and she had no trouble persuading him to go to bed early.

She went to bed at the same time, feeling better for combing the flour out of her hair. She used a dampened cloth to try to get it clean, but it didn't feel much better. As she lay down on her bed, she felt sure she'd never get to sleep. Her mind was too active.

She'd see about passages tomorrow. She prayed a ship would be leaving soon, prayed even harder that *he* wouldn't find them. And she'd have to work out a better disguise, one that would look all right from close to. They should change lodgings tomorrow so that the landlady wouldn't remember changes in her appearance.

Perhaps she could persuade Ben to dress as a girl . . . no, she doubted he'd agree . . . well then, how about . . .

★ ★ ★

Jacinta was amazed to find she'd slept right through until morning. Luckily the proprietor of the lodging house was able to tell her not only how to set about booking a passage, but also how to buy an outfit for the journey to replace the

88

luggage she said had been stolen, and even where to buy a second-hand trunk.

As the woman didn't seem to notice her changed appearance, and was so busy she didn't try to chat, Jacinta decided to stay on there. The food was quite good and it was clean.

When the shipping agent said a liner was leaving in two days, she could hardly speak for relief. Surely Gerald wouldn't find them in that short a time?

She whisked Ben round the ships' chandlers, who seemed able to supply everything they might need. She hated to spend so much money but had no choice. It'd take two months to get to Australia, even with the new Suez Canal shortening the transition time from the Mediterranean to the Orient. She and her son had to have not only clean clothes to bring up from the hold at regular intervals, but something to occupy themselves with during the voyage.

The shipping agent looked down his nose at her when she requested a cabin instead of the steerage accommodation he'd assumed she wanted. 'Are you sure you can afford it, madam?'

'Of course I am. Our trunks and cases might have been stolen, but luckily, I kept one bag with me and my money on my person. Not a first-class cabin, though.'

She didn't show that she'd heard him mutter, 'I should think not!'

By the end of the day she was exhausted again. Ben had been wonderful. But then, he was used to doing as he was told and keeping quiet. She worried about that sometimes. She promised to spend hours playing with him and reading to him on the ship, and that brought a smile to his face.

'And if you meet any other children of your own age, I hope you'll play with them too.'

That made him look at her doubtfully.

'Your father was wrong to stop you playing with others.'

'I don't know how to play with other children.'

'Just watch what they do. You'll soon learn to enjoy yourself,' she promised rashly. Oh, it hurt her what Claude had done to their son.

And she wasn't going to let another selfish man treat him even more unkindly. Not while there was breath in her body.

★ ★ ★

The next day they had to go for a medical examination. Jacinta put on some of her new clothes and made sure Ben was well turned out. She looked in the hall mirror in satisfaction before they set out. There! They both looked more respectable now.

The lady waiting beside her at the depot for the same purpose was about her own age and seemed pleasant. When there were delays, caused by a passenger being suspected of having consumption, they had to sit in a waiting room together for nearly two hours, so inevitably began to chat.

The clerk supplied Ben with a couple of books and smiled at Jacinta. 'Easier to keep children occupied than leave them to get in trouble.'

90

Ben beamed at his mother. 'I haven't read these.'

'That's good.' He'd not had much to read at home, just a few tattered books passed on by the Squire's wife.

The lad immediately settled down to read, lost to the people around him.

'Nice to see a child eager to read,' the lady next to Jacinta commented. 'I'm Eleanor Prescott, by the way. Are you going to Australia as well?'

'Yes. I'm ... Mrs Jackson, and that's my son — um, Billy.' She didn't find it easy to call him that. 'I wonder how long this is going to take. Our luggage was stolen and I need to do some more shopping.'

'How terrible for you! Is your husband waiting at the men's side?'

'I'm a widow.'

'So am I. But I'm out of deep mourning now.'

'Me too.' As if she'd ever mourn for Claude.

When they eventually got to see the doctor, it was a very cursory examination and they walked out of the depot together, Ben trailing behind, sad to lose the books.

'Mother, that man's still there, watching us,' he said suddenly. 'I saw him when we were coming here. He's over to the right.'

As Jacinta stole a glance sideways, her companion slowed her pace to match. 'Which man?'

'The one with the brown jacket.'

He was big, with a brutal face. Ben might be wrong, but if he wasn't, this man looked to be just the sort Gerald Blacklea would send to take her son away from her, by force if necessary.

What was she to do? For a minute, Jacinta's mind went blank, then she took a risk. 'Could I please ask your help? My husband's relatives don't want us to go to Australia and will do anything to stop us — or rather, to take Be — Billy from me. They don't care if *I* leave the country, in fact they'd prefer it. But I don't want them bringing him up. They're very strict and joyless. And anyway, I love my son very much.'

Eleanor looked at her in surprise, but seemed to see something in her face that was convincing, because she said quietly, 'Tell me what I can do to help.'

'Could we link arms as if we're friends, and could we go to your hotel, please? Maybe Billy and I can sneak out the back way.'

'Yes, we can go to my hotel. And I'll call you 'cousin' in case that man gets close enough to listen to what we're saying. What's your first name?'

She'd said 'Jacinta' before she realised. 'Thank you, Mrs Prescott.'

'Cousin Eleanor.'

'Yes. Ben, stay close to me.' She realised she'd used the wrong name. 'We've taken different names, but I'm so upset, I'm having trouble remembering. His real name is Ben, not Billy. I'm not a skilled liar, am I?'

'No, but that's a good thing, surely?'

'Is it far to the hotel, Mrs Prescott? Would we be better catching a cab?'

'I was going to walk.'

'Ben, can you sneak a look behind and check if he's still following?'

There was silence behind them for a moment, then the boy said, 'He is, Mother.'

'Oh dear.'

'We'll take a cab, then.'

But when they got out of the cab and were walking into Mrs Prescott's hotel, they saw another cab pull up and the same man got out.

'He's definitely following you,' Eleanor said. 'We'll go straight up to my room.'

As they started up the stairs, she said suddenly, 'No, we'll go to my friend's room. I'm sure he'll be back by now.'

She knocked on a door and an older man opened it.

'Can we come inside quickly, Mr Saxby?'

'Of course.'

They entered and she closed the door immediately.

'What's wrong, Eleanor?'

The man had a kind look to him, which reassured Jacinta.

'This lady is having trouble with her relatives. I said I'd help, but I think we need your help too.' She explained the situation.

There was a knock on the door.

'He's followed us,' Jacinta said involuntarily.

Mr Saxby put one finger to his lips and gestured to them to hide at the side of the L-shaped room where they couldn't be seen from the door. While they were doing that, the knocking started again.

He opened it to find the bell boy there.

'Gentleman is looking for Mrs Prescott, sir. I thought she might be with you.'

'I haven't seen her for a while. She went out shopping.'

'She came back, though. I saw her come in, sir. Only she isn't in her room. I've knocked three times there.'

'How strange. Well, I'm afraid I don't know where she is now. Possibly she's made friends with another lady and is taking tea somewhere. You know what ladies are like.'

As he started to close the door, the bell boy edged forward, trying to look into the rest of the room.

'Excuse me.' Quentin pushed him back and closed the door, turning to the others. He waited to hear footsteps moving away and when they didn't, he opened the door again to reveal the boy, trying to eavesdrop. 'Did you want something else?'

'No, sir.' The lad turned round.

Quentin stayed in the doorway until the bell boy had disappeared round the corner, and only then did he close the door. 'That lad is obviously trying to spy on you for someone.'

Jacinta was relieved to have his help. 'So you believe me, then?'

'Oh yes, my dear. I've been a lawyer for a long time and I pride myself on being able to judge someone's character or to notice when a bell boy behaves in a suspicious manner. The cheek of it, trying to push his way into my room!'

'Thank you.' Jacinta sniffed and had to blow

94

her nose before she could start giving him the details.

When she'd finished her tale, he said, 'I think we may need to board the ship rather carefully tomorrow, and keep you out of their way today. But first, I'll go and speak to the manager about the boy spying and ask if we can use the back entrance to the hotel to get you out.'

He came back twenty minutes later, looking smug. 'I have the manager on our side and he'll see us out of the back door if you still wish to leave. I told him I was your lawyer. And he's absolutely furious about the boy's behaviour. I guarantee the boy won't even speak to the man following you from now on, for fear of losing his job.'

'Thank you so much.'

'However, he suggested I book a room for you and your son here tonight, Mrs Blacklea, and I've taken the liberty of doing that. Mrs Prescott and I will go back to your lodgings and get your luggage, if you'll give me a note for your landlady.'

She stood for a moment staring, unable to believe in such kindness, then said, 'I can't thank you enough.'

'It's my pleasure to help you.' He leaned forward to pat her hand. 'Don't worry. We'll think of some way to get you both safely on board tomorrow.'

Jacinta felt numb with fear and could only sit in the lawyer's room with Ben and wait for Mr Saxby and Mrs Prescott to return.

Every time footsteps passed the door, she

listened carefully. But no one knocked, or even stopped outside.

Ben sat very quietly and they both kept away from the window as the minutes crawled past.

'We'll be all right,' she said in a low voice. 'We've found friends to help us.'

He shivered. 'I don't want to go back to that man.'

Children shouldn't live in fear, she thought angrily. And nor should I.

5

Western Australia

In Fremantle, Mitchell Nash stopped at the entrance to his timber yard, feeling great satisfaction at what he saw: a thriving business with a new house being built for him to one side of the yard.

Near the gate was a shack in which Tommy lived. His employee was an ex-convict and was learning the timber trade, as well as acting as general labourer and night watchman. Mitchell had taken a risk giving him a job, but he was proving a good worker. Tommy had to report each week to the magistrate, but Mitchell had told the authorities what a good worker he was proving.

Yes, all was well here now, except . . . Mitchell sighed. Except that he longed for a normal family life. He envied Bram his new baby, and the other two children that made up the family. He'd have liked other children too.

He'd had a disastrous start in Australia, coming here in search of his wife, who had run away with another man. He hadn't wanted Betsy back, but he had been determined to find his son, Christopher, whom he loved dearly.

Sadly, he'd had to chase them all the way to Sydney and hadn't caught up with them in time to prevent Betsy being murdered by the madman who had taken her away. The poor woman hadn't deserved that. But thanks to a neighbour's kindness in hiding him, Christopher had been saved.

He'd brought his son back to the Swan River Colony, where he'd made friends, and had set up as a timber merchant in Fremantle. This had been his family business in England and he had a passion for wood in all its forms. The timber Mitchell sold in Western Australia wasn't the same, of course, but he'd soon learned the qualities of the various trees here.

While he was standing there, Bram came walking along the road, whistling cheerfully, as usual, and stopped for a chat. 'You're running short of timber.'

'I've more coming in from the country. I got word that there are two big loads of jarrah on the way, felled by a new settler who knew his business.'

'Jarrah's my favourite Australian wood,' Bram said. 'Lovely colour it has when polished, such a rich deep brown. I like it better than mahogany. Lee Kar Ho has asked me to tell you that he'd like more jarrah sent to him in Singapore. His carvers love it.'

Mitchell smiled. 'I'll set another man on, then.' He already had two men scouring the countryside for timber and seeing it brought safely back to Fremantle, the sort of men who enjoyed travelling round and hated the idea of settling anywhere. There were quite a few like that here, some surprisingly knowledgeable about wood.

'Can't beat good trading links for making money,' Bram said. 'I'd trust Lee Kar Ho with my life.'

'Building's doing as well for me as selling timber.' Since so many houses here were made of wood, Mitchell had found himself doing alterations and now one or two whole buildings. He might not be a trained architect, but such men were in short supply in the colony and he knew how to build wooden houses safely.

His eyes went to his own home. He had an eye for style, too, if he said so himself. The house was going to look good.

'Watch out! Here comes trouble,' Bram joked.

Mitchell's heart lifted, as it always did when his son came running along the street to join them, shouting at the top of his voice.

'Dad, Dad, I had such a good time at school. Wait till I tell you.' At ten, Christopher was a sturdy lad who promised to be as tall as his father.

'You haven't said hello to Mr Deagan.'

'Sorry, Mr Deagan. I hope you're well. And that your wife and baby are well, too.'

'We're all well. I'll leave you to tell your father about your day.' Bram walked off down the street and was soon whistling again.

Mitchell put an arm round his son's shoulders and they walked up to the shack where they were living till the house was finished. Sadly, the boy's clothing never quite looked as well cared for as that of lads with mothers, and Mitchell felt the same way about himself. Which was one of the many reasons he'd plucked up the courage to write to his cousin in England asking if Peter could find him a suitable wife.

Anyway, a man wasn't made to sleep alone. Mitchell was still young enough to need a woman in his bed, yes, and to want other children, since his son had given him such joy.

As the weeks passed in the slow wait for a reply from Peter, and the new house neared completion, Mitchell alternated between two states of mind. Sometimes he hoped his cousin would know a lady willing to come out to Australia and marry him. At other times, he bitterly regretted ever sending that letter, because who knew what sort of woman would take up the offer to marry a complete stranger?

Bram said he was borrowing worries from nowhere and should wait till he received a reply. Things weren't likely to happen quickly, after all.

But what if some really unpleasant woman turned up in the colony unannounced, expecting Mitchell to marry her? What would he do then? At the very least, he'd be responsible for her.

He definitely wasn't going to marry anyone who wouldn't care for Christopher properly. His son had had one bad mother and suffered for it.

★ ★ ★

Bram Deagan stood in the chaotic workshop, surrounded by bits and pieces of machinery, and looked at the engineer in dismay. 'You can't possibly need *more* money, Chilton! Look at all the equipment I've bought you.'

'We're very close now, but I need some better

100

quality metal parts and that costs more than I'd expected. They have to be specially made in Melbourne, you know, then shipped across here to the west.'

'Well, I'm sorry, but I have no more money to give you. You'll just have to stop the experiment till I can spare more.'

It was Chilton's turn to look dismayed. 'But I've pledged your name to the order and sent it off by the mail ship. I didn't want to wait weeks to send it on the next ship. You *said* you'd set me up with a bigger ice-making manufactory.'

Bram stared at him, aghast. 'I know I did, but you weren't talking about such high costs then. You asked for a far lower sum when I first agreed to put money into your business.'

Chilton turned sulky. 'I didn't realise how much it'd cost. I'm an engineer and inventor, not a businessman.'

'Don't do anything else, and do not order a single other item. I'll have to see what I can do.'

Bram walked home feeling terrified. This situation was going from bad to worse. What if something else cropped up that needed money, only he didn't have it? What if he went bankrupt and lost everything he'd earned? He couldn't pay the bill for the new machinery, he knew that — well, not all of it. He'd have to wait till Adam's ship returned from Singapore with a new cargo and then sell part of it for less profit to get the money quickly.

That wasn't a good thing for a trader to do, not a good thing at all.

How was he to tell his wife about this? Isabella

was a full partner in the Bazaar and kept track of their finances. What would she say?

When he went into the house, she was just handing the baby to their young maid, Sally.

He went across to look at little Neala and Isabella whispered, 'Don't you dare wake her up.'

As he turned to join her, she stared at him, eyes narrowed. 'What's wrong?'

'Nothing.'

'Tell me.'

He looked meaningfully at Sally and the children. 'We'll go into the parlour for a little chat, shall we?'

There was no furniture in the best parlour yet, only the promise of an elegant, spacious room where he would one day be able to entertain all his friends and family — if he still owned this house, if he could afford to keep it.

Since he couldn't think of any way to soften the blow, he blurted it out. 'Chilton has pledged my name to a bill for some new equipment without asking me. I don't think, in fact I'm sure . . . Isabella, we don't have enough money to pay it.'

'How much?'

When he told her, she stared at him in dismay, then frowned and began biting her thumb, as she did when thinking hard. He waited, not knowing what to say or do. As he looked round, he wished he hadn't bought the big new house, or at least hadn't had it extended and repaired. What had he been thinking of?

She came to link her arm in his. 'I have some

money saved. I was going to use it to open a proper shop to sell my silks. That can wait. I'll have to do some calculations, but I'm sure there's enough to pay the bill.'

'Oh, my darling, you're so generous.' He gave her a cracking hug, and kept her in his arms, speaking softly close to her ear. 'I don't want to take it. I know how much getting a proper shop means to you, how you love dealing in silks.'

'You mean more to me than a shop, Bram, far more. Only . . . there are other bills coming due soon, so don't let him spend any more money. Not one single penny more.' She moved away from him, laying one hand on her breasts, swollen with milk.

He placed his hand over hers. 'We've expanded too fast, haven't we?'

'In one sense. Everything we import from Singapore is selling well, though. We've made a lot of money, but are still putting it into the business.'

She didn't say it, didn't have to. Everything would have been all right — more than all right — if he hadn't put so much money into the ice-making machinery, and into a couple of other small businesses, whose owners were Irish like him.

She turned to kiss his cheek. 'Adam is due back soon and he'll have a cargo for us. We can have a grand sale and rake in money more quickly than usual. And Dougal will be coming back a few weeks after him with another cargo. We'll manage.'

'Yes, we always manage, don't we?'

103

She looked at him severely. 'But you are not to help anyone, *anyone at all*, from now on, Bram, without consulting me. What's more, you are not to spend a single penny unless I allow it. *Not one penny.*'

He knew what she was getting at. He was often generous with his loose change. The trouble was, when he saw people in the street looking poor and hungry, he wanted to help them. He'd gone hungry many a time, knew how bad it felt.

Not everyone had been as lucky as him. But now, it seemed his luck was failing.

Dear heaven, what if he went bankrupt? What would they all do then? He had a wife, young children, a new baby. Everything they owned could be taken away from them.

He felt an icy shiver run down his spine at the mere thought of that. He knew from his own youth how hard it was to live in poverty. He wanted so much more for his family than that.

★ ★ ★

When he took over as captain, Adam Tregear renamed his schooner the *Bonny Ismay* after his wife, delighted that it was usual for a new owner to rename a ship. It was his first command and he quickly grew to love the ship almost as much as he loved Ismay herself.

As they headed south from Singapore, moving down the West Australian coast, the weather grew steadily rougher. He watched the sky anxiously, noticing high, streaky white clouds

104

moving in from the south-west. These were likely to be the sign of strong winds to come.

The barometer bore this out, showing the pressure dropping. As it continued to drop, he became concerned enough to prepare the ship for an uncomfortable blow.

The wind built up and the sea began to look almost black, with foam streaking the surface and a large swell. A line of rain-bearing clouds moved towards them across the lowering sky.

The crew didn't need telling to check and re-check everything, and all those going on deck donned wet-weather gear, with safety harnesses secured to the deck.

Similarly clad, Adam and his mate, Tucker, stood together watching the southerly wind approach, taking over from the warm air that had been pushing them along so far. The safest course of action was to stay on the same course and maintain as much forward motion as possible, but he ordered the top sails pulled in and the main sails reefed.

The waves were now mountainous, with the ship riding up one side and then falling down into the trough, making even experienced sailors' stomachs churn.

Thank goodness his ship was seaworthy, with an A1 rating from Lloyds. And thank goodness this wasn't the cyclone season.

They were lucky. Within an hour or so the wind strength started to abate and the wind direction slowly moved clockwise. It was still uncomfortable weather, but he was able to continue towards his home port of Fremantle.

But he remained on edge, unable to settle to anything for more than a few minutes.

He had a full cargo on board and was worried about that, too. Lee Kar Ho, a Singapore trader and friend, was proving an excellent partner for their group of people based in Fremantle. Bram and Dougal were benefiting greatly from the association, as was Adam now.

A rising man, their Mr Lee, and very shrewd. He was having a huge house built in Singapore, and had invited Adam to bring his wife on the next voyage, and to stay with them in their new home.

This was a rare honour from a Chinese family, but Bram's wife had a special relationship with them. Isabella had lived with the Lees for over two years, while teaching them English, and was very close to Mr Lee's sister, who was her partner in the silk business.

Adam would love to take Ismay back to Singapore, which she'd visited once, and he knew she'd love to go. The trouble was, his Aunt Harriet was a poor sailor and had vowed never to set foot aboard a ship again, unless it was safely moored to a quay. He didn't feel it right to leave her alone in Fremantle for several weeks, since she'd come to Australia specially to be with him.

If he had his wishes, he'd take Ismay to sea with him all the time because she loved being on the water. He didn't care if people mocked what they called 'hen frigates', where the captain's wife, and sometimes even his children, lived on board with him.

You had to believe that you'd continue to

weather the storms to do that.

Adam shook off thoughts of his family and returned to keeping an eye on the storm.

'I think we've avoided the worst,' Tucker said.

He nodded. Tucker was older than him, not interested in becoming a captain, but with many years of experience and a lot of common sense.

Most of the crew were below, only those essential to running the ship braving the dangerous weather. They'd change places every two hours, to give them some respite.

Just as Adam was thinking they really had come through the worst, he saw some objects bobbing about on the surface of the water ahead of the ship, large objects.

'What are they and where the hell are they coming from, Captain?' Tucker asked.

'Damned if I know. Flotsam from another ship, I'd guess.'

A few minutes later they saw the wreckage of the ship, no pieces with her name, though she looked to be of Asian make. There was no sign of living men or even of floating bodies.

They met more of her cargo, now recognisable as bundles of planks floating just below the surface, except when they crashed into one another and bobbed up as if to salute the storm.

Adam had no way of avoiding all of the wreckage, because the sea was still rough. He tried to steer so as to avoid the thickest clumps of planks, but it was impossible to avoid them all. He and his men could only watch the bundles of timber and the wreckage being tossed by the waves, watch them coming closer and closer to the *Bonny Ismay*.

They'd avoided the worst of the storm only to run into another danger. He prayed as he'd never prayed before.

But prayer wasn't enough. The sea heaved up and down in the aftermath of the storm, tossing pieces of timber at the *Bonny Ismay*. Inevitably some speared into her.

The sailors on deck clung to rails and ropes, yelling and cursing, dodging flying pieces of smaller debris. One man's yell was cut off abruptly as he was tossed overboard, but his safety harness held and he clawed his way back up the rope, helped by his shipmates.

Adam groaned aloud as one huge plank punched a hole into the roof of the main cabin, lodging there half in and half out. Water immediately began to cascade through the hole each time the ship broke through a wave.

Some planks and wreckage didn't lodge anywhere on the ship, but they still managed to leave a trail of damage behind as they bumped and slid across the deck.

'Some poor devils have lost their ship!' Adam yelled.

'And their lives.' Tucker quickly crossed himself, then clung on again as they breasted another wave and plunged into the trough behind it.

The waves might be smaller now, a mere ten feet or so, but they were still big enough to toss the ship around — and to hurl more flotsam on to the vessel.

Thank goodness no one seemed to have been

108

seriously hurt, though the helmsman was pale, his hand bloody and bruised where a piece of debris had slashed it.

Adam cursed as several more planks crashed end on into the forward part of the ship, hitting the central cargo hull and letting in more water.

No orders could have been heard, but more men came up on deck without needing telling, trying to make good whatever damage they could, all wearing their safety harnesses.

Following the mate's hand signals or lip reading his commands, some began to wrap ropes around pieces of timber and hammer them down into the holes to seal the damaged decking.

Once that was done, other areas were secured with a cover of canvas. The men had difficulty lashing it in place, because the ship was still rolling and pitching, but eventually they managed to stop most of the water cascading down into the hold.

Adam moved among them at the start, then pulled himself along his safety line to stand by the wheel again. He ached to do more, but his job as captain was to keep an eye on the overall situation.

Slowly, too slowly for safety, the situation improved. No more big clumps of timber hit them, though an occasional one floated past still.

Unfortunately, they could do little about the water inside the cargo hold while the ship was still tossing around like a cork on a pond.

It seemed a long time until the sea became merely rough. Although they'd known water must be sloshing around in the hold before, they could now hear it in the lulls between wind gusts. At least very little new water was getting in now. The men had done well.

As he looked round at the damage, Adam felt as if he'd let Dougal down, though what he could have done to prevent this, he didn't know. For such damage to happen on his first voyage as captain was devastating.

'You couldn't have stopped it,' Tucker said abruptly. 'The sea's a fickle mistress. We all know that. And who'd expect to run into wreckage? We were weathering the storm well, because she's a good ship and we've a good crew. But we could do nothing about the rest. That was sheer bad luck.'

Floating bundles of timber and pieces of wreckage could still be seen and some seemed to be paralleling the ship's course.

It seemed a very long time until the storm eased and left them floating on calmer seas.

And still pieces of wreckage mocked them from nearby, seeming to be accompanying the ship down the coast.

When Adam judged it safe to inspect the hold, he groaned as he saw the damage to the cargo. Some of the crockery would be smashed, however carefully it had been packed, but worst of all, most of the boxes of silks had been smashed by the blunt spears of timber. The sea water would have got in, in spite of the oiled wrappings. Their contents would be ruined.

Some of the crates of furniture were intact, but the pieces inside must surely have been bumped around and damaged.

Bram would have to wait weeks for another cargo. He would make little if any profit from this voyage.

Neither would Dougal and Adam. And the ship would need repairing before she could put to sea again.

Adam felt something nudging at his brain, some idea of how to make the most of this. But he couldn't quite grasp what it was, maybe because he was exhausted. It'd be a while before he'd dare let himself sleep, though. He was the captain. Responsibility for the ship, cargo and crew was his.

★　★　★

On the other side of the world, Quentin and Eleanor left the hotel in Southampton by going through the servants' quarters and used a cab the manager had summoned. This belonged, he'd told them, to a very reliable man, who had undertaken other confidential work for the hotel's clients, to everyone's satisfaction.

The lady at the lodging house seemed a bit furtive, so acting on one of his hunches, Quentin went back outside and asked the cab driver to stop anyone who looked as if they were taking a message from the house.

He went back inside to join Eleanor in the bedroom, where she was packing the few things Jacinta had left around, putting them quickly into the suitcases and trunk. She and Quentin then carried the smaller bags out.

He dropped his when he found the cab driver forcibly detaining a lad, who was protesting loudly. 'Keep hold of him!' he called as he ran across.

'I've done nothing,' the lad protested.

'And you're not going to,' the cab driver said; then, turning to Quentin: 'I can hold him but you'll need help with the luggage. Hoy, you! Want to earn a quick shilling?'

A sturdy bystander grinned and went inside to help Quentin get the trunk down, past the scowling landlady. After they'd lifted it on to the cab's luggage rack at the rear, the man walked off whistling happily, jiggling the shilling in his pocket.

Only then did the driver look at Quentin for permission to deal with the boy.

'I'll see to this.' Quentin turned to the lad, staring at him coldly till the boy wriggled uncomfortably. 'If I see you anywhere near me again, or if you try to follow us now, I'll call the police and ask them to lock you up. I'm a lawyer and they'll listen to me.'

A woman had come to the door and was watching them sullenly, but still didn't protest. When they let him go, the lad ran to her side and she cuffed his ears before following him inside. Perhaps she was his mother. Perhaps she too had been involved.

They drove back to the hotel, using the rear entrance again, but Quentin was afraid that now they'd been seen helping Jacinta, they'd have to face more trouble, outright attacks even, as they tried to board the ship.

How best to guard against Ben being taken from his mother?

When Eleanor had gone into the hotel with the luggage, Quentin lingered to ask the driver's advice.

'When I take you to the ship tomorrow morning,' the man said, 'I could bring along a friend, in case we're attacked.'

'Good idea.'

They discussed how to manage this, then Quentin gave him an extra big tip and they separated.

But he still wasn't satisfied this would be enough to protect the boy from being kidnapped.

The luggage had been taken up to Jacinta's room and he joined the ladies there. She was looking so upset, he guessed Eleanor had told her about the landlady's son.

'Thank you so much, Mr Saxby. I'm grateful to you for fetching our things.'

'But . . . ' he prompted.

'What if they stop us boarding the ship tomorrow?'

'We'll think of a way to get you both on board,' Quentin said. 'Trust me. Oh, and will you kindly appoint me as your lawyer? Then I shall have the right to defend and help you.'

'Whatever you think best. I'm happy to have you as my lawyer.' But now she was looking even more worried.

He smiled reassuringly, guessing what was upsetting her. 'My fee will be one shilling precisely.'

The relief on her face was its own reward.

He left her with Eleanor and after pacing up and down his room for a few minutes, decided to ask the manager's advice again.

* * *

At five o'clock in the morning, a man with a small cart delivered some fresh vegetables to the hotel. He was delighted at the chance to earn a whole half guinea extra by obliging Mr Saxby and the manager.

It was easy to conceal a small boy beneath some empty sacks on the cart. The driver assured them he had friends on the docks who would help out at that end, since he supplied some of the ships regularly with produce.

More money changed hands to reward the friends.

Quentin felt intense satisfaction at helping someone in distress. If you couldn't do good in this life, you weren't worthy of being called a decent human being.

They hadn't thought it wise to draw attention to their actions today, so had advised Jacinta to stay in her room while her son was hurried outside.

* * *

Once her son had left their bedroom, Jacinta couldn't stop worrying. She hadn't wanted to let Ben out of her sight at all, let alone send him to the ship ahead of her, but Mr Saxby had

114

promised her that the boy would be safe and well looked after. The manager had said he'd stake his life on the market gardener's integrity, because he'd known him for many years.

And anyway, she didn't have any real choice but to take this risk. She didn't know what Gerald had planned, what inducements he'd offered his henchmen, but she was quite sure that something would be attempted today.

Time dragged and each minute seemed an hour long as she waited to go on board later that morning with her new friends. She shuddered to think what might have happened if she hadn't met them. She'd been very lucky. First Mr Stanwell, the kindest clergyman she'd ever met. Now this lawyer and her new friend Eleanor.

She prayed that her luck would continue till she got Ben away from Gerald Blacklea. And that this man in Australia who wanted a wife would be a kind person. She didn't dare expect much from him beyond that, had barely had time to wonder about him because she'd been too busy protecting her son.

Now, the thought of travelling so far and marrying a complete stranger had resurfaced and would no doubt haunt her dreams during the voyage — if they ever managed to leave England.

Mr Saxby had lent her his travelling alarm clock so that she could wake early and get Ben ready to travel. Now, it sat there cheerfully ticking away the minutes following his departure, as if mocking the anxiety that made it hard for her even to breathe at times.

She let out a groan of relief when the hands at

last crawled round to breakfast time and she could go down to the dining room. The manager was waiting in the lobby and had a quick word with Mr Saxby, who beamed at him and clapped him on the shoulder.

When they were seated Mr Saxby leaned across. 'Everything went smoothly. Your package has been delivered into the care of one of the stewards.'

'You mean, he — it's actually on the ship?'

'Yes, my dear.'

She closed her eyes for a moment in sheer relief.

Even knowing Ben was safe, Jacinta couldn't eat anything, though she did manage to drink two cups of tea.

And then she had to wait once again until it was time to board the ship.

Never in her life had the minutes passed with such agonising slowness. She tried to chat to Eleanor, tried to be polite, wasn't sure she'd managed even to make sense.

She just wanted to be reunited with her son, to see for herself that he was safe!

★ ★ ★

At last, at eleven o'clock precisely, the three of them went to sit in the lobby. They could see the street outside and kept careful watch.

'Ah, here they are!' Mr Saxby said suddenly.

Jacinta watched two cabs arrive at the hotel, one driven by the same man as the previous day, the other by a burly stranger. The two of them chatted with the ease of old friends as they walked into the hotel to collect their passengers and the luggage. She could see their eyes darting here and there, as if checking for trouble.

The ladies got into the first cab with Mr Saxby as the luggage was being loaded into the second one.

Jacinta could hardly breathe, she was so afraid of what might happen during this short journey to the docks. Someone could even try to kill her, because that would solve Gerald's problem completely.

She could tell that her two companions were also very tense.

When the cabs stopped on the docks near the ship, both drivers summoned lads to hold the horses then walked along behind Mr Saxby and the two ladies to the ship, carrying their smaller bags.

Just before they got to the foot of the gangway, three men stepped forward from behind some piles of cargo, big men with brutal faces.

It was happening! Jacinta's stomach lurched and she felt sick with fear.

As the men blocked the path, one said loudly, 'Just a minute!'

'Hoy, you! Clear off!' the sailor at the foot of the gangway yelled.

'Not till I've got this lady. She's wanted for theft.'

His words were so loud that everyone working nearby stopped to watch.

Mr Saxby moved forward, putting his arm round Jacinta's shoulders. 'Is that the best your master can do?' he asked scornfully.

He beckoned the ship's officer standing at the top of the gangway. 'Could we have some help here, please? This person is making fraudulent charges against my client, in an attempt to prevent her from leaving the country.'

The two cab drivers had already moved forward to stand protectively next to the ladies.

With a jerk of the head, the officer summoned some of the crew and hurried down to join them.

'Who are you?' he asked the men.

'Name's Pearson and I'm employed by Mr Gerald Blacklea. This woman's wanted for theft. She stole some silver from my master.'

'When is this theft supposed to have taken place?' Quentin asked.

'Before she ran away from her home.' Pearson waved a piece of paper at them. 'This is a letter from Mr Blacklea, accusing her of the theft.'

Mr Saxby took it, read it quickly and showed it to the officer, before turning back to say, 'If she's wanted for theft, why are the police not here with you?'

The fellow scowled at him. 'She's a relative. He doesn't want to involve the police.'

'And nor would I want to involve them, if I were making fraudulent charges.' Quentin turned to the officer. 'I'm this lady's lawyer, employed by her because she feared one of her relatives might try to stop her from leaving the country.'

He took out a business card and handed it over. 'My client did indeed run away from home, but she took nothing with her. She left because she was afraid of Gerald Blacklea, the man who wrote the letter. She certainly didn't steal any silver from him.'

As Mr Saxby was speaking to the officer, one man suddenly lunged forward and grabbed Jacinta while the other two shoved everyone else away.

A cab waiting further back was driven forward, the man cracking his whip to clear his way. In the mêlée they got Jacinta most of the way towards it. The crew members yelled in outrage at what was happening to one of their passengers.

Two of the sailors reached the cab before the kidnappers could shove Jacinta inside it, and general fighting ensued, punches flying and feet kicking out.

While this was happening, Jacinta got away from her captors and ran for the gangway.

The officer gestured to her to go up it and blocked the way to anyone else. By that time, the captain was striding across the deck to see what was happening.

Her breath sobbing in her throat, her heart still pounding, Jacinta tried to tidy her clothes and pin up her hair.

It was a while before things calmed down and Quentin could get on the ship and move to her side. The leader of the would-be kidnappers had managed to talk his way on, too, and was standing nearby.

'I have every right to take her back. She's a *thief!* She — '

Quentin cut the man short. 'It should be easy enough to check my client's story, Captain. Why

119

don't you examine her luggage for this silver she's supposed to have stolen?'

They had to wait for Jacinta's trunk to be brought up from the hold and then her luggage was gone through by one of the stewardesses, her meagre, ragged underclothing laid out on the deck for all to see.

The stewardess turned to the captain when she'd finished. 'There's no silver in there, sir, no money either, and no sign of her spending much. She has only the bare minimum of clothing for the voyage.'

'What did I tell you?' Quentin asked.

The captain turned to the kidnapper. 'Well, Pearson, I'm satisfied that there are no stolen goods in this lady's luggage, so kindly leave my ship and think yourself lucky we don't have you charged with assault.'

'What about the boy?'

The captain looked at them in puzzlement.

'She won't have left without her son.' Pearson turned to Jacinta. 'Where are you hiding him?'

She didn't know what to say.

He turned back to the captain. 'The son is the one my employer really wants. You can keep the woman and welcome to her. Mr Blacklea is the lad's guardian and she has no right to take him anywhere, let alone to Australia.' He held out another letter.

There was dead silence and Jacinta felt as if she'd faint. What if the captain believed him, or was so annoyed at their deception, he threw her and Ben off the ship?

She'd be helpless to protect her son then.

6

Jacinta saw the captain watching her, waiting for an answer. She pulled herself together and said quietly but firmly, 'Gerald Blacklea is *not* my son's guardian! He's only a distant cousin who had never even seen Ben until a few days ago, when I sought his help after my husband left me penniless. Claude hadn't communicated with his family for years, you see, because they'd disowned him, but I was desperate.'

'She's lying!' Pearson shouted. 'Don't listen to her.'

'I told you to be quiet! If you can't do that, then you'll be put off this ship,' the captain snapped.

He turned to study Jacinta and by the time he'd finished she felt as if he knew how every hair grew on her head. But that didn't daunt her, because she knew she had right on her side. 'I have complete charge of Ben now that his father is dead.'

'Why would this cousin claim guardianship, then?' Quentin prompted quietly.

'Because Gerald Blacklea has no male heir. He wants to bring up my son and later marry him to his daughter.'

'That would be to your son's advantage, surely?'

'There is no advantage to being brought up by a cruel man. And in any case, I love my son dearly and would never give him away. Never.'

'Why were you seeking help from me?' Quentin prompted again, wanting to make things plain to the all-powerful captain.

She hesitated, then admitted, 'Because I have very little money.'

'How are you going to support your son in Australia, then?'

She looked meaningfully at Pearson and then asked the captain, 'May I tell you this in private? I don't want to get other people into trouble.'

When they'd moved to the other side of the deck, she said in a low voice, 'I met a very kind clergyman in the village near Mr Blacklea. He has a relative in Australia who wishes to find a wife and he thought I might be suitable. The gentleman and I both have sons to bring up, you see.' She could feel herself flushing.

The captain gave a wry smile. 'That happens quite often, Mrs Blacklea. I've taken other brides out to Australia. I dare say such marriages stand as much chance of happiness as any other. Thank you for telling me. We'd better rejoin Pearson now before he explodes.'

With a sigh she followed him and her lawyer back to the group near the top of the gangway.

'Where is your son now?' the captain asked.

Jacinta didn't want to tell him till after they'd sailed. She looked pleadingly at the lawyer.

Quentin gave her a sympathetic glance and a quick shake of the head. 'My dear, we can't hide Ben any longer. The captain is in charge of this ship and must be the one to say who travels on it. Explain what we arranged and why.'

She wished he'd do that, couldn't understand why he was leaving it all to her. She could feel tears welling in her eyes and her voice kept breaking because she was so upset. 'Ben was brought to the ship very early this morning by one of your food suppliers. We were afraid of him being kidnapped on the way here, you see. And our fears have been proven correct.'

'Your officer can confirm what happened on the dock today,' Quentin put in.

'Nothing happened,' Pearson said. 'We merely needed to talk to the lady, to persuade her to do the right thing.'

The captain scowled at him. 'You're lying, and that doesn't do your case any good. I saw most of what happened for myself.'

'I'm not sure exactly where Ben is now,' Jacinta said, 'but I'm sure someone on the ship will know.'

The captain turned to the stewardess who'd checked the luggage. 'Have you seen him, Jane?'

'The lad's helping the cook in the kitchen, sir. He was worried sick about his mother, so they've been trying to take his mind off it. He's a nice lad, very well-behaved. Cook's taken a real fancy to him, and you know Cook doesn't usually like having children around.'

'Fetch the boy here.'

Pearson took a quick step forward. 'And then you'll have to hand him over to me.'

The captain drew himself up. '*I* will decide what is to be done.'

Pearson took a deep breath and said in what was clearly meant to be a conciliatory tone but still came out sharply, 'I'm sorry, sir. I didn't mean to be rude. But my master is very eager to get hold of the boy — I mean, to get the boy *back*.'

It wasn't long before the stewardess reappeared, followed by Ben.

The minute he saw his mother, he flew across the deck to hurl himself into her arms. She cuddled him close, closing her eyes in relief and praying with all her heart that the captain wouldn't let them take her son from her.

'As you can see,' Quentin said quietly, 'the boy is devoted to his mother and she to him. Why should she wish to hand him over to a distant cousin?'

'Hmm. Let me see this letter of yours, Pearson.' The captain held out his hand. He studied the letter, then handed it back. 'Anyone could have written that. Is there a will, leaving the boy in your master's guardianship?'

'I'm sure Mr Blacklea will have whatever's needed to prove his case.'

The captain passed the letter on to Quentin. 'You're a lawyer, sir. What do you believe to be the truth of this document? On your word of honour.'

Quentin studied the letter and shrugged. 'As you say, anyone could have written this. It has no legal standing that I can see. What's more, I believe what Mrs Blacklea has told us. Like you, I trust in the evidence of my own eyes and I've seen how low this fellow' — he flicked the piece of paper with one finger — 'would stoop. He's sent bullies to kidnap the boy and his mother.

How would he treat a boy in his care?'

'Hmm.' The captain again studied Jacinta. 'Mrs Blacklea is obviously a good mother. My own stewardess has told us that Ben is well-behaved and she has no reason to lie. So we can't fault the way Mrs Blacklea is bringing up the lad.'

Jacinta waited to hear her lawyer plead for her to be allowed to keep her son.

He didn't. He merely added quietly, 'I'm well aware that the final decision rests with you, Captain, so I shall say no more.'

The captain pursed his lips, then said, 'I shall set sail as planned and allow my passengers to do the same.' He turned to Pearson. 'You, sir, can leave my ship at once and tell your master he must find himself another heir.'

For a moment all hung in the balance, then Pearson swung round and strode down the gangway. He immediately sent one man running somewhere and remained on the dock with his other companion. Taking out his pocket watch, he studied it, frowning at the time he saw and scowling up at them. He didn't put the watch away, but kept it in his hand.

It looked, Jacinta thought with a catch of breath in her throat, as if Pearson was waiting for someone. Not Gerald Blacklea, oh, please not him! She realised the captain was speaking to her.

'The stewardess will show you and your son to your cabin, ma'am, and I'd advise you to stay there until the ship has put out to sea.' His voice softened. 'Don't worry. You'll be safe on this ship.'

125

'Thank you.' She knew tears were rolling down her cheeks but didn't waste time wiping them away because she wanted to get out of sight. Putting one arm round Ben's shoulders and forcing her shaking legs to move, she followed the stewardess across the deck.

The captain looked at Quentin. 'You're a wise man to recognise whose decision it was.'

'And I am, I hope, wise enough to know who was telling the truth, as well.'

'Yes. I agree with you there. I didn't like the look of that Pearson fellow at all. *Like master, like man* is a saying I've found to be true more often than not. What will Mrs Blacklea do when she gets to Australia if she doesn't like this fellow she's being sent out to marry? Has she any family there?'

'I don't know. If necessary, I'll help her, because I've quickly come to respect her, in a purely *fatherly* way, I might add, and have enough money to do as I please. But I hope things will work out for her. A lad needs both a father and a mother.'

'She's lucky to have met you, Mr Saxby. Now, I must get this ship to sea.' The captain nodded and walked away.

Quentin turned to Eleanor, who had been standing quietly to one side while everything was settled. 'Shall we too seek our cabins, my dear? Though perhaps you could check first that Mrs Blacklea is all right? She was very distressed and no wonder.'

* * *

126

Two hours later, just as the ship was starting to move away from its mooring, a cab rattled on to the docks and a man jumped out, waving a paper at the vessel. An older man followed him.

'Hoy, you! Stop this ship!' the younger one yelled. 'I have a magistrate here with an order for me to take the boy into my care.'

The older man moved forward to stand beside him, hands clasped across the top of a silver-headed walking stick.

Quentin, who was on deck watching the departure, went across to the First Mate, who was supervising the departure and scowling down at the pair. 'That must be Gerald Blacklea, the man who wants to take her child.'

'What does he think we can do now, however many pieces of paper he waves? Time and tide wait for no man.' He waited a few more moments, winking at Quentin as the ship continued to move slowly away from the figures on the dock, before sending a lad with the news to the captain.

The lad came back alone. 'Captain says he's not stopping now, not for anyone, or he'll miss the tide.'

The officer smiled grimly, muttering, 'Good!' before turning to look across the strip of water that was gradually widening between them and Gerald Blacklea. He yelled in a very loud voice, 'Sorry, sir! It's too late to stop the ship now.'

Blacklea let the walking stick fall, shaking his fist at the ship, just about dancing in rage. His face was so red with anger you could see it, even from a distance.

'You have no *right* to take a boy away from his lawful guardian!' he yelled. 'Damn you, I *demand* that you bring him back.'

No one answered and his threats continued, fading gradually as the ship pulled away.

The last words to float across the water to them were, 'You'll be sorry, Jacinta Blacklea. I'll come after you. You'll never be safe. Never.'

'Listen to that fellow ranting on,' the officer said. 'I can see why she doesn't want to hand her son over to him. I'd not give a brute like that a puppy to raise, let alone a boy.'

Quentin shook his head sadly. He doubted anyone would really travel all the way to Australia for such a purpose, not unless they were completely deranged. More than ever, he hoped this Mitchell Nash would prove to be a suitable husband for Jacinta. She needed someone to protect her, just in case.

Eleanor came out on deck to join him. 'I'd not like to be in that man's power.'

'No. Neither would I. Where are Jacinta and Ben? Don't they wish to catch a last glimpse of England now that we've left the docks?'

'They're still in their cabin. Jacinta didn't want to come on deck until we were at sea, out of the reach of the tugs and the pilot boats. She thought the sight of her and Ben might make things worse.'

'She can come out now. We're gathering speed and he won't be able to distinguish one figure from another among this crowd of passengers. She'll be quite safe.'

'I'll tell her.' Eleanor smiled at him and paused

to add, 'You seem to enjoy helping people, Mr Saxby.'

'You're the second person to say that to me today. I do my best to be a good Christian and a friend to all in need.'

'I'm very glad I have you to help me as well.'

He watched her go, then sniffed the salty air, enjoying the breeze in his face as he listened to the sailors calling to one another, raising their voices above the sound of the steam engine. The other passengers were smiling. The weather was calm, a very auspicious start to their voyage.

He was glad he'd decided to travel to Australia, whatever came of it. At least he'd have an adventure or two before he died.

Even if Harriet didn't want to marry him, he thought she would be as glad to see him as he would be to see her again, and they could still be friends.

What if she did want to marry him, though? His breath caught in his throat. Ah, then, he'd be the happiest man on earth.

Perhaps Harriet might consider herself too old for love. He didn't feel too old, and indeed, he was feeling younger every day, now that he had some purpose to his life.

Ah well, he'd done all that he could for the time being. His happiness now rested in the lap of the gods. But a man could hope. And pray. And enjoy some wonderful dreams of what might be.

★ ★ ★

Bram walked along the Fremantle street and couldn't help slipping a penny to a woman begging on a corner. She had hunger written all over her face. Isabella had made him promise not to give any money away, and he'd cut down, he really had.

'Bless you, Mr Deagan,' she said in a hoarse voice.

He sighed as he walked on. 'Bless you,' she'd said, and all for a penny.

But maybe her wishes had brought him luck, because when he got to the ice works, he was met by a smiling Chilton.

'The new parts have arrived,' he said, not bothering with greetings. 'I'll be making more ice from next week onwards. You'll see.'

'I hope you're right, lad.'

Chilton looked embarrassed. 'I'm sorry to have taken so much money, Mr Deagan. I was sure I knew how to do it.'

'And this time? How sure are you that you've succeeded?'

Chilton wriggled. 'I *think* I've got the problem fixed. We'll see on Sunday. I'll be setting it off then.' He gestured to the shop. 'We could sell three times as much ice as we do, easily. And we will. You'll see.'

'What time on Sunday?'

'About midday.'

'I'll be here. I want to see it.' And because he didn't want to see any doubt on Chilton's face, Bram turned without another word and left the ice works.

He walked to the port but there was no sign of

130

the *Bonny Ismay*. Where was Adam? The ship was well overdue.

What if something had happened to the *Bonny Ismay?* What if she'd been lost at sea? The worst of that would be how heartbroken his sister Ismay would be if anything happened to Adam, but Bram would be bankrupt if he lost this cargo, and that too was an unbearable thought.

He knew then that he'd never, ever put his family in jeopardy again, no matter how tempting an investment might seem.

★ ★ ★

The night was fraught for those on board the *Bonny Ismay*, because the sea wasn't really calm yet, and the timber and wreckage were still floating around nearby. A very careful watch had to be kept.

Adam lasted as long as he could, but in the end had to snatch a couple of hours' sleep or he'd have collapsed where he stood. But by the time he came to that conclusion, his mate had had four hours' sleep, so could take over.

'Thank heavens it's almost a full moon!' Tucker said. 'We can see well enough to steer clear of any of the bigger masses, Captain. Or at least to fend them off.'

But no one could steer clear of the smaller pieces and some of them were large enough to damage a ship, Adam thought, as he lay down fully clothed on his bunk, sure he'd not sleep.

He jerked awake instantly when someone shook him. 'What's wrong?'

'Nothing, sir. But you said to wake you after four hours. It's nearly dawn and the mate thinks — ' The sailor was talking to himself. Adam was already out of the cabin and up on deck, staring at the water round the ship.

'No trouble, Tucker?'

'No, sir. Couple of those big planks bumped against us but only gently, sideways not head on. Did no damage and we captured them. I think we've picked up the ship's name from among the smaller stuff floating past.' He pointed to some wreckage lying on deck. 'Chinese, isn't it, that writing? We fished this one out of the water just before the sun rose.'

'Well done.' Adam took his time, quickly scanning the sea round the ship, then studying the ship more carefully. 'Are we taking in water anywhere?'

'Not now the storm is over. The hull wasn't damaged much. It was the deck that took the worst hits and let water in. The men did well, plugging the leaks. They're fine lads. We should be able to pump the water out of the hold soon.'

'Good. Tot of rum all round to start the day, don't you think? Warm our bellies.'

'They'll be pleased about that.'

'They've earned it.'

With the warmth of rum in his own belly, topped with a piece of stale bread and jam, Adam felt much more alert.

Strange how the timber had followed them, or perhaps not so strange. The storm must have swept everything in the same direction. The planks he'd seen were of good quality and

132

... 'Get the ship's carpenter up,' he called suddenly as the idea that had been hovering blossomed.

When Harry joined him by the wheel, stretching and yawning, Adam gave his carpenter time to come fully awake, then asked, 'Is it my imagination, or are those planks made of teak?'

Harry went to lean over the rail and stare at a nearby plank in the water. Clearly this wasn't wreckage from the ship but part of the cargo. He took the telescope to look carefully at it, then at some others. 'Looks like teak to me, sir. Well milled, too.'

'Yes.' Adam studied the pieces. 'I wonder . . .'

Harry and Tucker looked at him but didn't say anything, though he could see them gradually begin to realise what he was thinking.

'Be a valuable cargo, wouldn't it?' He looked sideways at them and waited.

Two heads nodded slowly.

'It wouldn't make up for the cargo we've had damaged, but it'd help. I'm not sure of the price of teak, but we'd get a reward at the very least, or maybe even the whole value, given it'd be hard to trace a Chinese ship. The sea won't have damaged the teak, will it, Harry? Well, except for where pieces have crashed into one another, of course.'

'I doubt it, sir. It may even help age the timber.'

Adam looked at the mate. 'Can we do it? Can we find a way of transporting as much timber as we can salvage? We'll not be able to lift all that lot on to the deck.'

'I've heard of it being done. Never thought to try it myself, though. And while we're doing it, we'll have a chance to have a good look round for survivors.'

Harry shook his head sadly. 'I don't think there could be any. Not after such a storm. That Chinese ship's smashed to pieces. Must have been old. The few pieces we've collected have signs of rot.'

'I agree. It's not likely there'd be any survivors, but it'd still be good to check, don't you think?'

'Yes, I do. And the men will think so, as well.'

It was what all sailors hoped for. If they were in distress, someone would try to come to their aid.

'We can't do anything till it's really calm, sir. Maybe tomorrow morning. But we can work out how to do it and make our preparations.'

'And we can stay near the planks,' Tucker added. 'Won't be hard, because that's where this wind wants to take us.'

★ ★ ★

Now that they had what they hoped was the Chinese ship's name, they didn't bother to collect other pieces of wreckage. A watch was kept on the floating timber and bets were laid about how much could be collected and what it'd be worth, since all would get a share in the prize.

Every single member of the crew was up early the following morning, before it was fully dawn

134

even, some staying on deck after being on watch instead of seeking their bunks. Spirits were high because of the possible bonus, though it would depend on how much timber they managed to salvage.

They'd kept watch the previous day and during the night, but had seen no sign of survivors, only the occasional dark shape heaving up and down in the water — oblongs, pieces of wood mainly, or smashed ship's timbers, definitely not bodies.

The new day was calm and sunny, with only a gentle swell. It took them less than an hour to find a big mass of planks, so they put down a sea anchor to keep the ship near these. Then they let down strong new rope, two thick strands twisted together, behind the ship before launching the bigger of the ship's two boats.

Adam watched his men row across to some nearby planks, joking and calling out to their comrades on board. He had a good crew, was proud of them, he thought with a smile.

The men secured the first bundle, which was still lashed together, to the rope strung behind the ship. They'd attached a sea anchor at the furthest point, so that the timber wouldn't overtake them or ram into the rear of the ship.

By working hard all day and taking turns on the salvage boat, the crew retrieved not only every bundle of planks they could find, but the occasional single plank. The latter were hauled up the side of the ship and fastened down securely on the deck.

Nowhere did they see any signs of bodies, let

135

alone survivors from the wreck. Adam suspected the Chinese ship had been squarely hit by the storm. The vessel might have been heading for any of the small countries north of Australia, or for the Swan River Colony itself. Unless someone was waiting for the cargo in Fremantle, they'd never know.

Harry stayed on board, his job to ensure that their makeshift repairs were more secure, which was much more important than him taking part in the salvage work. Men took it in turns to pump the rest of the water out of the hold.

There was nothing else Adam could do about his original cargo at this point. Most of it was ruined or at least so badly damaged as to fetch only a fraction of its expected price. Some of it was his, the rest belonged to Dougal and Bram. He dreaded telling them what had happened. None of them was so rich as to be indifferent to such a loss.

The ship made much slower progress once they set off again, taking a long time to settle on its new course.

At the end of their long string of planks they'd lashed two bundles together side by side and secured a small mast to this, flying flags to signal to other vessels that something was under tow, a red and white vertically striped pendant above a flag of blue with a white St Andrew's cross. Not that you met many ships in these waters.

7

It took Eleanor a while to persuade Jacinta to let Ben go on deck without her. Now that the crisis had passed, Jacinta was fighting back tears, obviously not in a fit state to take him herself.

The boy was so quiet, sitting on the edge of the bed staring down at his hands, that Eleanor worried about him. She had a sudden idea. 'If you don't want to go deck yet, my dear, how about we ask Mr Saxby to keep an eye on Ben?'

Jacinta looked doubtfully at her son. 'Will Mr Saxby want to be troubled?'

'Oh, I'm sure he will.' Eleanor didn't wait for permission, but said cheerfully, 'Come along, Ben. Let's go and find him.'

But even so, the boy looked at his mother first for permission and didn't move till she nodded.

Mr Saxby was delighted to look after Ben, so Eleanor went back to Jacinta. As she'd suspected, Jacinta was indulging in a hearty bout of weeping.

Eleanor hesitated. She didn't know the other woman well, but in the end couldn't stand seeing such pain and went to sit beside her, putting an arm round her shoulders, making soft comforting noises and letting her weep it all out.

Gradually the tears subsided and she passed Jacinta her own handkerchief, since the one that had been wept into was sodden.

'I thought I would lose my Ben,' Jacinta kept

repeating. 'I thought that horrible man would win.'

'Well, he didn't, thanks to Mr Saxby.'

Jacinta blew her nose and eventually managed to stop weeping. 'I'm sorry. I don't usually give way.'

'We all need a weep now and then.'

'What good does it do?'

'Not much except to give a little relief to the heart.' Eleanor heard the bitterness in her own voice and sighed. 'I didn't have a happy marriage, either. In the end, I could only endure. I wept a few times in secret, I can tell you. When I was sure Malcolm wouldn't find out. He'd have been so scornful.' She patted Jacinta's hand and waited, hoping for an exchange of confidences.

'I was forced to marry Claude,' Jacinta said abruptly. 'All my family were dead except for the aunt who'd arranged the marriage. She'd already told me she would do nothing more for me. She said it was the poorhouse or Claude, and he seemed pleasant enough when he was first introduced, so I agreed to the match.'

'Men like that can be pleasant when they want something,' Eleanor said grimly.

'I suppose so. But he turned out to be utterly and totally selfish. He wanted an unpaid servant more than a wife.' She blushed as she said in a low voice, 'He didn't even want me in his bed after the first year, and I slept in the same room as Ben. If I hadn't had my son, I might have tried to run away — though where I'd have gone, I have no idea.'

There was silence and it was clear that no

138

more confidences were to be offered as Jacinta got up to wash her face, squeezing past her companion in the tiny cabin to reach the small wash stand with its ewer of cold water.

'Come up on deck now,' Eleanor coaxed. 'Let the fresh sea air and sunshine blow away the last of your worries. You and Ben are free now to build a better life.'

Jacinta swung round. 'Are we really free, though? You heard what Gerald shouted after me.'

'It's one thing to threaten in the heat of the moment, another to carry out such a threat. Why, it'd mean him following you to a place ten thousand miles away. Didn't you say he was a landowner? He'll not leave his home and family to chase after you. No sane person would even contemplate that.'

'Perhaps he isn't sane. He was very strange, so cold and vicious. His wife was terrified of him, and he seemed to enjoy his power over her, ordering her around all the time.'

'Even so, I don't believe he'll chase after you. Anyway, by then you'll be married to Mr Nash, so there will be no point.'

'I hope you're right. But I'm not marrying any man unless I'm sure he'll be kind to me and my son.' Jacinta hesitated then gave her companion a hug. 'Thank you.'

'For what?'

'Being with me today. Talking. I've not had a woman to talk to since before Ben was born.'

'You'd do the same for me, I'm sure. Come on. We'll go up on deck now.'

Still Jacinta hesitated. 'People will see that I've been crying.'

'They'll be looking at the sea, not at you. Besides, you won't be the only one to weep. Some of them will be leaving family behind, not expecting to see them again.'

And so it proved. There was, Eleanor thought, a great deal of sadness as well as hope when people started such a long journey. They knew they'd probably never see the loved ones they were leaving behind again.

★ ★ ★

When Quentin was left on deck with Ben, he noticed that the boy was looking up at him warily, as if nervous and not daring to do anything until given instructions.

He tried to sound cheerful. 'We'll leave the ladies to have a chat, shall we? I'm sure Mrs Prescott will be able to cheer your mother up. Would you like to stroll round the deck or just stand by the rail?'

'Whatever you wish to do, sir.'

'I'm happy to do either. I've never been on a big ship before, which is strange considering I've lived in the port of Liverpool nearly all my life, don't you think?'

The boy nodded. 'Yes, sir.'

Quentin decided on frankness. 'Ben, I'm not like your father. I don't expect you to agree with me all the time, nor do I want you to stay silent. When I chat, I like to hear what the other person really thinks, not an echo of my own opinions.'

Two lads ran past as he spoke, and he added, 'You'll want to play with boys your own age for part of the time, too. Lads like to be noisy.'

'My father didn't allow me to play with the village boys. And there weren't any others.'

'Your father's dead. It's what your mother wants which will matter from now on . . . and what you want.'

Silence, then, 'I don't know how to play with other children.'

'Then watch them. You'll soon learn what to expect. But always remember not to let anyone persuade you to do anything dangerous, because that might upset your mother, and she's had enough to bear.'

Still Ben hesitated. 'Are we really safe from *him* now?'

'Yes. We left him behind on the dock.'

'I heard what he shouted to my mother, though. He frightens me, Mr Saxby. He frightens his daughter Elizabeth, too, *and* the governess. They didn't say anything, but I could tell.'

'How did you get on with Elizabeth? She's a sort of cousin, isn't she?'

A shrug was the only answer.

'Didn't you play with her?'

'The governess read us stories or we drew or went for walks. We had to be very quiet, so as not to disturb her father.'

'Well, you don't have to be quiet now. You can run about and shout just like the other lads.'

After letting that sink in, Quentin changed the subject. 'Do you know much about Australia?'

'No, sir.'

'We'll have to see if there are any books about it in the ship's library. And you'll want to choose some classes to attend, to help pass the time, won't you?'

Another grave nod, then the boy's face lit up at the sight of something.

Quentin turned to find out what it was and saw Jacinta come out on the deck. Her face lit up too when she saw Ben.

Such great love! Quentin thought. It was a pleasure to see love in any form. He hoped the man she was going to marry would be an affectionate person. She would be easy to love, he was sure. But if things didn't go well for her in Australia, then Quentin would continue to help her.

He was praying things would go well for him in Australia, too. He was longing to see Harriet again. Surely she'd be glad to see him?

★　★　★

Gerald Blacklea walked up and down the dock for a while after the ship had set sail, unable to think for the rage that still pulsed through him. He was vaguely aware of Pearson following him, but didn't speak to the man.

As the hot anger gradually began to fade, one thought took its place: whatever it cost him, in time or money, he wasn't going to be bested by that woman. *She would pay for what she'd done and he'd get the boy.*

But it never did to make plans while he was upset, so he waited for the pounding in his head to die down. At last he stopped and looked at Pearson. 'We need to visit the P&O shipping agent. Do you know where to find him?'

'Yes, sir. This way.'

The agent told them it was possible to catch up with the ship if they went by train to Marseille, but they'd have to leave London the next day at the latest, to be sure of it.

'I want to book a berth on that ship, in steerage.'

'Yes, sir. In what name?'

Pearson tugged at his master's sleeve and whispered, 'I don't think you'll want either of us linked to this, sir. Best to take another name.'

Gerald paused. 'You're right.' He turned back to the agent. 'I'm not sure yet which of my men will be going to Australia for me. Put him down as Mr White's manservant.'

The agent hesitated, looked at him, then said quietly, 'Yes, sir.'

On the train to London, the two men were alone in the compartment, so Gerald took Pearson into his confidence, talking to him, but not waiting for answers, as he worked out exactly how to get hold of the boy. One thing was certain. He'd have to dispose of the mother first. Yes, that was the thing. She'd never let Benjamin go.

As the latter idea settled firmly in his mind, he said, 'So it's decided. We need to get rid of the woman permanently, if I'm to keep the boy unsullied by her stupidity.'

'Yes, sir.'

'I think *you* should be the one to go after her.

You've the wit and cunning to do this carefully and you've never let me down yet.'

Silence, then, 'I can't do that for you, sir.'

Gerald scowled. 'I pay you to do as I say, whatever I ask. Where have such scruples suddenly come from?'

'It's because — '

Gerald could feel the anger rising again. 'If I say you're to follow her to the moon, then that's what you'll do, Pearson. I pay you well. I expect to be served well.'

'I'm sorry, sir. I phrased that badly. What I meant was, if we're to take her by surprise, then it can't be me who goes, because she'll recognise me. And so will that lawyer who was with her *and* some of the crew. I spent time with them, so it just won't work.'

Gerald sat drumming his fingers on his knees in time to the rattling of the train, frowning, hating to admit that Pearson had a point. 'Hmm. Perhaps you're right. Trouble is, there's no one else I can trust to do the thing properly.'

'Well . . . '

'We've no time for hesitation if we're to catch the ship at Marseille. Do you know someone else who could do this at short notice?'

'I have a nephew, sir, a likely young fellow, very keen to make something of himself. Alfred, he's called. Smart lad, my brother's only son.'

'I don't want your damned family history, Pearson!'

'Sorry, sir. Anyway, my nephew could go instead of me. He's a brawny fellow, if force is needed.'

144

'How old is he?'

'Twenty-five, sir.'

'Married?'

'Yes, sir. With three children.'

'Good. He'll be more likely to do the job properly and come back afterwards.' Gerald chewed his thumb, not saying anything for a while.

Pearson waited. He'd lasted longer than anyone else in this job of general assistant to the master mainly because he knew how to tread carefully and was willing to do anything, legal or not. He'd done very well for himself out of it and was keen to keep his job. Blacklea could be generous when he wanted something difficult done.

As long as he was well paid, Pearson's nephew would no doubt act in a similar fashion. Alfred hadn't had many chances to better himself . . . yet. But he was always short of money because his silly bitch of a wife didn't know the meaning of the word 'careful'. Pearson realised his master was speaking again and fixed his eyes on Mr Blacklea's face.

'I'll have to meet your nephew and quickly, too. We don't have much time. As soon as we get back to the village, go and find him. Bring him up to the house. He does work nearby, I trust? Otherwise there won't be time to get this arranged.'

'Oh, he's close by, sir. Alfred works in the stables at the inn, but there's no future in it like there used to be, with railways and branch lines springing up everywhere.'

'Tell whatshisname who owns the inn — '

'Mr Jeavins?'

'Yes. Tell him I need to see Alfred urgently.'

'Certainly, sir. He'll be happy to oblige.'

'If I like the looks of your nephew, we'll send him after that female.'

Hiding a grin, Pearson went to do as he'd been ordered as soon as he got off the train. This could be just what Alfred needed to get him out of the job in the stables. It was all right Alfred saying he liked working with horses and enjoyed driving the landlord's cart around, but if there was money involved, Ruth would make sure her husband did what Mr Blacklea wanted.

* * *

Peter Stanwell saw Blacklea return to the village and to his enormous relief, there was no sign of a boy or a woman.

The landowner's scowl was clearly visible through the carriage window. Something must have gone wrong.

Peter said a quick prayer that poor Mrs Blacklea and her son had got away. And that Blacklea didn't take out his anger on any of his tenants.

Peter would listen carefully to gossip, but had no way of finding out directly what had happened, because he and Blacklea didn't see one another socially, or even do more than nod when they passed in the street.

He'd not find out fully what had happened until the ship had taken Mrs Blacklea *and* his letter to Mitchell Nash to Australia, and another ship had brought back a letter from his cousin Mitchell. That'd take at least six months, probably longer.

It was a long time to wait for news.

'Lord, grant me patience,' he muttered. 'And give me some hint of what's going on.'

* * *

Pearson went first to find the landlord of the inn. 'Mr Blacklea wants to see Alfred. And quick smart.'

Mr Jeavins scowled. 'What for?'

'I don't know but the master said to hurry.'

'Well, Alfred had better get back here *quick smart*, too. He has work to do and I'm the one who pays him, not your master.'

'But Mr Blacklea is the owner of this inn.'

Jeavins sighed and didn't raise any further objections.

Pearson went to find his nephew. 'Mr Blacklea wants to see you. Get yourself smartened up a bit.'

Alfred washed his hands and face quickly, hoping he didn't smell too strongly of the stables. 'What's up, Uncle Bernard? Why does he want to see me?'

'Not for me to say.'

Ruth came running out as they walked past the cottage. 'What are you doing, Alfred Pearson? You've never got the sack?'

He scowled at her. 'No, I haven't. Mr Blacklea wants to see me. And no, I don't know what for.'

Pearson intervened, not wanting them to start

quarrelling. 'Let us get about Mr Blacklea's business, Ruth. The master's in a hurry to see my nephew. It could be to your advantage.'

She stared at him, eyes narrowed, then shut her mouth on a complaint and stepped back.

Alfred walked along, wishing his uncle hadn't let him in for whatever Mr Blacklea wanted doing. A more chancy fellow than the owner of the Hall, gentleman or not, you'd be hard put to find. And treated his horses badly, too, which Alfred didn't like.

He was shown into a big room full of books. First time he'd been in the front part of the house and he looked round with interest. His uncle went to stand near the desk, a little behind the master, leaving his nephew on his own in front of it.

When they explained what they wanted him to do, Alfred looked at his uncle in dismay, then gasped, 'I don't know nothing about ships and going to Australia.'

'You know about needing money and you'll be paid well for this,' his Uncle Bernard said curtly. 'Listen to what the master's telling you.'

Alfred listened all right, astonished at how much he was being offered for this job. He'd sell his soul for fifty pounds. It might even stop Ruth nagging — till she'd spent it all. But to kill someone. He wasn't sure he could do that. He looked at his uncle and opened his mouth to say so, but his uncle signalled to him to keep quiet, so he did.

'The money won't be paid till you get back, mind,' Mr Blacklea said.

148

'Then how's my wife going to manage? There are three children to feed while I'm away.'

Gerald scowled at him, glancing sideways at Pearson, as if for a solution.

'They're tenants of one of your cottages, sir, so you can let them stay rent-free. And they'll need a little money each week to eat, sir,' Pearson said. 'But a few shillings isn't much to a man like you, not when you want an important job doing. You can count on Alfred, you really can.'

'Hmm. You can arrange a suitable payment for this wife, then. Not too much. I'm not paying for her to live in idle luxury.'

'Of course not, sir. And Alfred will need clothes for the journey as well. When someone went to Australia from the next village they had to take enough clean clothes to last the voyage, and that's two months. We don't want Alfred drawing attention to himself by not having the same sort of luggage as the rest of them.'

It took them an hour to work out all the details, after which Alfred and his uncle walked back to the village to tell Mr Jeavins and pack his things.

Alfred stopped when they were out in the lane, putting a hand on his uncle's sleeve. 'I don't think I can kill someone.'

'Of course you can. Think of the fifty pounds.'

'I can't do it.'

'It'll be easy. Just shove her overboard. No blood and no fuss. If you're careful how you do it, no one will know. They'll think it was an accident.'

Alfred stared down at his feet. 'I still don't think I can.'

149

His uncle punched him in the belly, waiting till he'd got his breath, then saying, 'You'll do it. I've given him my word and he'll raise hell if you don't do it. Probably take it out on your wife and kids, then kick you out of the village.'

Alfred rubbed his sore belly, not knowing what to say.

'You're very fond of that eldest, aren't you? Callie, isn't she called?'

He nodded.

'Well, if you don't do what we tell you, I'll make sure she's the first one to suffer.'

'If you hurt her — '

'You'll do what? No one gets the better of the master, you should know that by now. So you're doing it. Right?'

Alfred could only nod.

'He's given me this gun for you. In case you need it.'

'I don't like the idea of carrying a gun. Dangerous things, they are, and I'm not used to them, and that's a fact. I bet I'd be in right old trouble if anyone found it on me on the ship, too.'

'Hmm. You may be right. Well, we don't need to say anything to *him* about that as long as you do the job. Hide the gun under the thatch of your cottage and take a knife instead. You're allus whittling bits of wood so no one will be surprised if you take some pieces along to pass the time with. You can kill her just as well with your pocket knife as with a gun. And it'll be a damn sight quieter. But best of all if you push her overboard. You take my word for it.'

150

Alfred sighed. He'd thumped Ruth a few times, and who wouldn't? She did nothing but nag, nag, nag. And when they were babies, the children never stopped yowling. It drove him mad sometimes, especially as they were all girls. A man wanted sons, not daughters.

But still . . . to kill someone. That took a lot of doing in cold blood. And if he did manage to do it, he'd have to make sure no one suspected him. Easier said than done, that was. He didn't intend to hang, not for anyone.

But you couldn't say no to the master.

Or to his damned uncle.

And when he came to think about the rest of it, well, he wouldn't mind seeing a bit of the world. This was the only way he was likely to get the chance.

So be it, then. He'd do what he was asked to . . . somehow bring himself to the sticking point. He had to.

★   ★   ★

Bram went to the ice works on the Sunday, as planned, trying to speak cheerfully as he told Isabella where he was going.

'Is it working properly now?' she asked at once.

He'd known she'd be hard to fool. 'We think so. This is the big test.'

She sighed and shrugged, so he left before she could come up with any of her penetrating questions.

Chilton was waiting for him at the ice works.

151

'The ice should be ready soon. I started up the new machinery early this morning.' He led the way into the manufacturing area at the rear, whistling cheerfully.

Did nothing ever upset the fellow? Bram wondered. Well, why should it? The money that had been thrown into this wasn't his, it was Bram's. He'd come to hate this place, the smell of it, the lumpy machinery. He still didn't really understand how it made ice, could never figure out machinery.

He couldn't think of anything to say till he saw how successful this test was, so he kept quiet.

When he took out his pocket watch some time later, he frowned. 'Wasn't the ice supposed to be ready by now?'

Chilton shrugged. 'It's taking a little longer than I expected, but it has cooled things down, it *is* making ice.' He went over to drip oil on some machinery and wipe another bit with a stained cloth, then he started fiddling with some other machinery in a corner.

Bram told himself to keep calm, but it was hard, very hard.

There were all sorts of bits and pieces lying round. He couldn't have borne to work in such an untidy place. He didn't let himself check the time. Not yet. He just stood and waited, enduring, as he had learned to do when he was a lad working in the stables of a vicious master.

Just as Bram thought he could bear it no longer, Chilton took out his battered pocket watch. 'Should be ready now.' He went across and opened a compartment, pulling out a tray

152

and holding it out to Bram, smiling. 'There. It worked.'

Bram reached out to touch the ice with a finger that trembled, then closed his eyes in relief so deep he felt almost sick with it.

'I'll have to get it working faster, Mr Deagan, but this should give us more ice to sell every day.'

'Don't do anything to change the machinery till it's paid back the money I invested. Not another change, nothing! I've no more money to spare for new machinery.'

'Don't you want it to work properly?'

'I just want it to make some money, to pay me back.'

Chilton shrugged. 'All right. We'll see how it goes.'

Bram walked home slowly, feeling like a man reprieved from hanging. All right. The machinery wasn't working as well as he'd expected, but it was working. What mattered was that it'd bring in some money, instead of draining it from him. That was all he cared about at the moment.

★   ★   ★

Maria Blacklea hadn't meant to eavesdrop. She was sitting in her favourite corner in the garden, on the old stone bench in an angle of the house, enjoying the warmth of the sun, when she heard her husband's voice. Too late to move. He'd see her as she walked past the window.

The bench was outside the library, just to one side of the big windows, a real sun trap, and she

153

often sat here. If the servants knew about her coming here, they never said.

Gerald didn't care where she spent her days, as long as she didn't leave the house and gardens, or visit anyone without his permission.

When the wind was in a certain direction, it brought her husband's conversations with it if the library windows were open, which they mostly were. Gerald believed firmly in fresh air and never seemed to feel the cold.

She'd been terrified the first time, because if he found out she'd heard what he was saying, he'd be furious. But he didn't find out and oh, she did love the peaceful warmth of that corner on sunny days, so she continued to risk sitting there.

She'd never told anyone that she eavesdropped, but what she heard had saved her from getting into trouble more than once, so she continued to listen attentively.

Today she listened in horror to the plans to pursue and kill Jacinta Blacklea, then bring back the boy.

Not that Maria would have minded Benjamin being raised to marry her daughter Elizabeth. He'd seemed a nice quiet lad, free of the taint that made her husband so terrifying. Benjamin's father, Claude, didn't sound to have been a very nice man, either. But at least the boy's father had been obsessed with his studies, not with his self-importance and pride.

'We Blackleas go for what we want and we don't stop till we get it,' Gerald had told her many a time. 'I'll be a titled lord before I'm through, see if I'm not.'

She knew how ruthless he could be. He'd decided to marry her for her connections and had pursued her single-mindedly. Even though she'd been in love with someone else at the time and expecting to marry John, her parents had insisted on her accepting Gerald's offer.

She wouldn't have dared refuse him, anyway.

Best not to think of John. He was long married to someone else. *He* was probably happy.

But to go as far as murder! She wouldn't have believed that even Gerald could do such a dreadful thing if she hadn't heard him planning it.

She shivered. If he was going to murder one person, he might murder another. It had crossed her mind before now that he might wish to look for a more fertile wife and sire a son or two. He was still a man in his prime, if a little full-bodied these days, while her health wasn't at all good and the doctor said that having another child would kill her as surely as poison or a gun.

But her family were there, with her brother as head, not her father, and he made it plain that he was keeping an eye on her and her husband.

But Gerald might still decide to get rid of her. He was so strong he could break her neck easily, then toss her down the stairs and say she'd fallen. Once or twice in his anger he'd half-throttled her, and she'd had to cover her throat with a scarf till the bruises faded. Her maid must have guessed what had happened, but she'd said nothing.

Maria had had nightmares about that ever

since. The lack of air. Her terror. Gerald's enjoyment of her fear.

As for that horrible Pearson fellow, with his smarmy smile, he was as completely lacking in morals as her husband. Look at the way he treated their tenants, doing anything Gerald wanted to terrify them into submission.

His nephew was probably just as bad. Well, he must be to have accepted the task of killing Jacinta.

Maria lay awake for half the night, worrying. But there was nothing she could do to help poor Jacinta, not without risking her own life.

She wished there was. Oh, she did! She'd go to hell after she died if she didn't manage to do something to redeem herself.

Dare she?

* * *

Peter heard the news within hours because the whole village was full of it. Mr Blacklea was sending Alf Pearson to Australia on an errand for him, though no one was quite sure what sort of errand that could be. Even Alf's wife Ruth didn't know that.

Peter's heart sank. Did that mean Gerald Blacklea was trying to kidnap the son or . . . His breath caught in his throat. Surely Blacklea wouldn't try to harm the mother?

It didn't take much thought to realise it was very possible that the landowner was planning to get his way by force. People from the village who'd upset 'the master' had been attacked and beaten up. Others had left the village in a furtive midnight flit.

Was there anything he could do to warn the poor woman?

He couldn't think of it. According to his cousin Mitchell, the colony was very backward, with no railways, let alone telegraphs.

All Peter could think of to do was pray, and he did that most fervently.

Since he could think of no way of resolving the dilemma, he left it in his Maker's hands, simply begging the Lord to intercede and save Jacinta and her son from that evil man.

Yet again, Peter considered asking to be moved to another parish, one where the local landowners were more Christian in their nature. But something held him back. He wasn't sure what.

Perhaps it was his pity for Maria Blacklea that kept him here. The poor woman was extremely unhappy in her marriage. Everyone knew that. And she was terrified of her husband. With good reason.

Yet he could see no way of helping her.

Perhaps it was also his own dislike of giving up when he'd set out to do something that kept him from asking to be moved.

After all, he had managed to help some people secretly, most recently Jacinta and her son. At least he'd done that.

8

The next morning, his head spinning with information, Alf boarded the train which would take him to London. From there he had to cross the English Channel and travel all the way across France to Marseille. The master had shown it to him on a map.

Five days, it'd take, what with changing trains here and there, and overnight stays.

He kept trying to imagine doing nothing but sit on a train for all that time. He wasn't looking forward to that. He didn't like being boxed up indoors.

He had all his travel instructions written down in his uncle's clear hand, and the papers were safe in his inside jacket pocket. But the information was locked in his head, too, because he didn't want to risk going astray or missing the ship and upsetting Mr Blacklea.

He was good at memorising things. If he'd known as a lad what he knew now, he'd have worked harder at school. But he'd been eager to get outdoors, away from the dusty classroom that made him sneeze, and especially to avoid the schoolmaster's cane. The old man had had a heavy hand.

Alf enjoyed working with horses. He just wished it paid better or that he had a horse of his own. That was his fondest dream.

To his astonishment, he'd been given a pile of

new clothes, old-fashioned stuff that had belonged to Mr Blacklea himself, from when the master was thinner. And other stuff from his uncle, who was about the same size as him. All for use on the ship. He'd never had so many clothes in his whole life. He hadn't thought of himself as being the same size as the master. Just fancy that.

He had most of his money in a belt round his waist, for safety, with some in his pocket for the expenses during the journey. It was a lot of money, but his uncle said it'd take all of it to get there and bring the boy back. His uncle had taken two guineas out of the money when he handed it over, and Alf hadn't dared protest about that.

Mr Blacklea said he was to write down every penny he spent, and his uncle had told him the same thing. The master checked everything, it seemed.

'You'll soon make up my commission,' his uncle said. 'Add a penny here, a penny there to the accounts till you've made up the two guineas.'

Alf could only nod, feeling aggrieved at his uncle's theft. Then he realised it'd given him a sharp lesson on how to get hold of some of the money for himself. What he wrote down had to sound right, but it wouldn't necessarily be what he spent. If he was careful, he could feather his nest nicely on this journey and come back with money saved.

If he earned the bonus by getting rid of the woman who was in Mr Blacklea's way, he'd use it to set himself up in a business, and would go as far away as he could get from the village and his uncle.

And Ruth could like it or lump it.

★　★　★

They were lucky in the Bay of Biscay. The weather was overcast and there was some drizzle, but there were no storms.

Jacinta proved to be as good a sailor as Eleanor, and the two of them spent a lot of time on deck with Mr Saxby, who was a little pale at first, but soon got his sea legs.

Ben didn't even seem to notice the rougher weather and laughed when the ship bobbed up and down, making them move in short runs from one place to the next.

The other passengers were pleasant enough, but the trio were soon fast friends and spent most of their time together, keeping an eye on the boy and chatting amicably about all sorts of things.

Remembering his conversation with Ben, Quentin took one of the other mothers into his confidence about the boy's strict father and him not being allowed to play out. She told her son a little of what he'd said.

Neil had previously been rather scornful of such a quiet lad, but he was kind-hearted, so made an effort with Ben. As they were the only boys of that age among the cabin-class passengers, they soon formed the sort of friendship between opposites that happens when people are thrown together temporarily and don't actually hate one another.

'I keep holding my breath about Ben,' Jacinta said to her friends one day. 'He's never had a friend before. Look how happy he is playing with Neil, who's such a kind lad.'

Eleanor smiled at the two boys, thinking Neil's kindness was probably because Ben let Neil boss him around. 'I told you he'd cope.'

'The classes help. He meets people there, as well.'

'They'll also help us. Two months is a long time to be shut up on a ship, even with good friends. I'll be glad when we get there.'

Jacinta nodded. She wasn't sure whether she'd be glad or not.

'Still worrying about Mr Nash?'

'How can I help it? I'm going out to Australia to marry a man I've never met before. What if I don't even like him?'

'Then you'll stay with me and Mr Saxby until you find another husband.' Eleanor added with a sigh, 'Don't forget that I'm going to see someone who said he loved me but who doesn't know I'm now free. I have to hope Dougal won't have changed his mind. If he has, I'll be like you . . . husband hunting.'

'You speak so glibly about that.'

'Because women are in short supply there. I've been to Australia and I've seen it. Even ugly ones have men courting them and soon marry. You're pretty enough to take your pick now you're eating properly.'

'I suppose so. Thank you for the compliment. I

'. . . don't think about my looks.'

'Well, you should. Not many women have such lovely silver-blond hair. When we've finished altering a couple of the dresses for you from those I got from Daphne, you'll look even better.'

'You're sure you can spare them?'

Eleanor laughed. 'Certain. I took every garment I could when she offered them, in case I had to sell them to survive. By the time we get to Australia, I'll make sure we're both well dressed and fashionable.'

'That'll be wonderful.'

*   *   *

By the time the train got to Marseille, Alf was heartily sick of travelling and was almost ready to burst with unspent energy. At first he'd looked out of the window, eager to see what France was like. But it wasn't much different from England: fields, cottages, trees, animals, and the occasional town sitting like a smoky mess on the countryside. That was his first disappointment.

His second disappointment was his fellow passengers, with whom he had nothing in common. As day followed day, he felt as if he'd go mad boxed up in the train. The man sitting next to him left the train at some town a day south of Paris — Alf couldn't get his tongue round the word — and offered Alf his English newspaper.

'Thank you. Much appreciated.' Alf wasn't very good at reading, but it'd be something to

162

do, at least, spelling his way through all those damned words.

The next day a most depressing thought crept into his mind. He'd have all this to do again on the way back, as well as looking after a lad who probably didn't want to return to England. No one had told him how he was to persuade the lad to come back with him.

For a start he'd have to make sure Ben didn't realise who'd killed his mother, or Alf would have no chance of doing what Mr Blacklea wanted.

He frowned every time he thought of killing a woman, still hadn't got used to the idea. It wasn't going to be easy. Not half as easy as his uncle made out. He felt he could strangle Ruth sometimes, but that was in anger, and anyway, Ruth was a nag. What if this woman was really nice and he liked her?

He looked at the old couple who had got on the train at the last stop and were now sitting next to him. Frenchies, they were. Jabbering away to one another. Who could understand such nonsense? No wonder the British ruled the world.

The young couple opposite mustn't have been long married because they were always whispering to one another and holding hands when they thought no one was looking. They'd soon get over that sort of nonsense. Everyone did.

In case he got chatting to someone, Alf had a tale ready, that he was a widower and was travelling out to Australia to join a cousin who was doing well there. But as he didn't find anyone to talk to on the train, he didn't have to use it. The tale was his uncle's idea and he wished it was true. By hell, he did.

When this adventure was over, he'd have to go back to Ruth and a house full of little girls. At least Ruth couldn't have presented him with another baby in the meantime. He knew for certain she was having her courses when he left, so he'd mentioned this to his uncle and asked him to keep an eye on her, to make sure she didn't flirt or worse.

By the time the train got to Marseille, Alf was hot and sticky. He hadn't bothered to wash himself at the overnight stops, except for his hands and face — well, he'd had a good wash all over before he left England, so there was no need. He was ready for another wash down now, though, and a change of clothes. He changed his underwear every Sunday back home and his wife had made him promise to do the same while he was travelling.

But first he had to find the damned ship. He asked the older man who'd sat quietly in a corner for most of the journey how to do that.

'If you help me with my luggage, lad, I'll show you. I've been to the docks before. Yes, and travelled out to Australia. After my wife died, I went back to see my family in England, but I doubt I'll do it again, at my age.'

'Is Australia a good place to live?'

'My son and I have done well there. It's what you make of it. Hard work, though. You'll be going on the P&O ship?'

'Yes.'

'Come along, then.'

Alf didn't mind helping Mr Cantley, who seemed a decent sort. The old man told him first to find a porter to carry their trunks, then warned him to keep an eye on the porter as they walked along the docks. It was a relief that Mr Cantley knew a few words of French. You couldn't help learning it when you travelled. Even Alf had learned what *bong-joor* and *mercy* meant.

He stopped dead in shock at the sight of the ship. It was huge, far bigger than he'd expected. He started moving again, staring up in amazement as they walked along beside it. He hadn't realised ships could be so big. Still, it was probably a good thing. Safer, like.

But as he went on board, he felt as if he was being swallowed up, especially as Mr Cantley was travelling cabin class and went straight to another part of the ship, while Alf had to queue up with the steerage passengers.

Alf didn't like the feeling of being helpless that he kept getting on this trip. He was taller than everyone else and stronger too. Normally he spent his time outdoors, not shut up inside. But what was normal about this?

★   ★   ★

At Marseille, Jacinta and Ben stood together by the rail, watching new passengers board the ship. They seemed to be mostly steerage, but two elderly ladies were escorted to the first-class cabins, with the stewardess fussing over them as

165

if they were royalty. Then an elderly gentleman followed them, but without as much fussing. He was in a second-class cabin.

One man stood out among the steerage passengers because he was so tall, also because he was scowling and looking round as if uneasy.

Eleanor came to join them. 'Those two ladies don't look a very interesting pair, do they? I bet they don't join in the concert. The old man looks nicer. I could wish for some younger companions. It's a long way to Australia.'

'The children's choir is going to sing three songs at the concert,' Ben said. 'Mr Teesdale says I hold a tune nicely. I like singing.'

Jacinta looked at him fondly. He was enjoying the various activities and beginning to do things without clinging to her. He followed Neil around a lot, but then they were the only boys of that age. 'I suppose that means you'll be having more rehearsals.'

'Yes. It's fun travelling on a ship, isn't it?'

Eleanor chuckled. 'You must be the only person enjoying it so much, young fellow.'

He gave her one of his shy smiles. 'There's lots to do. I like that.' He turned to watch the steerage passengers, who were now on deck and waiting their turn to go below. 'That man's very big, isn't he? I bet he's the strongest person on the ship, stronger than the sailors, even.'

Jacinta didn't comment, but she didn't like the new passenger's face. He looked . . . brutal.

She didn't usually take a dislike to someone on sight and couldn't help wondering why she'd done so now.

And there was something else. It was as if she recognised him from somewhere. Which couldn't be possible. He hadn't even joined the ship in England, so how could she have met him before?

She was glad he was in steerage and that she wouldn't have much to do with him.

★ ★ ★

Once he got on the ship, Alf found some things just the same as back home. People ordering him around, even less chance to choose where he went or what he did than at home.

He could see some rich folk at the front end of the ship, wearing their fancy clothes and sitting around doing nothing. Lazy sods! Those with more money made sure they got the best of everything, whether they deserved it or not, and left the rest to manage as best they could.

Alf queued to go below, going down some stairs that were more like a ladder and were called a companionway, of all the silly names. His feet were too big to fit comfortably on the narrow treads and he nearly fell.

Once down, he was directed to a cabin which he'd be sharing with seven other men. It wasn't all that big, either. He scowled at the sight of his bed. How someone over six foot tall was expected to sleep in such a small, narrow bunk, he didn't know.

The supervisor of the men's side watched him put down his suitcase and said with a sniff of disdain, 'I hope you're going to have a good wash and change your clothes now, Mr Walsh.'

It took Alf a minute to remember his new surname. Walsh, his uncle had decided, because they didn't know anyone called that. Alf had to ask the steward to repeat the rest of what he'd said.

'Are you deaf or what? I said you're sweaty and grimy after your travel, and quite frankly, you smell bad. If you want to get on with the fellows you're sharing with, you'll need to wash regularly. We like people to keep clean on these ships because we're all living so close to one another.'

Alf could feel himself flushing in embarrassment and was relieved that there was no one else in the cabin to hear this.

The steward's voice grew a little less hostile. 'It's all right. The others from this cabin are on deck, getting a bit of fresh air. I'll show you where to get some water for a wash. I hope you've got some clean clothes.'

'Of course I have.' He forced himself to add, 'Thanks for your help. I've been wanting a good wash. Didn't get a chance the last few days.'

Once the supervisor had gone, Alf set to and washed himself all over, which made him feel cooler. Hot it was here, and would get hotter still, the old man who'd helped him had said.

He'd glanced in the mirror someone had fastened to the wall in the cabin. He'd have to spruce himself up every day from now on. Not because he cared how he looked, but because he didn't want to draw attention to himself. Bad enough how big he was. He always stood out in a crowd and some people were afraid of him

168

because of that. It was useful at times but not here, well, he didn't think it would be, not with what he had to do.

Feeling refreshed and understanding now why he'd had to bring so many clothes with him, Alf decided to go up to join the rest of the passengers on deck.

Most of them were standing around chatting or staring across the water at the city. He didn't know a single person and he'd had enough of sitting still, so began to walk about briskly. But when he tried to go right to the other end of the ship, he was stopped by one of the crew members.

'Why can't I go past here?' he demanded. 'There are lots of other people up at the end.' He could see them.

'That space is reserved for the cabin-class passengers,' the sailor told him. 'You're in steerage, so you're not allowed beyond the funnel.'

They called the front part of the ship 'forward' it seemed, pronouncing it 'forrad', and they kept all that space for just a few nobs, squashing everyone else into the back part. As Alf looked down at his hand he saw a black smut drift down and settle on his newly washed skin. When he looked up to see where it came from, he saw smoke trickling out of the funnel.

'They're firing up the engines,' the chatty sailor told him. 'You'll get more than a few smuts landing on you before you're through.'

Alf shrugged and continued to walk up and down the back part of the ship, studying his fellow passengers in steerage. A meek, miserable bunch they seemed, too. Townies, most of 'em, he reckoned.

When his walking took him near the funnel again, he stopped to watch the nobs, wondering which one was Mrs Blacklea. Even without finding out their names, he quickly narrowed it down to six ladies, then decided that two of them were too young. That left four of the right age.

An old fellow was chatting to two of them, who looked a bit older than the others, but were still quite pretty. Well, rich folk didn't wear out like poor folk did. Ruth looked a right old mess these days and she'd been pretty once, prettiest girl in the village.

Then a lad came running up to one of the ladies and she gave him a hug, something you didn't usually see the nobs do in public.

I bet that's her, he thought. *And that'll be Ben*.

The loving way she looked at the lad surprised Alf. No wonder she didn't want to give her son to Mr Blacklea. No one had ever looked at Alf like that in the whole of his life, though his gran had been quite fond of him and had often slipped him a bit of food. His mother had always been too busy with a new baby to fuss over any of them.

There'd be time enough to find out if his guess was right about her being Mrs Blacklea. They'd got a long way to travel yet, so he didn't need to rush into anything. But he felt pretty sure she was the one.

Then he shivered as it occurred to him: *the one he had to kill*.

170

He pushed that thought to the back of his mind and began to make plans.

What he'd do first was get talking to the lad. He was good with lads — well, with village lads anyway. They liked to help him in the inn stables or watch him whittle his little animals out of wood. He had his knife and some wood with him.

He didn't think that lad would be very different from the village lads. He looked a quiet sort. Nice lad, probably.

He wouldn't have a happy life with Mr Blacklea, poor little sod. But that wasn't Alf's business. Definitely not. He had his own family to look after. Mr Blacklea would toss them all out of the village if he didn't do what he'd been sent for.

Alf had to remember that and not get soft. When you had a job to do you just got on with it.

★ ★ ★

When they got near Fremantle, the *Bonny Ismay* attracted a lot of attention, both because of the battered state of the ship and the strange floating cargo trailing behind her.

Adam took his time edging the ship into port, with the help of more tugs than usual to help them manage the waterlogged timber.

Once they were safely anchored, he started the crew working on pulling the timber in, setting up extra pulleys to hoist it on to the docks and then stacking it carefully.

As soon as that was under way, he sent a lad running to fetch Mitchell Nash, the timber merchant, because he trusted the man to deal honestly with them. He also sent a message to a local magistrate about the salvage, because he'd have to declare it and check that no one else was laying claim to it. That could make the difference between a hefty profit from his hard work and a lesser amount as a reward.

When Bram came hurrying down to the harbour, Adam went to meet his brother-in-law himself.

'Is it true?' Bram asked, even before he got on board the ship.

'Is what true?'

'That the cargo has been badly damaged in a storm.'

'I'm afraid it is.'

'Dear heaven, what am I going to do? I was counting on the money we got for it to pay some pressing bills.' Bram sank down on the edge of the nearest hatch, his face ashen.

Before Adam could ask what this was about, Mitchell arrived.

Adam left his brother-in-law and went to explain what had happened to the newcomer.

'I'll make you a decent offer to buy every bit of the timber, if it's in good condition,' Mitchell said at once. 'You won't need to find any other buyers.'

Adam stuck out his hand and they shook on that. 'We'll have to wait for the magistrate to pronounce on the status of the cargo before you can take it.'

172

'From what you've said, it'll be yours without any trouble. It'll take a day or two, though.' He glanced sideways. 'What's the matter with Bram?'

'He needed the money from our cargo, which got damaged,' Adam whispered.

'Poor fellow. He doesn't deserve that, does he?'

Bram got heavily to his feet and came to join them. 'No use hanging around here, then. You'll send what's left of my cargo to the Bazaar, Adam?'

'Yes. As soon as I can.'

As he was supervising this, he saw his wife and aunt coming towards the ship and prepared to explain yet again what had happened during the journey.

He ran towards them and hugged Ismay, then Aunt Harriet. Then he had to hug Ismay all over again.

When he told her about her brother's losses, Ismay looked at him in shock. 'Bram's lost his cargo?'

'A lot of it. And he said he was counting on it.'

'It's that ice-making business. Isabella is worried sick about the money it's cost.' Ismay hesitated, then looked from him to his aunt. 'I'll have to go to him. There must be something I can do to help.'

When she'd gone, Aunt Harriet said quietly, 'I do hope Bram will be all right.'

'So do I.'

'Was he . . . very upset?'

'Yes. He turned white and sat down. I've never

173

seen him like that. He's usually so optimistic and cheerful.'

'If he's going to be short of money, I could help him a little till he gets on his feet again. I'm sure he'd soon pay me back.'

Adam sighed. 'I can't do much for him, I'm afraid. I'm still making my way in the world and I've lost money on this storm damage myself. But I'm hoping the salvage money will make up for that.'

'Perhaps I should give you some of my money, then, Adam dear.'

'No, no! I've not lost more than I can afford. I'm being a bit cautious in my trading at this stage.'

'Are you quite sure you're all right? You know you're welcome to every penny I've got.'

He pulled her into a quick hug. 'You should keep your money, Aunt Harriet, and don't lend it to anyone. You need it to live on. And I hope you live for a good long time.'

*　　*　　*

Gerald Blacklea prowled round the house, finding things to complain about everywhere he went. He'd always been a difficult master to work for, but he'd become far worse lately.

The maids lived in terror and Cook gave notice, saying she was too old to live in fear.

Maria persuaded Cook to stay and then took refuge in her bedroom to escape Gerald's anger at her bothering to coax a servant.

That afternoon she went down to the church

174

to arrange the flowers, knowing Mrs Percival was ill. It was one of her rare opportunities to leave the house on her own, because Gerald approved her doing this task and few people came into the church at that time of day.

Mr Stanwell strolled along the side of the church just as she was finishing the first vase. He paused beside her.

'Your flower arrangements are exquisite, Mrs Blacklea.'

'Thank you.' She couldn't remember when she'd last been complimented about anything. Suddenly her burden of fear overwhelmed her, so heavy that she had to share it. 'Could I . . . talk to you? In confidence?'

'Of course.'

She didn't say anything but gathered up her equipment and put it behind the other big vase, hoping that no one would come looking for her.

She paused outside the parson's room. What would she say to Gerald if he found out about this? She almost turned tail, but then she remembered what she'd overheard and couldn't bear to carry that knowledge alone for a minute longer.

Mr Stanwell's voice was gentle. 'Please sit down.'

She sat and struggled not to weep because she mustn't go home with reddened eyes and a tearful appearance. Her tale came out in jerks, and in between each spurt of information, she had to pause and struggle to keep control.

When she'd finished she sat there, numb, with no hope in her of anything helping.

'My dear, this is a terrible burden for you to bear alone.'

She nodded.

'I'm sorry, but I can't see any way of helping you, except . . . '

As he hesitated, she looked at him, not hoping for anything, really, just the sympathy of a fellow human being.

'If you ever need to escape from him permanently, come to me and I'll help you get away.'

Oh, the thought of that. But the brief hope died as quickly as it had flared. 'I couldn't leave my daughter. I can sometimes protect Elizabeth from him, deflect his anger on to myself. It's not much, but it helps.'

'Unfortunately, I can't think of any other way of helping you.'

'It helps that you wanted to, that you cared.' She got to her feet, relieved that she hadn't wept, well not more than a tear or two, so there was nothing to show that she'd been upset. She looked sideways into a small mirror and saw her face becoming expressionless again. That was the best weapon she had against *him*.

'Thank you, Mr Stanwell. I'll show myself out, if you don't mind.'

She went and began to work on the second flower arrangement. As she was finishing it, she heard *his* footsteps coming towards the front of the church. He had such a distinctive and heavy tread.

'There you are,' he said.

She waited. Was Gerald going to stop her

doing even this now?

'It looks good. You have a talent for arranging flowers.'

'Thank you, Gerald. And I do think it sets a good example for the congregation that I participate in the life of the church.'

'It looks better for us, too, that someone from the big house is involved in church matters.'

She knew he could never join in anything, not even giving a reading as part of the service, because he and Mr Stanwell were like two fires, each politely holding back from the other. Their mutual dislike was so strong it was almost visible.

'Yes. I always think so too, Gerald. I like to help you present the best face to the world.'

'Good, good. Are you ready to go home now?'

'Yes. I've finished here.' She shoved her implements into the canvas bag she'd brought them in. She didn't clear up as carefully as usual, because he hated to see her doing such menial tasks.

When she turned, he offered his arm and escorted her out to the carriage. She was feeling almost dizzy with relief that he hadn't come to spy on her sooner and caught her with Mr Stanwell.

And if she ever had to flee for her life, she had found a way. Though she'd have to be desperate to go, because that would mean leaving Elizabeth.

9

It took the ship only a few days to cross the Mediterranean, and most people on board seemed to be enjoying the warm days and calm seas. A few complained of the heat and while the stewardess was always polite, she told them it'd be much hotter when they got nearer to the equator, so it was as well to get used to the heat now.

She offered all the ladies the same advice as she'd given to Eleanor and Jacinta, and which they'd found helpful: to wear fewer clothes and especially for the ladies, to leave off their stays and corsets. But some ladies found the idea of doing that horrifyingly indecent and preferred to suffer.

When the ship arrived at Port Said, at the northern entrance to the Suez Canal, even the most aloof cabin passengers went to the rail to watch. Everyone had heard so much about this modern marvel of a canal, reading about it in newspapers, seeing images of the ships passing through it. But that was nothing compared to the reality.

Moving more slowly now, the ship passed between the two huge obelisks at the entrance and entered the famous new waterway. The water there was calm and a heat haze shimmered over the land, making the air look like clear, rippling water in places.

'The canal's much narrower than I'd expected, not even wide enough for ships to pass one another,' Jacinta said. 'How do ships manage when they meet one another?'

A young officer standing nearby, who had several times tried to flirt with them, volunteered the information.

'Ships can pass one another at the various lakes. One of these, the Great Bitter Lake, is quite large. And there are special passing places built into the canal itself, where one ship can anchor while the other passes. They call these by the French word *gares*.'

'Thank you.' Eleanor spoke coolly, not encouraging him to linger, and after a few moments his attention was sought by some other passengers.

His eyes still lingered on Jacinta occasionally, but she stared back with an expression of utter indifference and muttered to her friend, 'I'm grateful to you for answering him. I do wish the stupid creature would stop hovering near us.'

'He's clearly taken with you,' Eleanor teased.

'It's all very well for you to find it amusing, but I'm not taken with him. And even if I was, I wouldn't do anything about it because I'm going out to the colony to marry another man, who has paid my fare. Besides, that particular officer smiles at *you* quite a lot, as well, and at others. He's a terrible flirt.'

'I don't smile back, though, do I?' Eleanor compared the young man mentally to Dougal. She often sifted through the memories of her captain. He wasn't handsome but he had a kind face and nature, and she valued that far more than good looks after her years at the beck and call of a totally selfish man.

The previous year, while they were sailing from Western Australia to Suez on Dougal's ship, she hadn't done anything to betray her husband, of course she hadn't. Not physically, anyway. But she hadn't been able to keep their captain from finding a place in her heart. She'd felt so *right* when she was with him. The two of them had never been short of something to talk about and even their silences were comfortable.

A pang of longing shot through her. Only to herself did she admit how much she was longing to see Dougal again. He'd sent money to his lawyer, so surely he'd meant what he said about loving her, wanting her to join him if she ever got the chance? Surely he'd welcome her?

For all her brave words to Jacinta and Mr Saxby, she couldn't help worrying about that sometimes during the hot, weary hours of the night. It took two months or more to travel between Australia and England. She'd spent several weeks waiting for her husband to die, had not even let herself write to Dougal during that time. Perhaps he'd met someone else in the meantime and changed his mind. He would make some woman a wonderful husband, she was sure.

She saw her friend looking at her with a worried expression and forced herself to smile and say brightly, 'Are you coming to the reading group this morning?'

'Definitely not. I'd rather get on with my sewing and anyway, I don't like being read aloud to. I'd not have joined the group if I'd known we'd be expected to sit and listen for a whole hour each time. I thought we'd be sharing books, reading them ourselves and discussing them.'

'Mrs Morton is a good reader, though, you must admit.'

'It's got nothing to do with her.' Jacinta sighed. 'It's because of Claude. He used to read aloud to me and Ben all the time, and such boring books, too. He got angry if Ben fidgeted, even when he was quite small, and once tried to beat my poor boy for not paying attention. Only I pushed between them and stopped him.'

And then Claude had beaten her instead. When she'd protested afterwards, he'd yelled, 'A man has the legal right to chastise his wife if she misbehaves.'

Soon after that incident, he'd sent her to sleep with her son in the other bedroom, which had been a great relief. And he'd never attempted to use her as a wife again. But he'd beaten her occasionally, for all she tried to defend herself.

She realised Eleanor was looking at her anxiously and managed to speak in a lighter tone. 'Well, those days are done with for ever, thank goodness.'

'I don't believe in beating children for being children. They should only be chastised for serious misbehaviour like stealing or lying.'

'I couldn't beat Ben, whatever he did. I love him too much. Though I don't think he'd steal or lie to me. Anyway, I need to get on with my sewing, so my time will be much better spent on that than on listening to someone read. I'd like

181

to have a few decent clothes to wear when I meet Mr Nash. I'm so grateful for your generosity, Eleanor. I can't thank you enough.'

'Oh, pish to that. I was given a great many clothes, many of which don't even fit me and they're all old-fashioned. I can easily spare what I've given you and you'll be doing the hard work on them, not me. I think you need a few more as well, if you're to face a new husband.'

'I can't possibly accept any others.'

'Of course you can. In fact, when we get the shower this afternoon let's ask the stewardess if we can go down to the hold and look through my other trunk to sort out some more things for you to alter. It's strange, isn't it, to have such short sharp showers? I'll be glad when we move further away from the Equator and don't have to take shelter every day.'

When Jacinta didn't say anything, Eleanor said, 'If we take the stewardess into our confidence, I'm sure she'll be sympathetic.'

'Yes, but I don't like to . . . to . . . '

'You'll need more underwear and I'm sure there's some in the other trunk.'

Jacinta couldn't deny that need. 'I shouldn't accept them.'

'Oh yes, you should. I keep telling you: I took everything I was offered, whether it fitted me or not. Just in case.'

'But if things go wrong, you may need the other clothes to sell. You said that was why you'd accepted them.'

Eleanor changed the subject firmly. It gave her pleasure to help the woman who had so quickly

182

become a close friend. As Malcolm Prescott's wife, she'd never managed to keep a friend, thanks to him moving around so often.

She hadn't even had a child to love. Not an affectionate man, Malcolm Prescott. He'd got married because his mother had died and he wanted to be looked after. Selfish to the core, he'd never once considered his wife might have needs of her own.

As the ship continued to move slowly along the canal, Eleanor helped her friend keep an eye on Ben and his friend. Mr Saxby joined them sometimes or walked about speaking to other people.

Everyone was watching the scenery and two other vessels ahead of them. There were more ships following them, but it wasn't possible to make them out clearly because they were further away.

From time to time groups of Arabs could be seen to the sides of the canal, dressed in flowing robes, with strange head coverings. And the boys were not the only ones to be excited by the sight of camels plodding along with their loads.

All in all, the day passed pleasantly enough.

This voyage was a sort of limbo, Eleanor decided. They were simply biding their time till they got to Australia.

★　★　★

After the ship had gone through the canal, it speeded up again as it began to cross the Indian Ocean. Sails billowed and thank goodness the engine wasn't in much use, because the noise got on your nerves after a while.

Ben came running up to his mother one day, very excited about a new class that was to be held for boys.

'Start again and speak more slowly!' his mother commanded. 'I can't understand what you're going on about.'

'There's a man who carves little animals — Mr Walsh, his name is — only he calls it whittling not carving. He's going to teach some of the boys how to do it. Say I can join the class, Mother! Do please, *please* say I can.'

'Does that mean you'll be using a sharp knife?'

He looked at her as if she was stupid. 'How can we do the carving if the knife isn't sharp?'

'You don't even have a knife.'

Mr Saxby, who had been standing nearby, moved across to join them. 'I can lend Ben my pocket knife. But only if you approve, of course, my dear Jacinta.'

She looked at him, frowning. 'I must admit, I don't like the idea of him using a sharp implement. Who is this Mr Walsh?'

'A fellow from steerage who boarded the ship at Marseille. He does some beautiful carvings, has a real gift for it.'

'I'd have to speak to him first, find out what he's like and see what's involved.'

'I'll go and fetch him, shall I?'

Without waiting for an answer, Mr Saxby went off towards the more crowded deck where the steerage passengers took the air. She could hear him humming cheerfully. He sounded so carefree, Jacinta envied him. Their lawyer friend got on well with passengers of every class, as well as the crew, who were always willing to do extra to help him.

He came back a few minutes later followed by the tall man who had made her feel uneasy when he boarded the ship at Marseille. Her heart sank. Did it have to be that man?

But she couldn't fault Mr Walsh, who answered her questions about safety patiently and smiled at her son from time to time when Ben interrupted their conversation.

The boy was so wild with excitement at the prospect of learning to carve that in the end Jacinta hadn't the heart to deny him this treat. Her poor son had years of missed boyish activities to make up for.

She looked very directly at Mr Walsh as she laid down her main condition. 'If my son proves clumsy and injures himself, I shall have to reconsider him attending. I shall expect you to keep an eye on the boys' safety at all times.'

'I won't let any of them hurt themselves, Mrs Blacklea, barring a small nick or two — and those can't be helped. Before we even touch any wood, I shall teach all the lads how careful you have to be with knives. And anyone who messes around with his knife will be sent packing, I promise you.'

He fumbled in his pocket and pulled out a small carving of a bird. 'Perhaps you'd do me the honour of accepting this? It's just a small example of what can be done.'

She took it from him and turned it round in her hand. It was indeed a pretty little thing. A

185

wren, perched on a piece of branch. Correct in every detail, as far as she could tell. She couldn't refuse it without giving offence, but she'd rather not have taken anything from him. 'You're very skilled, Mr Walsh.'

Her compliment seemed to make him uncomfortable and he flushed slightly, shuffling his feet as if he wasn't used to praise.

'It's just something I do to pass the time, Mrs Blacklea. I don't make my living as a wood carver. I work with horses.'

Again, as she watched him walk away, she had a vague feeling that she'd seen him before, not his face particularly, but the way he moved, the whole man. How could that be possible? He must resemble someone she'd known, only she couldn't think who. She should have asked where he came from. That might have given her a clue.

She put the bird in her cabin and Ben at least got a great deal of pleasure from fiddling with it. He kept hoping he'd learn to carve as neatly. She tried to tell him that it took years of practice to reach that stage of skill, hoping he wouldn't be too disappointed in his own efforts. But he was quite sure he'd succeed.

They were used to sharing a room, she and her son, used to turning their eyes away at delicate moments, but they'd never before shared such a small space. She had to ask him to lie in the bunk and turn his face to the wall when she was washing and changing her clothes, and she sat on the end of her bunk and averted her eyes when he performed his daily ablutions.

They'd never had such freedom, and both

were relishing that. They were still getting used to being able to do things as and when they pleased, or to say what they wished.

The thought of how wonderful it was to be free of Claude didn't make her feel at all guilty. He hadn't deserved her love, hadn't even won her liking, had only used her.

But was she really free of his cousin Gerald Blacklea? She couldn't stop worrying about him. Such an evil man! Surely he wouldn't pursue them all the way to Australia? No, how could he?

★   ★   ★

The days passed so peacefully as they sailed towards their next port, a place called Galle, that Alf pushed his purpose in coming here to the back of his mind.

To his surprise, he was enjoying teaching the small group of boys, and was proving a good teacher, too, if he said so himself.

He was also enjoying the hot days and balmy nights, enjoying this whole experience in fact. Even the food was more than adequate, especially after Ruth's hit and miss cooking.

He didn't think his uncle or Mr Blacklea would approve of him enjoying himself, well, he knew they wouldn't. They were a miserable pair and deserved each other. He didn't like what he was supposed to do, especially now he'd got to know more about the lady in question, who was a good mother.

There was no hurry to kill Mrs Blacklea,

though, no hurry at all.

Besides, Alf still hadn't worked out how to do it. The best way he could think of was to push her overboard, as his uncle had suggested. But there were so many people on the ship, it'd be hard to make certain no one saw him do it.

He woke in the night a couple of times, sweating profusely after nightmares of sinking down in the water, struggling to breathe, calling in vain for help.

Could he really do that to someone? To a woman who had never done him any harm?

But if he didn't his family would suffer. He might not be fond of Ruth any more, but he was fond of little Callie.

He had other nightmares of people putting a noose round his neck and the words 'to be hanged by the neck until dead', echoed in his dreams.

He didn't want to end his life that way.

The man in the bunk above his shook him awake from these nightmares several times, complaining about the noise he was making. Alf had to apologise to the whole cabin and pretend he'd always been prone to nightmares. He felt such a fool.

★ ★ ★

The following day Ben arrived early at the section of the deck where the class was held and sat down beside Alf to wait for the other boys. He was such a cheerful little lad, though from things he'd let fall, he hadn't had a very happy life until now.

'You look tired today, Mr Walsh. Didn't you sleep well?'

'I — um, had a bad dream.'

'I used to have bad dreams. I don't have them any more.'

'What did you dream about that was so bad?'

Ben looked round to make sure no one was near and whispered, 'My father. He used to hit my mother and I was too little to stop him. But he's dead now, so that's all right.'

And Alf, who knew from his uncle that Mr Gerald Blacklea sometimes hurt his wife, and seemed to enjoy it too, couldn't help wondering what the landowner would do to this cheerful little boy once Ben was in his power.

He had to give himself a real telling off that night as he lay waiting for sleep. It wasn't his business what happened to Ben. He was here to do a job, and do it he must, or his own family would suffer.

He had *no choice* but to obey orders.

★   ★   ★

Just over two weeks after leaving Suez, the ship was due to arrive at Port de Galle in Ceylon. Here the passengers going to Australia would have to change to another ship. Ben was very excited about that, but it made Jacinta feel nervous because it would be the last leg of their journey.

Once they arrived in Australia, she would meet Mitchell Nash and unless he was a horrible man, she'd have to marry him, with all that a marriage involved. It wasn't very enjoyable for the woman, but it was the price you had to pay, and maybe from the unpleasant act she'd have other children to love. That would be such a comfort.

And there was no denying that life in general would be easier if she had a husband, if she wasn't on her own. Not just because of the money, but because it'd be safer for her son if anything happened to her.

When they were lying in bed on their last night before Galle, Ben asked suddenly, 'What do you think Mr Nash is like?'

'You've seen the photo. You know as much about him as I do. But he's related to Mr Stanwell, who is a very nice man.'

'Mr Nash isn't old, like my father was, but he isn't smiling in the photo, is he?'

'People can't always smile to order and you have to stand still for a long time to have a photograph taken, so it's hard to keep a smile on your face.'

'His son looks nice.'

'Yes, he's called — '

'I know. Christopher and he's ten. You told me that. But will they *like* us? Will they be kind to us?'

'I hope so. If Mr Nash doesn't seem kind, I won't marry him.'

Silence then, 'How will you find out what he's like?'

'I'll wait and try to get to know him a little before I do anything. We can both listen to what people say about him, as well.'

'What if he isn't nice?'

'Mr Saxby has said he'll help us.'

'That's all right, then. I like Mr Saxby.' There was silence, then, 'Couldn't you marry him instead?'

She laughed. 'No, my darling, I couldn't. He's too old and anyway, he's going to Australia to see another lady he hopes to marry.'

She heard the sound of a yawn in the darkness and then steady breathing from the bunk above hers. She smiled in the darkness. Ben never had much trouble getting to sleep and she'd slept better while they'd been at sea.

★ ★ ★

Gerald Blacklea entered the library earlier than usual, to find a maid still laying the fire.

'What are you doing here at this hour?' he roared. 'You've been told to finish well before I get up.'

With a squeak of terror, she stood up, letting the rest of the kindling fall from her sacking apron, scattering chips of wood across his favourite armchair.

'Look what you've done now!' Suddenly he couldn't bear the sight of the stupid woman. Without considering what he was doing, he backhanded her away from the fire, away from his chair.

She fell over like a skittle, letting out one scream, abruptly cut off as her head hit the leg of a table.

He stared down at her, waiting for her to get

up, and when she didn't move, he grunted angrily and walked out of the room.

Moving as quietly as he'd entered, he went into the dining room and rang the bell for his breakfast.

As the butler brought him a pot of tea, he heard a scream from the library.

'Mr Marston! Mr Marston! Come quickly!'

Frowning, the butler murmured, 'Excuse me a moment, sir.'

'Pour my cup of tea first.'

Only when that was done did he gesture with his head to indicate that Marston could attend to whatever was causing voices to echo across the main hall.

★ ★ ★

In the library, Marston found the housekeeper and one of the maids bending over Megan, the parlourmaid, who was holding her head and moaning.

'What has happened? Whatever it is, keep your voices down. You're disturbing the master.'

Megan sobbed. 'He hit me, sir, knocked me senseless.'

'Who did?'

'The master.'

There was silence then the housekeeper said, 'I don't know what to do, Mr Marston.'

'You're sure it was the master?'

Megan nodded, then winced and put up one hand to her head. 'I'm not staying to be beaten for nothing.'

When she'd explained what had happened, Marston drew in a deep breath. His eyes met those of the housekeeper, but neither said what they were thinking.

'Pay her what's owing and give her a good character reference, Mrs Phillips,' Marston said at last. He turned to the maid. 'If you say one word about what happened, Megan, he'll come after you. You know that, don't you?'

She nodded, sniffling and wiping away a tear.

'So keep quiet. You'll have a good reference and you can add this to your money to tide you over till you get a new job.' He fumbled in his pocket and produced a guinea, grateful that Mr Blacklea at least wasn't stingy with the money needed to run the house.

When the maid had gone to help Megan start packing, the housekeeper looked at Mr Marston.

He held up one hand to stop her speaking and moved closer. 'Only in a whisper,' he mouthed.

'He's getting worse. I'm not sure I want to stay on myself.'

'Give it a little longer. He does pay well.'

'If he attacks any more of the maids, I won't stay.'

'I'll have a word with him.'

She looked at him in amazement.

He let out a dry little laugh. 'I shan't say anything directly, but I think I can phrase it so that he knows he'll lose his staff if he does this again.'

'You're a braver man than I, Mr Marston.'

He smiled grimly as he went to seek his master. He'd managed all these years in this monster's service and could manage two more. Then he'd leave with enough money to retire and open a boarding house for gentlemen, a long-time ambition.

★ ★ ★

At Galle all was bustle as the passengers travelling to Australia were helped to disembark. The second ship was going to somewhere called Albany in the south-west of the country, then Melbourne and Sydney in the east. Jacinta had been surprised at how far the distance was between Albany and these places, as far as from London to Moscow. She hadn't realised Australia was quite so big.

The second ship was a little smaller and looked more worn, but she wasn't all that different from the first ship. She still had a funnel for her steam engine and two masts to make use of the wind.

The cabin Jacinta had to share with her son was even smaller than the previous one and she sighed as she tried to fit their possessions under the bunks and in the corner.

There was a knock on the door and Eleanor peeped in. 'They're smaller cabins this time, aren't they? I have to share with another lady.'

'Is she nice?'

'No. She's very sour-faced, has hardly said a word.' Eleanor grimaced. 'Thank goodness this is the last stage of the journey!'

'Is Mr Saxby's cabin all right?'

'I haven't seen him, but he can afford to book

a bigger cabin on his own, so it'll probably be reasonably comfortable. I do envy him that.' She leaned against the door frame. 'I preferred it on the *Bonny Mary* last year. She was a sailing ship and much smaller, with only room for a few passengers. She mostly carried cargoes. But I enjoyed being on her. Everyone was so kind.'

'And you had Captain McBride to chat to.'

'Yes. That was the best thing about it.'

Jacinta looked at her friend, then at her son. 'You can go on deck, if you like, Ben, but don't mess about near the rail.' When he rolled his eyes, she chuckled. 'I know I always say that, but I don't want to lose you.'

'I'm nine years old, Mother. A boy not a baby.'

As she watched him go, she had to acknowledge how quickly he was growing up.

When the two women were alone, Jacinta looked at her friend's expression and said it baldly. 'Are you feeling nervous now we're on our final stage?'

'Yes, I am. And you?'

'I'm terrified. I made such a bad mistake when I married Claude. What if my judgement of men is faulty?'

'I know Dougal is a good man, so I don't have that worry, but I can't help wondering if he'll still want me. Really want me. He may have met someone else, or changed his mind. Who knows? I don't want a man to feel obliged to marry me out of pity.'

'Ah, there you are, ladies,' a voice called from just outside the cabin.

They turned as Mr Saxby joined them.

He studied their faces. 'You two are looking rather worried. Is something wrong?'

'We're worrying about the men we're going out there to marry.'

He gave them one of his shrewd looks. 'You don't need to marry anyone if you don't want to. No one can force you to do it.'

'We do need husbands, though.' Jacinta sighed. 'Life is difficult enough for a woman on her own, and a boy needs a father.' She didn't mention their lack of money, but he knew about that.

'If there are any problems with the two men you're going out to meet, I hope you know that I meant it when I said you could count on my help. In any way necessary.'

'We don't have any claim on you,' Jacinta said.

'But you're very kind,' Eleanor added. 'And if we're desperate, we'll definitely come to you for help.'

He gave them one of his sad smiles. 'I wish you did have a claim on me. If I'd had daughters, I'd have wanted them to be just like you two.'

Without thinking, Jacinta gave him a hug and after he'd hugged her back, he turned to Eleanor, who promptly did the same.

He hesitated, then said softly, 'Why don't you both adopt me as an uncle, even call me uncle? I'd love that.'

'I'd love it, too,' Jacinta said without hesitation, seeing Eleanor nod agreement.

'That's settled, then.' He blinked his eyes

furiously. 'So please . . . call me Uncle Quentin from now on.'

While he took out his handkerchief and blew his nose vigorously, Eleanor and Jacinta exchanged quick smiles.

After folding his handkerchief carefully and putting it back in his pocket, he beamed at the two women. 'Now, I think we should go and find out what your young rascal is doing on deck, Jacinta my dear. And tell him you've adopted me as your uncle, so that makes me his great-uncle. Goodness, how old that sounds!'

Ben wasn't on deck and Jacinta felt a moment's panic, then she saw him on the steerage deck, talking away to Mr Walsh, eyes flashing, hands waving. That boy never seemed to stop talking these days.

She hadn't realised Mr Walsh had also transferred to the ship sailing to Australia.

She wished he hadn't.

It'd be helpful if she could work out why she didn't trust him and why something about him seemed so familiar. But although she'd racked her brains, she'd not come up with any reason.

10

After breakfast, Ismay and Aunt Harriet walked across town to the docks to look at the salvaged wood. Adam had said over an early breakfast that it had all been properly stacked and the ship made tidy again, so that they could start on the repairs.

Ismay tugged Aunt Harriet to a halt just before they reached the *Bonny Ismay*, because it still gave her a thrill to see her name on the rear of the ship. She'd been thrilled to pieces when Adam, Dougal and Mr Lee had chosen her name for their new purchase.

She mouthed the words *Bonny Ismay*. She always wanted to say the name aloud as she passed the ship, but of course she didn't. She was a captain's wife now and mustn't lose her dignity. Though when she got excited, she sometimes forgot that.

'I'd love to sail on her with Adam,' she said without thinking.

Aunt Harriet immediately looked guilty. 'You're staying behind because of me, I know. I'm grateful for that, because I haven't been here in Australia for long enough yet to feel totally at home.'

'You're still missing your old friends, aren't you?'

Harriet sighed. 'Some of them, dear, I must admit. Especially Quentin. There's nothing like people who have known you in your youth. They can see beyond the wrinkles of a sixty-year-old woman to the girl beneath.' She gave a wry smile. 'I may be older in body, but I still feel young in my mind. Do you suppose one ever feels old inside? I certainly don't.'

'I hope I'm just like you when I'm sixty,' Ismay said at once. 'Your hair may be grey but your face is hardly wrinkled and your skin's beautifully soft. Best of all, you're fun to be with.'

'Flatterer. And I suppose I still have the trim waist I had when I first married?'

Ismay laughed. 'No. But you're what I call nicely plump. I shall probably be a scrawny old woman, like the lady who lives across the road from us. I never seem to put any weight on.'

They stood together at the bottom of the gangway.

'What a fine ship she is to come through a raging storm like that. I hate to see the damage, but I'm sure Adam will make sure that everything is properly repaired.' Ismay suddenly spotted her husband and was off running up the gangway, calling 'Adam! Adam!' at the top of her voice.

Harriet chuckled. So much for her young friend's dignity.

She watched the man who was like a son to her turn to greet his wife by swinging Ismay off her feet then plonking a big kiss on her rosy cheek, heedless of who saw them. Those two were so much in love, it brought tears to Harriet's eyes sometimes.

You missed the cuddles and closeness after you lost your husband. You missed a lot of things.

But she couldn't complain. She'd looked after Adam when he was a lonely lad, born out of wedlock and grudgingly provided for by his father. Now, Adam was looking after her. It was the way things went and she knew she was lucky to have him.

No use pining for those she missed. She'd write a letter to Quentin this very evening, telling him about the storm and the clever way Adam had salvaged the wood. He'd be interested in that, she was sure.

Smiling, she moved forward to join the young couple.

★   ★   ★

A week into the voyage from Galle to Australia, the weather grew suddenly rougher. It wasn't cold and the passengers were told this wasn't a storm, just a bit of heavy weather.

Ben wasn't affected by the way the ship heaved and rolled, but Jacinta felt a little uncomfortable and insisted her son join her in the cabin.

She lay down for a while, and managed a short nap, but when she woke, she was on her own. She'd distinctly told Ben not to go out without her and since the ship was still heaving about, she immediately began to worry about his safety.

When she peered outside, she could see a few hardy souls still on deck, their hair and clothes whipping about in the wind. But there was no sign of her son and it was growing dark, something which happened very quickly in the tropics, where there seemed to be only a very brief period of twilight.

Feeling annoyed at Ben for disobeying her, she wrapped a shawl round her shoulders and left the cabin, staggering as she walked, and holding on to things. She checked the forward deck carefully but there was no sign of her son.

Had he gone to see Mr Walsh? He often did, because he was absolutely fascinated by wood carving and eager to practise, so that he could make her a birthday present.

There was no sign of Uncle Quentin or Eleanor on deck. In rough weather like this, they were probably sitting in the day cabin, chatting to fellow guests as they waited for the evening meal.

Ben wasn't likely to be there with them, however, because he scorned being indoors when he could be out in the fresh air. She'd join the others as soon as she found him and insist that he too took shelter, in case the weather got worse.

As she was making her way towards the rear of the ship, she had to go round a crate containing a miserable group of chickens. The poor creatures supplied the passengers with eggs and never looked happy. She was out of sight of the other passengers for a moment or two.

The wind whirled round her, blowing her hair out of its pins and into her eyes, so that she didn't see anyone coming till she bumped into that person good and hard. She spun sideways, crying out in shock as she careered towards the rail. When she reached out to grab it, the other person bumped into her again, so hard she fell sprawling across the rail.

As she scrabbled to catch hold of the slippery metal, the ship dropped abruptly into the trough of a wave and she was flung forward again, tumbling right over the side.

Panic lent her strength and somehow she kept hold of the rail, hanging down from it, screaming for help at the top of her voice.

Everything seemed to happen slowly, so slowly. She looked up into the eyes of Mr Walsh, shocked to see the hatred in them.

His hands moved towards her in the gesture of someone about to push hard and she screamed again, sure she was about to die, sure he was going to push her away from the ship.

Seconds ticked slowly past and his hands stilled in mid air. He made no move to save her, though.

Was he going to leave her to die?

'Help me!' she pleaded, feeling her arms losing strength and not daring to wriggle or try to get her feet on to the outer edge of the deck. It was so hard to hold on and she knew she couldn't manage to do it for much longer. *'Please . . . help me!'*

With a curse he suddenly grabbed her by the hair and one arm, yelling for help as he struggled against the wind and the heaving ship to pull her back over the rail on to the deck.

She kept hold of the rail with her other hand, terrified he might let go of her again. He didn't speak to her, not a single word.

Suddenly there were other people crowding round, grabbing her, dragging her over the rail to safety.

She collapsed on the deck in a sodden heap, her whole body shaking after her narrow escape. She was unable to think or speak coherently, could only draw in deep gulps of air and fight to control the terror that was still pulsing through her body.

It took a while for the understanding to settle into her mind that she was still alive, safe on deck. Mr Walsh *had* saved her in the end.

But why had he hesitated for so long?

As she looked across at him, she saw that he was still glaring at her, as if she'd done something wrong. Why?

She closed her eyes, not wanting to see such hatred, then opened them as someone flung his arms around her. It was Ben and she clutched her son thankfully.

Over his head she saw Mr Walsh take a step backwards, his face expressionless now.

She hadn't imagined it, though, she knew she hadn't. He had definitely been going to push her into the sea. Then he'd hesitated, and nearly left her to fall to her death.

He must be the one who'd pushed her in the first place. No one else had been near them.

Why?

She watched a man clap him on the shoulder. 'You're a hero. You saved her life.'

The crowd around them cheered and applauded.

But Walsh shook his head and backed away, then turned and pushed through the crowd.

'Modest,' a woman said.

'He *is* a hero, though,' a man repeated.

She knew differently. She hadn't imagined it. Walsh had pushed her towards the rail on purpose. There had been no one else around and she'd been bumped into twice. If it'd been an accident, it wouldn't have happened a second time.

A stewardess and an officer pushed through the crowd and moved Ben aside. They helped Jacinta to her feet, supporting her and telling people to stand back as they took her to her cabin. She was still shivering and shaking, couldn't stop.

She had so nearly died and that made you realise how vulnerable you were, made fear crawl through you to the depths of your soul.

Ben hurried ahead of them, turning once as if to make sure she was still there.

Jacinta tried to pull herself together, for his sake. She was safe, that was the main thing. Alive. She didn't want her son so upset by this accident that he would become too cautious and cling to her side.

He opened the cabin door and moved out of their way.

To Jacinta's relief, her friend Eleanor took over from the stewardess, helping her into her cabin, one arm round her shoulders. She half-turned and saw Uncle Quentin put an arm round Ben's shoulders.

'I'll take care of him,' he told her. 'You know

204

you can trust me. Get out of those wet clothes quickly, my dear. You're shivering.'

She knew she could rely on him. But she had to tell him one thing. 'Don't let Ben go off with Mr Walsh alone.'

He looked at her in surprise and she glanced quickly at Ben, trying to signal that she couldn't talk now.

Uncle Quentin nodded, seeming to understand her silent message. 'I won't let him leave my side for a second.'

Only then did she allow herself to give in to her weakness and sag against her friend, who felt warm and strong.

She was safe. But how would she manage to stay safe from now on? Would Walsh regret changing his mind and make another attempt to kill her? He must have stopped because someone had seen them. He was a big man. Dangerous. She must be on her guard every second from now on.

Someone was speaking to her. It was the stewardess. She forced herself to pay attention, though everything seemed very distant.

'You must get out of those wet clothes, Mrs Blacklea.'

She looked down at herself in surprise.

'I'll fetch you some hot water to wash the salt off your skin. And I'll bring a cup of tea. There's nothing as comforting as a cup of hot, sweet tea.'

'Thank you.'

The cabin door closed behind the stewardess.

'Let's get those wet clothes off you,' Eleanor said.

Jacinta looked at her friend, uncertain whether to reveal her suspicions.

'How did that happen? You're not usually careless when you move round the ship.'

'I'm not sure, but I think — ' Jacinta broke off, then said in a rush, 'I can't prove it, but I believe Mr Walsh tried to push me overboard, and then . . . I know it sounds stupid, but then he dragged me back on to the deck again.'

Eleanor stared at her in horror. 'Why would he do that?'

There was dead silence for a moment or two, then Jacinta answered the question, feeling quite sure she was right. 'There's only one person I know who wants me dead. *You* heard that person threaten to kill me.'

'Gerald Blacklea.'

'Walsh only joined the ship at Marseille. I think Blacklea must have sent him to kill me. There would have been time for him to get there. I keep thinking I recognise him. I've racked my brain but I can't remember where from. Perhaps I saw him in the village when I was staying with the Blackleas.'

'Are you quite certain of this?'

'I'm sure Walsh tried to kill me, but unless someone else saw him do it, I have no proof. So I can't accuse him of anything, can I? But why else would he have tried to push me overboard?'

'It could have been an accident.'

'I don't think so. Unfortunately the wind had blown my hair loose from its pins and I didn't even see him coming.'

'Maybe he was just thrown against you by the

movement of the ship.'

'Twice? With a pause before the second bump, which shoved me in a completely different direction? It was such a hard bump I nearly went over the rail. Luckily, I managed to grab it with both hands. Then the ship dropped suddenly and I did go overboard. But I kept hold. Dear heaven, I'd be dead now if I hadn't managed to hold on.'

She looked down at her hands and let out a bitter laugh. 'Who'd have thought that the hard physical work in house and garden would have saved my life? Things like chopping the firewood have given me more strength than most women, I think.'

They abandoned the discussion as the stewardess brought in a steaming copper ewer and a hot-water bottle, promising a fresh pot of tea as soon as it had brewed.

Within minutes Jacinta had used the hot water from the ewer to sponge the salt water from her shivering body. After she'd put on her night-gown, she realised something was missing. 'Oh, no! I've lost my shawl. It must have fallen overboard.'

'I'll fetch you one of mine.'

'Thank you.'

With her friend's shawl wrapped warmly round her shoulders, she curled up in bed cuddling the earthenware hot-water bottle in its flannel wrapper. 'I'd like to rest now, to think about . . . what happened. Can you and Uncle Quentin please keep an eye on Ben for me?'

'Of course we can.'

'Don't let him out of your sight for a minute.'

'I promise we won't.'

Jacinta snuggled down, feeling exhausted, glad when the cabin door closed.

She roused when the stewardess brought in her tea, but just asked her to pour a cup of tea then leave the tray on the floor near the bunk.

She sat sipping it, her hands round the warm cup, once again going over in her mind what had happened. Mr Walsh had tried to kill her. She was quite sure of that. But why had he rescued her at the last minute? That was what puzzled her most. It would have been so easy for him to let her fall overboard.

Was she still in danger? Would he change his mind again and make another attempt on her life?

She woke from an uneasy sleep and sat bolt upright when Ben came to bed.

'It's only me, Mother.'

'Thank goodness. Put the tea tray outside, will you, dear?'

Once he was safe in the bunk above her, she had a sudden idea and stuffed Ben's shoe under the door so that no one could open it without alerting her. He thought that was amusing. She didn't argue with him.

Afterwards she fell into a better sleep, waking a couple of times during the night.

Once she thought someone had tried the door, but the shoe held. Or was that just a dream?

★ ★ ★

It was a relief when daylight brightened the cabin. The stewardess woke her, bringing their morning tea and calling out anxiously when she couldn't open the cabin door. She brought the welcome news that the weather was calmer today.

'I don't want you leaving the forward deck,' Jacinta told Ben.

'I won't. I'm going to look after you. Mr Saxby told me I ought to.'

That was as good an excuse as any to keep him nearby, she thought.

When they went to the day room for breakfast, the other cabin passengers fussed over her, helping her into a chair as if she had suddenly turned into an invalid. She knew they were trying to be kind, but she wished they'd leave her alone.

Ben remained very subdued, not chattering as he ate.

They'd been told that it would take just over two weeks to get to Western Australia, so they still had about ten days to go. Jacinta wondered how she was to pass the time, and especially how to keep her son entertained and yet close by her side.

The lady sitting next to her said, 'Have you heard? They're asking for people to run some classes and activities for the steerage passengers.'

'For all passengers,' Eleanor corrected.

The woman sniffed. 'Well, I'm sure *I* don't need entertaining and I've no intention of mingling with the great unwashed.'

'I thought I'd volunteer to run a sewing class,'

Eleanor said. 'That will mainly interest steerage passengers, I should think, though I don't find them unwashed, I'm sure. Well, I will run a class if the stewardess can find us some pieces of material to use. We could make aprons or . . . small personal items. Why don't you join me and help out, Jacinta?'

'I'll think about it.' Her eyes went involuntarily to Ben.

'He'll be all right,' Eleanor said in a low voice. 'No one has tried to hurt *him*. In fact, if it's what you think, he's very safe indeed.'

Uncle Quentin came in just then and sat down opposite them. 'How did you sleep, Jacinta dear?'

'In fits and starts. I kept reliving my . . . accident.'

'Could we have a little chat after breakfast? I'm a little concerned about . . . a few things.'

Ben was invited to play with another boy, under the watchful eye of his parents, who seemed strict but kind.

Jacinta couldn't help asking, 'You won't let him out of your sight?'

The man shook his head. 'We'll treat him as we would our own son. You must be nervous after what happened. Are you sure you're all right now, Mrs Blacklea?'

'Thank you, yes. I'm just going to have a quiet, restful day. My friend and I will probably do some sewing.'

It was calmer today, thank goodness, so after breakfast Jacinta went with Uncle Quentin and Eleanor to a corner where they could be private.

'This is the first time I've managed to get you on your own,' Uncle Quentin said. 'Tell me exactly what happened yesterday.'

'I was pushed. Then pushed again,' Jacinta said baldly. 'By Walsh.'

He looked at her in consternation. 'Are you sure?'

'Very sure. Though I can't prove it. I think Walsh must have been sent to kill me. Why else would he try to push me overboard?'

He was silent, then said, 'Gerald Blacklea.'

'Exactly.'

'But if what you suspect is true, why didn't Walsh finish the job? No one else was around just then. He could easily have shoved you overboard, instead of rescuing you.'

'That's what I don't understand. He may have heard someone coming.'

'Perhaps I should have a word with him?'

'No, please don't. He won't be sure whether I realise what he tried to do. But if he thinks I could accuse him of attempted murder, he might try again to get rid of me.'

'I suppose you're right. We must make sure you're never alone.'

She hesitated. 'Actually, I thought someone tried our bedroom door during the night. But I'd stuffed one of Ben's shoes under it, so whoever it was couldn't open it without making a noise.'

He looked at her in consternation. 'How are we to keep you safe?'

She shrugged. 'I'll be very careful, I promise you.'

Eleanor looked at them thoughtfully. 'I wonder

if the male steward could arrange for a bolt to be put on the cabin door, or even a lock? You could say you're worried about Ben sleepwalking during the night and the fear is disturbing your sleep.'

Silence, then Uncle Quentin nodded. 'Good idea. I'll have a word with the man.' He rubbed his fingers together in an age-old gesture. 'A little persuasion should make him eager to help you.'

'Am I worrying over nothing?' Jacinta asked suddenly.

There was silence, then Uncle Quentin shook his head. 'I don't think you're a fanciful woman, and we all heard Gerald Blacklea shouting threats as the ship sailed from Southampton.'

'What will happen when we get to Australia?'

'If you find Mr Nash acceptable, we'll tell him about this incident. He'll know what to do to keep you safe.'

'Or it may put him off marrying me.'

'I doubt that. Have you looked in the mirror, my dear?'

She stared at him in puzzlement.

'You're a very pretty woman and a good mother. I think he'll be pleasantly surprised by you. And want the same loving care for his own son.'

'Oh.' She could feel her cheeks growing warm at his compliment. 'But I'm too thin.'

'You were quite gaunt when we set off, but you've filled out nicely with all the good food. I promise you, any man would be proud to have such a pretty woman on his arm.'

'Uncle Quentin, I think you're a flatterer.'

'Not at all. I'm telling the simple truth.'

She had to give him a quick hug. He had calmed her fears and managed to make her feel much better about herself. What a lovely man he was! She couldn't imagine his Harriet being anything but delighted to see him.

★ ★ ★

That afternoon, Ben went to speak to Uncle Quentin. 'I don't understand what I've done wrong, sir. When I saw Mr Walsh, he told me to keep away from him from now on. And he's not going to take any carving classes on this ship.'

'No one can force him to do it.'

'But I haven't finished my present for Mother and he won't help me. It's her birthday soon and I'll have nothing to give her.'

'We'll have to think of something else. You could write her a special birthday poem.'

'That's not a proper present.'

'I think she'd prefer it to a carving. She doesn't really like Mr Walsh.'

'But he saved her life! I thanked him for that and he got even angrier with me. I don't understand.'

'Well, maybe he doesn't enjoy being a hero.' Maybe, Quentin thought, it made Walsh feel guilty when people praised him. And so he should!

Ben scowled. 'I think grown-ups are very strange sometimes.'

'All people are strange at times, my dear boy. Anyway, from now on keep away from the man.

I'd welcome your company, though. And I could
help you with the poem, if you like. We could
write it together, then you could copy it out in
your best handwriting and decorate the corners
of the pages with drawings. Ladies like that sort
of thing, I promise you. I have some drawing
materials in my cabin. You can work on it
secretly there.'

'I suppose so. Thank you very much, Mr Saxby.'

'Uncle Quentin now.'

That brought him a smile.

'I like having an uncle — no, you're my
great-uncle, aren't you?'

'Yes. And I like very much having nieces and a
great-nephew.'

Later, when Ben was safely with his mother
and Eleanor, Quentin went for a stroll along the
rear deck. He didn't approach Walsh, but
nodded as he passed him because not to do so
would have made the fellow suspicious about
what Jacinta might have said about the accident.

Jacinta was right about one thing. It would be
far safer if Walsh didn't know she'd realised what
had really happened. And guessed why.

Walsh was looking angry, scowling at the
world. What had caused that? Was he angry at
himself for failing to complete his mission?

That thought immediately started his lawyer's
mind thinking. What if, for all their care,
something happened to Jacinta? What would
become of the boy then? Walsh could say he
knew Ben's only remaining relative in England,
and any judge would send the boy back to
Blacklea's care.

214

On that thought, Quentin turned round and made his way slowly back to join the others, working out what to do.

Later, Ben came back into his care and they retired to Quentin's cabin. The boy finished drawing and painting the first two corners, then helped him to clear up the mess.

'We'll do the rest after that's dried. I have something to do now, so I'll take you to find your mother.'

Ben looked at him in puzzlement. 'I can find her myself, Uncle Quentin.'

'She's worried about your safety, so let's humour her, shall we? If you're never alone, that's one less thing for her to worry about. You know what women are like.' He felt guilty about maligning Jacinta, who wasn't a weak, clinging type of woman, but Ben shrugged and accepted his reasoning.

When Quentin returned to his cabin, he got out his writing slope and began to draw up a simple will, giving guardianship of Ben to himself and Eleanor, in case anything happened to Jacinta before her son reached his majority.

He hesitated, then added a line saying she didn't trust her husband's Blacklea relatives to deal kindly with her son, so particularly didn't want him to be looked after by them.

He didn't know whether the will would hold firm if a rich man like Blacklea contested it, but he intended to make very sure that Jacinta was carefully watched for the rest of the voyage. Once they arrived in the Swan River Colony, he'd ensure Mitchell Nash was made aware that

215

his intended might be in danger.

It was sad that you had to take such precautions, very sad. But a wise person did whatever was necessary to protect his loved ones. Jacinta had come far too close to death this time.

Loved ones. Quentin smiled and admitted to himself that he'd grown to love the two women and the lad. He hoped both Eleanor and Jacinta would remarry and have other children.

He felt as if he hadn't been able to use up all the love he'd been born with. Until now.

11

Mitchell Nash studied the piles of salvaged timber stacked neatly on the docks. It was good quality teak and well milled. Those pieces ought to make him a lot of money, both as a timber merchant and as a builder.

He turned at the sound of footsteps to see Bram walking in his direction. He smiled and raised one hand in greeting, but for once his friend didn't notice him. Bram seemed lost in thought and was looking extremely worried. And no wonder. The majority of his trading goods had been damaged in the storm, and Mitchell guessed that as a newly established trader, Bram didn't have comfortable reserves.

One man's bad luck was another's good fortune, Mitchell thought, feeling guilty about his own pleasure at being able to purchase the salvaged wood. 'Good morning, Bram.'

'What? Oh, sorry. I didn't see you there. I was . . . um, having a little think. Good morning to you, too.'

Mitchell hesitated, then bit back the questions he longed to ask. If Bram was in financial trouble, a dozen people would help him without thinking twice, just as they knew Bram wouldn't hesitate to help them if they were in trouble — well, Bram had helped a lot of people. But you couldn't ask bluntly if someone was short of money. No, you had to wait until he confided in you.

Still, it might be possible to approach the subject in a roundabout manner. 'Not a good trading trip for you. I'm sorry about that. Your goods weren't insured?'

'The ship was, but it's not easy to insure a cargo.'

'The salvaged timber will help, surely?'

'It'll help my brother-in-law, yes, and I'm glad for Adam and Ismay, I am so. But I don't own a share of the ship, so it'll not help me.'

He sighed and again stared into space.

Mitchell waited.

Bram seemed to be speaking more to himself than to his companion. 'I've lost a lot of stock due to storm damage, and at a bad time after my recent expenses, which ate into our reserves. But that's not your concern. We'll come about. We have a thriving business. It's just . . . a little harder to get good stock here in the Swan River Colony to replace what was lost. It takes weeks to bring in supplies from Singapore, d'you see?'

Mitchell watched his friend dredge up a smile, but it wasn't at all convincing. Bram's smile usually lit up his whole face and made anyone with him feel good. Today's smile was a travesty, a mere lifting of the corners of the lips.

To hell with tact! he decided. 'If you need help, my friend, I have some money set aside and you're more than welcome to borrow it.'

Bram blinked his eyes hard and said in a hoarse voice, 'That's . . . um, very kind of you! Yes, very kind. But I'll not be troubling my friends with this. Isabella and I can manage. We

218

will manage.' He touched his hat in a gesture of farewell and continued walking.

Mitchell watched him go, seeing one hand come up to flick away a tear. He shook his head sadly at the way Bram's whole body drooped. He didn't like to see such a good man in trouble. He'd keep his eyes and ears open from now on, and if Bram Deagan needed help, Mitchell would not only offer it, but force it upon his friend, if necessary.

If only he had a wife, he could ask her to talk to Isabella Deagan — it wasn't easy for a man to talk to another man's wife privately.

And that set off another train of thought that had Mitchell taking his turn at standing frowning into the water that was slapping gently against the side of the dock. It was months since he'd written to his cousin and it was about time he heard back. Only, what answer did he want from Peter? He still wasn't sure. He did need a wife, but did he want to marry a complete stranger?

Why the hell had he acted so rashly? It wasn't like him.

There was a P&O ship due at Albany just about now, he couldn't help but notice in the shipping lists in the newspaper. What if a woman turned up out of the blue on her? What would he do then? The only sort of woman who might be willing to travel to the other side of the world to marry a complete stranger was surely one who hadn't been able to find a husband in England. Probably ugly, or shrill-voiced, or prone to nag — a spinster desperate for a man.

He wanted a wife for all the usual reasons, not

just the housekeeping. He was a man with a man's normal physical needs, which were causing him some restless nights. His son spoke wistfully sometimes about how nice it'd be to have brothers and sisters. Christopher was such a joy that Mitchell would like to have other children too.

To make matters worse, Mitchell had had some rather unpleasant experiences with would-be matchmakers in the past year. He'd been invited to take tea with several families who had unmarried lady relatives to display to him, and he hadn't been able to refuse the invitations, because this was a small town and he didn't want to alienate anyone.

He shuddered at the memory of those tea parties, the way everyone in the room had stared at him as they tried to gauge his reaction to the poor unmarried female, who usually blushed and fluttered, ready to please, agreeing with every word he said and not putting forward any views of her own, so that he had no idea of the woman's real character.

Was he being fussy and unrealistic? After all, marriage was a business arrangement as much as an emotional one. Yes, perhaps he was being fussy. But he had good reason: he wanted a better woman than his first wife, someone he could trust to be loyal and behave decently.

He stepped back from the water, annoyed with himself for going over all that again. He should stop worrying till he had something to worry about. If his cousin Peter did find a lady willing to marry him, she wouldn't be a nag, at least, he could be sure of that. So he would accept her with a good grace.

But for both their sakes, just in case they were totally unsuited, he'd find her somewhere to live after she arrived and get to know her better before committing himself to marriage.

Yes, that was the way to do it.

Feeling somewhat better, he went back to his timber yard.

★   ★   ★

When the captain announced that they were approaching Albany and would arrive there the following afternoon, it caused a lot of interest among all passengers, whether they were disembarking or not.

Quentin had read everything he could about Western Australia and the port to which he was travelling, and he'd been surprised by what he found. Albany lay on the south coast of a colony which was at least ten times as big as Britain and which comprised about a third of the land surface of Australia. And yet, people talked about the west as the Cinderella colony, because it didn't have a large population or valuable agriculture and industries. In fact, there were only about thirty thousand people in the whole colony, one article in the newspaper had said.

Those who would be leaving the ship were warned to pack their bags before they went to bed, and be ready to stuff in the last few items the following morning, because they'd be disembarking immediately after breakfast.

The newcomers were naturally eager to see their new country, and only one man was returning there from a trip to Britain. He was the target of many last-minute questions and worries, bearing it all with good humour.

The steward in charge of service to the cabin passengers had informed them the previous day that the captain was obliged to inform the authorities of any infectious diseases on board and give details of any cargo being landed, also give the nationality of any foreign passenger disembarking — though as there were only British citizens this trip, the latter wasn't necessary.

The passengers who were going on to Melbourne welcomed any distraction in the monotony of their days, and lined the ship's rails, watching what was going on.

Even before breakfast, signal flags were hoisted to inform the port authorities of the ship's intention to stop at the port, though everyone agreed that with such sparse traffic and the fact that the steamer had already entered the inlet, this must have been fairly obvious.

'It's good to arrive at last,' Jacinta said.

'Yes, but Albany isn't our final destination,' Eleanor reminded her. 'And it'll take us a few days to get to Fremantle, since there aren't any railways here.'

'At least you have some idea of what Western Australia is like.'

'Not much idea, actually, because I didn't see a lot last time. Since my husband had been very seasick, he insisted we got off the ship for a night on shore, and then we missed its departure. Malcolm was always sure he knew best and insisted on arranging our lodgings, but he failed to inform the landlady that we needed to be woken early. She thought we'd come to stay in the colony. So there we were, stranded.'

Jacinta had heard this before but still found it amazing. 'I can't believe your husband forgot such a simple instruction.'

'He was a poor organiser. And yet he hated me to make the arrangements because *he* was the man. We were lucky that Captain McBride agreed to give us passage to Galle on his schooner.' Eleanor smiled into the distance as she always did when she thought of how she'd met Dougal.

Uncle Quentin let her have a moment to dream, then said gently, 'We still have to make our way to Fremantle, which is about six hundred miles further north, the steward tells me. But we're all booked on the coastal steamer, which departs tomorrow, so that shouldn't be too difficult. And *we* won't forget to ask to be woken in time.'

'We shall have to take great care of Jacinta if that man is still following us,' Eleanor said. 'It'll be much easier for him to attack her on land.'

'Yes. I've been wondering what would be the best thing to do. Perhaps this young rascal should share a bedroom at the hotel with me, while you and Jacinta share one? That way no one will be on their own. What do you think?'

'I think that's a good idea,' Eleanor said at

223

once. 'I too would be happy not to be on my own.'

'That's settled, then.' He ruffled Ben's hair and the lad grinned at him.

When they disembarked, they found a man waiting for the cabin passengers who would be going on to Perth. He had a large cart with benches along the inside, and *CHUSAN HOTEL* painted on the outside.

'It's a strange name for a hotel,' Jacinta commented.

The man returning to Australia was standing nearby and said, 'It's called after one of the first big steamers to use this port. You'll be quite comfortable there. A cousin of mine owns it. And you're only staying one night anyway. I should think you'll — ' He broke off to yell across to a group further along the quay, 'I'm here, Mary Ellen! I'm back.'

A woman waiting for the ship burst into tears and a young man patted her on the back.

'My wife cries when she's happy as well as when she's sad.' Their companion gave them a wry smile. As soon as he could, he said goodbye and went hurrying across to embrace her and tease her out of her tears. His voice rang out as he commented on how much his son had grown while he was away. His wife was smiling now as she linked her arm in his while they waited for his luggage to be unloaded and given a cursory check by the solitary customs official.

'I like to see people who're fond of one another,' Quentin said wistfully watching the newly reunited couple chatting and smiling.

224

'So do I.' Eleanor clutched his arm to steady herself. 'Oh dear. Sorry to grab you but I still haven't got my land legs.'

'It'll be wonderful to go for proper walks again,' Jacinta said. 'I've missed being active.' She turned to her son. 'But you'll remember your promise, Ben?'

'Yes, Mother. No going outside on my own.'

'No going *anywhere* on your own, even inside the hotel.'

'Yes, Mother.' But he didn't look happy about this.

The only thing to mar the joy of their arrival in Australia was the sight of Walsh waiting with the other steerage passengers to leave the ship once the cabin passengers had been dealt with. He scowled down at the group on the quay.

She turned to Uncle Quentin. 'Why does that man always look at me as if *I* have done something wrong?'

'Guilty conscience, I suppose.'

She shook her head slowly. 'I don't think so. He doesn't seem the sort. There's something else upsetting him, but I can't think what. You've got the will safe, haven't you? Just in case anything happens to me.'

'We'll make sure both you *and* the will are kept safe, my dear.'

★   ★   ★

When they got off the ship, Alf followed his fellow passengers to a lodging house, annoyed to be told he still had quite a way to travel. He

225

should have asked about it before now, but he'd been so angry about missing his opportunity with *her* he'd kept himself to himself.

'If Fremantle is the port for the capital, why do the ships come here to Albany when it's hundreds of miles away? I call that stupid.'

'Shows how much you know about ships and harbours,' the man next to him said. 'This is a fine deep-water harbour, and Fremantle hasn't got any deep water close to shore. Ships have to anchor in the sea there and unload on to lighters.'

'They're improving things,' another added. 'They've extended the jetty and some ships can now tie up there. But big ones like the P&O liners still use Albany.'

The lodging house was another place where men were stacked on bunks and kept separate from the women, even if they were married. Alf didn't miss his wife, but he did miss his bed play. And he was fed up of sleeping on hard, narrow bunks.

He'd noticed one woman on the ship, and she'd smiled encouragingly at him, but he'd been too worried to pursue her. And anyway, he was a married man, wasn't he? However much he wished he wasn't sometimes.

He made enquiries about how to get to Fremantle, hoping to avoid another damned ship, but it took even longer by road, it seemed, and anyway, he didn't want to lose sight of Mrs Blacklea. He had to rush out to book a place on the coastal steamer before the shipping agent closed down for the day.

When the ship was pointed out to him in the harbour, it looked very small after the P&O ship, but if that was the only way to get to Fremantle, then he'd have to be on it. All he could get at this late stage was a seat in the common cabin, which sounded uncomfortable when it was going to take three days to get to their destination.

He had to board very early, but he couldn't see why, because after that he spent the morning hanging about in a small area of the deck, forbidden to move elsewhere as they waited for the ship to finish loading and leave. At least it didn't look as if the weather was going to be stormy, but it wasn't all that warm, either, after the heat of the tropics.

Mrs Blacklea and her friends boarded the ship just before midday with the other cabin passengers, and they all went below straight away. No doubt they'd be travelling in comfort, the lucky sods, not crammed into one small area.

The lad looked at him reproachfully as he passed, which made Alf feel guilty. Ben was such a nice youngster. Any man would be proud to have a son like that.

What was he going to do about the lad's mother, though? The worry of that was keeping Alf awake at night, because he wouldn't dare return if he didn't do as Mr Blacklea and his uncle had told him.

Why hadn't he pushed Jacinta Blacklea overboard when he'd had the chance?

Well, he knew why: he just hadn't been able to do it with her looking at him so pleadingly, just couldn't.

He'd have to find a way to kill her where he didn't have to look her in the eye. He yawned. And if he could . . .

He woke abruptly to find the woman who'd sat down next to him cuddling close. He couldn't see what she was like, because they'd turned the single lamp down low. Anyway, he was too tired and cold to care, so he let her stay there. At least it warmed that side a little.

Three days of sitting around in this hole were going to be hard going.

All because he'd been too soft to do the necessary. He cut off that thought and closed his eyes. Couldn't do anything about *her* on this crowded little ship.

★　★　★

Jacinta saw Walsh as she and her friends were boarding the coastal vessel which looked rather small and run-down after the spick and span P&O ship. She tried to ignore the man, but his glare made a shiver run down her spine.

She was glad when they went below deck and were shown to their cabins.

'Goodness!' Eleanor exclaimed. 'This is even smaller than the cabin on the last ship. How on earth are we going to manage to get dressed and undressed?'

'What worries me is the door. It doesn't have a lock on it.' Jacinta rattled the knob. 'This seems quite loose and there's no chair to put behind it.'

'Good thing there are two of us. You take the upper bunk. You'll be safer there. We'll put our

228

luggage behind the door at night.'

'Am I being cowardly, seeing trouble where there is none?'

'No, you're not. That man tried to kill you, Jacinta, and he nearly succeeded too.' She put an arm round her companion and gave her a quick hug.

'I don't know what I'd do without you and Uncle Quentin.'

'You'd manage. You're a capable woman or you'd not have raised such a delightful lad in difficult circumstances.'

Jacinta couldn't prevent herself from smiling at this compliment to Ben.

'Anyway, it's only two nights and three days to Fremantle. I think they have to stop on the way at places called Busselton and Bunbury.'

The two women exchanged smiles. They knew they could depend on one another, whatever happened.

★   ★   ★

Alf found out that his unknown cuddler of the night before was the woman he'd noticed on the ship. She was about his own age, an Irishwoman, with a soft, lilting voice and a nicely plump body.

'You're a good sleeper,' she said by way of a greeting.

'You didn't do so badly yourself.'

'I'm Bridie Folane.'

She stuck out a hand just like a man, so he had to shake it. Nice soft hand, she had. 'Alf Walsh.'

'Pleased to meet you. I'm a widow, come out here to join my cousin. He sounds to be doing well in Australia, though that may all be lies, of course.'

Alf had to go on chatting. He was trapped in the corner and couldn't get away without pushing past her. Anyway, where would he go? He noticed that Bridie had a scar on one cheek. It puckered that side of her face and gave it a permanent smile, but since she seemed to smile a lot, the unmarked side matched the damaged one most of the time.

Anyway, who was perfect?

To his surprise, he found he enjoyed listening to her voice, and since chatting to her helped pass the time, he kept her talking. 'No children?'

'None. I never fell for a baby, not once in twelve years of marriage, I'm glad to say.'

'Most women want children.'

'Not me. The Mammy had one nearly every year and I had to help look after the little ones from the time I could manage to hold a baby without dropping it. Though some of them died, poor little things. Don't they always? When I married Perry, I insisted we left the village and went to live in Enniskillen to get away from them all, or they'd never have had their hands out of our pockets.'

A woman of sense, he decided. He wished his wife was more like her. 'That place — Enniskillen did you say? — it's in Ireland, is it?'

She grinned. 'Yes. It's a fine little town. Ah, you English! You have no idea what Ireland's like or where the towns are, have you?'

'I've never been rich enough to travel. And Ireland can't be all that wonderful if so many people leave it.' England was full of the Irish but Mr Blacklea wouldn't have them working on his estate or even in the village.

'Ireland's a pretty country, Mr Walsh, but there's not enough work and that's a fact. Even if you do find a job, it doesn't pay much. I grew sick of eating potatoes when I was growing up. That's all we had at home, potatoes, with a bit of flavouring now and then. Da had meat sometimes or an egg, but all we children got was the gravy or a dip of the yolk.'

'We did a bit better than you, but not much. Go on.'

She smiled at him. 'Really? I know I talk too much, but I can keep quiet if you'd prefer it.'

'I don't talk enough, so we're well matched.'

'Well then, we had a good life together, me and Perry, even put a little money aside for the bad times, and I made sure we ate well. We both worked in a pub, you see, and customers would buy him a drink now and then, so he'd no need to spend our money on booze. I'd not have let him drink our money away, anyway.'

She stared into space for a few seconds, then sighed. 'I wanted to get right away, make a better life. England next, I'd decided.'

Her smile faded. 'Then Perry got himself killed, the fool, trying to stop a runaway horse from trampling a little girl. The man whose daughter he'd saved gave me ten guineas afterwards and so did the owner of the horse — I made sure of that — but it didn't make up for losing all the years of a husband's earnings, did it? I don't know why they always pay men more in wages. Women have to eat too. Yes, and put clothes on their backs.'

Alf found he only had to ask a question now and then to keep her chatting and it was soothing somehow. 'What did you do after your husband died?'

'I already had a job in the pub so I kept on working. But I didn't like it there without a man to protect me, and I had to move to a small room in the attics to make ends meet. Some customers think you're easy game if you're a widow, and I'm not.' She looked him in the eye and repeated firmly, 'I'm not easy game to anyone, and you'll kindly remember that.'

'Have I done anything to offend you that makes you say that?'

'Not you. But there's a couple of other men asked me to sleep next to them tonight, and I know why. They've already tried to lay their hands on me.'

'Stay near me, if you like. I'll keep an eye on you.'

'I'm not doing anything to earn your help, mind.'

'You said already that you aren't easy.' He gestured round them, angry suddenly. 'Do you think I'd do that sort of thing in public, like an animal?'

She studied him. 'No. And neither would I. So that's all right, then.'

'Go on. What brought you to Australia?'

'I wrote to my cousin — Rory, he's called — and asked if there was work for a woman like me here. He wrote back and said there was plenty of work, especially for a woman. And plenty of men looking for wives. He'd sponsor me and help me settle in, but he just got married so I couldn't stay with them for long. I don't mind that. I'm a good worker. If there are jobs going, I'll soon find one. I'm not so sure about another husband, though.'

She waited, looking at him thoughtfully, then prompted, 'Here's me talking your head off about myself. What about you? Why are you going to Australia, Mr Walsh? Have you got a wife and children back home, waiting to follow you out here?'

He didn't even want to think about Ruth: the quarrels, the dirty house, the children whining and the constant lack of money. 'No. I'm the same as you. I'm a widower. No children.'

That seemed to satisfy her and she started talking again. He let her. This journey was going on and on. The coastal steamer wasn't travelling as fast as the other ship and didn't seem to use her engine much. There was nothing to do but wait to arrive and the mate said he didn't want you cluttering up the deck, so you were squashed into this cabin with its hard wooden benches.

'Go on,' Alf repeated. 'What are you going to do in the colony?'

Bridie was full of plans to make a new life by starting a boarding house.

'Is that your ambition?'

'I'd rather run a pub, but I can't do that without a husband. There's not much else a woman on her own can do but open a boarding house — if she's respectable, that is. But I'll have to save some more money first. I've had to spend some of my savings on the fare and my clothes for the journey. That's why I'm travelling the cheapest way I can.'

'It must be a fine life, running a pub.'

'It's hard work, but at least you can earn good money if you do it right. There aren't many ways people like us can make money that leaves you with some to spare, are there? I don't spend a farthing I don't have to, and one day I'm going to live like a lady.'

He looked at her admiringly. 'You'll manage it if anyone can.'

He wished his wife was like that. Ruth never spent one penny when she could get rid of two. She'd even wanted him to stop having his beer money so that she'd have more to waste, something he'd refused point blank to do. A man had to keep his head up in the village, and who'd have respected a man who couldn't afford a sup of ale?

During the second day they chatted amicably, or rather Bridie chatted and asked questions, and Alf answered.

He smiled at her at one stage.

'What are you looking at me like that for?' she demanded.

'I'm thinking what a fine woman you are.'

'Is that so? And are you a fine man, Alf Walsh?'

'Probably not. I know about horses and not much else.'

'What was your wife like?'

He shrugged. 'All right. Not as strong as she looked. Died of a summer fever. There was a bad one going round last year.'

'Well, I'm sure a sturdy fellow like you will soon find another wife.'

'Mmm.' He didn't know what to say to that. He wished he was free, he did indeed.

As darkness fell on the second night, Bridie asked him to keep her place while she went to the necessary. When she came back she wrapped her blanket round her and sat down.

'I'll scream if you touch me,' she warned, as she had the night before.

'And I'll scream if *you* touch me,' he joked. 'So hands off.'

There was enough moonlight for him to see her smile. 'Ah, you're a good man, Mr Walsh, sure you are. You've never offered me any insults and we've sat as close as two peas in a pod.'

He wasn't a good man, though she made him feel to be a better one. And she made him laugh. It seemed a long time since he'd had something to laugh about.

At some time during the night, her head found its way on to his shoulder and he smiled in the near darkness. It felt good to be close to someone so cheerful.

He was enjoying this short journey and was glad the ship had stopped twice, because it made it last longer.

The other thing could wait. Mr Blacklea had no way of knowing how Alf was getting on, after all, and never would know the true details.

12

When Pearson came to take his orders for the day, Blacklea greeted him with the statement, 'They'll be arriving in Western Australia round about now.'

'So they will, sir.'

'If your nephew has done his job properly, *she* won't be with them.'

As his master stared blindly into the distance, Pearson waited. He knew better than to interrupt or try to introduce a new topic of conversation when Blacklea was in this mood. And what did it matter, after all? He was paid his wages whether he did anything to earn them or not.

'Do you think your Alfred will have done it, got rid of her, I mean?'

'Oh yes, sir. He's a very capable young fellow.' Pearson hoped he sounded confident. He'd been having doubts about Alf's suitability for such a job ever since his nephew left for Australia. Alf was like a horse that mostly jogged along steadily, but every now and then developed a kick in its gait that could toss you off its back if you weren't expecting it.

No, Alf wouldn't dare disobey Mr Blacklea. He wasn't that stupid.

'It'll be months before he brings the boy back, though.'

'I'm afraid so, sir.'

'Australia's a damned long way. Why do you think she went there?'

'I can't say, sir. Who knows what makes some women do things?' He suppressed a smile as he saw his master nodding agreement. Mr Blacklea had a very low opinion of women, even of his own wife.

Pearson reckoned Mrs Blacklea must be a very clever lady to have survived this many years with a husband like that. And her unable to have more children, too. Though of course she did have good family connections. That'd probably be the reason she was still alive.

One day Pearson was going to leave this job and move to another district, but how to do it without upsetting his master was something he'd not yet worked out. He would, though. His life probably depended on it.

*   *   *

When they reached Fremantle, Quentin was surprised at how small the port was, not only the port itself but the town, which had houses dotted haphazardly up a gentle slope, with some large buildings in what was presumably the town centre and some smaller ones with gardens in between them.

One of the passengers returning to Western Australia had told them it was a very sandy place and that was only too obvious. Some of the buildings were built of what looked like limestone, and were dazzling white in the sunshine. Quentin could see two churches, one of them distinctly larger than the other.

As usual, the cabin passengers were allowed to disembark first, which Quentin thought was a good thing for young Ben, who was nearly bursting with excitement at the thought of actually arriving after such a long journey.

'The ground doesn't feel any different from England,' Ben confided as they at last stepped ashore.

'Did you expect it to?'

'I thought *something* would be different from England.'

'Well, the sun's warmer, don't you think? And this is September, which is spring here. The weather will soon get very hot, I'm told.'

'No ice and snow, ever. Imagine that, sir.'

Quentin thought that sounded wonderful. He wasn't fond of winter weather.

Once their trunks had been retrieved from the hold and brought down to the quay, they accepted a lad's offer to take their luggage on his handcart, because it'd not fit into a cab as well as the people.

'Can you fit all our luggage on?'

The lad studied the pile, then shook his head. 'No, sir. Can't do it. We'll need another handcart. It'll cost a shilling for each of us. Is that all right?'

'That's fine. Please find us another cart.'

The lad put two fingers into his mouth and whistled loudly, then made urgent beckoning signs. Another boy arrived at the run, pushing a slightly smaller handcart whose wheel squeaked loudly.

By the time they were ready to go, the afternoon was nearly over and it'd soon be dark, so the first thing was to find somewhere to stay. They'd already agreed not to try to contact anyone until the following day.

'We need to find a hotel or a lodging house,' Quentin told the handcart lad. 'Somewhere comfortable and clean. If you take us somewhere good, there's another shilling in it for you.'

'My aunt's place is the best there is,' he said confidently. 'She doesn't take scruffy folk and she's a good cook. She'll look after you properly. Will you be staying in Freo for long?'

'We don't know how long yet. Is that what you call the town, Freo?'

'Most people do.'

They decided to walk along beside the handcarts because they'd been told distances weren't great in the town centre and they were all longing to stretch their legs.

Quentin was pleased to see that the steerage passengers hadn't been let off the ship yet and the crew were still unloading luggage. Alf Walsh was scowling at them from near the top of the gangway, looking as if he wanted to follow them. Fortunately, he would still have to retrieve his trunk so they could be free of him for a while.

And by then Quentin would have taken advice about how to deal with the fellow.

By the time they reached the boarding house, they were all feeling the pull on muscles not used properly for over two months and were glad to stop walking.

Their guide vanished inside and came out a moment later with a sturdy woman, who was wiping her hands on a small towel.

'This is my aunt.'

She dug him in the ribs. 'Didn't I tell you last time to introduce me properly, Dennis?' She turned to them, saying nothing but studying them carefully. After a minute or two, she gave a little nod, as if they'd passed some test. 'I'm Mrs Haslop, proprietor of this boarding house.'

'I'm Quentin Saxby and these are my nieces, Mrs Blacklea and Mrs Prescott. This fine young fellow is my great-nephew, Master Benjamin Blacklea. We'd like two rooms. The ladies will be sharing and I shall be with the boy.'

'I have more rooms if you'd prefer to sleep on your own, sir.'

'No. We like to be together.'

'How long will you be staying?'

'A few days, possibly longer.'

Eleanor stepped forward. 'Could we see the rooms first, please, Mrs Haslop?'

The landlady shrugged and led the way inside, calling over her shoulder, 'You keep an eye on their luggage, Dennis.'

The rooms were comfortably furnished and clean but not all that big.

'Is there somewhere to store our trunks, somewhere safe?' Eleanor asked.

'I can let you have a third bedroom. That way, your things will be inside the house and you'll be able to get to them easily. It's what other people have done who've come straight from a ship. But I'll have to charge for the third room — half price because I'll not need to supply meals and linen.'

Quentin looked questioningly at Eleanor and received a nod in reply. 'That's fine. I'm sure we'll be very comfortable here.'

As the two ladies went back into the rear bedroom to decide who was having which bed and wait for Dennis to bring up their luggage, he lowered his voice and said to Mrs Haslop, 'I'll be paying this bill, so please don't trouble the ladies with it. My nieces are both widows and have to be careful with money but they don't like to be beholden.'

She nodded. 'Very right, too. Will you be wanting a meal tonight, sir?'

'If it's not too much trouble.'

'It won't be anything fancy, but it'll be good, hearty food. I have two other gentlemen staying, so I was cooking anyway. Six o'clock sharp, if you please.'

'Fine.' He turned to Ben, moving aside as Dennis and the other cart boy panted up the stairs with two of their suitcases. 'Let's choose which bed we each want and unpack our things for tonight.'

'It feels strange to be on land again, doesn't it, Uncle Quentin? My head keeps feeling as if the ship is still moving about.'

'You'll soon grow used to land again. It's good to arrive at the end of a long journey.' He could see the lad frowning. 'Is something worrying you?'

'I was just wondering about Mr Nash, if he'll like us.'

'I'm sure he will.'

'How can you be sure?'

'Because your mother's not only very pretty, but she's a nice, kind person.'

'He might not want another son. He has one already.'

'He told his cousin in England that he would be happy to take a child as well.'

But poor Ben still looked doubtful. He stepped back as the two cart boys puffed their way up the stairs again, watching them, head on one side. 'If he doesn't like us, I wouldn't mind getting a handcart and carrying people's luggage for money.'

Quentin hid a smile. Ben was well-grown for nine years, but not nearly big enough to haul luggage around. 'I'm sure that won't be necessary. The best thing you can do is work hard at school so that you can find a good job when you grow up.'

'I've never been to school.'

'You haven't?'

'No . . .'

They broke off their conversation as Dennis and a man who was presumably Mr Haslop brought up the first of the trunks and took it into the third bedroom.

'Why didn't you go to school?'

'Father didn't like me to spend time with the village children. He said he'd teach me himself, but he was always too busy, so Mother taught me how to read and write, and we learned all sorts of other things, too. I don't think I know as much as other boys, though. We didn't have

242

a lot of school books.'

'I've noticed what a quick learner you are. You'll soon catch up, and you may be ahead of them in reading.'

Ben gave him an uncertain smile and Quentin's heart filled with love for him. How he'd have loved a grandson like this one!

'You've no need to worry, Ben. I've told you before and I meant it: if nothing comes of this Mr Nash, I'll look after you both.'

The boy suddenly launched himself at Quentin and gave him a hug, then moved away, cringing slightly, as if fearing he'd done something wrong.

Quentin pulled him back and returned the hug, then clapped him on the shoulder. 'Let's go and find out how the ladies are getting on. And I have to pay the cart lads, too. It's nearly time to go down for our meal.'

He gave the two cart boys four shillings between them, and saw their faces light up at the tip.

'Are you ready, my dears?'

He let Eleanor and Jacinta precede him down the stairs and gestured to Ben to follow the ladies.

He was glad they weren't going to look for Mr Nash and Captain McBride until tomorrow. He always found it best to tackle important business with a clear head and he was feeling rather tired now, though he wasn't going to admit that.

And there was the matter of Alf Walsh to be resolved. It seemed clear that the fellow intended to keep an eye on them. Why? Surely the man wouldn't attack Jacinta here in the port, with so many people around?

But what other reason would he have for following her?

Then it occurred to him that the man might still try to snatch Ben. Only, how would he manage that in a place so isolated, with no railways and such a reliance on coastal shipping?

★ ★ ★

Dougal McBride stared at the ocean ahead of the *Bonny Mary*, enjoying the sight of the waves glinting in the sunlight but feeling restless. Normally, he felt happiest when he was on the ocean, in charge of his ship, but in all the long months since leaving Eleanor and her husband at Suez, he'd felt restless, unable to settle to anything for long. It was as if he was waiting . . . waiting for something very important to happen.

He couldn't know for certain that she would come back to him, but he could hope. Sometimes the hope burned brightly, at other times he felt despondent.

Even his friend and partner in Singapore, Lee Kar Ho, had noticed Dougal wasn't his usual self and asked if he needed help about something. But Dougal didn't want to tell anyone how he felt about Eleanor. Which wasn't to say that his clever friend wouldn't have found out about the lady. Even the most loyal crew members could let something slip in a casual conversation.

Dougal sighed, then got angry at himself for

sighing after her like a lovesick youth.

He knew what had made him more restless than usual. In Singapore, he'd received a letter from his sister Flora, left for him with Mr Lee when her husband's ship docked there. She sounded very happy with Josh, whom she'd married recently, after they'd been kept apart for years by the lies their mother had told.

Even though his mother was now dead, Dougal was still angry with her for fooling both him and his sister about Josh's intentions. Cruel, that had been, and all to ensure she had a spinster daughter to care for her in her old age.

Well, Flora and Josh were married now, and she'd written to say she was expecting her first child. He was concerned about this, since Flora was thirty-three, but she sounded confident of a happy outcome.

He'd like to have children, too — Eleanor's children. Though she hadn't borne any to her husband. Was that because she was barren or had it been Prescott's fault? The fellow had seemed effete, as if he had no red blood in him, and had looked increasingly ill and drawn during the voyage. He'd spent most of the time lying down in his cabin.

It had taken Dougal until he was nearly forty to find his love. He longed to see her again. He remembered so clearly the restrained beauty of her face, the alertness of her mind, her kindness. He could think of a dozen good qualities she possessed.

He'd written to his friend Adam's lawyer in England, sending his letter by the same ship as took Eleanor and her husband to the same destination. Adam had often talked about Mr Saxby, who sounded to be a kind and sensible fellow, so Dougal had sent him a draft on a bank in London, with a request to help Eleanor in any way necessary, including buying her a passage back to Australia.

He had to believe she'd come to him.

★ ★ ★

Alf walked slowly down the gangway to the dock, then waited impatiently for his trunk to be brought out from the hold.

He turned to say farewell to Bridie and saw her run to greet a thickset fellow with a woman by his side. This must be her cousin Rory. He looked like a surly bull, strong, the sort of man you wouldn't want to cross.

As Alf walked along the dock, wondering where to go, he heard her calling him and swung round.

'Got a minute, Alf?'

He went to join them. 'I've got plenty of minutes.'

'Rory, this is Alf Walsh, who helped me on the ship. Alf, this is my cousin Rory Flynn and his wife Jilleen.'

The two men shook hands and Alf nodded to Mrs Flynn.

'As I told you, Alf helped me on the ship, so I reckon we owe him a bit of help in return. He's really good with horses and he's looking for a job. Do you know anyone who wants help?'

Rory studied him, eyes half closed, a shrewd expression on his rather brutal face. 'How are you with cows?'

Alf blinked in surprise. 'I'm good with all animals. Treat 'em right and they'll most of 'em do what you want. But I've never been a cowman, if that's what you're asking.'

'I need someone to help me with my cows. If you haven't got a job, and you're willing to learn, I'll offer you a try-out. If someone helps my family, then I do what I can for them in return.'

He stopped talking to scowl, not at Alf but at some memory. 'Bridie says you're not stupid, so that's in your favour. The last fellow was too stupid to remember what I'd told him and he did more harm than good, the idiot.'

'What are you offering in wages?'

Rory hesitated.

Alf grinned. He knew that look. 'I'll not take any job without checking what they pay cowmen here in Australia.'

'As if I'd cheat you, when you've helped my cousin.'

'As if you'd not try to get me as cheaply as possible, you not being a stupid man.'

Rory rolled his eyes heavenwards, grinned and named an amount. 'That's top money for here, minus ten shillings for your housing and keep, which is only fair. Not only do you get your keep, but you can sleep on the veranda. We turned one end of it into a sleepout and the weather isn't cold at this time of year.'

Alf nodded thoughtfully.

'Since I'll want you there first thing in the morning for early milking, it'll suit me to have you live in. Jilleen here is a good cook. I'm getting a name for selling good clean milk and the shops want it delivered as early as possible. You'll be helping with the deliveries as well. The weather gets hot later on in the year and we have to milk the cows early to sell the milk and cream before they turn sour.'

Alf turned to look at Bridie, who blushed and began to fiddle with her bonnet strings. She'd asked about a job for him. That must mean she was interested in him. Did he want to be beholden to her? Was it fair to make her hope he was interested in return, when he was already married?

He looked round the busy quay. He didn't know a single person here. This was as good a chance to get a start as he was likely to find, so, fair to Bridie or not, he was going to accept the job. It'd give him time to think about what he was supposed to do here and work out a way to do it. He'd not dare to go back, otherwise. 'All right. We'll give each other a month's trial.'

Rory held out his right hand. 'We'll shake on it.'

They did this then Alf added, 'You'll find me a hard worker. I like animals. They don't mess you around like people do.'

Bridie was talking to Rory's wife, but Alf noticed her glancing his way every now and then.

If he was free, he'd court her, damned if he wouldn't. He didn't know when he'd met a woman he actually liked, as he did her.

Fate was unfair. It didn't give you what you wanted or thought you were getting. He'd been really deceived by Ruth. Then fate showed a much better woman, one out of reach, as if to torment you.

13

Quentin noticed at breakfast that the two ladies were showing signs of being nervous, fidgeting with their teacups, not eating much, sighing for no reason. He couldn't talk to them privately because Mrs Haslop was in and out bringing the food, and anyway, there were two other guests dining at the same table.

Ben was too interested in what he was eating to notice anything, bless him.

Quentin waited until the meal was over before suggesting they all go out for a stroll.

He'd already asked the landlady for directions to the three places they needed to visit: Mr Nash's timber yard, Captain McBride's house and the address Adam had sent him. Quentin had written down her instructions carefully. He patted his pocket where the piece of paper was safely lodged.

The directions for finding Harriet had instantly fixed themselves in his mind. Seeing her was the most important thing of all, and if it was up to him, they'd go straight there. But he couldn't abandon his two adopted nieces now, especially not when they were looking so nervous.

Once they were away from the house and able to speak privately, he stopped to ask, 'Shall we go and see my friend Harriet first or do you two ladies wish to find your men straight away? I'm happy to do what suits you best. I can come with you or you can visit them on your own. Whichever you prefer.'

Jacinta shook her head vigorously. 'I don't wish to meet Mr Nash on my own, not the first time, anyway. And I'm not only nervous about meeting him, I'm afraid of Walsh attacking me in the street.'

'I'd rather you accompanied me to Dougal's house as well, Uncle Quentin,' Eleanor admitted. 'It's daunting, the thought of asking a man if he still wants to marry you.'

'But he sent the money for you to come here.'

'Yes, but even though he said he'd never change his mind, he might have done so by now. So I think we should go and find your Harriet first. I know you're eager to see her again.'

It was what he wanted, so he didn't argue. 'Very well. I think Adam's house is quite near.'

Jacinta beckoned to her son and Ben came back to join them from where he'd been looking in a shop window. Then he walked quietly behind the adults.

That lad never protested about what they were doing, Quentin thought. He was far too docile. What had his father done to him?

On the way they passed Deagan's Bazaar and stopped to admire the neat, tidy grounds and the big sign over the building at the top of the slope. 'That shop belongs to Adam's brother-in-law,' Quentin said. 'He's been very successful in the colony as a trader.'

As he was speaking, a man passing by stopped. 'Excuse me for interrupting, but I couldn't help overhearing what you said. Are you looking for Adam? I'm Bram Deagan, his wife's brother and owner of the Bazaar.'

'It's his Aunt Harriet I've come to see, though of course I'm looking forward to seeing Adam again as well. I've known him since he was a lad. I haven't met your sister Ismay yet and am looking forward to getting to know her as well.' He realised the man was looking puzzled and introduced himself. 'I'm Quentin Saxby. Adam or Harriet may have mentioned me.'

'Oh, yes. You're the lawyer. Adam's told me how kind you always were to him when he was a boy. Was he expecting you to come here? He didn't mention it.'

'No. I decided to . . . um, surprise him.'

'It's a long way to come for a surprise. Welcome to Australia, Mr Saxby! I'm sure Adam and Ismay will be delighted to see you. Harriet, too, of course. I hope you'll enjoy your time here.'

'Thank you.' Quentin introduced his companions.

'I'm pleased to meet you, ladies. Are you joining family here as well?'

Both ladies flushed and looked embarrassed. Bram shot a startled glance at Quentin, clearly wondering what he'd said.

Since Bram was now related to Adam, and since he'd taken an instant liking to the man, Quentin had no hesitation about taking him into his confidence. 'I think it may be useful if I have a chat with Mr Deagan. Why don't you ladies go and look round the Bazaar for a few minutes?'

He watched them go with a wry smile. It wouldn't be correct to say that they fled from him and Mr Deagan, but they certainly moved up the slope quickly, with Ben trailing behind them.

'What did I say to upset them?' Bram asked once the others were out of earshot.

'It's a delicate matter and as Adam has spoken warmly of you, and we could almost think of each other as relatives, perhaps I might ask your advice?'

'I'm always happy to help a friend of Adam's.'

'I'm here because the two people I love most are here, Adam and his aunt. I hope to settle near them for the rest of my life.' It was Quentin's turn to feel a little embarrassed, since he wasn't used to sharing his feelings with strangers. 'The thing is, I've missed Harriet greatly and I want to find out if she's missed me too. Then we might, um, do something about it. We're both . . . unmarried.'

'She's a charming lady, to be sure, and I wish you well.'

'The two ladies who travelled with me aren't really relatives, but we grew close enough on the voyage to decide to adopt one another as uncle and nieces. Mrs Prescott visited the colony briefly last year. She and her husband were stranded in Western Australia and sailed to Suez with Captain McBride in order to continue their journey to England. She is now a widow and . . . um, has returned here at the good captain's invitation.'

Bram beamed at him. 'She's his Eleanor!'

'Yes, that's her name. Has he mentioned her, then?'

'Mentioned her? He never stops talking about her. Heaven be praised! It'd have broken his heart if she hadn't come back to him. I'm assuming she's free now?'

'Yes. It happened a few weeks after they reached England.'

Bram glanced up the slope, as if he could still see her. 'She's as lovely as he said.'

'You know about their . . . friendship?'

He gave Quentin a twinkling smile. 'More than a friendship, surely?'

'Well, yes. She hopes so.'

'She can be certain of it. Dougal is a good friend of mine and did me the honour of confiding his hopes to me. He hasn't changed his mind. In fact, he's been moping about like a lost soul.'

'Is he . . . in port at the moment?'

'Sadly, no.' Bram suddenly lost his smile. 'And we have bad news for him when he does return. The ship Adam was captaining, a ship in which Dougal had a share, met a bad storm.'

Quentin felt as if his heart had skipped a beat. 'Adam's safe, though?'

'Oh, yes. They didn't lose any lives, but the cargo was badly damaged.'

'Ah. *Your* cargo I assume, Mr Deagan?'

Bram had lost his smile completely. 'Adam and Dougal had some cargo, but it was mostly mine, I'm afraid.'

'I'm sorry to hear that. Did you lose much?'

'We did, yes. But we'll come about.'

254

'But Adam is in port?'

'Yes. Are you on your way to see him?'

'Actually, I want to see his Aunt Harriet.'

'If you like, I'll give myself the pleasure of showing you the way to their house. I'm glad you've come to visit. We could all do with some good news to cheer us up. Shall we go and find the ladies?'

Quentin took another decision, because Deagan was such a sympathetic listener. 'In a moment. The other lady, Mrs Blacklea . . . This is in confidence, mind.'

Once again, Bram was all attention. 'You can trust me, Mr Saxby.'

'Jacinta is a widow too, and in impoverished circumstances. A man called Mitchell Nash wrote to his cousin in England, asking help in finding a wife and well, Mrs Blacklea was alone in the world, so Mr Stanwell suggested she come here to fulfil that role.'

Bram beamed at him, good humour restored. 'Oh, that's excellent news. *I* was the one who gave Mitchell a nudge last year to do something about finding himself a wife. He'll be very pleased to see her.'

'You think so? Even though he's never met her?'

'Well, there aren't a lot of unattached ladies in the colony and a man needs a wife, especially a man with a son. Arranged marriages happen regularly here, though things take a long time to arrange, given how long it takes to send letters to and fro.'

'Jacinta won't seem . . . too unusual, then?'

'Definitely not.'

Quentin's sigh of relief was heartfelt. 'She's brought a letter from Mr Stanwell to Mr Nash, but I thought I'd deliver it for her so that he can read it before they meet. I'd like to find out how your friend feels. He may be regretting his request and I don't want her upset.'

'I'm sure he isn't regretting it, but that'd be a tactful way to arrange a meeting,' Bram agreed. 'I think Mitchell is a little nervous about marrying a complete stranger. Who wouldn't be? But she's a pretty woman and looks to be pleasant-natured, so I'm sure once he meets her, his doubts will vanish.'

'She is a lovely person. I'm grateful for your advice, Mr Deagan. Shall we join the ladies now?'

Bram led the way up to the Bazaar, stopping in the doorway to study the two women, who were admiring his wife's silks. 'Is it the taller who knows Dougal?'

'No, the dark-haired one.'

'And the boy is Mrs Blacklea's son?'

'Yes. That's . . . one of the things which worries her, how Mr Nash will feel about taking on another man's child.'

'He looks a fine lad to me.'

'He is. I've grown very fond of young Ben.'

Eleanor and Jacinta caught sight of Quentin just then and murmured something to the lady displaying the silks, before coming across to where the men were waiting.

Bram smiled at his wife, then turned to the others. 'I hope you won't mind if I join you for a street or two, ladies. I've offered to show you and Mr Saxby the way to Adam's house. I'll just say goodbye to my wife before we leave.'

They went to wait for him in the doorway and after a quick word with Isabella, he led the way out into the sunshine.

'I like spring best of all in Australia,' he said cheerfully. 'It gets too hot for me in summer. Though we get plenty of sunny days in winter too here.'

Quentin turned his face up to the sky for a moment or two. 'I'm looking forward to not having English winters and snow. Sunny days cheer you up.'

And the day would be better still if Harriet was glad to see him. Surely she would be? He'd known he'd feel nervous of seeing her, but hadn't expected to feel this nervous.

★ ★ ★

Jacinta watched Mr Deagan smile at his wife, and it was such a loving smile, she felt a pang of jealousy twist through her. She had once dreamed of meeting a man who would look at her in just the same way, but poverty had forced her to abandon that girlish dream for the harsh reality of Claude Blacklea as a husband and provider. But oh, she wanted her dreams and hopes back.

Was she wrong to accept another marriage of convenience? Surely, if the man were reasonable and kind, it couldn't be as bad as marrying Claude?

She hadn't exactly accepted Mr Nash yet, though, had she? Uncle Quentin had said he'd help her if she decided not to marry, and it was a great relief to know that.

But still, life would be a lot easier if she did marry Mr Nash, for both her and Ben.

She'd studied the man's photograph many times during the long voyage and knew every detail of it by heart. Mitchell Nash seemed like a decent person, not exactly good-looking, but with an honest face. And at least he wasn't old. He was resting his hand on his son's shoulder in an affectionate gesture, at least, that was how it looked.

She shivered. The trouble was, you never really knew what someone was like till you lived with them.

They walked along in two couples, with Ben following on his own.

'This is my house.' Bram stopped to indicate a wooden structure, two storeys high. It was larger than its neighbours and surrounded by verandas on the ground floor, as so many of the houses were.

He moved forward but stopped at the next house, which was much smaller. 'This is where Adam lives at the moment.'

'You're neighbours, then, as well as relatives.'

Bram grinned. 'More than that. I'm his landlord too.' He stepped back and gestured to Quentin to knock on the door.

The lady who opened it was too young to be Aunt Harriet and clearly didn't know who her caller was, though she smiled at Bram, standing to one side.

Quentin didn't feel he could bear to wait another second. 'Is Harriet at home? I'm Quentin Saxby, you see, and — '

The woman exclaimed in surprise at his name, then beamed at him. 'You came all the way to Australia to visit us? Oh, Adam and Aunt Harriet are both going to be so happy to see you. I know they've missed you dreadfully. But only my aunt is at home just now.'

She turned to call out, 'Aunt Harriet, see who's come to visit you!' Then she stood back and shooed Quentin into the house. 'Go straight through to the back.'

Bram nodded approval of his sister's action.

Eleanor moved closer to Ismay. 'Could we give them a moment or two alone together, do you think? He has something of a private nature to say to Mrs Seaton.'

Ismay clapped her hands in delight. 'I was right in my guess, then? He's come to be with her?'

'Yes. He's missed her dreadfully.'

'She's tried to hide it, but she's missed him too.' She waited as her brother introduced Eleanor, Jacinta and Ben properly.

But they didn't start chatting. They were all straining their ears, wondering what was happening inside the house.

∗　∗　∗

Quentin strode quickly along a narrow corridor to a room at the back of the house, eager to see Harriet. He stopped in the doorway of a room

259

which seemed to be a combined kitchen and living room. She was looking well, hadn't really changed at all.

She was standing next to a table, where some mending was spread out, holding a piece of cloth in one hand and studying one corner of it, so didn't immediately turn to see who had come into the room. When she did, she dropped the cloth, mouthing his name and pressing one hand to her breast, as if to hold in her feelings.

'No words of welcome?' he teased. 'When I've come so far to see you.'

'Oh, Quentin! It really is you. I thought I was dreaming.' She ran across the room and flung herself into his arms, hugging him as if she never wanted to let go.

Hope flooded through him in a tide of bubbling joy as he held her close and dared to drop a kiss on her hair, then another on her soft cheek. 'Oh, Harriet, I've missed you so much. I couldn't bear to be apart any longer, so I sold up and booked my passage.'

She looked up at him, her eyes bright with happy tears. 'I've missed you, too, my dear, dear friend. I knew I would, but not how much it would hurt.'

Words tumbled out and he made no attempt to stop them, speaking from the heart. 'I didn't realise I loved you until after you'd left. Oh, Harriet, my darling! Say you love me too.'

For answer, she raised her face in a mute invitation and he obliged her with a quick kiss on her lips, then another more urgent one.

He held her close. 'We must never be apart

again. Never, ever. Will you marry me, dearest Harriet?' Which was not how he'd intended to propose to her. He held his breath as he waited for her answer.

'Of course I will.' She leaned her head back a little, still with her arms round his neck, and smiled mistily at him. 'Why did we waste so much time? We could have been together years ago.'

'Because we were set in our ways, and because we saw one another often. But your leaving jolted me out of my rut, showed me how stupid I'd been.'

Her smile faded and she faltered, 'You . . . won't want us to go back to England, will you, Quentin darling? We could make a very pleasant life here, I promise you. I've grown so fond of Ismay — the one who answered the door is Adam's wife.'

'No, of course I don't want to go back. I'd like to live near Adam as well, and his wife looks to be a delightful woman. She has such a warm smile.' He suddenly realised that his hostess hadn't followed him into the house. 'Goodness! They must be waiting outside, letting us meet in private. What must they be thinking?'

'I'd still have rushed into your arms even if they'd come in with you. Am I absolutely shameless?'

'No. You're the same loving Harriet, only we've both brought our feelings out into the open now.' He took her hand in his and tugged her to the front door. 'Let's tell them.'

The five people standing on the small veranda

turned to look at them expectantly.

Quentin let go of Harriet's hand to put his arm round her shoulders. 'Ladies, Mr Deagan, Ben ... Mrs Seaton has just done me the honour of accepting my proposal and we intend to get married as soon as possible.'

There were exclamations of happiness, then the two younger women kissed and hugged Quentin, while Ismay did the same to Harriet, before hugging him.

Bram shook his hand, before congratulating Harriet and wishing her well. 'We've needed some good news, we have indeed. You must all come and take tea with me and my wife on Sunday. Isabella will be so pleased for you both.'

He took out his pocket watch and clicked his tongue in surprise. 'Is it that late already? I'd better get back to the Bazaar. I'll leave you all in peace now to catch up on your news.'

As the door closed behind him, Harriet went to the stove to turn up the damper and increase the heat. 'Let me make a pot of tea. And we have a fruit cake. Are you hungry, Ben? Boys usually are.'

He nodded shyly.

She bustled round the kitchen getting things ready, but her eyes kept going back to Quentin, and the smile never left her face.

He didn't attempt to talk, but smiled at her just as foolishly.

Ismay nudged Eleanor and whispered, 'Isn't it lovely to see the two of them.'

'Wonderful.'

'Tell me about yourselves,' Harriet said, as she

262

joined them at the table. 'I want to know about everything that's happened on your journey.'

★ ★ ★

Once they'd finished their refreshments and Quentin had explained about the two ladies he'd travelled with, he looked at Jacinta and stood up.

'If you can direct me to where Mr Nash lives, my dear Harriet, I'll go and speak to him, prepare the way, as it were.'

Ismay at once suggested the other visitors stay with her till he returned.

'Thank you.' He studied Jacinta. 'Unless you've changed your mind and want to come with me?'

She shook her head, unable to hide her anxiety. 'No, I think it's best if you tell him about me, so that he can ... feel free to say he's changed his mind.'

He patted her shoulder. 'I doubt he'll do that. Leave it to me, my dear.'

When the two men had left, Jacinta appreciated her hostess's tact in not talking about Mr Nash, and tried to seem interested as Ismay told them about life in the colony and the differences she had found.

But it was hard to concentrate.

14

Mitchell was hard at work in his timber yard. With Tommy's help, he was sorting out the first consignment of the wood he'd bought from Adam. He enjoyed physical work, which had always annoyed his mother, who had wanted him to act more like a gentleman.

The work of rearrangement fitted in well, because at this time of year, when the weather wasn't too hot, it was good to check through his stocks of wood to make sure no white ants had got into his yard to nibble things away to sawdust.

He loved the smell and feel of wood, and was happy that people were beginning to trust him, not only buying his dressed timber, but asking him to do small building jobs, such as adding on a room or veranda. Alterations were so much easier to do with wooden houses.

Tommy came across with big enamel mugs of tea for them both, the half pint mugs that were so popular among Australian working men, and both of them took a break.

Hiring Tommy had been a piece of luck for Mitchell when he first decided to settle in the Swan River Colony. As a former convict desperate for a job, Tommy had offered to work for a lad's wages if he could sleep in the yard in an old shed. He'd been struggling to find work after he was granted his ticket of leave, because people didn't trust ex-convicts.

Mitchell had taken that chance and now that Tommy was properly fed, he'd built up some decent muscles. He was eager to learn the trade properly, asking questions all the time, and had become a great help in many ways.

'I see from the newspaper that the mail is in from Albany,' Mitchell said. 'Perhaps your wife will have written back to you from England, Tommy.'

'I doubt it, sir. She's not replied to my other letters. I wrote to my cousin as well, and hoped he would at least write back to tell me how she was, but there's been no word from either of them.'

'Give them time.'

Tommy shrugged. 'You couldn't blame her for making a new life, could you? She's probably found herself another man. She couldn't feed herself and three children on a woman's wages.'

'But she's married to you.'

Tommy flushed and stared at the ground. 'We're not exactly wed. We just . . . told people we were.'

'Oh. But I have a feeling she will still get in touch.'

'I hope you're right, sir. I was very fond of my Dora and the kids.'

'If you give me your wife's address, I'll write to her and offer to pay their fares out here. I can easily sponsor them.'

Tommy gulped and stared at him, with tears starting in his eyes. 'You'd do that, sir?'

'Yes. You're a good worker and I'd like to keep

you happy. I'm sure your wife would help around the place, too.'

'She would, sir, she would. She's a good housewife, my Dora.'

'That's settled, then.' Mitchell gave him a moment to gain control of his emotions, then changed the subject. 'I've put an advert for a housekeeper in the newspaper. I need to find someone to replace Mary as soon as possible.'

'She should have give you proper notice. It weren't right, just upping and leaving.'

'I agree.' His so-called housekeeper had been a rather slovenly woman whose only real talent was for washing, but her efforts had been better than nothing. She'd sent a badly spelled note yesterday to say that she was getting married and wouldn't be coming to work for him any longer. There was a PS in another handwriting, asking him to send the wages owing to her husband at their new address.

He supposed he'd have to do that, though it went against the grain to pay her anything after she'd let him down so badly.

Mitchell wasn't enjoying the thought of cooking the evening meal tonight. He supposed it'd have to be ham again. At least he knew how to fry that, and if her hens were laying, he'd buy some eggs from the woman down the street to go with it. His son wouldn't complain. Christopher would eat anything put before him, however badly cooked, and usually asked for seconds as well.

When he saw Bram approaching, Mitchell tipped out the dregs from his mug and handed it to Tommy. 'You carry on checking the piles of wood for white ants while I see what Bram wants.'

His friend was accompanied by an older man, who for all his kindly expression, held himself with the confident dignity of a gentleman of means. A customer, perhaps?

'I see you're still idling your days away, Mitchell,' Bram teased. 'And the sawdust in your hair looks pretty.'

Mitchell grinned and brushed his hair, sending a shower of sawdust flying. 'We're getting the wood piles rearranged to accommodate the new pieces, and we've started sorting out the smaller salvaged stuff.' He looked at the stranger and waited to be introduced.

Bram waved one hand. 'This is Mr Saxby, who has just arrived from England. He's a lawyer and a good friend of Adam's.'

'Then I hope you'll become a friend of mine as well, Mr Saxby.' Mitchell gave his right hand an extra wipe on his trousers before shaking the hand that was offered to him.

'I hope so too.'

Bram took a step backwards. 'Mr Saxby has a private matter to discuss with you, so I'll leave you now. Come and visit me at the Bazaar any time, Mr Saxby. And if you need help with anything else, you've only to ask.'

Mitchell studied his visitor, who was studying him in return. 'Would you like to come into my office?'

'Yes. I think we should do this somewhere private.'

Do what? Mitchell wondered. Frowning, he led the way across to the wooden building, which had once been his home but now housed Tommy and the business's records and equipment.

When they were seated on the hard wooden chairs which were all he had to offer, he waited again.

'You wrote to your cousin Peter Stanwell,' Mr Saxby said.

Mitchell stiffened. 'Yes. You . . . know what I wrote about?'

'I do, though I must be honest and admit that I've never met your cousin. On the voyage from England, I became acquainted with the lady who came in answer to your request. She's brought a letter from him for you.' He took the letter from his pocket and handed it over. 'It'd perhaps be best if you read it first, then we discussed what to do next.'

Mitchell took the letter, walked over to the window and opened it with his back to the room.

My dear cousin,

I was delighted to hear from you and know that you've settled happily into the Swan River Colony.

You asked about my well-being. I can't say I'm enjoying life in this parish, because the local landowner is a cruel man and regularly causes trouble for anyone who offends him. I tell you this because it's relevant to your request, as you will appreciate when you read on.

I can understand your need for a wife

and I don't find it at all strange that you should ask my help. I've heard of several other people from the colonies asking their families to find them suitable ladies to marry. We clergymen are particularly sought after for this sort of task, though I'm not sure we're any more omniscient about matchmaking than the next man.

I hadn't even begun to look around for a suitable lady when I chanced to meet Jacinta Blacklea, a young widow with a son nine years old. That would make him about the same age as your Christopher, I believe.

She's a poor relative of the landowner I mentioned earlier and he intended to treat her most cruelly. He wanted to take her son away from her and bring the lad up as his heir, while sending her out to the colonies to get rid of her. She was never to see the boy again.

She's a most loving mother, and this would have upset her dreadfully. And in any case, I'd not let Gerald Blacklea rear another child. His own daughter, to whom he'd planned to marry young Ben, is cowed and terrified of him, as is his poor wife.

I mentioned your need to Jacinta and showed her your photo. She welcomed the chance to leave the country, seeing marriage to you as the only way she and her son could get far enough away to escape Gerald Blacklea.

*I was impressed by her gentle nature
and her love for her boy. I also think it not
unimportant that she's a pretty woman
with a neat figure.*

*I have therefore used your money to
send her to Australia and will give her this
letter for you.*

*My dear cousin, I hope all goes well for
you, and that Jacinta Blacklea proves an
acceptable wife.*

*If you're not interested in marrying her,
it would be kind of you to help her find a
position as housekeeper or similar. I
believe these are in short supply in the
colonies.*

*Please write and tell me how things work
out.*

*Yours very sincerely,
Peter*

Mitchell couldn't move for a moment or two,
or even think clearly. At times he'd regretted
sending the letter to Peter, at other times he'd
hoped his cousin would know someone suitable.

Now it had happened.

What was she like, this lady Peter had sent?
Mitchell didn't care much about whether she
was pretty but he did care whether she was the
sort of person who'd look after his son, treat him
kindly and understand that his terrible experiences had made him rather quiet.

Would she be a good mother to Christopher,
when she had a son of her own? Would she be
able to love him as well as her own child?

270

He'd said in his letter to Peter that it'd be all right if she already had a child, but somehow he'd expected her to have a daughter not a son. How stupid of him!

He had a sudden, desperate wish that he'd not started this, and couldn't think what to do next.

His visitor's chair creaked and Mitchell turned round. 'I'm sorry. I was just . . . surprised that my cousin had found someone so quickly.' He held out the letter. 'Here. Read it.'

'You're sure?'

'Yes. You and she will want to know how much Peter has told me about her. No doubt you'll want to enlarge upon it.'

Quentin scanned the letter quickly. A good summary, but Nash was right. He needed to know more.

'You must be wondering about Jacinta.'

Mr Saxby said her name with such familiarity and yes, fondness, that Mitchell frowned. 'Well, yes. I wonder what would drive a lady to this extreme.'

'Desperation, to put it bluntly. Because of the way she was treated, first by her husband, then by his relative. Look, please feel free to ask me any questions you like. I travelled with two young widows, Jacinta and Mrs Prescott. We all grew to be close friends and now consider one another as honorary uncle and nieces, since none of us have any close relatives.'

'Oh?' He sounded surly, Mitchell realised, but it was a lot to take in, not only a woman sent out to be his wife, but another man growing close to her during the journey.

Mr Saxby studied him for a moment, then added quietly, 'I came out here to marry a lady called Harriet Seaton, who lives with Ismay and Adam Tregear. You might be acquainted with her?'

Relief ran through Mitchell and he felt ashamed of his suspicions. 'Yes, I am. She's a very pleasant lady. Congratulations.' He hesitated, then blurted out, 'I don't know what to say, let alone what to do next.'

His visitor smiled. 'Jacinta is feeling exactly the same, which is why she sent me to speak to you.' His smile faded. 'If you've changed your mind about finding a wife, you should say so straight away. You need have no concern about Jacinta's welfare. Harriet and I will take care of her and Ben.'

A moment before Mitchell had been wishing he hadn't arranged this, but perversely, he didn't now want to take up Mr Saxby's offer of stepping away from the bargain. He said so quickly before he could change his mind yet again. 'I do still wish to find a wife, so I'd like to meet Jacinta Blacklea. I just . . . don't want to rush into marriage. There's my son to be considered as well, you see.'

'Her son, too.'

'Yes. Her son, too. I'd never hurt a child, I promise you, and would do my best for him. Could we take this slowly: meet, get to know one another before we decide to go forward with it? The boys will need to meet one another, too. I'd be happy to pay the cost of their lodgings.'

'You're absolutely sure you wish to continue?

272

You don't sound all that certain. Jacinta has had one unhappy marriage and I'd not like her to rush into another.'

Mitchell stiffened. 'I'm not the sort of person to ill-treat a wife, but I do think it's wise to see if we suit before we agree to marry.'

'We'll do as you wish, then, but it'd be better if I paid for their lodgings, in case things don't go well between you. I wouldn't wish Jacinta to be under any further obligation to you than the cost of her fare to Australia.'

Quentin stood up and retrieved his hat. 'As I'm getting married shortly, I need to find a house to rent before we can do much else. I'll let you know where we're living. Jacinta and Ben will, of course, stay with Harriet and me.'

Mitchell seized on the one thing he did know about. 'There aren't a lot of decent houses to rent in Fremantle — or even in Perth. I do know of one which is about to be offered for rental, because I've been doing some work on it. But perhaps you'd like to find your own home?'

'I'd be grateful for any help you can offer. It's a very big undertaking, moving to a new country, setting up home there.'

'And . . . surely Jacinta and I could meet fairly soon?' Mitchell wanted to get that over with, not hang around waiting for other people to get married and set up house together.

Mr Saxby gave him another of those piercing looks that seemed to see right into his soul. 'I'll ask her if she'll agree to see you tomorrow.'

'I could take you all to see the house tomorrow, if it's still available. That'd be a good way to start, don't you think? Mrs Blacklea will feel safe with you beside her. I'll send a message to your boarding house if the house is still to let.'

'Thank you. I'd appreciate that.' Mr Saxby moved towards the door. 'Goodbye, Mr Nash.'

Mitchell escorted him to the gate and watched him walk away, letting out his breath in a long, groaning sigh as the tension of the meeting ebbed.

He'd handled that clumsily, he knew. But he'd been shocked to have a woman suddenly arrive in the colony. He hadn't expected Peter to find someone for him so quickly. He'd expected to receive a letter giving details, and be able to take his time about deciding whether or not to go ahead.

Take his time! He shouldn't try to fool himself. He'd already had several months to get used to the idea of a second wife and it still seemed strange to him. That was the worst thing, not being sure of what he really wanted.

He *needed* a wife, though. And Christopher needed a mother.

Perhaps that would be enough.

Perhaps he should just . . . do it. Marry her. At least then he'd be comfortable again, not living in a chaotic household, making do with unsuitable servants, while struggling to fill a mother's role as well as a father's.

★ ★ ★

Alf wasn't sure what he thought about Rory Flynn. Looking round the place showed that his new employer was a capable cowman. The beasts were well fed and sleek, the small farm Rory rented was kept immaculate out of doors and in, as were the cowsheds.

And Jilleen was an excellent housewife. She and Bridie seemed to get on well from the start, which was a good thing, because the wooden house they'd all be living in was little more than a hut.

As the day passed, Alf came to the conclusion that he'd never seen any women work as hard as those two did. Ruth had been lazy compared to them.

By teatime it had been decided that they would share the housework, but Jilleen would work on the garden, which she much preferred to cooking. Bridie seemed more than happy to take over the provision of meals.

As promised, Alf was given the 'sleepout'. The room made by enclosing one end of the veranda was tiny and narrow, with only just enough room for a single bed and his luggage, which had to be pushed under it before he could occupy the narrow space beside the bed. Bridie would have to sleep on the sofa.

Just before he went to bed, she caught him on his own. She glanced quickly over her shoulder and said in a lowered voice, 'Alf, I'd appreciate it if you don't say anything to my cousin about me having a bit of money. He's all right, Rory is, and he'll see I don't go hungry, but he'd take the money from me and pretend he was going to look after it. I'd never see it again and I'd be tied to working for him. He married Jilleen to get work out of her, I'd guess. He's changed so much, is so ambitious now, wants to be a rich man.'

'I won't say a word. It's not my business, anyway.'

She fiddled with the button on her blouse and said just as quietly, 'Might be your business one day . . . if you're interested.'

He stared at her longingly and the words came out before he could prevent them, 'I might be interested once I find my feet here.'

She let out her breath in a whoosh of air. 'I'd like that, so I would. We'd make a good pair running a pub, don't you think?'

He couldn't imagine anything better. Nodded. Sighed. Looked at her again. It'd be a dream come true, living with a woman like her and working at a job like that.

When she slipped her hand into his, he pulled her towards him and kissed her, hoping for more. She'd been a married woman, after all.

But as the kiss deepened and passion rose in him all too obviously, she put both hands on his chest and pushed away. 'No more. One kiss is enough. I'll not be giving myself lightly to any man, not even you, Alf. I did it once when I was a girl, and look where it landed me.'

He took a few deep breaths and stepped back. They stood looking at one another for a minute or two, then she turned and went into the house.

Once he was in bed, he lay awake for a long time, finding it impossible to sleep and cursing himself for saying he'd be interested in Bridie. It wasn't fair to her and she deserved better.

It was true in one sense, though. He wanted

very much to take her up on her offer. Oh, he did, definitely! Not just for her money, but for herself. He'd never wished for anything this much in his whole life before.

What would his uncle say to that, though?

And what would Mr Blacklea do if Alf didn't carry out the job he'd been given? That worried him a lot. The man was mad, everyone in the village knew that, and was quite capable of hurting Alf's family, as well as sending someone else to Australia to kill Mrs Blacklea and get hold of the boy. He'd try to get his own back on Alf while he was at it. Blacklea was noted for that sort of thing, which was why people feared him so much.

And where could you hide in a scrubby little place like Fremantle?

Western Australia was a real let-down. Alf couldn't understand why people would ever choose to come here. He'd have gone to London if he'd had any choice about where to live. He'd been there once when he was a lad, to see the Great Exhibition. His father had insisted on the whole family going on one of the shilling days. That had been the first time Alf rode in a train, first time he'd had a fizzy drink or an ice cream too.

He'd never forgotten that day, the best of his whole childhood.

★   ★   ★

When Quentin got close to Adam's house, he found himself walking more quickly, so eager was he to see Harriet again.

He knocked on the front door and Ismay came to open it. She gave him one of her delightful smiles and led the way to the back room, gesturing to a chair. 'How did you get on?'

He looked at Jacinta, not sure whether to speak of her affairs in front of the others.

'They know about Mr Nash,' she said quietly. 'Or at least, they know as much as I do about the arrangements. Which isn't much. What is he like?'

'He's very like his photograph and seems a decent sort of fellow.'

'Does he still want a wife?'

'It took him by surprise that you'd come out to Australia so quickly.'

'Does that mean he's changed his mind?'

'No. Just that he doesn't want to rush into anything.'

'Did you tell him why we left in a hurry?'

'Mr Stanwell had given him the gist of it in the letter. It'll be for you to share further details with him.'

Ismay leaned forward. 'I like Mitchell, Jacinta. And you're right, Mr Saxby, he *is* a decent sort of man. He's faced tragedy and rebuilt his life.'

'What's his son like?' Ben asked suddenly.

It was so unlike him to ask questions that Jacinta was surprised. But of course he'd be worrying.

'I didn't meet his son,' Mr Saxby said. 'He must have been at school.'

'Oh.'

'Christopher's a quiet lad,' Ismay said. 'But he

seems nice enough to me.'

Ben nodded. 'Thank you, Mrs Tregear.'

Quentin looked at Harriet. 'Mr Nash knows of a house to rent, and if it's still available, he's going to take us to look at it tomorrow.' When she nodded, he turned back to Jacinta. 'Living there with us would allow you to spend a little time with him, and gain a first impression of whether you like him or not. Would that suit you?'

'Yes. That'd be fine.'

'He's to send a message to our lodgings tomorrow morning. Eleanor, what about you? What are your plans?'

'Ismay's coming to pick me up tomorrow morning and she'll take me to see Linney, who is Dougal's housekeeper. I found her a very capable woman when my husband and I were staying there before. I'll leave a message to be given to him when he returns. Until then, I'll just have to wait.'

'If we take this house, you can stay with us, Eleanor.' He frowned. 'If there's room, that is.'

'If Aunt Harriet moves out of here, you can have her room,' Ismay offered.

'Are you sure?'

'Of course I am.'

'That's settled, then.' Quentin took out his silver pocket watch and opened the cover. 'My goodness, is that the time already? I think we'd better get back to our lodgings. Our landlady sounds very keen on people being on time for her meals.'

15

Mitchell explained to his son what had happened, and Christopher listened with his usual grave interest. Then he looked round the untidy room and smiled at his father. 'It'd be good to have the house clean and tidy again. Mother always kept things nice, even though we didn't have much money.'

'Yes. She was a good housewife, at least.' It always made Mitchell feel uncomfortable to talk about his late wife, but Christopher sometimes spoke about her casually and it didn't seem right to blacken Betsy's memory to her son.

'What if I don't like Mrs Blacklea's son?' Christopher's face clouded as he added, 'What if he's a bully?'

'We'll have to see what he's like. His mother seems very pleasant. I wouldn't put up with anyone bullying you, though.'

Christopher's voice was a near whisper. 'You might not know.'

'I'll keep a careful watch on how Ben behaves, I promise you. He's a little younger than you, anyway, so he'll probably be smaller. He'll be coming with us to see the house later this morning so that I can meet him as well as his mother.'

'If I could stay at home from school today, I could meet him too.'

Mitchell grinned at his son. 'Oh no, you don't.

You've missed enough school as it is. But I *will* introduce the two of you before I do anything about the situation. Then you can decide how you feel about him.'

When he'd seen his son walk off to school, Mitchell tried to smarten himself up. He was wearing a shirt which was clean but crumpled, because when he'd tried to do some ironing he'd scorched a couple of garments before giving up in despair. Mary had been about to do this task when she stopped working for him, so now he had only one nicely ironed shirt left.

He needed to find a laundress as soon as possible, and buy some new clothes as well. But he'd been so busy. And buying new clothes would probably mean him going into Perth, twelve miles up the river, and seeing a tailor, then going back for fittings. Then there was underwear to find, shirts to have made.

He had a sudden inspiration. He'd ask his friend Bram, who would know where to buy clothes. Maybe there were tailors and seamstresses in Fremantle.

A group of people was waiting for him outside the lodging house, chatting to one another. He stopped at the corner to study them: Mr Saxby, Mrs Seaton, a lad of about Christopher's age. The other lady must be *her*, Mrs Blacklea. She had blond hair and was looking nervous. But another younger woman came out of the house with Ismay just then, and he was no longer sure. No, the lad was blond too, so the first one he'd seen must be her.

Ismay caught sight of him and waved

281

cheerfully, so he had to move forward, feeling his stomach churn at the thought of this meeting.

Mr Saxby introduced him to everyone. The lady with Ismay was Dougal's Eleanor, it seemed. Which meant the other one was Jacinta Blacklea, as Mitchell had guessed. She and the boy bore a distinct resemblance to one another, not only in colour of hair, but in their features.

She didn't offer her hand, but stood looking at him, hands clasped tightly at her breast, her expression solemn, as if her emotions were under tight control. He guessed she was just as nervous about meeting him as he was about meeting her, and that made him feel slightly better. He wasn't interested in an insensitive woman.

'I'm pleased to meet you, Mrs Blacklea.'

'I'm pleased to meet you, too, Mr Nash. And this is my son, Ben.' She placed her hand on the boy's shoulder, as if for comfort. It looked a very familiar action, something she'd probably done many times before because Ben didn't pull away but gave his mother a quick smile.

Mitchell studied the lad, pleased to see that he had a neat, quiet look to him. You could usually tell the rowdy ones at first glance. The quiet ones weren't always as easy to understand, though, and it was important to him that Christopher get on well with any child who joined their household.

'I'm taking Eleanor to see Dougal's house,' Ismay announced in her usual cheerful way. 'We'll call in if Linney is there, otherwise we'll go back another day. Afterwards, I want to call in

282

and see Maura or she'll think I'm neglecting her.'

She turned to explain to the newcomers. 'Maura is Bram's aunt, but she's nearly the same age as him. She came out here to live at the beginning of the year. We're filling the colony with Deagans.'

The two women walked off, chatting before they'd gone even ten paces, and he wished he could talk to people as easily. But he couldn't, never had been able to.

He realised the others were all looking at him, waiting for him to show them the house, and dragged his mind back to that important matter. 'I have the door key.' As he took it out of his pocket, it caught the sun, the brass gleaming as if full of promise. He hoped that was an omen.

Mr Saxby turned to Mrs Seaton and offered her his arm. She took it with a glorious smile that made Mitchell blink in surprise. Suddenly he could see what she'd been like as a young woman — very pretty indeed.

Mr Saxby's smile wasn't that of an older man, either. The two of them were . . . could only be when they looked at one another like that . . . head over heels in love. The sight made him feel good and he was still smiling as he turned to Mrs Blacklea and copied Mr Saxby's gesture by holding out his arm.

As she took it, he could feel her hand shaking. He tried not to show that he'd noticed, but her nervousness pleased him rather than upset him. Betsy would have begun flirting with him. This lady stared straight ahead, swallowed hard and said nothing.

The lad began to walk at her other side. He didn't look at Mitchell, either. He seemed a sturdy child, with an open face and was about Christopher's height.

It was hard to think what to say. 'The house isn't far from here, Mrs Blacklea, but then nothing is very far away in the centre of Fremantle. Caswell Street is just off High Street, and lies between Adam and Ismay's house and mine.'

'And your timber yard? Is that far?'

There was a slight wobble to her voice. That pleased him too. 'No. My house is right next to it. I can show it to you afterwards, if you like.'

'I should be interested to see it.'

'I've never seen a timber yard,' Ben said suddenly.

'Then we must definitely visit mine.'

'Thank you, sir. I like to learn new things.'

'I shall look forward to explaining how I run it to you. My son loves to help out there.' He raised his voice. 'Turn right here, Mr Saxby.'

About fifty yards along the street, he called again, 'It's the next house on the left.' Everyone stopped in front of it.

★ ★ ★

The house was neat but smaller than Quentin was used to. He looked at Harriet, frowning, trying to gauge her reaction and she said quietly, 'Houses are generally much smaller here,

284

Quentin dear. Shall you mind that?'

'Not if you're in it.'

They exchanged warm smiles.

Mitchell let go of Jacinta's arm to open the door. 'Shall I lead the way?'

He waited till they were all in the house out of the sun, to say, 'There are four rooms, two on each side of the breezeway, a kitchen at the rear and a lean-to intended for a maid — if you can find one.'

'Is the servant situation so bad here?' Quentin asked in surprise.

'It is, but I know a maid who's looking for a place. She's the sister of Ismay's maid,' Harriet said. 'Tabby's only sixteen but she's been in service for two years already. Her present employers are moving across the country to Sydney and asked her to go with them, but she doesn't want to leave her family. She's a very willing girl, though how long she'll stay, however well we treat her, is anybody's guess. They marry young here and few women of any age are left unwed.'

Quentin saw Jacinta blush and stare at the floor in an effort to hide her embarrassment, poor thing. He didn't comment but went off with Harriet to explore each of the rooms and discuss how it could be used. After that they stood together by the kitchen window, looking out at the large garden to the rear. To his delight, a lemon tree was offering a few ripe and ripening fruits, and other plants seemed to be flourishing, though he didn't know what all of them were. He thought he might enjoy gardening, but someone would have to show him what to do.

The others hadn't yet joined them. 'Shall we go outside and stroll round the garden, my dear?'

'Good idea.' Harriet's eyes twinkled with amusement, probably because she'd guessed he was trying to give Jacinta and Mitchell time together to chat in privacy.

Ben had joined them and now asked, 'Can I come outside, too, Uncle Quentin? I'd like to look at the lemon tree more closely. I've never seen one growing until now. It's very different from an apple tree, isn't it? The leaves are nice and shiny.'

* * *

Dougal's housekeeper Linney wasn't in, which disappointed Eleanor. She'd written a letter to Dougal and was disappointed and yet relieved as well not to have to explain anything till he'd read her letter.

'I'll just push this through the letter box,' she said.

'We'll put it on the kitchen table with a note to Linney. I know them well enough to go inside. Most people don't bother to lock their doors here,' Ismay said firmly and led the way inside.

What memories it brought back to be in this house again! Eleanor had to stop in the hall to pull herself together. She half expected to see Dougal coming through a door towards her. Which was stupid.

'Come on!' Ismay called.

Eleanor went into the kitchen and waited while Ismay scrawled a message, saying this letter for Dougal was

VERY IMPORTANT INDEED

She'd written it in huge letters and underlined it twice. She finished with a swirling line and looked at Eleanor challengingly. 'Well, it *is* very important, isn't it? Important enough to bring you ten thousand miles from your home.'

'Yes.' Eleanor walked forward to lay her letter on the table next to the note.

Not content with that, Ismay weighed down the letter with a knife. 'We don't want it blowing away.'

'No. No, we don't.'

But Eleanor was quiet as they left the house and continued their walk. Leaving the letter had made it all seem so very real.

Surely he wouldn't have changed his mind?

* * *

Left alone with Mr Nash, Jacinta felt her face go warm again. It was years since she'd blushed so often. He must think her a timid fool. But she was determined not to let her nervousness prevent her from talking to him and trying to find out what sort of man he was.

He spoke first. 'This is typical of the houses here, with the passage acting as a breezeway through the middle to help keep cool in the hot weather.'

His tone was cool and impersonal, which sent a little shiver of apprehension down her spine. Claude had often spoken in just that chilly tone. She didn't think she could face a lifetime of men like that.

Mr Nash continued as if giving her a lecture, 'People sometimes build on lean-tos at the backs of their houses, if they need more space and have room in the garden. I'm starting to build such improvements for customers.'

She decided to turn the conversation back on to him. 'But your main income comes from the timber yard, doesn't it?' Then she suddenly realised how mercenary that might sound and tried to think how to correct it. But his expression had gone even more wooden, so she didn't dare because she might make things worse. She changed the subject. 'Tell me about your son.'

She could see Mr Nash immediately start to relax and when he spoke, his voice was warm with love.

'Christopher is ten. He's a quiet lad because he's seen some dreadful things. You know what happened with my wife?'

'Yes, Ismay told me. It must have been dreadful for you both.'

'It was. I try not to speak of it now and wish Christopher could forget it, but he still has nightmares occasionally.'

'Poor boy.' She tried desperately to think of something else to say.

Mr Nash seemed equally tongue-tied and at last said brusquely, 'Shall we join the others?'

'If you wish.' Did that mean he didn't like the look of her? Well, come to that, did she like the look of him? She did, because he was quite good-looking, better than she'd expected from the photo. Why was he having trouble finding a wife? Even if women were in short supply, he'd surely be one of the more successful gentlemen because he had a good business as well as looking attractive?

At the door, Mr Nash stopped to watch the older couple standing outside in the garden. They were chatting away to one another, looking completely at ease.

'Mr Saxby seems like a pleasant gentleman.'

She found it easier to talk about others. 'He is. And very kind. I'm so glad Mrs Seaton feels the same way about him. He was a little anxious about that.'

'She's well liked in the town, a kind and generous lady.'

Mr Nash didn't move outside so she waited and his next remark surprised her.

'Your name is unusual, and rather pretty.'

'Jacinta means hyacinth. It's one of my favourite flowers.'

He nodded and held the door open for her, so she had no choice but to lead the way outside. How little they'd found out about one another! How they'd struggled to find common ground.

Was it because they were both nervous or because they didn't feel at ease with one another?

She watched Ben talking to Mrs Seaton, waving his arms about wildly as he spoke. 'My husband hated Ben to get excited and used to scold him. But I like to see my son acting as a boy, not an old man.'

'Your husband was much older than you, I believe?'

'Twenty years older. It was . . . a marriage of convenience . . . and Claude was very set in his ways. But at least he gave me Ben. It's been worth everything to have my son.'

His voice was warmer. 'I feel the same way exactly about Christopher and his mother.'

'I'm looking forward to meeting your son. So is Ben. I wonder, could you tell Christopher that Ben isn't unfriendly, but he's quite shy with other children. He's never been to school, you see, and he wasn't even allowed to play with the other children in the village.'

Mitchell didn't try to hide his shock. 'Why did you decide on that rule?'

'I didn't. It was Claude's idea. To maintain our dignity, he said. I tried to change his mind about it several times. But opposition to my husband's wishes only made him bad-tempered, then Ben and I bore the brunt of his temper. In the end I stopped trying.'

The others had turned and were smiling at them, so there was no further chance to chat. And maybe it was as well, she thought. Their conversation had been strained and it worried her that Mr Nash hadn't really said much of importance. She'd been so nervous, she hadn't been much better.

In fact, she must have sounded stupid, which Claude had often told her she was.

★ ★ ★

Mitchell followed Jacinta across the unkempt garden, admiring her trim figure and graceful movements. What he liked most of all was the warmth of the smile she gave her son.

He realised the couple near the lemon tree were waiting for him to speak. 'Well, Mr Saxby, what do you think? Would you like to rent this house? I don't think you'll find anything better at the moment.'

'I must leave it to the ladies to decide.' Quentin looked at Harriet. 'What do you think, my dear?'

She chuckled. 'You can guess what I think, probably the same as you. We should take this house because we don't want to delay our wedding. We can look around for something bigger later on, perhaps, or even buy a home of our own, once you've settled in here.'

He beamed at her. 'I should certainly hate to delay our wedding.'

For a moment their eyes held and their love showed so clearly that Jacinta sighed in envy. She checked on her son, but he appeared to be watching a tiny lizard climb up the wall of the shed, dark grey against the silvered, unpainted wood, as delicately made as a piece of jewellery. He seemed hardly aware of what the grown-ups were doing, but his face was alight with interest in the little creature.

Please, she prayed, *let nothing quench that enthusiasm. Let my son enjoy his life from now on.* She realised Uncle Quentin was speaking and forced herself to pay attention.

'Perhaps you can introduce me to the owner, Mr Nash, so that we can make the necessary arrangements?'

'I'll take you to see his lawyer later today, if you like. I've just finished renovating the house and clearing it out for them. Oh, and the bits and pieces of furniture you saw in the sleepout were left by the owner. He and his family have moved to Sydney, so they're not likely to be living in the colony again. The lawyer asked me to dispose of them, but if you think they'll be of any use to you, it'd save me the trouble.'

'Yes, do leave them, please,' Harriet said. 'I brought a few of my favourite pieces of furniture to Australia but there isn't nearly enough to furnish a whole house.' She turned to her betrothed. 'We shall have to visit Bram's emporium, Quentin dear. He sometimes clears out houses and keeps the best pieces to sell.'

She hesitated then added, 'Don't tell him I said this, but the more custom we can give him at the moment, the better. He lost a lot of trade goods when they were damaged in a bad storm Adam ran into on his way back from Singapore and I think he's rather upset about it all. He's such a lovely man. Well, all the Deagans are delightful people. Bram and Ismay in particular have a real gift for friendship and happiness.'

Mitchell nodded. 'You're right about the Deagans. They've been very kind to me and my son. It's agreed, then, that you'll ask to rent the house. Now, if it's all right with you, we can walk back via my timber yard. Mrs Blacklea has expressed a desire to see it and I want to check with Tommy that everything is going well. He's a good fellow and a hard worker, but is still learning the trade.'

'I shall be very interested to see the yard,' Jacinta said.

'It'll be my pleasure to show you round it.'

As they strolled through the streets, Jacinta couldn't help noticing that Mr Nash's shirt was crumpled and his hair needed cutting. She wondered if she dared ask what his house was like and suggest they look round that too, but she didn't want to sound mercenary. It was so difficult, talking about personal details to a stranger, and yet they needed to know far more about one another before they risked getting married. At least, she did. A wife was so much at her husband's mercy, in law as well as in person.

She glanced sideways and again met Mitchell's gaze. This time he gave her a faint smile instead of a cool frown, and that gave her the courage to say, 'It's a difficult situation we find ourselves in, isn't it?' She held her breath, hoping her frankness hadn't upset him.

'Very difficult. I hadn't thought about how to proceed if some lady came here, just that I needed a wife and Christopher needed a mother. I'm not . . . good with words, either.'

'I think — ' She broke off, wondering if she dared say it.

'Please go on. I much prefer you to be frank with me.'

'I'd prefer both of us to speak openly.' She took a deep breath. 'I think we should get to

293

know one another before we do anything that's legally binding.'

His face showed only relief. 'I'm of the same mind.'

'And our sons . . . they should get to know one another as well.'

'You're right, Mrs Blacklea. I can tell how much you love Ben and I like to see that. I'd want a new wife to become a true mother to my Christopher. I also want him and your son to be happy about any new arrangements we make.'

'Good. Then the first thing is, I wonder if you would call me Jacinta from now on. I loathe the name Blacklea. I've been badly treated by two Blackleas, first my husband, then his terrible cousin.' She shuddered at the mere memory of Gerald Blacklea.

'Jacinta, then. And I'm Mitchell.'

She stumbled and he caught her arm. For a moment or two, they were close together and that was not . . . unpleasant. He smelled of soap and clean flesh, not of an old body in clothes which were changed less frequently than Jacinta had liked. Then Mitchell moved away and the moment was over. But still, it had been useful to know that she didn't mind being close to him.

'We're there.' He stopped and gestured to a piece of ground covered with neat piles of timber of various sizes.

She tried to pull herself together. It was as if she could still feel his touch. His hands had been warm on her arms, but not sweaty. She'd already noticed that although they were clean, his hands were quite rough, not those of a gentleman.

Claude's skin had been white and soft, his palms always a little sweaty.

It showed that Mitchell wasn't afraid of hard work.

Nor was she.

'It looks a well-organised place,' was all she could think of to say.

He nodded, seeming pleased by this remark, thank goodness. 'It was a mess when I bought it, but it's now in good order and I have a good man to help me look after it.'

She had been intending to tell him more about Gerald Blacklea and the ongoing threat to her life from Mr Walsh, but there wasn't time to do that now as the others started to comment on the yard.

Mr Nash didn't invite them to see his house. Perhaps it wasn't ready for visitors, so she didn't press to see inside. A man on his own might not keep things in good order.

She wondered if she dare ask Eleanor what it had been like when she and Dougal were alone together on his ship. Did they have trouble conversing? Or were they like Uncle Quentin and his beloved, chattering away happily?

Bram Deagan seemed particularly happily married. You could tell that at once. He'd smiled so warmly at his wife. He'd been very loving with his sister, too, and charming with Aunt Harriet, who was no relation to him.

And when she came to think of it, Ismay's voice softened whenever she spoke of her husband.

Facts had to be faced, however. Jacinta must

always keep in mind that she had only a little money left, was in a new country and needed to provide for her son. She couldn't be too picky, needed to find a breadwinner for them.

If she'd taken a dislike to Mitchell, she would have turned to Uncle Quentin without hesitation and asked his help, much though it went against the grain to be dependent on anyone's kindness and charity. But she hadn't taken a dislike to Mitchell. He seemed decent and polite.

As they parted company, Mitchell said, 'Would you like to come and look inside my house tomorrow? Just you, Jacinta?'

She was surprised, and thought it sounded, well, more hopeful. 'Yes, I would like to do that.'

He looked uncomfortable. 'It's not very tidy.'

Ah. She'd guessed right, then.

'Our maid left us without notice last week. Only, if you can forgive the untidiness, it should be easier for us to talk freely when we're not with other people.'

'It doesn't matter if the house is untidy. That's not important to me at this stage. I'd be happy to set it in order . . . if we come to an agreement. I'm not afraid of hard work.'

He frowned, opened his mouth, closed it again, then cleared his throat and asked, 'What is most important to you?'

'How you and I get on. How our sons get on with one another.'

He nodded, his relief showing in his face. 'I agree. I'll call for you at ten o'clock in the morning, if that's all right. If it's not too early?'

'I'm an early riser, so it's fine.'

She watched him walk briskly away. That invitation boded well, didn't it? He wanted to see her on her own.

She wanted to see him on his own, too, spend time with him.

16

Later that afternoon, Jacinta decided to go for a short walk. She'd grown very fond of the people she was living with, but felt she needed time on her own to think quietly about what she wanted to say to Mitchell the following day.

None of them liked staying in the boarding house's cramped rooms, and Ismay had invited them to spend their days at her house. But it wasn't a big house, so that still meant people were always around, chatting and asking questions.

At the moment, Ben was learning to play chess with Uncle Quentin and kept yelling in pleasure when he took a piece. Eleanor was altering another of the dresses she'd been given, while she chatted to Aunt Harriet, who was helping her with the easy bits.

Ismay had decided to go down to the docks to find her husband and intended to call at her relative Maura's house on the way back, then the two of them might visit her brother's Bazaar. Jacinta had been invited to go with them, but she'd declined.

'I think I'll go for a walk,' she announced after Ismay left.

'Do you want me to come with you?' Eleanor asked.

'No. I'll just walk up and down this street and the next. There always seem to be people

298

around, so I should be safe. I need to be on my own to have a think about . . . things. I won't go far. Is it all right if I leave Ben with you?'

'Of course it is.'

Jacinta walked slowly, enjoying the gentle warmth of the winter sun, enjoying being alone with her thoughts.

Not looking where she was going, she bumped into someone, letting out a squeak of shock as she realised it was Alf Walsh. He grabbed her arm to stop her running away.

She didn't want to make a scene and anyway, there were enough people in the street to make her feel safe. They'd come running if she shouted for help. 'Let go of me at once or I'll scream!'

He let go but continued to block her way. 'We need to talk, you and me.'

'We do *not* need to talk about anything.'

'Mr Blacklea sent me.'

She clutched her chest. She'd guessed correctly, then. 'I'm not giving up my son to that man, not for anything, and that's all there is to it.'

'You know what Mr Blacklea's like. He's rich and he always gets what he wants, one way or another. Look, if you let me take your Ben back to him, you can be sure the boy will be well looked after, because Mr Blacklea wants an heir. I'd leave you in peace and just tell the master you're dead. He'll never know it isn't true. You'll be safe then.'

There was a pause, then she asked in a choked voice, 'So he *was* paying you to kill me?'

Alf nodded, looking uncomfortable.

She asked the question that had been puzzling her. 'Then why didn't you let me fall over the side of the ship in that storm?' The memory of that incident was still giving her nightmares.

'Because I saw someone coming.'

'That's a lie. There was no one nearby. I'd have seen them first if there was. You were looking towards the sea; I was the one facing the ship's deck.'

His scowl deepened.

She looked at him in surprise and took a guess. 'You couldn't do it, could you?'

He gave the tiniest of shrugs. 'I'd rather not do it. Especially when we could easily come to an agreement about the boy. That way, everyone would be happy.'

'I wouldn't be happy. Nor would Ben. Not in that man's power. So I'm *not* giving up my son.'

'You'll lose him one way or the other if the master wants him.'

'Gerald Blacklea is ten thousand miles away and he's not master of anything here.'

'He's *my* master still, so I have to do as he orders. Look, I've got children of my own. If I don't obey his orders, they'll suffer. Little girls, they are. Three of them. And my family is living in one of his houses, as well as depending on my wages to buy bread. He'd make sure I got sacked if I went back without the lad. I *have to* take your Ben back, I tell you.'

Suddenly she lost all confidence in his inability to commit murder, staring at him in sick horror as the words sank in. He too was fighting for his children. That made him much more dangerous.

'Think about it. You'll see I'm right.' Alf stepped aside, waving her on.

She fled then, running down the street as if all the demons in hell were chasing after her, not caring that people stopped to stare.

Or perhaps it was just one demon called Gerald who was chasing her still.

But whatever the danger to herself, she wasn't going to send Ben back to *that man*. That would be to sentence her son to a miserable life. Far better to find herself a protector. Which probably meant marrying Mitchell Nash, or someone in an equally strong position in the community.

★ ★ ★

Alf went back to the farm, satisfied with his unexpected meeting. He'd come into town with Rory to bring the milk and learn the daily routine. Then Rory had said he had something to do and could they meet in a couple of hours?

Which left Alf free to explore the town and get to know it, which would no doubt come in useful. It'd been sheer good luck that he'd run into Mrs Blacklea today, though he'd have found her sooner or later. Oh, yes.

He'd made her what he considered a very fair offer, but would she even think about it? No, she damned well wouldn't. Yet she was young enough to have other children and what was so bad about letting this son go back to a life of luxury? The lad would be set up for life. Gerald Blacklea couldn't live for ever and then the boy would be rich enough to send for his mother.

Alf sighed and walked on, automatically taking note of the streets and businesses, learning his way round. What he saw made him feel more and more unhappy at the prospect of living in this small town, even temporarily. He hated the place. Hadn't wanted to come, couldn't wait to leave.

He saw one or two of the people from the ship and nodded, but didn't stop to talk, wasn't in the mood. Eventually, he wound up at the docks — if you could call such a small place 'docks'. He found a pub and went inside, ordering a glass of beer. It wasn't good to drink at this time of day, and he wasn't a boozer, but he was thirsty.

When he got into conversation with another man, he found a fellow sufferer, but this fellow had arranged to escape.

'I'm off to Sydney by the next ship. Sydney's much bigger than this dead-end hole. A man can make himself a fortune over there in New South Wales. And if that city is too big, there are all sorts of towns over there as well, not like here.'

'How will you get there?'

'By steamer. There's no road across the continent and anyway, it's two thousand miles away. It'd take for ever to get there, even if there was a road.'

'I'm not so fond of ships.'

'Me neither, but there you are. It's the only way to get anywhere from Western Australia.'

Alf pulled out his battered pocket watch and saw that it was time to meet Rory. He envied his drinking companion, envied anyone who was free to do what they wanted.

He was supposed to murder someone, and he didn't like the idea of that at all.

Then he'd have to travel all the way back to England, trapped on a ruddy great ship with a lad who didn't want to go and who would no doubt make a fuss.

Life wasn't fair. Some people had all the luck and power, while others had all the trouble.

★ ★ ★

Maria Blacklea sat in the sun in her sheltered place, feeling even more miserable than usual. She only dared come here when Gerald was busy. She'd had to spend so much of her life cowering in her bedroom, pretending to be an invalid, and that definitely wasn't fair.

Gerald had become even more bad-tempered since Jacinta had run away. Was it her imagination, Maria wondered, or was he not looking as robust as usual? She didn't dare stare at him, and as he no longer shared her bed, she didn't get a chance to see him without his well-tailored clothes. Thank goodness!

She frowned, trying to picture him at breakfast this morning. He seemed to have put on even more weight and it didn't suit him. He was a pig about food, always had been, eating far too much. Unless she was much mistaken, his belly looked to have puffed out. What did the French call it? *Embonpoint.* A polite word for fat.

Why had her family given her to a man like him? He must have some hold over them.

She sighed and closed her eyes, letting the sun

warm her skin, listening to the birdsong and the busy, gently humming insects.

This was the best time she ever spent, sitting out here on her own in the sun, without servants nearby to report on her doings to her husband. She didn't even dare spend more than a few minutes a day with her own daughter, because Gerald had chosen a strict governess and wanted Elizabeth brought up to be meek and obedient. He considered Maria far too soft with the child.

Even the strict governess was afraid of him and Elizabeth was utterly terrified of her father, didn't dare open her mouth when he was near.

Poor child! Her life wasn't very pleasant, and Maria was quite sure that Gerald would marry his daughter off one day to a man of his own ilk, so things wouldn't get much better.

Or, if he got hold of that boy, he'd bring Ben up in his own image before marrying him to Elizabeth.

None of it was fair and however hard Maria prayed, nothing ever seemed to improve. The main object of her prayers was that something better would happen for her daughter.

She didn't even plead with her Maker for herself. She had no hope whatsoever for the future. Gerald was a strong man and she was sure to die before him. She'd be glad to go, too, if it wasn't for Elizabeth.

★ ★ ★

Renting the house was arranged very quickly and Quentin decided to arrange a wedding equally

304

quickly, in fact as soon as they could purchase the furniture and oddments needed to move into the house. He was finding the boarding house with its strict rules, watery stews and greasy fry-ups very hard to take. And the landlady was always checking on them. Did she think they wanted to steal her worn old blankets?

Harriet was in full agreement with all his suggestions and when Jacinta came in just then, she told her what had been arranged. 'My main problem is what to wear for the wedding.'

'You should ask Eleanor. She has excellent taste in clothes and can alter things if you need her to. She made a big difference to my appearance.' She could feel herself flushing as she added, 'I was very shabbily dressed, because my husband wouldn't spend money on anything but books. He even resented what I spent on food and clothes for Ben.'

'That must have been hard,' Harriet said gently.

'Yes. That's why I must be more careful who I marry this time.'

'I like Mitchell Nash, if that's any help. And I'll take your advice about Eleanor.'

When they asked Ismay how to find furniture quickly, she said at once, 'You should go to Bram's shop first. You'd have to wait to have new furniture made, but he has a lot of second-hand things, good ones too, brought out from England or from the Orient.'

Harriet beamed at Ismay then turned to Quentin. 'Shall we do that, dearest?'

Before he could even nod, Ismay clapped her

hands and said, 'Let's all go. I know you're meeting Mitchell this morning, Jacinta, so Ben can come with us to look for furniture. I'm sure we'll all enjoy rummaging through the second-hand stuff at the back of the Bazaar. I've picked up some real bargains there.'

Ben was scowling at them, clearly not considering shopping a treat.

'You'll love the Bazaar,' she told him. 'Really you will. There are all sorts of strange things there, some of them from Singapore. It's a treat just to look at them.'

Jacinta managed to have a word with her son, apologising for not being able to give him even a few pennies to spend. 'If Mr Nash doesn't want to marry me, we'll need every halfpenny for necessities till we can make a new life. So neither of us can buy things we don't need.'

'I do understand that, Mother.' He stared down at his foot, tracing the pattern in the rug with the toe of his shoe. 'Father was mean, wasn't he?'

She answered honestly because neither of them had good memories of Claude. 'He was mean with everyone except himself. A very selfish man.'

'I won't be like him when I grow up.'

'You're not the selfish sort.' She gave him a hug. 'But you can look at what's for sale in the Bazaar and if things work out well for us, we'll go there and buy some things for the sheer pleasure of it one day.'

When the group arrived at the shop, they found Bram staring blindly into space, looking

306

downright miserable, but he pulled himself together when he saw them, greeting them with his usual friendly courtesy.

As they explained what they wanted, he brightened up considerably and led the way to the back of the shop.

Quentin was soon lost in admiration at the way Bram seemed to know where every single item they needed was located, and they quickly began to gather a collection of very suitable furniture.

Occasionally Bram was unable to find something they asked for, but if he couldn't supply it, he always seemed able to give them the name of another shopkeeper who might be able to help.

He certainly knew his job as a trader, telling them about the things that would be on his next shipment from Singapore, which Dougal was due to bring in any day now, and promising to make a list with them after the wedding of things they could order from Mr Lee, his partner in Singapore.

'Tell me the truth: do you mind having second-hand things?' Quentin whispered to his intended when they were looking through some smaller items together. 'Only, Bram says it'd take ages to order some new furniture and have it made.'

She hugged his arm, bubbling with excitement, not looking at all her age, he thought.

'I don't mind at all buying these things as long as I like the style of what we buy. Oh, Quentin, isn't it exciting putting a home together again? I thought I was past all this sort of thing, but I don't like living in someone else's house, even when it's people I love. I'd have been looking for a home of my own, even if you hadn't come after me.'

'That's good, then.'

'What about you? We won't be able to find somewhere as big and elegant as the house you were living in.'

'Anywhere will be home to me as long as you're there.'

She smiled at him so sweetly, he had to kiss her cheek and whisper, 'You're making me feel young again, my darling Harriet.'

★ ★ ★

It was Ismay who noticed that Ben had gone to stand outside the shop and was scuffing his feet in the rolled gravel that went all the way round it to provide a path for the night watchman to do his patrols.

She smiled. The poor boy must be tired of looking at pieces of dusty furniture. There was no sign of other children around the town. They were probably all in school.

He was a lonely child, she could tell, and it sounded as if he'd been brought up in a stupid way by that father of his. Fancy stopping a lad from playing with other children.

She went to stand beside him. 'Would you like to choose a book to read from Bram's shop?'

He looked at her as if she was speaking a foreign language.

'I've seen you with your nose in a book, but mine aren't really suitable for a lad your age. Bram has some second-hand books. I'll buy you one, if you like.'

His face lit up, then his smile faded and he said quietly, 'I don't think Mother would approve of that.'

'It's all right to give a friend a present, you know. It won't be an expensive book.'

He looked at her hopefully. 'Well . . . '

'Come and choose one.'

She watched the neat way he moved things about on the little stall, the way he checked the prices pencilled into the books, putting one aside regretfully after shaking his head at the price. She could tell he'd always been short of money. Well, it took one to know one, as Aunt Harriet said.

Ismay remembered being poor, she definitely did. But it must have been even harder to be genteel poor with a crazy father who wouldn't let you do anything.

She picked up the book he'd put regretfully aside. 'I think this one might be rather interesting.'

'It costs too much.'

'I'm not short of money, Ben, and I love to buy presents, so don't try to stop me. Do you like this book?'

He nodded, clearly torn between hope and good manners.

She turned to her brother. 'Bram darling, this boy needs a book or two. Come and tell me what to buy him. This one, I think, and what else?'

Ben tugged at her arm. 'One will be enough.'
'Oh, pish!'

Bram joined them and picked out a couple of other books. 'These are very popular with boys in the colony. No need to pay for them, Ismay. I don't like charging my own sister.'

'If I don't pay you, they won't be a present from me to Ben, will they?'

'Well, all right.'

Ben walked out clutching three books under one arm, his eyes bright and happy now. He kept looking down at them, and once his other hand went up to stroke the binding of the biggest book.

Ismay came away from their shopping expedition feeling thoughtful. When Uncle Quentin came to walk beside her, she said impulsively, 'My brother's worried.'

'I gather he's had a few financial reverses lately.'

'He could manage normally, because he always kept money in reserve. But that stupid ice works has eaten up his reserve.'

'Oh? Do tell me about it. Ice-making sounds like a good business proposition in a hot climate.'

'And so it would be if the man who started it knew what he was doing.'

'Tell me how it happened.'

'Ice helped save Bram's son's life when Arlen had a fever. But the owner wasn't making much each day and it was expensive. Bram thought if they could make it more cheaply and in bigger quantities, it might save other children's lives.

310

He's like that, my Bram is.'

'A kind man. It's very obvious.'

She beamed at him. 'Yes. It is, isn't it? Only the owner of the ice works isn't a very good engineer, for all his big talk, and poor Bram's had to pour in more money or lose his investment completely.'

'He needs to find a better engineer, then.'

She spread her hands in a gesture of helplessness. 'How do you do that here?'

'Ah. A big problem given the distance from everywhere. But if your brother needs a loan, I'm happy to help him. I'm quite comfortably circumstanced.'

'He won't take it. I've offered him some money. I've a little saved myself from the housekeeping. Adam's so generous with it. But Bram says I may need my savings one day. What does 'one day' matter if my brother needs money now? He does so much for other people. Why won't he let anyone help him?'

'He seems to have a gift for making friends. I hear nothing but good of him. But perhaps he wants to sort this out himself.'

'Well, I think he's being stupid. He's a lovely fellow, but Deagans can get very pig-headed, especially the men.'

With a sigh, she changed the subject, because what could you do with a stubborn Irishman like her brother except leave him to go his own sweet way?

★   ★   ★

311

Mitchell arrived outside the boarding house at ten o'clock promptly. Jacinta was ready and went out to meet him, hoping things would go better between them today.

He didn't smile, just gave her one of his little nods and offered his arm. 'I — um, hope you slept well, Jacinta.'

'Not very. I'm suffering from a lack of something to do, so I'm not really tired when it's time to retire. And I can't read in bed because that would disturb Eleanor. I'm used to being busy, you see.'

'How did you fill your time . . . before?'

'It filled itself. I didn't have help in the house during the last year or two, so there were never enough minutes in the day. I didn't have much help before that, either, if truth be told. And I was trying to teach Ben as well as do the housework.'

'But you had help with the rough work, surely?'

'Not during the last two years. Claude lost our money through a series of stupid investments, you see, so we couldn't afford to hire a maid, though there was always money for him to buy books.'

'That must have been hard.'

'At least I didn't get bored.'

He smiled. 'And you're bored now?'

She could feel herself flushing. 'It sounds ungrateful, doesn't it? Only I like to keep busy.'

'I do too.'

He looked at her with what seemed to be approval, then said quietly, 'I can provide my wife with a maid or two and any extra help needed. I'm not looking for someone to spend all her time doing housework.'

'What exactly are you looking for in a wife?'

'A companion, a helpmeet really. I need someone who'll organise the domestic side of my — our life.' His step faltered for a moment, then he added, 'You must have noticed that my shirt hasn't been ironed. I'm ashamed to appear like this. I did try to do some ironing when the maid left suddenly, but I don't have the knack for it, and after I'd scorched two shirts, I abandoned the attempt. I was going to find a laundress, but I've been so busy and then, well, there you were. The best you can say of my own and my son's appearance at the moment is that we're clean.'

'I could iron your shirts for you today, if you like.' He was silent for so long she wondered what she'd said wrong.

'That's very kind. I ought not to accept that sort of help from you until we . . . decide what to do, but I'm desperate and if you could do some ironing, I'd be most grateful. I don't mind so much for myself, though it doesn't look good for a man in my position to be so untidily dressed, but I mind very much for my son. The other boys at Christopher's school are much better turned out than he is. *He* doesn't care whether his shirts are ironed, but I do. The problem is, he gets them dirty so fast.'

She laughed. 'Ben is the same. He seems attracted to mud and dirt, or else they throw themselves at him.'

Mitchell smiled down at her, a warm smile

this time. He was much better looking when he smiled like that. Why had she not noticed that before? Because she'd been so nervous, that's why. But she was feeling less nervous now.

They turned a corner and he stopped to gesture to their left. 'This is my house.'

The wood it was built from was raw and new, and it was bigger than the one Quentin would be living in. She liked the balanced look of it, though.

'It's not finished off inside, because I keep getting jobs to do for clients, and they must come first, as must feeding and caring for my son, but I'm gradually getting things sorted out.'

The garden in front of the house was small, with no fence as yet and no plants in it, only bare, sandy ground.

He stopped at where the gate would be, gesturing to her to go ahead, but she paused briefly to study the front of the house. 'I like the balance and symmetry.' That won her another smile.

'I do too.'

The short path led to two broad wooden steps going up to the veranda. She laid one hand on the reddish wood of the little fence along the side of the steps and veranda — well, it would be a fence when it was finished, she supposed, but at the moment it had only the sturdy upright posts and the crosspieces along the top.

He moved ahead of her to unlock the front door. 'Some people don't bother to lock their doors, but I prefer to be careful. Please come in.'

She walked through shafts of sunlight shining

314

through narrow windows to either side of the front door, and that felt like an unspoken welcome.

'If I could find someone to do stained glass panels, I could make the hall much prettier,' he said. 'At the moment the windows just do the job of letting light in.'

'Stained glass would be lovely.'

He led her round four rooms downstairs, three bedrooms upstairs and some echoing attics with timber posts here and there. 'I'll put in the dividing walls up here one day, but they didn't seem as important as the rest of the house.'

When they went down again, he took her into the kitchen which he'd only pointed to before.

'I saved this area till last on purpose. My brother's an architect and he's been sending me magazines, sketches and brochures from England, so that I can keep up with how modern houses are being built. I tried to incorporate some of the recent improvements to domestic amenities into this part of the house.'

'The magazines must be very interesting.'

'Yes. I managed to order the equipment to set up a bathroom and laundry at the rear of the house. The things have to be shipped out from England, of course, but in the meantime I've installed hot and cold water taps in those two rooms.'

'That seems a great luxury to me.'

'An absolute necessity, to my mind, now that I've tried to keep myself and my son clean without help.'

He opened a door to one side of the kitchen

and showed her the laundry and storerooms, which formed a right angle with the main house. All the rear rooms looked out on to the garden, or what would be a garden one day. It was a sandy desert at present.

She was struck dumb as she realised how much she wanted to live here. If the quiet, spacious rooms of the house reflected the character of the man, then there was something wholesome about both of them. Wasn't there? Surely she couldn't be that wrong about him?

Most of the rooms they'd looked at had been unfurnished and she'd love to help turn them into a home. Then she chided herself. She mustn't rush into this, for Ben's sake. It was a man she was marrying, not a house, however lovely it was.

She'd said she would be honest with him, though, hadn't she? He was looking at her with a guarded expression, waiting for her to comment.

'I'd have thought myself in paradise if I'd had facilities like these. What a beautiful house this is! And the bathroom is an excellent idea. Imagine not having to lug buckets of hot water to fill a bath then empty it all out again afterwards.'

His face brightened. 'I'm hoping people will like it. I'm thinking of shipping bathroom equipment out from England and setting up a business. Sanitation and the supply of water inside houses are by way of being an interest of mine and I'm sure it's a field that's going to expand.'

'What a clever idea! I should think ladies will

be queuing up at your door to ask you to install bathrooms and proper laundries for their families, especially if maids are as difficult to find as people tell me.'

His face had completely lost the tight expression, so she could tell how pleased he was by her reaction to the house he'd built with such love and care.

'Would you like a cup of tea, Jacinta? I can get the fire burning quickly and the water in the kettle should be warm already from sitting on top of the stove.'

'I'd love a cup of tea. And while we drink it, there's something I must tell you about myself before we . . . go any further.'

His frown returned and her heart sank, but she couldn't leave it any longer to warn him about her problem with Gerald Blacklea and the man he'd sent to kill her. Who knew when she'd bump into Alf again? Or what the man would do when he accepted that she wasn't going to give her son away?

Once they were sitting at the kitchen table, she sipped her tea, but couldn't swallow more than a mouthful. Taking a deep breath she tried to keep her voice steady as she said, 'It wouldn't be fair to you and your son if I didn't tell you about the trouble that's followed me to Australia.'

'Trouble?'

She nodded and told him about Claude, his cousin Gerald and the pursuit of her and her son by Alf.

'The man tried to push you overboard!' Mitchell exclaimed when she'd finished her tale.

'Why didn't you complain? Have them arrest him?'

'I couldn't have proved it. It looked as if he'd played the hero and saved my life. They *congratulated* him!' She couldn't help shuddering and was surprised when Mitchell laid his warm, strong hand over hers.

She looked up, dreading to see scorn and disbelief on his face, unable to hold back a sob when she saw only compassion. 'You believe me, then?'

'Oh, yes. Not many people could act the part of a distressed mother so convincingly, only a professional actress, I think. And anyway, you don't have a lying face. Nor does your son.'

She gave him a watery smile. 'No. Ben is more likely to offend someone by blurting out the truth than by lying.'

'My Christopher's the same. Look, I'm glad you told me about your problem. I need to feel you'll be honest with me.'

'Your wife wasn't.' It wasn't a question, merely a statement of fact.

'No. But I don't think you're a liar.' He hesitated, frowning as if searching for words.

'I'm not, if I can help it, though I had to lie sometimes to Claude to protect Ben from him.'

He gave her a wry look. 'I'd lie too, to protect my son.'

She waited but Mitchell didn't say anything else, so she stood up. 'I'd better be getting back. And . . . you'll need to think about what to do next, about us.'

'I don't, actually. I needed to talk to you, get

to know you a little better without a crowd of people around.'

'One private meeting isn't enough to get to know one another well, surely?'

'No. But it's enough to come to a decision. Your need for a husband and protector is urgent and my need for a wife is urgent too.' He gestured to the untidy kitchen. 'Though not as urgent as yours, obviously.'

She continued to wait, letting him speak at his own pace.

'It seems quite clear to me now, Jacinta, that if we're going to marry, we need to do it as quickly as possible, so that I'm better able to protect you.'

He took her hand in his. 'In fact, we should get a special licence and marry immediately.'

It was the last thing she'd expected to hear today and she could only stare at him in open-mouthed shock.

17

Bridie came to stand in front of Alf after he'd finished his work for the day. Arms akimbo, unsmiling, she said, 'We'll go for a walk, just you and me. We need to talk.'

Rory looked across at them sharply. 'There'll be no messing around with my cousin.'

She swung round to glare at him. 'I'll do my own telling about what to do and not to do when it comes to my life, and that includes my dealings with men, Rory Flynn.'

'Not when you're living under my roof, you won't. And not after what I've just told you.'

'I'll move out tomorrow, then.'

'And I'll go with her,' Alf said at once.

For a moment she and Rory stared at one other, then his wife laughed. 'She's right, you know, Rory. She's a widow, not a young girl, and she knows what she wants. You'll have to trust her to be careful.'

'Well, I won't be supporting someone else's get.' He patted an imaginary belly suggestively.

'I wouldn't ask you to support me,' Bridie snapped, then her face grew sad. 'Not that it'd be necessary, more's the pity. If I didn't fall for a child in all the time I was married to Perry, who liked his bed play as well as any man, let me tell you, then I can't see me falling for a child now.'

'He could have been the one unable to get

320

children, so just be careful what you do,' Rory said.

'You must think I'm stupid, and I'm not.' She held up one hand to stop him as he opened his mouth to speak. 'Oh, I will be careful, don't worry. But not at your telling. Come on, Alf.'

He followed her outside, not happy to be ordered around by a woman. Once they were away from the house, he pulled her into his arms and gave her a sound kissing, which took a lot of the anger out of her.

She sighed and nestled against him for a moment or two, then pushed him away.

He knew better than to try to force her. She was a determined woman and anyway, he both liked and respected her. A strange thing for him, that. He didn't usually pay much attention to females and what they said.

'Who was that woman you grabbed hold of in Fremantle?'

'How the hell did you know about that?'

'Rory saw you and stopped to watch. He said you were talking to her for a while and you both looked as if you knew one another.'

Alf was so surprised he couldn't think straight for a moment or two, then he took a deep breath. He thought of telling Bridie to mind her own business, but he couldn't do it. Instead, he took a deep breath and said, 'Let's go and sit on that fallen tree trunk. I need to tell you a few things.'

When they were seated, he took hold of her hand, just to give himself courage and patted it gently as he tried to think how to tell her. He couldn't find an easy way, so said bluntly, 'I've been sent to Australia to kill someone.'

The hand jerked in his and her voice was only a scratch of sound. 'You've *killed* someone?'

'No. I could have done it on the ship, I definitely had the chance, only I couldn't kill her.'

'Who?'

'Mrs Blacklea, one of the cabin passengers.'

'The blond lady with the nice young son? Why would you kill her?'

He let go of her and buried his face in his hands, so that his words came out muffled. 'What am I going to do, Bridie? What am I going to *do*?'

She put her arm round his shoulders. 'You're going to tell me the whole tale, from start to finish.'

'You'll hate me and I don't want that.'

'I don't think I *can* hate you, Alf Walsh.'

'For a start off, that's not my real name. I'm Alf all right, but it's Alf Pearson, and . . . and I'm married with three children. Only they're all in England.'

Breath whistled into her mouth and she moved away, punching him in the arm. 'So you're just like the rest of them. You've been playing me along for what you could get.' She sobbed and began to hit out at him, arms flailing.

He caught her hands, pulling her close to him, looking her straight in the eyes. 'I haven't been playing you along, Bridie. I wouldn't. I couldn't. I like you more than anyone I've ever met, and I

322

wish I'd known you before I got married, because then I might have married you and been happy. Some people are happily wed. I've seen them. Not many, though.'

'I wasn't all that happy. Oh, I wasn't *unhappy*, but Perry and me, well, we just rubbed along, working together. He was a nice man, but not . . . exciting.'

'Ruth isn't nice. I don't even like her. She's a right old shrew, she is. Nag, nag, nag. I don't want to go back to her. If I could do as I wanted, I'd stay in Australia with you.'

'You still haven't told me why you agreed to kill Mrs Blacklea?'

'I didn't get much choice.' He told her about Mr Blacklea and his Uncle Bernard, how they'd forced him to come on this mission to Australia. When he'd told her everything he could think of, he sat silently, expecting her to tell him to get out of her life.

Only she didn't. She took his hand in hers again and kissed it absent-mindedly. 'How could they think you a killer? You're an old softie. I bet those horses loved you and you fed them treats on the sly.'

He smiled. 'How did you know?'

'I've been working in a pub for years. I've seen a lot of men come and go, and I reckon I can tell a good 'un from a bad 'un.'

'I'm not good! I don't even go to church if I can help it.'

'Not goody-goody, like in church. They're too soft, them lot are. Like a flock of bloody sheep, doing as they're told. I bet you didn't beat your wife, even when she nagged you, and I bet you're good in bed.'

He wriggled uncomfortably, not used to hearing a woman say such things.

They sat in silence, then she said thoughtfully, 'If you could have what you wanted — '

'But I can't!'

'No, listen. If you could do what you wanted, would you choose to be with me from now on?'

'Oh, yes.' And then he said them, the words he'd never expected to use to any woman, 'I love you, Bridie lass. Surely you can tell.'

She searched his face, her eyes anxious, then softening at what she saw there. 'That's all right, then. I've grown fond of you, too, Alf.'

He could only squeeze her hand in response, or he might let the tears in his eyes spill out and how would *that* look, a grown man crying for what he couldn't have?

'Well, I believe in fighting for what you want, so we'll have to plan what to do so that we *can* be together. I'll come up with something, don't you worry. My whole life depends on it.'

He stared at her in amazement. 'You'll . . . take me as I am? A married man?'

'Heaven help me, yes. I'm not a good enough person to send you back to them. *I* want you for myself. And once we're sure of our plan, we'll tell Rory we're going to get married. Though what he'll say about it, I don't know.'

'He'll be angry. He doesn't think much of me. Look, there's one thing I heard that might help.' He told her about the man he'd met in the pub who was going to Sydney.

324

'There. I knew you weren't stupid, Alf. That's what we'll do, go to Sydney. I've heard it's a much bigger city than Perth, and it's far away from everyone who knows us. We'd be much better going there than staying here, because they knew you were coming here. But we'll have to work out the best way to do it and we'd better change our names.'

'I'd like to do that, I really would, but it doesn't solve my problem, which is the main reason I came here. I don't want Mr Blacklea hurting Ruth and the girls when he finds out I've not done what he wanted. It'd lie heavy on my conscience, that would.'

He remembered his eldest daughter, Callie, and told Bridie about her. 'She's my favourite. Eight years old and a real charmer. What if Blacklea kills her? Or turns them all out of the house and tells them to get off his estate? She could starve to death, or be put in the poor house, which is nearly as bad.'

Bridie stared at him thoughtfully. 'Would your uncle let that man hurt your family? From what you said, he looks after his own.'

Alf frowned. 'I don't know. He might let it happen if he found out I'd run away with you. He's got a temper on him, Mr Blacklea has, you see. Used to frighten me senseless when I was a kid, he did.'

'Then we'll have to make sure he doesn't find out what we're doing. I *will* find a way for us to be together, Alf.' She looked round and stiffened. 'That Rory's spying on us. Look at him watching us. Well, he's not taking over my life.

He's grown sharp and cunning since he came to Australia. If I'd known how he'd changed, I'd not have come to join him.'

They stared across the paddock to where her cousin was sitting outside his house, perched up on his cart to get a better view of the two of them. Rory wasn't attempting to hide, was making sure they knew he was watching them, making sure Alf didn't play around with his cousin.

'Leave it to me to do the rest of the planning,' she said again. 'I'm good at sorting out details.'

'All right.' Alf smiled suddenly. 'How about we give your cousin a little show?'

'What do you mean?'

'Let's have another kiss or two.'

She grinned. 'Why not? It'll drive Rory wild. But kisses are all you're getting from me, Alf, till I trust you enough to go further. And that'll be *after* we've got everything settled and have started pretending we're married.'

He couldn't blame her, even though he wanted her so much, he felt uncomfortable.

As they strolled back towards the house after a few kisses, he admitted to himself that the only thing he knew for certain was that he wanted her more than he'd wanted anything in his whole life. He didn't want to hurt his family, but he did want to leave them behind, especially Ruth.

Was Bridie right? Could they find a way to do it? Or was he fooling himself?

Damn Blacklea! And damn his Uncle Bernard, too, for getting him into this mess!

Dougal McBride stood on the deck of his ship, enjoying the warm breeze on his face. The *Bonny Mary* had made good speed from Singapore, probably the fastest trip back to Western Australia he'd ever made. Another couple of days should see them arriving at Fremantle. He was looking forward to getting home again, even if it was only for a short time.

He hoped Adam was having a good journey too. He should be well on his way back to Singapore by now. They'd probably passed each other en route, as usual, without knowing when it happened.

There would be a message from his partner waiting for him at Fremantle, and Dougal left messages for Adam in each port, too.

If only there were a system for sending telegrams to one another across the vast distances of the ocean. The first telegram had been sent in Western Australia the previous June, and typically, it had happened more than fifteen years later than the first one sent in Australia.

But the West Australian line only spanned the twelve miles between Perth and Fremantle. New lines had been authorised in June to other regional towns, but it would all take time. They still wouldn't be able to send telegrams overseas.

He sighed. New things took so much time to set up in Australia. People in Britain simply didn't understand how big the distances were.

He and his partners owned three ships now, one going from Singapore to Sydney, with his brother-in-law Josh as captain, the other two going from Singapore to Fremantle. You could make good money in a country hungry for trade goods.

They didn't allow themselves long turn-arounds at either end of the journey, even Adam who had a charming young wife. All the partners were hungry to make money: himself, Adam, Josh, Bram — yes, and Mr Lee, their Singapore partner. Having money made you feel safe, let you look after your family in comfort, opened many doors.

The desire to make money was one reason many men left England for the various colonies. Dougal reckoned it was because they wanted to try their luck in a country that wasn't crammed with people who'd already made their fortunes and weren't making it easy for others to follow in their footsteps.

That brought the inevitable question, the one that always insinuated itself in his mind when he thought of his future. What was he making the money for? Or rather, *who* was it for?

Nowadays he had a much firmer answer to that old question when he asked it: it was for Eleanor. He wanted to be able to support a wife in comfort and, he hoped, a few children too, if they were blessed. But it all depended on Eleanor trusting herself to him.

Would she come all the way to Australia to marry him once her husband died? That was the big, unanswered question. And the big hope in his heart.

Dougal couldn't stop worrying about her. It'd

been many months now since he'd left her and her husband in Suez. Surely he couldn't have been mistaken about her feelings for him? Or about her husband not making old bones?

No, he hadn't been mistaken about Malcolm Prescott, of that he was absolutely certain. There was no way the man could still be alive. He'd had the look of death and been so skeletally thin, Dougal had wondered if he'd even survive to reach England. That look was unmistakable.

But why was he going over the same old ground again? Picking at it like an unhealed sore.

He was a fool, that's why, a stupid romantic fool. He'd reached the age of forty without falling in love, and now he'd fallen very hard indeed.

'Come back to me, my lovely Eleanor,' he whispered into the wind. 'Please, come back to me.'

★   ★   ★

Jacinta realised she was still sitting at the table, but didn't remember whether she'd answered Mitchell or not. She looked across and saw him gazing at her with one of his wry smiles. She was beginning to like those smiles.

'I thought for a moment you were about to faint. Are you all right?'

She nodded. 'Yes. Sorry. I was just . . . shocked.'

'Why? After all, you came out to Australia to marry me.'

'Yes, but I thought we'd get to know one

another first. I didn't think you'd want it to happen so quickly.'

'I don't think you can afford to wait. You're not safe living in a boarding house, and if you're to become my wife, of course I want to be able to protect you. This place I've built' — he gestured round — 'is very secure. Probably more secure than is necessary, but my house in England was burgled once and I vowed no one would get into my house again without a lot of trouble. I also have good neighbours in this street. They watch out for one another. I know that already, too.'

She liked the sound of neighbours keeping an eye on one another.

He stared down at the table and said in a low voice, 'Or have you changed your mind about marrying me? I won't make a fuss if you have.'

She felt heat surge into her cheeks. 'I've not changed my mind. It's just that I wanted time to get to know you before we . . . well, shared a bed.' She shivered, as she always did at the memories of sharing a bed with Claude. How she'd hated it!

He stared at her, head on one side. 'Was it very bad, your marriage?'

She closed her eyes on the images that twisted before her, wasn't able to clear the memory of Claude's early assaults on her body from her mind. He'd hurt her, and mocked her while doing it. She'd felt dirty every time he touched her in that way, however much she washed herself afterwards.

And yet, from that sordid activity had come

her son, the light of her life.

Mitchell took her by surprise again. 'That worry is easily settled. We don't need to share a bed, or even a bedroom, until you feel ready for it.'

'You'd wait to consummate the marriage?'

'Yes. And I'd make sure you enjoyed love-making. A caring man can do that for his wife.'

She didn't see how anyone could enjoy it, but didn't say so, because she was sure it needn't be as bad as Claude had made it. 'Why would you wait?'

'Because I want a good marriage this time, a partnership with someone who will enjoy life by my side, and stand by me in the bad times. I think you're that sort of woman.'

'I don't abandon those I love.'

'Not even when it puts you in danger, as it has with your son. I like that. I want a woman who will love and care for *my* son, and who will, I hope, one day give me more children. I'm not just looking for bed play, Jacinta, but for a lifetime together. If we need to take our time laying the foundations for that, so be it.'

'I would like another child or two,' she admitted. She'd dreamed of a daughter, even chosen a name for her: Katie.

She looked at Mitchell again, feeling as if she was seeing him for the first time. He had steady grey eyes, but they weren't cold now. They had warmth and kindness in their depths. She felt safe with him, and he'd even convinced her that it might not be too bad to share his bed one day.

'I will, of course, care for your son as if he were mine, Jacinta. I like children, you know. Ben would be part of *my* family too.'

And suddenly she was weeping again, tears of relief, tears of hope, tears of cleansing.

He took her in his arms, his expression concerned. 'What have I said? What's wrong?'

'I'm just . . . happy and relieved,' she managed. 'All the way to Australia, I've been worrying about meeting you. All those weeks.'

He cradled her against him, rocking her slightly. 'Oh, if that's all, then cry away. I'm relieved too, you know. I was worried Peter might send someone I didn't like. But I do like you, and I think we'll do well, especially if we give ourselves time to grow together.'

She let him hold her for a moment or two, because it felt so good to be looked after, even in a small way. She couldn't remember the last time anyone had comforted her or held her close, not since Ben had been very small and had loved his cuddles.

Surely she would be all right with this kind man?

When she pulled away, Mitchell let her go, taking out a crumpled but clean handkerchief and offering it to her with a little bow.

She mopped her tears, laughing with him at her own silliness in crying because she was happy.

'Now, there's just one other thing,' she said when she felt calmer. 'Can you please find me those shirts that need ironing, get the stove hot and produce your flat iron. I refuse point-blank to get engaged to a man wearing a crumpled shirt.'

His chuckle melted something inside her still further.

Hope filled her instead, warm lovely hope. And though she didn't dare trust it completely, it did touch a corner of her heart and lodge there.

★   ★   ★

Quentin had to go up to Perth to complete the necessary paperwork to get a special licence for the wedding. It seemed a chancy business here how you got married, with the rules and requirements not always being adhered to. However, the clergyman he'd spoken to had insisted on doing things properly, adding darkly, 'unlike some'.

Thank goodness for the little paddle steamer that chugged up and down the Swan River between the capital and its port. For a fee of one shilling and sixpence, Quentin was able to ride in comfort up the river to Perth, enjoying the scenery, the small headlands, the places where the river widened, the dusty colours of the vegetation.

When he got back to Fremantle that afternoon, pleasantly surprised that he'd been able to do everything necessary in the one day, Quentin decided to pop into the Bazaar to see if he could find a present for his bride-to-be.

Once again, he found Bram standing staring into space, looking utterly miserable. This time he decided to be blunt, because he really liked

Ismay's brother. In fact, Quentin didn't know when he'd taken to a man so quickly.

'Come and talk to me about what's troubling you, Bram. As a lawyer, I'm used to helping people.'

Bram jerked round in shock. 'Sorry. I was miles away. And you don't want to be bothering with my problems.'

'I do. The people I've made friends with seem very strongly linked to your family, so since I don't have any close family, I intend to act as an honorary uncle to all of your generation.' He laid one hand on his companion's arm. 'Tell me about it, Bram. A trouble shared is a burden halved, in my experience.'

Still Bram hesitated, then he said in a voice more strongly marked by an Irish accent than usual, 'Will we go into my office at the back? I can't talk here.'

'Wherever you're comfortable.'

When they were seated, with the door shut, Bram began fiddling with some lists.

'Well? What's upsetting you?' Quentin spoke in a gentle but firm tone of voice he'd found worked well with young lawyers articled to him to learn their profession. They could so easily get themselves into a tangle through inexperience. Bram might be older than them, but he was young in experience of the business world, while Quentin had been successful in investing his own and clients' money for many years.

'It's the ice works that's my problem. I invested money in it, didn't I? I wanted to expand it, because ice can help people lower a high fever. It helped my son, ice did, helped save his life. I didn't want other children to die for lack of ice when they run out of it, as they do quite early in hot weather.'

He sighed and closed his eyes for a moment. 'I was a fool. Dazzled by what I'd done as a trader, thinking I had the golden touch with everything.'

'And . . . ?'

'Chilton at the ice works was very convincing. He said he needed money to manufacture better parts and make bigger machinery, so they wouldn't run out of ice. So I lent him some money, taking a share in the company in exchange. It's the only one in this part of Australia, after all. I thought it would make money for me, not a lot, but a steady trickle. Only he's not as competent as he made out. No, not nearly as competent.'

Another silence, another gentle, 'And . . . ?'

'Chilton may know how to make ice with other men's machinery, but he doesn't seem able to create machinery of his own. I've paid him more and more, money I could ill afford. He's been bringing parts across from Melbourne because he said there was no one to make them here in the west. And the new machinery still doesn't work properly. It's making more ice, but it keeps breaking down every few days.'

'He sounds completely incompetent.'

'He can't make efficient machinery, that's for sure. He's not a *bad* man, not trying to defraud me. At least, I don't feel he is. Only, when do you stop throwing good money after bad? When do you write off everything you've invested? I think

I'm at that stage now. Except we're making a little money here and there. But not enough. How can I be sure what to do? And then, to cap it all — ' He broke off, his face twisting with anguish.

Quentin took a guess. 'You lost most of your cargo in the storm.'

'Yes. It'd have set me right, that cargo would. You can make a lot of money here if you supply the right goods. But most of my goods got damaged. I won't make enough from them to pay my bills and order more.'

'Let me talk to a few people, Adam for a start.'

Bram flushed. 'I've not told them how bad things are.'

'You can't hide it for ever. And they know something is wrong.'

'I suppose so.'

'I'm sure Adam will keep it to himself. In the meantime, how much do you need to keep afloat?'

'A hundred pounds would do it for a while.' Bram laughed, a bitter spurt of sound. 'Two would be better. Only I don't have it. And who's going to lend money to a man who's been so stupid?'

'I am.'

'No. I won't take money from my family or friends. I must live with my own mistakes.'

'Let me tell you how big my fortune is, now that I've sold everything I owned in England.'

When he heard the amount, Bram gaped at Quentin. 'Then what are you doing here? There's hardly anything to spend your money on here, if you're not buying land.'

'I'm here to marry the woman I love. I'll be living near other people I've grown to love. Money doesn't buy happiness if it sits in the bank, however much interest it accrues. It's for using, especially for helping the people you love, as far as I'm concerned. I think you understand that better than most. I've seen how you care about your family and how you look at your Isabella.'

'I love her more than life itself.'

'Then let me give you a hundred pounds to be going on with, after which you can come back to me for another hundred as you need it. And no, we'll not be writing contracts about it. This will be just between friends. I'll bring the money from my safe box at the lodgings.'

When he'd gone, Bram buried his head in his hands and wept out of sheer relief.

Then he went to tell Isabella about this miracle, rejoicing at the way her face brightened.

After which, of course, he had to pick up his baby daughter and give her a cuddle. Miss Neala Deirdre Deagan gurgled and cooed at him, as always, kicking her feet and waving her arms about.

'She recognises you, you know,' Isabella said.

'Of course she does. Isn't she my best little girl?' He put his arm round his son, who'd run over to join them and encouraged the little boy to play with his baby sister. 'Ah, and here's Louisa, come to join us too.' He gave his adopted daughter a hug for good measure.

After a while, Neala stopped kicking and

Bram's playing gentled down. 'Arlen, will you help me lay your sister down again? Louisa, come and smooth her sheets down, will you, darling. I think she's getting tired now.'

When he came down, he played with the two older children for a while longer, then sent them out into the garden and sat down next to his wife, beaming at her.

'I love the way you always bring the other children into it when you cuddle Neala.'

'She's their sister too, and the only one they'll be getting if I'm careful, and I shall be, my love, for your sake.'

'I wish we'd met when I was young enough to give you more children in safety.'

'I wasn't worth meeting then. I was just an ignorant groom, without a thought in his head except for the horses.'

'Don't you miss working with horses?'

'Not really. I'm too busy with my family and my business.'

'I'm so grateful to Quentin Saxby. He's put the smile back on your face.'

'He's a grand fellow, that one. He says he's adopting us all as a family, and aren't we lucky to have him? And not because of his money, either. He's good enough to be a Deagan, that one is.'

18

Two mornings later, Eleanor and Jacinta helped Harriet get ready to marry Quentin. For some reason the idea of a wedding seemed to soften their landlady and she'd proved very helpful, even to the point of giving Harriet a very ugly little pottery bowl as a present.

They'd all worked hard and got the rented house ready for the newly-weds to move into, even if it was only minimally furnished, because Quentin kept insisting he didn't want to waste a day of their life together.

The wedding was to be a simple affair, with just their group of family and new friends, mostly Deagans, attending the ceremony at the church.

But there was no reason for Harriet to look anything but her best, her young companions insisted, and took charge of outfitting her.

The gown was of dark blue silk, and Eleanor had transformed the crinoline into a skirt that was almost straight at the front and had a small bustle at the back. They'd even found some matching fringing at Isabella's silk stall, to edge the apron front and the drapery over the bustle. The bodice had a high neckline edged in white lace, with the same lace at the cuffs.

When she was ready, the bride went down to stare at herself in the best mirror in the parlour, with the landlady standing in the doorway, sighing sentimentally.

Harriet had tears in her eyes as she turned to Eleanor. 'You are so good at altering clothes. I'm looking fashionable, yet I've had this outfit for years, ever since crinolines first came out.'

'It's easy to alter things when there's so much extra material.' Eleanor twitched a fold of the skirt into place, then stood back to admire the older woman, whose silver hair was twisted into a high chignon topped by a flat bow in blue velvet.

Jacinta was standing at the other side of Harriet. 'You look lovely.'

Harriet smiled. 'In spite of all the trouble you've taken, I don't think Quentin will pay much attention to what I'm wearing.'

Eleanor smiled back. 'Men don't notice the details, I agree, but he will see that you look lovely.'

Harriet turned to her other companion. 'What about *your* wedding, Jacinta? You've been very quiet about what's happening, yet you've seen Mr Nash several times.'

She took a deep breath and admitted, 'Mitchell's asked me to marry him and I've been, um, thinking about it.'

The others exchanged puzzled glances, then Eleanor asked, 'Don't you want to marry him? I thought you liked him.'

'Well, he's far nicer than I'd expected. But my first marriage was so awful, I'm finding it hard to contemplate marrying again.' She blushed furiously. 'With all that it entails.'

Harriet took her hand. 'My darling girl,

340

because you *are* a girl to me, most marriages tick along just fine. Some are very happy. I was lucky with my first husband and I'm sure I'm going to be equally lucky with Quentin. Few are as bad as yours sounds to have been.'

'But how can you be sure of someone you've never . . . um, shared a bed with? You can't try someone out before you marry, after all.'

'I trust Quentin absolutely. He'd never do anything to hurt or upset me. And the marriage bed can give a lot of pleasure, you know.'

Jacinta gave her a disbelieving look. 'Mine never did.'

Eleanor gave her a quick hug. 'Mine didn't either, not in that way. But I'm sure marriage to a loving man would be different.'

'My advice is not to marry anyone until you trust him fully,' Harriet said quietly.

'I'm starting to trust Mitchell a little, but I don't think I'll ever trust a man fully. Only, he's promising to protect me and Ben from that awful man, and I do need help. For my son more than for myself. I saw Walsh again in town yesterday and I was so glad I was walking with Uncle Quentin, so the fellow couldn't approach me.'

'Well, he won't be able to get near you today, either. We'll make sure of that.'

'I can't spend my life hiding from him, though.'

'What about Ben and Christopher?' Eleanor asked. 'Have they met yet?'

'No. Unfortunately, Christopher had arranged to go to tea at a school friend's yesterday and as it was the first time, Mitchell didn't want him to back out. But he's going to bring his son to the wedding so we'll be able to introduce the boys to one another today.'

'How does Ben feel about that?'

'He's nervous. But I expect things will go well. I found Christopher very polite and well-mannered when I met him, and he didn't seem rough-natured or hostile to me, so why should he resent Ben? But that's enough about us. It's *your* wedding we're getting ready for, Aunt Harriet, and now that we've got you looking so fine, I think it's time we set off for the church.'

The three women and Ben walked through the streets, to find Quentin waiting for them outside.

The way his face lit up when he saw Harriet made the fear inside Jacinta ease a little more. Those two were such a shining example to everyone.

Bram Deagan and his wife turned up shortly afterwards, followed by Ismay and Adam, together with a lady Jacinta hadn't met before, who was introduced as Livia Southerham.

Then came Maura and her husband, together with four children. Jacinta had only met Bram's aunt briefly, but had liked her. Maura was pregnant and looked to be in blooming health. Her husband Hugh was very protective towards her. It was lovely to see.

Eleanor nudged her. 'Look. These are all happily married people. Surely you and I can do as well for ourselves?'

Jacinta nodded, but her eyes were on Mitchell, who had just arrived at the church, accompanied by his son. He was looking very elegant today, with a well-ironed shirt, thanks to her efforts, and he came straight across to join her.

'You're looking lovely,' he said in a low voice, then drew his son forward and introduced him to Ben, who couldn't hide his nervousness.

They'd agreed not to comment on the poor boy's feelings, so Mitchell said only, 'I hope you two lads will become good friends,' and offered his arm to Jacinta. 'Now, let's go inside and find seats.'

So she found herself sitting in a family group next to the man she was going to marry. And yes, she definitely was going to marry him, and quickly, as he'd suggested, even if they didn't share a bed at first. That suddenly seemed very clear. As Harriet had said, most marriages were reasonably happy. And Mitchell was being very thoughtful about her worries and needs. Surely he wouldn't change after their marriage?

The boys were sitting on either side of her and Mitchell, stealing glances at one another across the two adults but not attempting to talk.

Jacinta listened to the minister's booming voice as he conducted the marriage ceremony. The bride and groom gave clear, confident responses, and she was surprised to feel tears welling in her eyes. She'd hardly noticed what she was promising at her own wedding, so afraid had she been of the elderly stranger she was marrying. Now, she found some of the words truly beautiful.

As the minister declared, 'What God has joined together, let no man put asunder,' she realised that was what was making her so

343

nervous of marrying Mitchell: once they were bound together, it was only death which could separate them.

She looked at him and found him gazing at her. She couldn't read his expression and hoped he couldn't see into her troubled mind, either. But when he took her hand, she let him, and when he patted that hand, which she couldn't prevent from trembling in his, she felt comforted.

Afterwards Jacinta was surprised to find they were going back to Maura and Hugh's house for the wedding feast, not to Ismay's.

'No one can organise a celebration like my aunt,' Bram whispered to her. 'She was an assistant housekeeper in a large country mansion in England, you know.'

'Did she come out to Australia to marry Hugh?'

'No. She was bringing the children here. Their parents had died in an epidemic of typhus in Ireland. She met Hugh and his daughter on the ship. All very romantic.' He grinned. 'My family's good at finding marriage partners, or nudging our friends into getting married. Ah, you haven't met Livia Southerham, have you?' He beckoned to a slender woman of about forty and as she moved across to join them, he added in a low voice, 'She's a widow like yourself and has been a dear friend of ours for several years. She has no one but us in Australia now.'

He greeted his friend by shaking her hand and then keeping hold of it. 'Your turn to find a husband next, Livia darlin'. You can't stay a widow for ever, not in a country that's so short of women.'

'Don't you start your matchmaking with me, Bram Deagan. I've enough on my plate with my maids.'

His smile widened. 'Are the two of them still looking for a husband for you?'

'They are indeed. I can't stop them scanning newspapers for advertisements and keeping their eyes open for a likely gentleman, but I *can* refuse to co-operate with any of their silly ideas.' She shook her head as if annoyed, but didn't seem too upset by this. 'Actually, I'm still thinking of opening a bookshop. Books are the thing I know most about. Surely I can make a living by selling them?'

'You'd be so busy reading your stock, you'd forget to take the money for the books you sell, or you'd charge the wrong price.'

She pretended to hit him, but didn't protest at this description of her absent-mindedness.

'Now, let me introduce you. You haven't met Jacinta Blacklea yet, have you? She's come out here to marry Mitchell.'

'So I heard.' Livia held out her hand to Jacinta and nodded to Mitchell who was standing patiently behind them. 'I hope you'll be very happy here. Mitchell's been a good friend of mine for a while.'

Which made Jacinta wonder why he hadn't married Livia when she was living so close to him. Or had she turned him down?

When the conversation moved on, Mitchell leaned closer to Jacinta and said, 'Livia is a good friend, but I could never see her as a wife.' He paused and added, 'I could see you as a wife from the start, though, even if we had things to work out first.'

★ ★ ★

Jacinta was amazed by the informal nature of the gathering at Maura and Hugh's house. Livia's two older maids were there to help the Beauforts' maid, together with Sally, Isabella's young maid, who had brought a friend in to help with the group of children. They took them outside to play games in the back garden until they were invited in after the adults had helped themselves to a splendid array of pies, cooked meat, potatoes and other dishes.

'Cheese!' Adam exclaimed. 'I haven't had any for months.'

'This cheese was made by a friend of ours,' Isabella told Jacinta and Eleanor. 'Cassandra and Reece have a small farm a day's drive to the south of Perth, and have started making cheese. It's hard to keep it cool in hot weather here, but luckily, they're in the foothills and they have caves on their property, where the temperature is more constant.'

'You seem to know a lot of people. Did you know any of them before you came to Australia?'

Isabella shook her head. 'No. I knew no one except Bram. I was very apprehensive. And pardon me saying it, but you must be too.'

'I am.'

'You'll make friends easily here, I'm sure.

People are much closer to their friends when the rest of their family is on the other side of the world.'

'Do you think so?'

'I know so. And you've got a good start on me. Mitchell knows lots of people already, because he's making a good name for himself with his timber and house building. Bram didn't know nearly as many when we were first married.'

When it came to the wedding speeches, Adam spoke about his love for his adopted uncle and aunt, before wishing them every happiness.

Then Bram insisted on making a speech too, which brought blushes to the cheeks of not only the bride, but Jacinta, Eleanor and Livia. He asked people to drink to these three lovely ladies' happiness and wish them luck in finding husbands for themselves.

The 'three lovely ladies' all glared at him.

He would have gone on for longer, but his wife tugged his sleeve and of course he turned instantly to her.

★ ★ ★

'Bram seems much happier today,' Eleanor said. 'Oh, my!' She clasped one hand to her mouth as a man came into the room.

Jacinta looked at her anxiously. 'What's wrong?'

'That's Dougal McBride.' She stood frozen, watching as he spoke to Bram and Isabella. Then he saw her and stopped speaking, his mouth dropping open in shock.

He didn't move, didn't speak, didn't smile — in fact he didn't do anything but close his eyes for a moment, as if he couldn't believe what he saw, then stare at her again. There was no other word for the way he was looking at her but 'hungrily'. Without a word to his companions he began threading his way through the crowd, ignoring the fact that Adam, whom he'd expected to be at sea, was there in the room.

Not till Jacinta poked her in the ribs and said, 'Go to him,' was Eleanor able to move.

When they met, he said only, 'You came.'

'Yes.'

'You're free now?'

'Yes, I am.'

He took her hand in his and raised it to his lips, then threaded her arm through his and led the way to the door.

She accompanied him without a word. Of course she did. She wanted to tell him so much, but not in front of other people, and she was sure he felt the same.

Outside, he stopped to say, 'Your face has haunted my dreams, but it's even lovelier than I'd remembered.'

He was taller than her, overwhelming in his masculinity and vigour to one who had spent years with a thin, peevish little man. Dougal was so different from Malcolm, so wonderfully normal that he took her breath away.

'Will you come to my house, Eleanor? We can't talk in the street.'

'Yes, of course I will.'

One moment more he stared at her as if trying

to read her thoughts, then smiled, a wonderfully soft smile, saying only, 'Good.'

The streets they walked through seemed unreal, other people they passed no more substantial than ghosts. Though some of them greeted Dougal, and he returned their greetings briefly, he hardly took his eyes off Eleanor. She knew, because she couldn't stop staring at him, either.

At last he spoke, his voice deep and gentle. 'I brought my ship in this morning, but for some reason I left the unloading to my mate. I saw the *Bonny Ismay* in the harbour being repaired, but somehow I felt a need to go home before I looked into anything else. When I got there, Linney told me about the wedding and I was so glad for Harriet, I came to wish her well.'

'Everyone is happy for her.'

'Linney didn't say anything about you, though.'

'I haven't managed to visit her yet so she might not know I'm here. I was helping Aunt Harriet with her wedding gown. We only had two days' notice to get it ready. I left a letter for you at the house, though. Didn't she give it to you?'

'I didn't give her time. I went straight out again.' He looked at her in puzzlement. '*Aunt* Harriet? I didn't know you had any family left.'

'Three of us became close on the journey from England — Jacinta, Uncle Quentin and I. He's the one who's just married Adam's aunt. They all feel like family to me now and they've asked to be called aunt and uncle.'

'It happens like that. The sea often strips away the social veneers and lets people get to know one another quickly.'

'It happened that way with you and me, didn't it?'

'Yes. But still I worried you wouldn't come to me.'

'I worried you wouldn't want me.'

'*Not want you?* There's nothing in the world I want more than to be with you. Seeing you today was the best surprise I've ever had in my whole life.'

Happiness bubbled through her. 'I'm glad.'

She could have walked beside him for much longer. She was getting used to the feel of his arm now and even the simple act of moving along the streets together felt wonderful. It was something they'd never done before, since their time had been spent on board his ship, with her sickly husband always nearby.

There were so many things they hadn't done before.

They both realised suddenly that they'd arrived at his house, and had stopped automatically. They were standing outside, still talking.

'What fools we are,' he teased. 'We can be more comfortable inside.' He opened the door and stood back to let her enter first.

At the sound of the front door, Linney poked her head out of the kitchen, beamed at Eleanor and said, 'I'm glad you're back.' Then she vanished again.

The maid was a very perceptive woman, Eleanor thought.

Dougal led the way into the parlour and swept her into his arms. 'Let me hold you. Let me get used to the fact that you really are here. I've dreamed of this moment so often, wondered what we'd say to one another.'

For answer, she nestled against him and said aloud the words she'd held back until now, though she'd said them often enough in her dreams, 'How about I start by telling you that I love you, Dougal McBride?'

'And I love you, Eleanor. How soon can you marry me?'

'As soon as it can be arranged. It took only a few days for Uncle Quentin to sort out their wedding. You'll have to buy a special licence, though.'

'We'll do that, then.' He pulled her closer. 'It's customary to seal such a bargain with a kiss.'

For answer, she lifted her face to his and the world faded again as her lips met those of the man she loved.

Her fears had been unfounded. He'd been waiting for her, wanting her. She was a very fortunate woman.

★   ★   ★

Jacinta watched enviously as Eleanor and Dougal met. Almost immediately they forgot about everything else but each other. She jumped in shock as a voice spoke beside her.

'It's clear they love one another dearly. I envy them that,' Mitchell said.

'So do I. It's lovely that they're together again.'

'Yes, very romantic, the stuff of foolish novels, some would say.'

But his voice sounded wistful, she thought.

'I'd be content with friendship and mutual support from a wife. That would be a big improvement over what I had last time.'

'One of the things *I* value highly is kindness.' She wished he didn't sound so jaded about marriage. 'And when ... if I marry you, I'd expect you to believe that I'd never betray a promise.'

His voice softened. 'No. I'm sure you wouldn't. Which is one of the reasons why I'd like to marry you. You haven't given me a firm answer yet, though. I'd like to set a date quite soon.'

Jealousy of Eleanor surged up suddenly, making her speak more sharply than usual. 'Is this the place to ask me such a thing?'

A young girl suddenly appeared beside her. 'Excuse me, but Ben fell over and he needs his cut washing.'

Jacinta forgot Mitchell and hurried after the child, finding her son as stoic as ever and protesting that he didn't need looking after, could wash his own cuts.

'How did you fall?' she asked.

'We were playing. I fell.' But he scowled at Christopher as he spoke and her heart sank as Christopher scowled back at him. Were the two boys quarrelling already? That didn't bode well.

She hadn't exactly quarrelled with Mitchell, but they hadn't been in accord just now and it might have led to a quarrel if they hadn't been interrupted. He hadn't followed her, either, to see if she needed help.

She'd had so many years of biting her tongue, she felt as if she couldn't hold back her thoughts and feelings any longer or she'd burst, so she said curtly to Ben, 'We'll go back to the lodging house and wash that knee of yours. We'll go out through the gate, so that we don't upset people at the party.'

'I don't want to go.'

That surprised her. He so rarely defied her. But then they'd usually been working together to deflect Claude's anger or manage some household task. 'Please don't argue, Ben. I have other reasons for wanting to leave.'

She turned to the girl, who was still standing nearby, looking embarrassed now. 'Can we get out to the street round the side of the house?'

'Yes, Mrs Blacklea. I'll show you.'

Outside, Jacinta started walking with Ben slouching along behind her.

'That's not the shortest way,' he protested.

'It's the way I know best.' It led past the timber yard, but Mitchell wouldn't be there, so that didn't matter. Anyway, she felt like a good brisk walk.

She heard her son mutter, 'I don't want to go that way.' But she didn't answer. She just continued walking, her emotions in a turmoil, and let Ben trail behind, checking every now and then to make sure he was still there.

She didn't know why it had upset her so much to see Eleanor's joy at meeting Dougal again, or his at seeing her. It hadn't seemed upsetting when Uncle Quentin and Aunt Harriet got together. Well, not much.

Someone grabbed her arm — Alf! — and she gasped as she realised that she'd stopped keeping an eye on what was happening around her.

As he dragged her into a passage between two houses, she opened her mouth to scream for help.

But he was too quick for her. As soon as she opened her mouth, he clapped his hand over it.

19

Ben kicked a piece of rubbish out of the way as he walked behind his mother, deliberately going slowly. He hadn't wanted to leave the party, because he was just getting to know Christopher.

They'd argued at first, then Christopher had pushed him, so he'd shoved back. But he'd tripped over a piece of wood, so falling over had been an accident not a fight, and Christopher had helped him up, hadn't he? Things had just been starting to go right when his mother came out and told him off for getting into a fight, then made him leave, as if he was a baby.

He looked up but couldn't see her, so hurried along the street to catch up.

As he passed a narrow alley, he saw movement out of the corner of his eye and stopped to look. His mother was struggling with a man — not just any man, but Mr Walsh. What was he doing to her? Why was he holding her?

Ben rushed to help his mother but Mr Walsh gave him a backhander that sent him slamming into a fence.

He'd tried to stop his father hitting his mother, and it had never done any good. Mr Walsh was far bigger than his father, so Ben rolled out of the way and ran out of the alley to get help.

But there were only two old ladies further along the street and even as he watched they turned the corner and vanished from sight.

Obeying his instincts, he ran back towards the house, which wasn't far away.

He sobbed in relief when he met Christopher and Mr Nash in the very next street. They must have left the party too and be on their way home. He rushed up to them, shouting, 'Come quickly. That man's grabbed Mother and he's holding his hand across her mouth. She's trying to get away from him.'

'Where?' Mitchell said.

'This way.' Ben ran back as fast as he could, with Mr Nash pounding beside him. He was so out of breath when they got there, he could only point down the alley, then lean against the fence to suck in air.

Christopher stood next to him. 'Are you all right? You're going to have a big bruise on your face.'

'He knocked me out of the way.'

'Don't worry. Dad'll save your mother.'

They were watching what was happening in the alley, knowing instinctively that the two adults wanted them to stay out of the way.

Ben leaned against Christopher, terrified, and the older boy put a hand on his shoulder. It was a comfort. 'I don't want my mother to be hurt.'

'It'll be all right. Dad's very strong.'

But Mr Walsh was strong too.

★ ★ ★

Furiously angry, Mitchell grabbed Jacinta's attacker by the collar. Yanking him away, he punched him in the face, then punched again.

356

The man fought back for a moment or two, but Mitchell was stronger, after heaving around big pieces of wood all his life.

He sent the fellow flying and was about to follow up with a kick or two, but the man rolled away, got quickly to his feet and ran off along the alley. Moving away from the street, he turned right at the top and vanished from sight.

Mitchell hesitated, wondering whether to follow him, but when he felt Jacinta's hand on his arm, he turned to look at her. 'Are you all right? He didn't hurt you?'

'I'm fine. Just . . . a bit shaken.'

Her voice wobbled, so he pulled her into his arms and held her close. 'Thank goodness. If he'd hurt you, I'd have gone after him and made him rue the day he was born.'

He could feel her clinging to him and couldn't resist dropping a kiss on her hair, then on her cheek. Just to comfort her. 'You're sure you're all right, Jacinta?'

'Yes.'

The world seemed to fade for a moment or two, and leave only the two of them, standing close, staring into each other's eyes.

It felt so right.

Then Ben's voice broke the spell. 'Are you all right, Mother? Why did Mr Walsh attack you?'

'This is the fellow you told me about, Jacinta?'

'Yes.'

'He's not given up, then.'

'It seems not.'

Mitchell stepped back but couldn't keep his eyes off Jacinta. Her hair had fallen out of its pins. He hadn't realised quite how beautiful it was, because she normally pinned it severely back. It rippled over her shoulders, gleaming in the sunshine like gilded silver and he wanted to touch it, run his fingers through it.

She saw the way he was looking at her and blushed, so he looked away, but the picture was still imprinted on his mind. Suddenly, things had changed and he wanted her as a man wants a woman; suddenly, it was just as important that she be a proper wife to him as a mother to their two sons.

Colour still high, she finished pinning up her hair, checked that her clothing was straight and turned to the boys. Tutting over the bruise on her son's face, she turned him towards the light to take a better look. Then she straightened Christopher's jacket in an automatic gesture, smiling down at him as she tugged his shirt collar gently into place.

Mitchell watched his son smile at her just as warmly as her own son was doing, and that simple gesture added another layer to his wanting to marry her. Christopher so desperately needed mothering like this.

'We'll all go to my house now and you can tell me what you know,' Mitchell said. 'You two boys can lead the way. Stay together. If you see the man again, run back to me.'

★ ★ ★

Jacinta watched both boys straighten up as he spoke, instinctively responding to Mitchell's quiet authority. She liked the way he spoke to them, firmly but politely, and not harshly.

When he looked at her again, she heard his voice become gentler. She liked that too.

'Shall we go now, Jacinta?'

'Yes.' She felt shy as she took his arm. 'Thank you for your help.'

'It was my pleasure and I hope it'll soon become my right, as your husband. We need to talk about this fellow, though, and work out why he's still pursuing you.'

She sucked in a deep breath, but her voice wobbled. 'Can we wait to discuss it until we get to your house? I can't talk here in the street.'

'Of course. I should have asked you first about going there, I suppose, but it seems the obvious thing to do. We can't talk privately in your lodging house, or at Maura's. Besides, Ben hasn't seen my place. Christopher can show him round while we have our talk.'

They walked along the next street and found the boys waiting for them at the end. Mitchell pulled a key out of his pocket, tossing it to his son in what was obviously a familiar gesture. 'You two go ahead. Open the damper and get the stove top heating up, Christopher. We'll all have a nice cup of tea.'

The two boys did as he'd asked, running flat out, but he didn't hurry after them. Indeed, he walked even more slowly, frowning now, looking as if he had a lot on his mind.

'Do you think those two will get on all right, Mitchell?'

'What? Oh, the boys. Yes, I do.'

'It's very important.'

'It's even more important that I keep you safe.' He smiled at her. 'Don't worry. I'm sure they'll rub along together. Christopher needs a good friend of his own age.'

'So does Ben.'

Another few paces then he said, 'I can't bear to think of you being attacked.'

'Since he made it look as if he'd rescued me on the ship, I'd have difficulty proving anything against him. You and the boys are the only ones who saw him today. What am I going to do about Walsh?'

'We should get married at once. You'll be far safer in my house.'

She looked at him uncertainly.

He seemed to guess her thoughts. 'It's not just to protect you, Jacinta. I *want* to marry you. I didn't realise how much till I saw Walsh hurting you. I wanted to beat him, teach him a lesson he'd never forget.'

She waited for the familiar fear of marriage to rise inside her, but there was no lurching sense of apprehension, just a slight nervousness.

'Look, I know it's important to you that we don't share a bed until you feel more comfortable with me, Jacinta. I won't force you into anything. I'm sad that your life with your husband was so bad that you feel like that, though.'

'It was . . . very bad. For me and for Ben.'

'I would never force myself on you or any woman,' he repeated emphatically.

Claude had never hesitated to force himself on

her. Aunt Harriet's words came back to her. *Don't get married till you know you can trust him.*

Did she trust Mitchell? Jacinta stopped walking for a moment, raised her eyes to his face and met his gaze squarely. Yes, she did. He had such a steady look, and although he was a strong man, he was also very gentle, with her and the boys.

She gathered her courage together. 'I appreciate your kindness and yes, we should marry as soon as we can, Mitchell. Then we can all get on with our new lives, I hope — you, me and the boys.' She could feel heat in her cheeks, but she didn't turn away from him. That would have been cowardly.

His smile lit up his whole face. 'I'm delighted.' He bent to kiss her cheek, then took her hand and started walking again.

The kiss had been light, like a butterfly's touch, and it hadn't been at all distasteful. He didn't frighten her at all now in public, she decided. If he would just keep his word for a while, she thought she might face the marriage bed with more courage. She still didn't believe anyone could enjoy *that*. But she didn't think it would be nearly as horrible as it had been with Claude.

He stopped at the garden path. 'I'll go up to Perth tomorrow and arrange for a special licence. We can marry a couple of days after that, if you can be ready by then.'

'Yes, I'll be ready.'

As she went into the house, it felt as if she was

coming home. The place wasn't finished and was untidy, yet it seemed to wrap around her. 'I feel at home here already,' she said in wonderment.

'Good.'

Footsteps thumped about upstairs and Christopher poked his head over the banister rail to yell, 'I've shown Ben round. Can we come down and get something to eat now, Dad?'

'I thought you both ate plenty at the wedding.'

'That was *ages* ago. You're hungry too, aren't you, Ben?' He nudged his companion.

'Very hungry,' Ben said.

'So it's not just me.' Christopher's voice was triumphant and he grinned at the other boy.

'Come down to the kitchen, then.' Mitchell turned to Jacinta and gestured round. 'I *will* finish the house as quickly as I can, and I apologise for the untidiness.'

'I don't mind. It'll be my pleasure to help set our home to rights. I haven't lived in a house this big since I was a girl.'

The boys came clattering down the stairs, holding back to allow Jacinta to go into the kitchen first, then letting Mitchell shoo them in with one gesture.

'It'll have to be bread and jam,' he said. 'It's all I've got. I need to buy another cake, so I'll send you two out to the baker's later. But before you eat, we have something to tell you.' He took her hand in his. 'Jacinta has agreed to marry me quite soon.'

'We knew that,' Christopher said scornfully. 'Everyone at the wedding knew that you were going to get married.'

'They did?' Mitchell exchanged startled glances with his intended.

'It was the way you kept looking at each other and smiling. Brenna told me her aunt was like that with Mr Beaufort for ages before they married, always smiling in a soppy way.'

'Soppy?' Mitchell chuckled.

Ben sounded cheerful as he asked his mother, 'When exactly are you getting married?'

'In two or three days. There's no reason to delay things. Is that all right with you?' Jacinta waited, needing her son's approval to set the seal on her decision.

'I'm glad, Mother. I don't like our lodgings. This is a lovely house, Mr Nash.'

'It will be when it's finished. You and Christopher can help me with some of the little jobs. He's quite a good little carpenter now.'

'You'll let me use the tools?'

Ben's ecstatic expression brought a lump to Jacinta's throat.

'Of course. As long as you learn to use them properly and never, ever mess around when you're holding them.'

'I will use them properly. I promise I will.'

'Can Ben have the room next to mine?' Christopher asked. 'We'll need to buy him a bed, though.'

'We'll have to buy a lot of new furniture.'

'That's all right then. *Now* can we have our bread and jam? And can we go and buy a cake afterwards? You have to have cake when you're celebrating.'

Jacinta felt happier than she had felt for a long

time as she took charge, cutting the bread, starting to learn where things were kept, making herself at home.

At home! Oh, she so wanted a proper home again.

And all the time she kept an eye on the boys. Her son was chattering away with Christopher, the two of them making plans in between stuffing bread and jam into their mouths.

When Mitchell caught her watching them and winked, she felt a rush of warmth.

It was all so blessedly normal. Like a real family. Already.

* * *

As the wedding guests chatted and ate, and Aunt Harriet beamed at her new husband, Ismay went to find Adam. He'd told her earlier that he'd have to set sail again in a day or two to fetch another cargo from Singapore. Mr Lee would need to know that many of his trade goods had been damaged and that Bram desperately needed new stock.

At first she'd not said much. The familiar feeling of sadness at the thought of him leaving swept over her and made her feel like weeping. She loved Adam so much, and knew he loved her, but she saw so little of him. It was what happened to sailors' wives, of course, and she'd rather have that than not be married to him.

But perhaps now they could change things. Oh, she did hope they could!

She found her husband talking to her brother

Bram, so decided to tackle the two of them together.

'I've been looking for you, Adam. We need to talk.'

'Shall I leave you two love-birds alone together?' her brother asked with a smile.

'No. You need to know what I'm going to say as well, Bram. It came to me this morning that I can come to sea with you now, Adam, because Aunt Harriet will have Uncle Quentin to look after her.'

He put an arm round her shoulders. 'I did consider it, but I don't want to put you in danger. That storm destroyed at least one ship and damaged the *Bonny Ismay*. I don't want to take such risks. I couldn't bear it if anything happened to you.'

'I want to be with you, Adam. Other captains' wives go with their husbands and take the risks. I've been thinking hard and my mind is made up. I'm coming to sea with you from now on.'

But he was still shaking his head.

Bram shuddered. He was a terrible sailor. 'How can you even think of spending your life on the sea, Ismay, with all the storms and rough weather?'

She smiled. 'Because I love being on the ocean and I don't get seasick like you do. Besides, there are sunny days and moonlit evenings, too. And what I need more than anything else is to be with my husband.'

She set her hands on her hips and stared challengingly at them both. 'I'm going to sea with you, Adam, if I have to stow away to do it.

So you'd better get used to the idea.'

'Oh, my darling . . . I shouldn't let you.'

'Your mate's wife goes with you. I shan't even be the only woman on the ship.'

'She's much older than you.'

He studied her face intently, as if he could read her very soul, so she moved closer and took both his hands, looking up at him. She could see in his eyes that he was dithering, almost ready to give in. 'I'm coming.'

'Oh, Ismay, are you sure?'

Letting out a crow of triumph, she flung her arms round his neck and plonked a kiss on each of his cheeks in turn. 'I'm very sure. You'll just have to get used to sailing on a 'hen frigate'. Isn't that what they call ships when the wives go to sea too?'

'It is. I don't know what the crew will say, though.'

She shrugged. 'You're the captain. They have to do as you tell them.' She tugged him into a little dance, plonked a kiss on her brother's cheek as they passed, then flung herself into her husband's arms and demanded, 'When do we leave?'

'As soon as we can make ready. Two days at most.'

'We'd better go and tell Aunt Harriet and Uncle Quentin, then I'll start making lists. Bram, will you tell Isabella for me, please?'

'Of course.'

As she dragged Adam back into the house, Bram stood watching them, his smile fading. 'Dear God, keep her safe,' he prayed. 'I've lost enough of my family.'

20

Eleanor and Dougal talked for hours. When she worried that people would be wondering where she was, he sent a message to Jacinta, telling her she was safe with Dougal.

Neither ate much of the meal Linney brought.

'Let me show you round the house, my darling,' he said when the food had been cleared away. 'You must choose a bedroom for us and then Linney can get it ready.'

She followed him round, marvelling at how spacious it was. 'There are so many rooms. I only saw the guest room and the living areas when Malcolm and I were here last time. Tell me which bedroom you'd like us to share.'

'The one my mother used to use. Trust her to take the best room. My sister Flora and I cleared it out when she left, so it needs furnishing properly, but it has a lovely outlook.' He opened a door and gestured to her to go inside.

She walked round the room, with its bare bedframe. 'We must get a new mattress.'

'Whatever you want.'

'Whatever *we* want,' she corrected. She checked that the drawers and wardrobe were empty, mentally deciding where she would put things, sighing in pleasure. 'We'll be happy here, I know we will.'

So he had to take her into his arms again and kiss her thoroughly.

When she pushed him away, her colour was bright and her dark hair had come loose from its pins.

He took a step backwards, breathing more rapidly. 'I'm longing to make you mine.'

'I'm looking forward to everything about us being married — except you going away.'

'I'm a sailor. I have no choice. Can you cope with that?'

'If I must. Maybe sometimes I can come with you? I've heard so much about Singapore.'

'Do you mean that?'

'Of course I do. I enjoyed it before when we sailed together.'

'Then why not make this a honeymoon voyage? I'm sure Mr Lee would be delighted to welcome you to his city, and we can buy many of the things we need for the house while we're there and have some clothes made for you, if you like.'

She stared at him, mouth open. 'Can I really come with you?'

'Yes. I don't want to be separated from you. There's time to arrange things because I'll be staying here for a week or two more. I need to have some maintenance done to the *Bonny Mary*.'

She didn't hesitate. 'I'd love to come with you.'

He grabbed her by the waist and waltzed her round the half empty bedroom. 'I must be the luckiest man in the colony! In the world, even.'

In the end, she had to say, 'Stop!' and lean

against him to catch her breath.

As they went downstairs, the grandfather clock in the hall struck the half hour. 'Oh dear! It's getting late. I'd better go back now, Dougal.'

'I wish you could stay.'

'And have that landlady tell everyone I'm immoral!' Her voice softened. 'It won't be long, Dougal darling.'

So he walked her back to the lodging house and lingered for a further ten minutes outside it to say farewell. He didn't embrace her in public, but his eyes spoke for him.

★ ★ ★

When Jacinta heard the landlady let Eleanor in, she opened the door of the guests' sitting room, a bleak unwelcoming room. 'Have you a minute? I've something to tell you.'

'As many minutes as you like. Is it what I think?'

'I've agreed to marry Mr Nash as soon as possible.'

'I'm so pleased for you. I took to him at once and Dougal says he's a good fellow.'

'He is. And Ben seems to be getting on well with Christopher, too.'

'So why are you still looking worried?'

'Mr Walsh grabbed me after I left the wedding. He dragged me into an alley.'

'Did he . . . hurt you?'

'No. I tried to scream, but he put his hand over my mouth. If Ben hadn't seen what was happening and fetched Mitchell to help me, I don't know what that horrible man would have done to me.'

'Quite the hero, your Mitchell.'

'He was wonderful.'

Eleanor looked at her earnestly. 'I keep telling you, Jacinta. Other men aren't like your first husband.' She waited, head cocked to one side. 'So, when are you getting married?'

'As soon as Mitchell can get a special licence.'

Eleanor let out a shriek of joy that brought the landlady running to find out what was wrong. The two ladies didn't share their news with her, and kept quiet as they were given a stern warning not to make such noise again, on account of it disturbing the other lodgers.

When Mrs Haslop had gone, Eleanor pulled a face at her retreating back, then closed the door firmly and gave Jacinta a big hug. 'I'm marrying Dougal quickly, too. He still loves me, wants me. I don't think I've ever been so happy in my life.'

So of course Jacinta had to hug her and wish her well.

After a moment, Eleanor said thoughtfully, 'Why don't we have a double wedding in two days' time?'

'What a lovely idea!'

'You still sound nervous. Don't be. It can be a pleasure between men and women, you know. Malcolm was as poor in bed as he was in everything else, but I know my mother and father were happy together. As a child, I used to hear laughter from their bedroom, and the way they smiled at one another made me feel happy. So I'm trusting in them, not the fool I married.'

370

Jacinta didn't say anything about that side of things. She still felt embarrassed even referring to it vaguely.

'So are we having a double wedding?'

'Yes. Oh, yes. I'd love that, Eleanor.'

'Good. We've only a couple of days to decide what to wear. We want to look as beautiful as we can on our wedding day for our new husbands, don't we?'

Jacinta didn't dare mention the condition she'd imposed on Mitchell, the fact that she wouldn't be sharing his bed at first.

As she snuggled down in bed a little later, she thought about what Eleanor had said about her parents, and about the joy on Harriet and Quentin's faces as they turned to one another.

She was beginning to believe her second marriage wouldn't be nearly as bad as her first, she really was.

★ ★ ★

When they went for their evening walk, Bridie waited till they were away from the house, then stopped and said bluntly, 'You may as well tell me what's wrong, Alf. How did you get those bruises on your face? And don't start pretending you had a fall, because I know a punch mark when I see one.'

He scowled and scuffed the sandy soil with one foot. 'I tried to talk to Mrs Blacklea again and she started screaming, so I put my hand across her mouth just till I could tell her what you and I had decided, and ask her help.'

'That's no way to get her to accept our idea.'

'Well, I didn't get the chance to tell her, as it happened. This fellow came along and punched me.'

'What fellow?'

'He's called Nash and he runs that timber yard.'

She raised her eyes to the sky. 'Heaven help us, he's well known and liked in the town. If he sets the law on you, you'll be in trouble, my lad. You can't go round grabbing people like that.'

'But how else was I to tell her what we want to do? If we can't get someone posh, someone that devil Blacklea will believe, to write to my uncle, I'll have to go back to England.'

'Oh, no you won't, Alf. You're staying with me and that's that.'

'It's what I want, you know it is. But I'm not letting Blacklea take it out on my kids, so how do we manage it?'

She frowned, staring at the ground, then at him. 'I'll go and talk to her.'

'You?'

'Yes. Woman to woman.' A smile crept over her face. 'I know what. I'll pretend I'm expecting your baby — '

'Fat chance of that when you won't let me do more than kiss you.'

'I'm not as stupid as your wife. I doubt I can have a baby, anyway, but I'm still not risking it.'

'How will you get Mrs Blacklea to talk to you?'

'I'll go openly, knock on the door of her lodging house and ask to see her.'

'What if she won't see you?'

'I'll stand outside till she does. But she won't refuse to talk to me, you'll see.'

★   ★   ★

The following morning Bridie did just as she'd said she would. Dressed in her Sunday best, she knocked on the door of the lodging house and asked to speak to Mrs Blacklea.

The landlady looked at her suspiciously. 'What's someone like you wanting with a lady like her?'

Bridie stiffened. 'That's my business and hers. But it's important.'

Jacinta, who had heard this exchange from the sitting room where she and Eleanor were sitting sewing, waited for the landlady to come and fetch her.

But all Mrs Haslop said was, 'I'm not having your sort in here. Go away.'

Shocked, Jacinta went out into the hall just in time to stop the landlady from closing the door in her visitor's face. 'I believe I have a visitor, Mrs Haslop.'

'I don't allow her sort into my house.'

Jacinta studied the woman, who was flashily dressed, but seemed clean and respectable enough, with a rosy face and eyes that looked as if they might smile easily in other circumstances. 'I don't think I know you.'

'You don't,' Bridie said bluntly, 'but I have information about your son and Blacklea. It's good news, I promise you.'

Jacinta stiffened. 'Perhaps you'd better come in, then.'

With a triumphant look at the landlady, Bridie followed Mrs Blacklea into the small sitting room.

Mrs Haslop opened her mouth to protest, then sniffed loudly and went back to her quarters at the rear.

'I'm Bridie Folane, widow. And I've come on behalf of Alf Walsh to talk to you.'

'In that case, I shan't invite you to take a seat,' Jacinta said in a chill voice, 'because if you've come from *that man*, I'll tell you now, I don't intend to get into discussions about giving up my son. I won't do it. What's more, I'm about to be married and my husband is an important man in this colony, so he will know how to deal with any further attempts from anyone to take my son away.'

'Best thing you could do, marrying is,' Bridie agreed. 'But my Alf doesn't want to take your son away from you. He never did, really. Look, I'd better start by apologising for his behaviour yesterday. Doesn't know the meaning of the word tact, my Alf doesn't. But I promise you, he didn't mean any harm.'

'Then why did he grab me, put his hand over my mouth?'

'Because he's a fool. He only wanted to stop you running away so he could talk to you. But like I said, he did it in a stupid way, so I've come to apologise for his behaviour, then do the talking for him, if you don't mind.'

Jacinta studied her, then said, 'Perhaps you'd

374

better take a seat after all.'

'Shouldn't we do our talking in private?' Bridie asked, with a glance at Eleanor.

'No. I prefer my friend to remain with us. She knows everything that's happened so far.'

'All right. I'll say it bluntly then: Alf never did want to kill you, he isn't the sort. But he was frightened for the lives of his children if he didn't agree to do it. And now, well, he doesn't want to go back to his wife, who's a shrew, but he does want to make sure Mr Gerald Blacklea doesn't take his failure to kill you out on his family.' She waited for this information to sink in.

Jacinta nodded slowly. 'I'm afraid of Blacklea myself and can well believe that he'd take his revenge if someone didn't do as he ordered. Go on.'

'Alf and me, well, there's no dressing it up. We got friendly on the ship and now I'm expecting his child.'

'But he's already married!'

'Yes. Pity, that. But he's not going back to his wife, whatever happens. And if me and Alf go to Sydney or Melbourne, I don't think this Mr Blacklea will find us. Only . . . well, Alf wants to make sure his kids are all right.'

Jacinta frowned. 'I don't understand why you're telling me this.'

'Because you're the only one who can help us.'

'Why on earth should I do that?'

'To keep your son safe.'

Jacinta exchanged glances with Eleanor, then said again, 'Go on.'

'You came out to Australia with that nice

lawyer, Mr Saxby. Everybody on the ship liked him. He would talk to anyone, he would, housemaid or duchess, politely as you please. Alf and me thought if *he* wrote a letter to Mr Blacklea, telling him Alf had been killed in a storm, well, Mr Blacklea and that Mr Pearson, who is Alf's uncle, would believe him. And if your Mr Saxby said you'd married and gone to Sydney, and he'd lost touch with you, I don't think Blacklea would send anyone else after you. He'd not know where to start, would he?'

Bridie stopped talking and waited, hands folded in her lap.

It was Eleanor who broke the silence. 'I think that's quite a good idea, actually.'

'You do?' Jacinta looked at them both. 'I'm not even sure Unc — Mr Saxby will do it.'

'We can ask him. And we should tell Mr Nash, as well.' She looked at Bridie. 'You've given Mrs Blacklea a lot to think about. Can you please come back this evening and we'll see what the gentlemen say about it?'

Bridie nodded and got to her feet. 'Thank you for listening to me.' She patted her belly. 'I want to keep this one safe, and keep my Alf safe, too. He's an idiot sometimes, knows more about horses than people, but I'm really fond of him. I'd marry him tomorrow if I could. Oh, and please don't tell my cousin Rory about this. Rory Flynn, that is. He sells milk in this town.'

Another pat of the belly. 'Rory will kill Alf if he finds out and probably beat me black and blue too.' At the door she turned and fumbled in her pocket for a piece of paper. 'Nearly forgot. This is where we're living. If you send a lad with a message, tell him only to give it to me, not my cousin Rory, not even Alf.'

When she'd gone, Jacinta shook her head. 'I'm not sure about this.'

'I think it's a good idea. Let's talk to Mr Nash and Uncle Quentin. I think they'll agree to it.'

'You really think so, Eleanor?'

'Yes. But let's be quick. We need to get on with our wedding preparations.'

'All right. I'll go and fetch Ben. I'm not leaving my son on his own here . . . or anywhere.' She sighed. When would poor Ben get a normal life?

Eleanor looked at her anxiously. 'I think Mrs Folane was telling the truth and her Alf doesn't really want to kidnap Ben. He didn't kill you on board the ship when he could have done, either, remember. We never could understand why not.'

'I still don't trust him, not an inch.'

'I think I'd trust her, though. She's rough and ready, but there's something about her that I rather like.'

Jacinta sniffed scornfully.

★   ★   ★

Quentin listened to Jacinta, who was clearly very agitated. By careful questioning, he made sure of the facts, then sat frowning at her.

'I knew you wouldn't want to do it,' she said. 'And I don't blame you at all. I don't want to do it, either. Only — '

He held up one hand. 'Give me a moment to think through the implications.'

She sat twisting her handkerchief.

'I'll need to speak to Alf before I agree.'

She looked at him in shock. 'You're thinking of agreeing?'

'It would tie up all the loose ends rather neatly.'

'But we'd be telling lies, and condoning immorality.'

He shrugged. 'The two of them won't be hurting anyone. Not really. From the sounds of it, his real wife can't stand him. She'll probably be happier without him. I've seen it many a time. Being locked into an unhappy marriage can ruin people's lives. Only it's so expensive and difficult to get a divorce that only rich people can do it.' He turned to Harriet. 'What do you think, my dear?'

'I agree with you.' She looked at Jacinta. 'It'd keep you and Ben safe. That's the most important thing, surely?'

Jacinta nodded slowly. 'Yes, of course. That's what counts, keeping Ben safe.'

Harriet took hold of her hand. 'And you'd be safe as well. You're important too.'

'Very well. I'll do it.' Jacinta let Quentin arrange to bring Bridie and Alf round to their house that very evening.

Safe. The word kept echoing through her mind. It'd be worth a lot to feel that she and Ben were truly safe.

★ ★ ★

'We'd better go and see Mitchell next,' Eleanor told Jacinta firmly. 'He needs to know what's going on.'

'What will he think of me, telling lies like that?'

'He'll think you're protecting your son, as any caring mother would.'

She was right. Mitchell listened with the same quiet courtesy as Uncle Quentin had, then volunteered to join the lawyer in interviewing Alf.

'There, that's settled,' Eleanor said as they walked back. 'Now, we have a lot of sewing and packing to do.' She ruffled Ben's hair. 'I think we should stop at the baker's and buy a nice currant loaf for this young rascal. I wouldn't mind a piece or two myself. Our landlady isn't the best cook in the world, is she?'

Ben grinned at her.

Eleanor saw how Jacinta's whole face softened as she watched her son and had a sudden longing for a child of her own. She'd been pleased at the warm looks Mitchell kept giving Jacinta.

Surely the two of them would find a way to make their marriage a happy one?

As Eleanor was sure hers would be. She'd worried needlessly about Dougal changing his mind. She was so happy to be marrying him.

★ ★ ★

Bridie had trouble convincing Alf to come with her to visit Mrs Blacklea at the lawyer's house that evening.

'They'll have the police waiting for me,' he said gloomily. 'I know they will. The gentry only ever think of themselves.'

'I don't think these people will. I liked Mrs Blacklea. And anyway, what will anyone accuse you of?'

'Attacking her yesterday.'

'If they do, we'll say you were upset about your children and got carried away. But I don't think they will. Come on, Alf. We have to try.'

So he spruced himself up and followed her into town.

When they arrived, she gave his hand a quick squeeze and let him knock on the door.

Mr Saxby opened it and gestured to them to enter. He looked solemn and serious, very much the gentleman.

Three ladies were sitting waiting for them, also looking solemn, and for all her brave words, Bridie felt intimidated by them and edged closer to Alf.

'Please sit here, Mrs Folane. Mr Pearson — I prefer to use your real name from now on — next to her, if you please.'

The lawyer waited till they were seated, then took a hard chair between the two groups. 'Now, explain to me again what you wish me to do and why. Take your time and tell me everything you think is important.'

'We thought we could pretend I'd died. Though we'd have to find someone to write to my uncle and tell him. He'd not believe just anyone. It'd have to be a priest or a gentleman at least. Someone who can write a good letter.'

Mr Saxby nodded encouragingly. 'Go on.'

'It'd be best if it was someone my uncle could check up on in England, if he's to convince Mr Blacklea that it's the truth. You're a lawyer. You must have connections there still.'

'Why should I lie for you?'

Alf looked at Bridie for help, so she said, 'Because you're fond of Mrs Blacklea, of course. And because she doesn't deserve treating like that. Any more than my Alf does.'

Mr Saxby asked several questions looking at her rather than Alf, and she grew even more fearful, because he was so clever in what he asked. If she'd been telling lies, he'd have found out, she was sure. But she wasn't. Well, only about the baby and he didn't question that.

When he fell silent she waited.

Mr Saxby looked at Jacinta. 'Are you still of the same mind as when we discussed this earlier?'

'Yes. I'm thinking of the children, my son and Mr Pearson's daughters. At least he seems to care about them.'

Bridie felt a tiny curl of hope and had difficulty keeping quiet, waiting, waiting . . . Why didn't they get on with it? She watched the lawyer. He was the one in charge, no doubt about that. When she glanced quickly at Alf, she saw him staring down at his clenched fists.

At last Mr Saxby spoke. 'Mr Pearson, you can be very thankful that Mrs Blacklea has a kind heart. I'd not be doing this except at her bidding.'

Alf looked up, his expression brightening.

Bridie glanced at everyone in turn, feeling heartened by the calm expressions on their faces.

'I shall write a letter to your uncle, Mr Pearson, if you'll furnish me with the address. How do you wish me to say you died?'

'Of illness at sea?' Alf suggested.

Mr Saxby thought this through, then shook his head. 'I don't think that would be wise. The shipping company would be obliged to keep records and report the death. May I suggest a runaway horse and cart here in Fremantle? You tried to save a little girl and were badly trampled. You died of your injuries, but not before you'd asked me to write to your family.'

'Whatever you think best, sir.'

'Very well.'

Bridie had suggested something to Alf. Surely he hadn't forgotten? She watched him expectantly and heard him take a deep breath as he looked up.

'Mrs Blacklea, I'm sorry for all the trouble I caused you. I really am. And . . . that's a grand young lad you've got there. I wish you both well.' Alf opened his mouth, then shut it again and looked at her.

She inclined her head but didn't speak. Miserable sod, Bridie thought. She could have spared a kind word for poor Alf. Oh well, that was the gentry for you. Never thought what hard lives others had.

Alf fumbled in his pocket. 'This is my uncle's address. He lives in the village near Mr Gerald Blacklea.'

Mr Saxby stood up. 'I'll write the letter. Now,

you won't need to see Mrs Blacklea again and I'm sure you won't linger in the colony. As far as we're concerned, the sooner you leave for Sydney, the better.'

Bridie stood up and followed Alf out of the house.

As they walked down the street, she linked her arm in his and forced herself to speak cheerfully. 'That went very well, didn't it?'

'Yes. You were right, Bridie love. Thanks.' But his voice was very subdued.

She decided to keep him busy. She didn't want him changing his mind about staying with her. 'Let's go and find out when the next ship sets sail. Then we'll have to tell my cousin Rory we're leaving. He won't be best pleased, but he'll just have to lump it.'

★   ★   ★

Quentin came back into the sitting room and looked at his companions. 'I'll write the letter now, so that it catches this week's post.'

Jacinta nodded.

'You've not changed your mind?'

She shook her head. 'No. I think Alf is telling the truth about his children. He was really good with the youngsters on board the ship. Besides, I've met Gerald Blacklea. I wouldn't put anything past that man. He's evil. There is no other word to describe him.'

Quentin sighed. 'We have no guarantee that Blacklea won't hurt Alf's family anyway, but we can only hope for the best. If I tell him you've married and moved to Sydney, there's a fair chance that he won't pursue you further.'

★ ★ ★

In England Maria Blacklea sat in the sun, eyes closed, not thinking about anything, just enjoying a rare moment's peace.

'What the hell are you doing sitting here?'

She started in shock and cowered back involuntarily as her husband yelled at her. He was standing right next to her. Why hadn't she heard him approach? How long had he been watching her?

'Well? Answer me! I asked what you're doing here.' He looked beyond her and his eyes narrowed as he saw how close the library window was. 'You've been eavesdropping, you bitch!'

'I haven't. Gerald, I haven't. I just sit here for the sun. It's protected against the wind and it's south-facing, so it's warmer than anywhere else in the garden, even this late in the year.'

He turned his eyes towards the nearby window, pursed his lips and shook his head. 'That's a poor excuse, if ever I heard one, but then, you're a poor sort of a woman in every way. I've put up with a lot from you over the years, but this is the last time. The very last.'

He dragged her to her feet and shook her hard to emphasise each point he was making. 'No son. Only one daughter. What sort of a wife are you? A useless one, that's what.' He threw her down hard on the wooden bench and pulled out a piece of paper, waving it at her. 'Well, I've just heard that your father has died, so I don't need to put up with you for a minute longer. *Not — one — minute.* I'm young enough to marry again and sire a son.'

Terror held her fixed to the spot. He was going to kill her, she knew he was. She'd always known he'd kill her one day.

Gerald leaned down and clamped his hands round her neck, smiling now. 'I'm going to strangle you slowly, and I'm going to enjoy every gasp.'

The grip on her throat tightened till she couldn't breathe. She'd have let him kill her, hated her life with him, but the thought of her daughter made her struggle. She tried to scratch out his eyes, but he shook her hands off.

She tried desperately to unclench the fingers that gripped her throat so tightly. But in vain. He had always been much stronger than her and he laughed at her, playing with her by allowing her to gasp in a couple of sobbing breaths, then squeezing her throat again, more tightly than before.

'Now,' he said softly. 'Now, you'll die.'

She looked up at his flushed face and staring eyes. She knew she was dying and stopped struggling, praying for mercy from the God who'd never listened to her prayers before.

Even that didn't please him and he slackened his grasp again, shaking her hard. 'Fight me, you bitch. Can't you try harder than that? You're useless . . . useless.'

But she couldn't find the energy to struggle

any more, was glad when the world began to turn black around her.

★ ★ ★

When she regained consciousness, she thought for a moment she was dead, then realised she was lying on the damp earth of the flower bed with a heavy weight on top of her legs.

Why had he let her live?

Feeling muzzy-headed, she pushed at the weight and realised it was Gerald. What torture had he dreamed up now? Was he pretending to be unconscious? Did she have to go through more of that agonising pain again?

But he didn't move.

Her voice came out hoarsely. 'Gerald! Gerald, please get off me.'

He didn't stir. She listened, and couldn't hear him breathing. One hand was near enough to grasp, though she hated to touch him. She couldn't find a pulse.

Was he dead?

God couldn't be so kind.

She pushed Gerald and he still didn't react.

With a struggle she managed to roll his body off her. Even when the thorns of her favourite rose bush scraped a bloody groove down his cheek, he didn't move.

It seemed to take for ever to sit up. When she turned sideways to look at him, she realised he was still breathing.

She screamed then, screamed in terror at the thought of having to go on living with him, or being killed by him.

But he didn't move, just lay there, still as a fallen tree, silent apart from sounds like faint snoring.

Servants came running, exclaiming, calling for more help.

One of the gardeners carried her inside and up to her bedroom. Others must have dealt with Gerald. She didn't care.

Only when Dr Robson arrived at the house did she rouse herself, relieved it was young Dr Robson, not his father, who was a crony of Gerald's.

It was a while before he came into her room, standing beside her bed, looking down at her sympathetically.

'My husband . . . is he still alive?'

'Barely. He's had a massive seizure. If he survives, he'll be as helpless as a baby.'

The room whirled round her and she had to close her eyes for a few moments. When she opened them, Dr Robson was still there.

'You're sure of that, doctor? He won't . . . recover enough to move around?'

He frowned at her, then touched her neck with one fingertip, answering her question with one of his own. 'How did that happen?'

'Gerald tried to strangle me.'

The doctor gaped at her. 'Why?'

'Because I'm a barren bitch who can't give him a son. Because my father has just died and so Gerald dared try to get rid of me.'

'But people would have seen your body, seen the marks on your neck.'

'He'd have found a way to keep that quiet. He always finds a way to get what he wants.'

The doctor sat down on the edge of the bed, his fingers gentle as he turned her head from side to side. 'How long has he been treating you so badly?'

'All our married life.'

'I knew things weren't right when I came to visit you before, but you said nothing, and I had no way of going against your husband's wishes. Why didn't you ask your family for help?'

'I didn't dare. I have a daughter.' She laid one hand on his sleeve. 'You're *sure* Gerald won't recover?'

'Very sure. With a seizure that bad, he won't be able to speak or move, though he might understand what's happening around him. But he'll gradually decline. We have no way of keeping people in that situation alive for long.'

She managed not to say 'Thank goodness' aloud. But she thought it. Oh, she did.

Looking grim, the young doctor stood up. 'Now that I know you're all right, I'll go and make arrangements for someone to care for your husband. But I doubt it'll be for long.'

She wished Gerald was dead already. She'd not feel safe until he was buried in his family vault.

That afternoon Dr Robson came to see her again. 'I've sent for an attendant for your husband. There's a man in the village who's done such work before. We're lucky he's between jobs. Or you may want to find someone yourself?'

'No. No, I'd be grateful if you could find someone.'

'Well, you really need to hire two strong attendants to care for your husband and keep an eye on him till the inevitable happens. I know someone else. I'll find the men and instruct them on his insanity, in case he does recover some speech.'

Terror lanced through her.

'It's not likely,' he said gently. 'But I want to protect you.'

She closed her eyes for a moment as relief washed through her in such a huge wave she wondered if you could die of it. Then she thought of something else. 'Please, don't let your father treat him. The two of them are friends.'

'My father isn't well, either. Too much eating and drinking has taken its toll. I'm taking over the practice and my mother's going with my father to live quietly at the seaside.'

Thank goodness, she thought.

When the doctor had gone Maria didn't weep, not a single tear. She got up and changed her clothes, wrapping a silk scarf round her bruised neck.

She paused to stare at herself in the mirror, straightening her shoulders and taking a deep breath. She felt lighter, younger . . . almost free.

Then she went to take charge of her household. First she would tell her daughter and the governess what had happened.

Then she would call the servants together. There were some of them who would be leaving immediately, the ones who hadn't been kind to her. There were others whose wages she would raise, whom she would thank for their surreptitious help over the years.

Later she would go down to the village church to say her thanks properly to her Maker, then to speak to Mr Stanwell.

Smiling, she opened the door of the schoolroom and held out her arms to her daughter.

* * *

Two days later, Maria went to see her husband. She'd stood at the bedroom door the day before, unable to force herself to go nearer to the bed, unable to believe that he couldn't harm her.

Today she felt more courageous and walked across to stand right next to him, sending the attendant away.

Gerald's colour was poor and his breathing laboured, but something about the way he was looking at her made her feel he could see her and understand what was going on. She could almost feel his fury.

She leaned forward. 'So, Gerald. I win. You'll not last much longer and I'm glad. For once, the Lord has smitten the wicked.'

He seemed to be straining to speak. His face turned a dark red with the effort and the skin around his mouth quivered.

Then he jerked and his eyes rolled up in his head.

She waited, watching carefully. But there was no sign of movement in his chest. He was dead.

She wasn't sorry, not a bit. If anyone deserved to die, he did.

'Enjoy your stay in hell,' she said as she stood up and called the attendant, pulling out a handkerchief to pretend to dab at her eyes.

As if she'd weep for that monster!

Then she went to spend an hour with her daughter, feeling as if a load was lifted from the whole house, as if a clean breeze had swept the last of the evil away.

21

Bridie did the speaking. 'Alf and me are going to get wed, Rory.'

He stopped eating to stare at her. 'You can do better for yourself than him.'

'No, I can't. I *want* to marry him.'

Alf reached out to take her hand. 'We're going to live in Sydney. We'll open a pub. More custom there, you see.'

'We're fond of one another,' Bridie added, sending a smile at Alf and getting one in return.

Rory scowled at this display of affection, repeating, 'He's not good enough for a Flynn.'

'He's the one I want. And I'm not a Flynn any longer.'

'You were born one.'

'You don't need to worry,' Alf said. 'Bridie will be all right with me. I look after my own.'

Bridie decided enough had been said. She wasn't answerable to her cousin. 'We have to pack now. The coastal steamer leaves tomorrow afternoon, so we'll be boarding it tomorrow morning. We were lucky to get the last cabin.'

'You're not wed yet, so you're not sharing a cabin and you're not going anywhere with him.'

'Don't be silly. We'll get married in Sydney.'

'Over my dead body. When I set up here, I promised myself me and my family would be respectable an' you'll not be spoiling it. If people

392

find out, I'll be the one left behind to face the sneers.'

She jumped to her feet and faced him, arms akimbo. 'I'm old enough to make my own decisions and you've no right to tell me what to do.'

He stood up and thumped the table. 'Might is right. If it comes to a fight, I can beat your Alf any day. What use will he be to you if I really lay into him?' He grinned as he added, 'Where it hurts a man most.'

There was dead silence as she looked from her cousin to Alf, then she said, 'You'll be fighting two of us. I'll not stand by and let you hurt him.'

'You'll be facing two of us, as well,' Jilleen said. 'I stand by my husband.'

Rory grinned at them triumphantly.

'But we can't get married before we go,' Bridie protested. 'There isn't time. It takes three *weeks* to call the banns.'

'They don't always stick to the rules about calling the banns here. They think it's better for folk to marry, more respectable like. Besides, I know a clergyman who'll do it. Not that starched-up fellow in the big church.'

'You'd still need a special licence.'

'He'll do it without on my say so.' Rory grinned and added, 'He's Jilleen's cousin. He'll not want immorality in the family, either.'

'I don't want to wed in a rush,' Bridie said. 'I want to do it proper. I'd rather wait, thank you.'

'You'll wed him or you'll neither of you leave tomorrow.'

Alf stepped forward to put an arm round her.

'We were going to marry, so it doesn't make much difference, love.'

She looked up at him and he gave the tiniest of shrugs. 'You'd better go and arrange it then, Rory. But I shan't forgive you for this interference.'

'Me and Jilleen will go and arrange it together. She'll weep all over her cousin, won't you, me darlin'? But first we have the milk to take to the shops, an' I need to find a new cowman, dammit.'

When Rory and his wife had left, Bridie looked at Alf and whispered, 'They put people in prison for bigamy. I didn't want to go through an actual ceremony.'

'Who's to know?'

'I am. I don't like doing it.'

'We've got no choice, love.'

'No. I suppose not. He always was a bully, my damned cousin Rory was.'

★ ★ ★

That afternoon, as Quentin and Jacinta were returning from posting the all-important letter to England, they saw what looked like a wedding group going into a small nonconformist church.

'What are Pearson and Mrs Folane doing going in there at this hour?' he wondered aloud.

'It looks as if they're about to get married. Surely not?'

'Come on. We can peep into the church and find out.'

'Shouldn't we just . . . leave them to work

things out for themselves?'

Quentin gave her a surprisingly boyish grin. 'I can't resist finding out.'

She let him tug her into the rear of the small wooden building and they stood near the door, half-hidden by the shadows.

At the front of the church, the clergyman was standing with Alf and Bridie in front of him, Rory and Jilleen behind them.

'They *are* getting married!' Jacinta whispered.

He was silent, then he said quietly, 'It's bigamy. I should report them.'

But neither of them spoke as the supposed marriage service was gone through very rapidly and the groom instructed to kiss his bride.

Afterwards the clergyman took them to sign the register and get their marriage lines.

Rory and Jilleen strolled towards the door, which prevented the watchers from slipping out without being seen. Rory stopped to frown at them, not recognising them in the dim light. 'Are you getting married next?'

'No. I just can't resist a wedding,' Jacinta said brightly.

The newly-weds came down the aisle and stopped dead at the sight of the watchers, whom they recognised only too well. Alf opened and shut his mouth as if unable to form a word. Bridie looked from her supposed husband to Quentin, then looked pleadingly at Jacinta and moved close enough to whisper, 'We're sailing to Sydney tomorrow. It was Rory insisted on the wedding.'

For a moment all hung in the balance, then

Jacinta tugged at Quentin's arm. 'Let's be on our way.'

'Are you sure?'

'Yes. Very.' She looked back at Bridie, ignoring Alf completely. 'I wish *you* well.'

Bridie closed her eyes, understanding the hidden message. 'Thank you. I'm grateful.'

'You've no need to be grateful to them,' Rory said loudly. 'As *my* cousin you're as good as anyone in the colony.'

Alf didn't speak, was still looking shocked.

Bridie tugged his arm and the quartet moved out of the church.

'We really ought to report this,' Quentin said.

'They're leaving the colony. All I care about is getting that man as far away from my son as possible. Besides . . . *she* doesn't deserve to be put in prison, does she?'

'Very well.' He smiled. 'Anyway, I think she'll make sure Alf behaves himself from now on, don't you? So he'll be redeemed, whether he wants it or not.'

Jacinta chuckled. 'Oh, yes. I'm quite sure she'll be in charge in that household. I just hope his children in England won't be in want.'

'Sadly there's nothing we can do about them, my dear.'

'No. I suppose not. Look, I have a few things to buy, women's things which won't interest you. Why don't you go and join Aunt Harriet? I shall feel quite safe walking back on my own now.'

★ ★ ★

396

After she'd made her purchases, Jacinta went into Deagan's Bazaar. She found Isabella there with her baby daughter, supervising a woman who was reorganising the display of silks that was attracting more and more attention from the local ladies.

'You have some beautiful materials,' Jacinta said wistfully.

'Perhaps Mitchell will buy you a length after you're married.'

'Oh, I couldn't ask for *silk!* It's too expensive.'

Isabella smiled. 'Not even for Sunday best?' She hesitated, then said quietly, 'Please forgive me for interfering, but I know you and Mitchell will be making what people call a marriage of convenience.'

'Yes.'

'Did you know that's how Bram and I started off?'

Jacinta could only gape at her. If she'd ever seen two people deeply in love, it was Bram Deagan and his wife.

'What's more, my Bram thinks you're well suited.'

'How can he be sure?'

'He seems to sense these things.' She clasped Jacinta's hand. 'I hope you're not upset at me speaking frankly about this, but you were looking so worried.'

'No. I'm grateful. My first marriage wasn't very happy, and my husband didn't encourage me to exchange visits with other ladies, even in the days when I could afford to dress properly. So I've little experience of what it takes to make a happy marriage, only a very unhappy one.'

'Don't let it blight your life.'

As she walked back, Jacinta was very thoughtful. She let out a cry of shock as Alf appeared suddenly from round a corner.

He stood facing her, making no attempt this time to touch her or pull her aside.

Before she could do anything, she was pushed aside and Mitchell placed himself between her and Alf.

'Get away from her.'

'I haven't touched her and I wasn't going to. I just wanted to thank her for not . . . ' he looked despairingly at Jacinta before finishing lamely, 'not interfering today. Bridie sent me.'

Alf began backing away. 'That's all it was, just to say thank you.'

He turned and ran off down the street.

Mitchell turned to Jacinta. 'He didn't hurt you?'

'No. He didn't even attempt to touch me.'

He put his arm round her. 'You look shaken, all the same.'

'I was surprised to see him. I thought he'd be on the ship by now.' She leaned against Mitchell for a minute. 'Thank you for coming to my aid.'

He smiled down at her, still holding her in the circle of his arm. 'I'll always try to look after you. Please believe that. I'd never willingly hurt you or let anyone else do it, either.'

'I'm starting to believe it.'

He bent his head, clearly wanting to kiss her, but giving her time to pull away. Only, she didn't want to pull away. She wanted the strength of his arms round her and the warmth of his lips on hers.

When the kiss ended, he grinned boyishly. 'You seem to be getting more used to my touch.'

She was surprised at herself, but was determined to be honest with him. 'I am.'

'That's good. Where are you going? May I walk with you?'

'I'm going back to the lodging house. Eleanor and I are getting ready for our weddings tomorrow.' She smiled. 'But if you and Christopher need any shirts ironing, I can spare time to do that.'

'I've found a washing woman who has taken the matter in hand. I'm not marrying you to gain a servant, Jacinta. Oh, and Bram knows a woman who may be able to find us a maid, but I'll leave it to you to speak to her.' Amusement lit his eyes. 'Bram always seems to know someone.'

'He's a lovely man.' She hesitated, then added, 'I was speaking to his wife and she said he was sure we'd be happy together.'

'He told me that, too. Give me half a chance and I will make you happy, Jacinta.'

'Give me half a chance and I'll make you happy, too, Mitchell.' She hadn't even had to think about that response and it brought the smile back to his face, which warmed her heart.

When she'd said goodbye to him, she went to the bedroom at the boarding house on the excuse of taking off her outdoor things, but really she wanted a few moments to think about what had just happened.

Nothing very special, if you told it to anyone.

And yet, she felt as if the whole world had changed and she with it. She felt free from the threat Blacklea had posed, and happier, much happier. She even felt right about her coming marriage, about sharing a life and eventually a bed with Mitchell.

And oh, that was so good a feeling.

Then the peaceful moment was lost as Ben came rushing to find her and tell her all about his latest visit to Christopher's house, where they'd all be living from tomorrow onwards. As promised Christopher had walked home with him.

She couldn't keep Ben guarded every single minute, she knew that. But each time she tried to relax her vigilance and tell herself not to worry, she kept remembering Gerald Blacklea's last threatening words: 'You'll be sorry, Jacinta Blacklea. I'll come after you. You'll never be safe. Never.'

But he was ten thousand miles away, and the man he'd sent after them hadn't even wanted to kill her. So perhaps she should stop worrying and go with her instincts, which said Mitchell Nash was a kind man who would make an excellent husband, and who wouldn't change as soon as they were married, and would never hurt her.

Besides, it'd be months before Blacklea could send anyone else. She certainly didn't intend to spend that time worrying 'in case'.

The load lifted still further and she twirled round, hands raised, skirts flying. No, she would *not* spend her life worrying. It said in the Bible:

400

Sufficient unto the day is the evil thereof. She would take that as her motto.

★ ★ ★

The wedding morning dawned bright and clear. Eleanor and Jacinta got up early and took it in turns to wash in the crowded bedroom.

'I'm all packed now, except for what I'm wearing,' Eleanor said.

'You're going to make a beautiful bride.'

'So are you. We aren't doing badly for two widow women, are we?' She chuckled and then went on, 'But I do wish you looked less nervous. You seemed more confident last night about marrying Mitchell than you do today.'

'I was. I am. But still . . . marriage.' Jacinta shuddered.

By mid-morning both ladies were dressed in their wedding finery. The silk of the remodelled clothes might have been old, but it was still good quality, and Eleanor's nimble fingers had worked wonders with the old-fashioned styles.

It was a relief when Uncle Quentin and Aunt Harriet came to collect them, so that they could all walk to the church together. Mrs Haslop's nephew and his friend were waiting with their handcarts to take the ladies' luggage to their new homes.

It seemed strange to Jacinta to step out of the lodging house for the final time. Everything seemed strange today.

To their surprise, Bram turned up just as they were about to set off.

'I hope you don't mind me walking with you, but one gentleman hasn't enough arms for three ladies. Mrs Blacklea, will you do me the honour of taking my arm, please?'

She did so with a smile. Who could fail to like this friendly Irishman?

But he didn't fill the walk with platitudes, he said straight away, 'You look nervous.'

'Oh. Do I?' She didn't know what to say.

'Isabella said I should come and remind you of how happy she and I are.'

'She told me you made a marriage of convenience. I was . . . surprised.'

'Ah, well, actually, she did that, make a marriage of convenience, I mean. But I fell in love with her the first time I saw her. And I only love her more with each day that passes.'

She stopped walking in surprise. 'I've never heard a gentleman speak so frankly about his love for his wife.'

'Maybe because I'm not a gentleman. Am I speaking too frankly for you? I can go back to meaningless chat, if you prefer it.'

'No, I prefer people to say what they think.' She decided to be equally frank and added, 'I'm just a bit surprised you're taking such an interest in my doings.'

'Well, to tell you the truth, I feel responsible for your being here. I'm the one who pushed Mitchell to find himself a wife, you see. I was a bit worried about who might come out from England to marry him, but when I met you, I lost all my worries.'

'Did you really?'

'Yes. Because for all you're nervous about marriage, your love for your son shines so brightly, so I knew you had it in you to love my dear friend as he deserves.'

She thought about that then asked, 'Do you do much matchmaking?'

He grinned at her. 'I do it when I see the need. I believe I have a gift for it.'

'I hope you're right.'

'I am. You'll see. You're just right for Mitchell.'

He stopped walking and she realised in surprise that they'd reached the church and the others were waiting for them.

'Here we are. I wish you happy, my dear.'

Eleanor was standing at the entrance to the church, ready for their double wedding. Ben and Aunt Harriet could be seen through the doorway, making their way down the aisle to the front of the church. Bram gave Jacinta's hand a quick squeeze and then he followed them inside.

Uncle Quentin surveyed the two ladies with a fatherly eye. 'You both look truly beautiful.'

Eleanor dipped him a mocking curtsey, so Jacinta followed suit.

As they walked into the church, they stopped in surprise, because all Bram's family were there, half-turning in their seats to smile at them.

Dougal and Mitchell were standing at the front of the church, waiting for their brides.

'Here we go,' Uncle Quentin said.

Time had gone slowly so far this morning, but as soon as they started down the aisle to their husbands-to-be, it seemed to speed up.

Jacinta made her responses in a daze, aware of little except Mitchell, his smiling eyes, his hand warm on hers, the kiss he planted softly on her cheek after they'd been declared man and wife.

It was done, Jacinta thought then, and that brought its own peace.

'Are you all right?' he asked in his quiet way.

'Yes, I am.'

'You'll not regret it. We'll find happiness. I'll make sure of it.'

'I'm getting more sure of it by the day.'

'Good.'

And then it was a blur as all Bram's family claimed the right to kiss the brides or shake the grooms' hands.

Out into the sunshine they walked, in a smiling, chattering crowd which spread out down the street as they went to drink the health of the newly-weds and eat a piece of wedding cake at Maura's house.

Dougal and Eleanor looked blissfully happy, as if they were hardly aware of the people sharing the celebration. Jacinta had no doubt their marriage would be a good one.

So many kind people wanting to befriend her, she thought in wonderment. And Ben, her darling Ben, racing round like a normal lad with his new stepbrother.

She smiled at Mitchell who was also watching the two boys. 'I think they'll do well together.'

'We'll *all* do well together.'

★ ★ ★

404

Jacinta's mood of elation lasted until the wedding night. With the boys long in bed and asleep, exhausted and happy after the party, she and Mitchell had lingered in the kitchen.

Then he stood up. 'Time to go to bed.'

Her heart lurched.

'Let me take you to your room.'

Did he mean she had a room of her own? Or would he insist on joining her there? Her heart began beating with apprehension.

At a bedroom door, he stopped, opened it and stood aside. 'I hope you sleep well, my dear.'

And he was gone into his room across the landing before she could say anything.

She walked into her bedroom, knowing he'd kept his word. He was giving her the time to learn to trust him. He was such a good man.

It was a lesson she'd learned far more quickly than she'd expected. She changed out of her finery into her nightgown, then, before she could lose her nerve, she walked barefoot across the landing to her husband's bedroom.

She didn't tap on the door, but opened it a little and saw him standing by the window in the moonlight. 'May I come in?'

His face lit up and he simply held out his arms.

She walked into them with a feeling of rightness and stood with him for a moment or two, in a simple embrace.

'Are you sure?' he whispered in her ear.

'Yes. I want to be a proper wife to you.' She took a deep breath and braced herself for what was to come.

Instead Mitchell asked quietly, 'Did Claude never please you at all in the marriage bed?'

'No. Nor made the attempt to do anything but relieve himself on me.'

'I shall always try to please you first,' he promised and kissed each of her cheeks, before escorting her across to the bed.

When he took her in his arms, he began to kiss her again, so sweetly, so gently, that she relaxed as she had never done with Claude.

To her wonderment Mitchell didn't climb on top of her and hurt her. He made love to her slowly and carefully, and she found it so different, so wonderful that afterwards she wept for joy.

'Did I hurt you?'

'No. Oh, no. You pleased me. I didn't realise it could be like that.'

'It'll always be like that, if I have any say in things.'

'Thank you.' She couldn't hold back a yawn because she hadn't slept well the night before. It felt good to nestle down beside him in bed. So good to settle quietly into sleep and . . .

* * *

In the morning Jacinta woke to find her husband watching her, lying on his side.

She reached out to take hold of his hand. 'Thank you, Mitchell.'

'For what?'

'For taking away my fears, for showing me that I had never before *made love* with a man.'

406

He reached out to smooth a lock of hair from her forehead. 'We shall do very well together, I'm sure of it.'

Which left her with only one real fear: that Gerald Blacklea would send another man after her. Surely he wouldn't go to such lengths again?

Well, she had several months' leeway before she need fear that, because mail between the two countries took so long. She would banish it from her thoughts until then and concentrate on making her husband, son and stepson as happy as was possible.

And then she had to explain to Mitchell that these were more happy tears, which made them both chuckle.

22

Almost three months later, Bernard Pearson arrived home to find a letter sitting on the mantelpiece.

'Did you . . . have a good day?' his wife Clara asked.

'Depends what you call good. It's easy enough working for Mrs Blacklea, that I will admit, but she could make far more money if she wasn't always remitting the rent to those who fall ill or sending a basket of food to people like old Mrs Brooking.'

'It's very kind of her, I'm sure.'

'Oh, kind. Yes, she's kind. That's why she kept me on here, to be kind to my family.'

'Well, you're not complaining about that, surely?'

He shrugged. 'I don't like to see how happy she is now that Mr Blacklea's dead.'

'He wasn't kind to her. She deserves some happiness.'

'Yes, I suppose so. But there's no excitement working for her, no pleasure in getting the better of someone.'

He picked up the letter, saying unnecessarily, 'It's from Australia, but it's not our Alf's handwriting. This is an educated hand.'

He turned it round, looking for a clue about who had written it, then shrugged and tore it open.

Cursing at what he found, he reread it before sharing its contents with his wife. 'Our Alf's dead. I might have known he'd mess it up.'

'How did he die?'

'Died trying to rescue a child from a runaway horse. He's another fool who's too kind for his own good.'

'What'll Ruth do now?'

He shrugged and stood thinking, then nodded as he came to a decision. 'She'd better throw herself on the mistress's charity. If Mrs Blacklea's going to waste her money on good deeds, she might as well spend some of it on my family. Until Ruth finds another husband, that is.'

'She wasn't suited with Alf. Maybe she won't want to marry again.'

'Nor was he suited with her. Flighty piece and always having children. But she's not one to sleep alone in bed. She'll find some fool to take her on.'

A little later, he yawned then said grudgingly, 'I'm glad *you* didn't present me with one every year or I'd never have got ahead.'

'You'd have got ahead whatever happened. But you were lucky to marry me.'

He grinned in the darkness of their bedroom. 'I was, was I?'

'Definitely. And you know it.'

★ ★ ★

The following day Bernard went up to the big house and asked to speak to the mistress.

He didn't waste time, but held out the letter.

'Your husband sent my nephew to Australia, chasing after Claude Blacklea's widow, wanting to persuade her to give him the child to rear. He had orders to kill her if she wouldn't. Now Alf's the one who's dead and he's left a widow with three children to raise here in the village.'

Maria read the letter carefully. 'I shall have to check this man's credentials. At least he's offered us references. Your nephew may have simply decided to abandon his wife and family, and stay in Australia.'

'I don't think Alf would do that, ma'am.'

'Nonetheless, if I'm to take responsibility for the family, I must be certain I'm not being tricked.'

Bernard looked at her with more respect than before. She'd been very cautious at first in managing the estate and he'd made sure she came to rely on his help, couldn't sack him out of hand as she had some of the others. He didn't want to lose his job and home. But she'd gradually started asserting herself and he'd grown to admire her.

He decided it was best to ally himself with her in this from the start. 'How best can we do that, ma'am? Shall you write to these people he mentions?'

'No. I'll go and visit them.' She stood thinking for a moment or two, then asked, 'Do you think your wife would accompany me? I've always found her a woman of sense.'

'I'm sure she would be delighted to, ma'am. You'll be wanting me along as well, to see to the arrangements.'

'No. I want you here to keep an eye on things. I must learn to deal with matters myself.'

'But — '

'If you don't want your wife to come with me, I can find someone else.'

'I'm very happy for you to take Clara, ma'am. I'm just concerned for your safety.'

'No need to be. I'm learning to manage for myself. And you must learn too, learn my ways of doing things.' She fixed him with a stern gaze that seemed to hold a warning.

She let the words hang in the air for a moment or two, then sent him off to ask Clara to walk up to the big house and speak to her.

His wife was even more delighted than he'd expected. And she refused to be given orders about what to do, saying she had enough sense to look after herself, yes and keep an eye out for the mistress too.

Which tried his patience to the utmost.

Things had changed for the worse, indeed they had. But financially, they weren't too badly off, so he'd put up with it.

⋆   ⋆   ⋆

It was four days before the mistress returned, and not a word from her or from Clara during that time, either. Bernard was twitching with impatience by the time he saw the cab from the station roll up the drive.

He ran across from the estate office to greet them at the door.

Both women looked pleased with themselves.

411

Maria smiled at him. 'You must be impatient to know how we got on. Come inside and take tea with me and we'll tell you.'

His wife ignored his whispered command to tell her about the letter writer and followed her mistress inside the house.

Maria sat down on the small sofa she favoured in the evening, looking round with obvious pleasure.

There was now no butler, because Marston had left to achieve his dream of running a boarding house for gentlemen. It was the head housemaid brought in a tea tray and set it before her mistress.

Bernard was almost bursting with impatience by the time the mistress had poured tea for them all, sweetened her own and drunk it sip by ladylike sip.

She set the empty cup down. 'Well, let's put you out of your misery, Mr Pearson. The man who wrote the letter is indeed Mr Quentin Saxby. They showed me other letters in his handwriting. You can't mistake it. And they spoke of him with great respect. In other words, we can believe what he's written.'

'Well, it's better to know,' was all he could think of to say.

'I shall make myself responsible for your nephew's widow.'

'She'll need — '

'I'll decide what she needs. This isn't your task. Now, I must go and see my daughter, and Clara will want to take charge of her own home again.' She walked with them to the door, a courtesy her husband wouldn't have dreamed of offering to employees.

When they were out of earshot of the house, he said, 'I want to hear every detail, Clara.'

'So you shall, but not till this evening. I want to make sure everything's all right in my home, and you have a job to do. She's a good mistress. See that you please her. No going back to your old ways.'

Mrs Blacklea was too damned good, he thought. Goody-goody, she was, spending her money on people who didn't deserve it. He'd have trouble lining his purse with her around. He was having trouble controlling his wife, even.

Fate could deal you some strange hands.

★ ★ ★

The following day, Maria wrote to Mr Saxby, thanking him for making them all aware of Alf Pearson's sad demise and letting him know that her husband had died suddenly.

She thought nothing more about the matter, and concentrated instead on training Bernard Pearson to work in her way, since she preferred the devil she knew. It gave her great pleasure to find ways to help people on the estate and in the village to enjoy better lives, and to raise her daughter to be happy.

In fact, life had never been so good. She would definitely not remarry, and intended to make very sure her daughter didn't fall into the hands of a fortune hunter.

It had surprised her how much money Gerald

had amassed, and it pleased her greatly to think how furious he'd be at the way she was using it to benefit people of all sorts. If he'd ever roused from his stupor, she'd have told him about what she was doing. It might have been wrong, but he'd made her life miserable for fifteen long years and she'd have liked to inflict a little misery on him in return.

Epilogue

Australia: 1872

The letter arrived at Quentin's house on a burning hot day in February. He opened it, read the brief epistle, then called for his wife.

'Harriet, look what I've just received.'

She read it and beamed at him. 'So dear Jacinta can now feel completely safe. She tries not to let it show, but she does worry about that man and what he might do. Nothing Mitchell says can convince her that Ben is safe.'

'Well, this letter will do the job. Let's go round to tell her straight away.'

But they met her in the street, so stopped to tell her the news there and then, that Gerald Blacklea was dead and had been for some months.

Jacinta stared at them for a long time, then swayed and closed her eyes. Quentin watched her anxiously, wondering if she was going to faint.

Then she opened her eyes again, her face still pale but her demeanour suddenly showing more confidence and happiness. 'Thank you for letting me know, Uncle Quentin. I must go and tell Mitchell at once.'

She didn't even wait for an answer, but turned and hurried away, breaking into a run.

At the timber yard, she burst into the office,

where Bram was chatting to her husband.

'Uncle Quentin's heard from Gerald Blacklea's wife. He's dead. Mitchell, he died months ago and we didn't know it.' Suddenly she burst into tears.

'I'll leave you to enjoy your news,' Bram said softly. 'We can complete our business another time.'

Jacinta was clinging to Mitchell, still sobbing, so he sat down in his big chair, pulling her on to his knee.

The storm of tears soon passed and he produced a handkerchief to wipe her face. 'Better now?'

She nodded. 'So much better, I can't tell you.'

'I would have protected you, you know.'

'I know. But I didn't want to put you at risk too. Anyway, that's all behind us now. We have two rascals to raise, and another growing inside me.' She pulled his head towards her and gave him a quick kiss on the cheek. 'I never thought to be so happy. I do love you, Mitchell.'

'I shan't believe you till you've kissed me properly.'

So she set about convincing him.

★ ★ ★

Bram hurried home to share the good news with Isabella.

'Are you satisfied now?' she demanded in mock fierceness. 'Gerald's dead and your matchmaking was successful. We need to concentrate on the business now. We've still to catch up on things after that storm. Though the last cargo did well, I must say. I wish the ice works wasn't all stop and start, but at least it isn't costing you money now.'

'We'll get through it all and I'll be more careful about money in future.' He frowned. 'But there's just one more person to settle before I stop matchmaking.'

She gaped at him. 'Who? And what do you mean by 'settle'?'

'Livia, of course. She needs a husband.'

'Livia will never remarry. Those two servants of hers have been trying to find her a husband for years and if anyone could make her do it, they could.'

'Perhaps they need a little help?' He grinned at her.

'Bram Deagan, you should mind your own business.'

'Oh, I will. Unless I see someone really suitable for Livia, I'll do nothing about it.'

She could only shake her head at him in mock anger.

'But in the meantime, I want to give a party to celebrate.'

'Celebrate what?'

He lost his smile. 'Jacinta's release from fear. But we'll make some other excuse for the party, of course.'

Then his smile returned and he pulled his wife into his arms. 'In the meantime, woman, you haven't kissed me for hours.'

Books by Anna Jacobs
Published by Ulverscroft:

FAMILY CONNECTIONS
KIRSTY'S VINEYARD
CHESTNUT LANE
SAVING WILLOWBROOK
FREEDOM'S LAND
IN FOCUS

GREYLADIES:
HEIR TO GREYLADIES

LADY BINGRAM'S AIDES:
TOMORROW'S PROMISES
YESTERDAY'S GIRL

THE KERSHAW SISTERS:
OUR LIZZIE
OUR POLLY
OUR EVA

THE MUSIC HALL
PRIDE OF LANCASHIRE
STAR OF THE NORTH
BRIGHT DAY DAWNING
HEART OF THE TOWN

THE STALEY FAMILY
CALICO ROAD

Other titles published by Ulverscroft:

THE TRADER'S WIFE

Anna Jacobs

1865. Singapore is exotic and yet terrifying for a penniless Englishwoman, alone and vulnerable after her mother's death. Too pretty to obtain a governess's job, Isabella Saunders accepts an offer from Singapore merchant Mr Lee — to teach him English and live with his family. Two years later Bram Deagan arrives in Singapore, determined to make his fortune as a trader. Mr Lee, wanting to expand his business connections, persuades Isabella to marry Bram. She sets sail for a new land and life. But the past casts a long shadow and she and Bram face unexpected dangers. Can they achieve their dreams of a successful trading business? And will their marriage turn out to be more of a love match than they could have ever dreamed?

THE TRADER'S SISTER

Anna Jacobs

Ismay Deagan wants to leave Ireland and join her brother, Bram, in Australia. However, her father wants her to marry their vicious neighbour, the loathsome Rory Flynn. But after Rory brutally attacks her, Ismay realises she must escape. And, disguised as an impoverished young widow, she sets sail for Australia, hoping to be reunited with her brother. When she meets Adam Treagar on the ship, she believes her dreams of future happiness may come true. But before reaching their destination they are flung into adventures in Suez, Ceylon and Singapore . . . Can Ismay tell Adam the truth about who she really is? What secrets does Adam hide? And will Ismay's past catch up with her and threaten her new life in Australia, before it's even begun?